Éilis from the Flats

Paul Larkin

ÉILIS FROM THE FLATS

(Part One of the
"Good Friday Sting" Hexalogy)

DALKEY ARCHIVE PRESS

Copyright © by Paul Larkin, 2018.
First Edition, 2019.

Names: Larkin, Paul, author.
Title: Éilis from the flats / Paul Larkin.
Description: First Dalkey Archive edition. | McLean Il : Dalkey Archive Press, 2018.
Identifiers: LCCN 2018026125 | ISBN 9781628972764 (pbk. : alk. paper)
Classification: LCC PR6112.A76 E37 2018 | DDC 823/.92--dc23
LC record available at https://lccn.loc.gov/2018026125

Co-funded by the Creative Europe Programme of the European Union

Dalkey Archive Press
McLean, IL / Dublin

Printed on permanent/durable acid-free paper.

www.dalkeyarchive.com

What to do when greed and avarice has replaced love in the hearts of the people?

Éilis from the Flats

Paul Larkin

The Regal Emissary

THE STAFF NURSE barely looked at Dawn as she walked into the ward. This boss of nurses glanced and then went back to her logbook, or whatever device it was that could make Dawn feel inferior to it.

The sixteen-year-old Dawn was nothing to look at. Tiny of stature, with a small, rotund bullethead to match, but with a mind as sharp as her elbows, and an attitude as tough as the Star of the Sea estate in which she grew up.

—Yes, the staff nurse said, can I help you, dear?

—If you don't mind. I'm not your "dear." My name is Dawn Kernan and I'm looking for Éilis Devanney.

The now-bristling staff nurse was joined at the shoulder by a junior nurse whose Betty Boop eyes widened at Dawn.

—Ah, so we have two troublemakers on the ward now. Wonderful. Watch your step, madam. Lady Devanney is down there.

The eyes of the junior nurse now widened at her overnurse.

—Tank you, Dawn replied firmly, now in an arch, inner-city Dublin accent. —And by dee way dere's nutten wrong wit' me step. That's not why I'm here. Can you bring some tea down to us, miss?

Dawn moved down the centre of the ward but already knew that Éilis would be in the corner. She would have asked to be put there. Made it happen. And there she was with her dense, red-auburn hair with that distinctive wave and curl at its lower reaches. Her pallid and shockingly perfectly elliptical face. Wide

3

mouth breaking to smile. Bright teeth. Flowers. One red rose. They hugged warmly. Up close now. Éilis's lack of flesh. Like she was just a limbless, thinking head. Dawn noting the set of crutches by her small bedside cupboard.

—Jesus, Éilis, you look wrecked.

—I look wrecked, Dawn? You should see my psychoanalyst.

—I heard you'd been put in, so I got time off from Wakefields.

—Look, Dawn. I've written this, was up all night writing it, which is why Big Bertha up there is annoyed, and Wakefields, the Wakefields shop is in it, and you are in it, Dawn!

—Hold on, tell me how you're doing?

—Ah, the usual, not eating, low blood count. Éilis the Vamp, basically. But listen, I want you to do something with this document. It's important, Dawn.

—Éilis, this is Dawn you're talking to. We grew up together, remember. People in the flats are saying you were attacked or something.

—I'll tell you what happened when I'm ready, Dawnie. Sure, you know me. I'll be all right because I want to be all right.

Dawn looked round and then lowered her voice still further.

—There's a big bruise on the side of your face, E.

—Yes. That's partly what this story is about. Fighting back.

Éilis reached down into a large, gaily decorated canvas bag, and Dawn watched her, wondered at her, needed to say it out.

—Sinéad and Deirdre told me to tell you they were asking for you. They're coming in tonight. Are you going to tell me what happened? Have you been self-harming again or is it true what I'm hearing? That someone tried to get into your room and you jumped?

—I didn't jump, I had bed sheets already tied. Loads of them.

—Éilis, you mad thing. You live on the third floor.

—I know, Dawnie, broke me ankle, but it worked!

—Who was it? Was it him? The fucking Lord of Darkness. Darth Vader himself. Dawn bit her lip to cut her tongue.

—Tell you again, Dawn. I'd say he'll try in the future, but I'm up to him.

Éilis began writing something at the top of the manuscript,

her hand and wrist flowing all leisurely now, like some pale wind that was predestined. Head cocked like a hawk. Then she put the document into the folder she had pulled out of her bag. Looking up and directly at Dawn now. Suddenly not a scintilla of bodily movement. All is spoken yet nothing happening.

Éilis wanted to say that if Antigone could face the world, assert her human right and endure . . . And if Antigone could die happy . . .

Dawn did not know Antigone but she knew Éilis. Dawn wanted to say that she was there and would ever be there. All these things in a look. Some chorus there also. Beings watching from some other time, or world. Flowing robes and appalling masks. Then the Queen broke the spell, handed the folder to Dawn.

Spoke.

—Dawn, I want you to take this to Empire Television. To a guy called Tommy Baker?

—Tommy Baker, who's that, Éilis? Another one of your admirers?

—Ha, ha. No. He's a journalist and writer. The best. He has personal problems, I think. But don't we all.

—How do you know him?

—I met him when I was in there doing an Irish-language interview.

—You just bumped into him? This Tommy Baker fella . . . ?

—No, I walked up to him after one of the TG4 guys pointed him out.

—And you said?

—I said, Hello there, Mr Baker, I'm Éilis Devanney from Star of the Sea flats. When are you going to do something about us? I think he's an alcoholic, God help him . . . broken veins. Very sharp though. Listened to my brain before sizing me up. Good sign.

Dawn shook her head.

—You want me to just walk into Empire and give this to him, Éilis?

—Exactly.

—Will I ring him first?

—No, get reception to call him and hand it personally to him.

—Éilis.

—Don't worry, it will work. I already know that it will work. I see you going in there and something positive happening. I can feel it in my rising blood count. Wriggling red corpuscles. Getting frisky again now. Great to see you. Will we get tea?

—I've just asked, but I think we better walk downstairs if you can get up and hop along.

A Prole Penetrates the Empire

Dawn marched up to the fantastic-looking lady with those shoulders at the main reception desk in Empire Television. The shoulders were friendly enough but rather nonplussed.

—Well, I'm not sure that Mr Baker will, well, just take a package from you, just like that. I'll call the department secretary.

—No, sorry, I was told to give it to him personally.

A young and tall researcher/runner is walking across the reception area and the sight of Dawn remonstrating with the receptionist arrests his progress. He is a country man with big hands. Hands that have lifted a turf-cutter and much else. Stared at death's eyes in animals and humans. Aware of life's deeper incongruities—the plush walls and polished floor, the wide expanse of Empire Television's reception area and all its livery surrounding the slight girl with the tough face and accent, she holding some package in the air in the manner of a lifebelt. James Tierney turned back and walked towards the reception desk.

—Sorry, but you'll understand, madam, that I can't just call Mr Baker, I'd need some . . .

—First off, I'm not a madam, and you are obviously not a lady. But I'm not moving till . . .

Tierney intervened his tall, rangy frame and disentangled the girl from the grip of the situation. He led her to a long, low sofa in Empire purple and told Dawn that he was working for that same Tommy Baker and that he could pass the document on to him. The girl clutched the parcel even more firmly to her breast but trusted his eyes.

7

In the Empire Television restaurant, this James talked to
Dawn and she could feel his empathy. He had eyes that she
could fall into because he let her, wasn't disgusted by her, sat close
and naturally placed his hand on her arm when he was making a
point. He was like a priest. Or like a priest should be. Not devi-
ous. Eyes also that had seen things, suffered things. Dreamy and
comic by turns, like he knew how to ridicule himself. Searching
eyes. Also the eyes of a fighter. Like he would fight for Éilis.
For justice. For poor people. For the things they still cling onto
about Jesus, Mary, and the Saints.

Dawn released her grip on the folder.

—So, this Tommy Baker's on leave, James?

—He is. He goes off to Spain a lot, Dawn. Well, Catalonia
actually.

Dawn handed him the package and said confidingly, —Éilis
says that he has problems?

Tierney looked at her directly.

—I mean, I couldn't possibly comment, Dawn, but all the
same . . . how the fuck did she know that?

—She's Éilis, sure. She's been here before and I love her more
than meself.

Dawn would not have been surprised that James Tierney
made a number of calls to say he would be indisposed that afternoon and got a fellow researcher to do runner in the news studio that afternoon. He then retired to a quiet place to read Éilis
Devanney's document.

Soiscéal; or, The News from the Street

IT WAS HANDWRITTEN and presented as a story, in the third person, with this Éilis one above everything like an interested, sometimes impassioned observer, even though she was often obviously describing herself. James lifted an eyebrow at several points. There were some drawings. Drawings and sketches. It was like reading and viewing a film. She knew her characters and could write, had sympathy for everybody, everybody, everybody in her remarkable story. Even the baddies had a reason and something beyond reason. Also her neat, precise hand, but with a flourish to cross-strokes and letter endings. He appreciated that—like some kind of street calligraphy. Was she an Irish Banksy?

James Tierney knew the area around Star of the Sea in north inner-city Dublin and knew vaguely (from Tommy Baker) about the major drug dealer that was being referred to—Jimmy Heffernan. But he had also heard that Heffernan was some sort of local hero. People, even celebrities, saying he was no longer a gangster. That he had taken on the system and beaten it. A very bright working-class boy made good, which is why he was resented so much by the old order.

By the time James had got around halfway, past Éilis's shocking description of Heffernan, then driving on to the next and the next chapter, then going backwards to check something urgent, he had to stop to clear his head, go home and read the story all over again. By the third reading, in the falling light in his kitchen, and he wolfing down pizza and a glass of cold beer, he wondered if it was his future that was being foretold even though he did not feature in the telling. He wanted to go the Mater Hospital and ask this Éilis right then and there how she could know such things when he knew that they had not happened. Anyway, she was too young if she was the same age as Dawn, about sixteen or seventeen, but then he leaned back, admitted he was jealous of her talent. Then he stooped his head over its pages, browsed some of the text and drawings and blew his cheeks in admiration.

The end he did not want to read. He could already feel it. Walked away from it. Went upstairs, brushed his teeth. Got ready for bed. Lay down, turned off the light. Eyes staring at the walls. His specially framed picture of Cantona kicking the hooligan. His piece of Galway bog. Scenting the wind off Lough Dearg—the long, red eye rimming land and water. He flung back the duvet, went back downstairs, and it was still there on the table.

When veteran journalist Tommy Baker got back from Girona that Sunday night, he was surprised to find a number of messages on his home phone (he never took his work mobile with him to his retreat in the hills of Catalonia). The messages were from James Tierney, his new researcher. The next minute, Tierney was at his door. He already liked Tierney, approved of his ferocious drive, his anger at the world, the fact of his clinically depressed mother, his bullying, absent father, two older brothers who seemed to resent his intelligence, and no sister to soften things. Baker felt sorry for Tierney also. Not doubting that Tierney carried the same canker, that insane impulse that he too carried. To open Pandora's box.

Not doubting that Tierney was on a road to destruction. This young, handsome man with his broad features and chiseled bones, almost-black hair and Atlantic eyes—a West of Ireland face. Here standing now before him, not cowed, but too earnest, too bright for this cynical world. For no single soul can survive the onslaught. Almost rocking on his feet as he stood there with his inner energy. A boxer. A young marathon man.

Tierney wondered at the utter quiet in this big house. Guessed that there no female was. No business. No alternative voice or design. A monk's place it was. No, not a monk. An erudite scholar. His larger, detached retreat. Baker's learned redoubt. The physical expression of his fortified mind. The books and wine his drawbridge into himself.

Baker gulped at his goblet of wine but left the glass in the sitting room and ushered James Tierney into his study.

—My God, James, I know I said, nay insisted, that you should ring or call any time of day if you thought it necessary but what . . . ?

James simply proffered Éilis's document.

—Sorry, Tommy, but I think you better read this. I made a copy for you. You are one of the main characters.

Wakefields

ÉILIS LOOKED INTO the mirror, *and then stared into the mirror.* For an age she looked intently at the mirror until she could face the truth in her eyes. So hard that the glass cracked and the truth shattered in smithereens across her body, her large dresser, and the bedroom floor.

Smidiríní, she mouthed in her ancient tongue.

The store manager noticed her the second she appeared like a vision bathed in sunlight just outside his premises. He guessed the girl was around twenty, maybe slightly older, and from the flats or thereabouts, because he had seen her talking to an old lady, a regular customer, whom she had kissed on the cheek or sort of hugged before coming into his store. To be accurate, the premises did not belong to him but were part of a Wakefields franchise. Young as he was, he had a good track record of managing difficult shops in poor areas and he had been given a very favourable commission to open and run the store, given the territory in which it was located. For him, it was very simple. You just made sure you knew who the Face was in the area and kept him happy. Peace of mind flowed from simply paying homage to the local gangster—some guy called Spanzo—whom he'd actually never met and, by the sounds of him, didn't want to meet. Paying a go-between was just fine. In fact, things had been so quiet that he had even been able to do away with the security man in the morning hours. Though he was about to regret that move.

The manager also knew that Wakefields had decided to locate

the store near the flats because the area around them was going upmarket fast. This part of north inner-city Dublin had been identified by their analysts in England as a major growth area. Gated yuppie communities, the new Super Court building, the huge student complex at Grangegorman. All the arms of the law and academia would be installed there.

In other words, the days of the flats were numbered—settled, old Dubliners in the surrounding streets, an ancient community, as well as the inveterate poor, immigrants, and skangers who had been dumped or abandoned there were yesterday's toast. History. If this young man could successfully run the business until the flats were knocked in around two years' time, he had it made. Or at least that was what Wakefields had promised him. More long term, he wanted to have the kind of business profile that would help him start his own set of chain stores, before retiring early to the Algarve. His real passion was snorkelling and studying wondrous fish, but he tried not to think about it, or dream about it in working hours.

Yet this one didn't look like she was from the flats. She was tall and her mane of long, lustrous, brown hair had a reddish tinge and a swing like the posture of a catwalk model. At the same time, she gave an air of being absolutely careless about the way she looked. Or maybe what people thought about the way she looked. The young manager realised that, in a reflex action to her appearance in the store, he had begun smoothing his hair back and checking whether he had applied deodorant to his underarms that morning.

He had experienced a variety of events in his role as a "troubleshooter" for Wakefields, but nothing could have prepared him for what happened next. Nor was he surprised when, not long after, this same girl's face was splashed all over the newspapers and on the television. Like some latter-day Marilyn. By then, however, and as a direct result of meeting this girl, he would no longer be a manager in a Wakefields store. He would not be a manager of anything.

He stood some distance away, at the far end of the dairy-products aisle, which offered a clear view down to the cash register where this beauty was having a conversation with Dawn, the assistant at the counter. They obviously knew each other very well. Smiles, eye engagement. Standing back to ponder a point. A range of understood assumptions that often made the need for words irrelevant. He could not hear what the redhead (auburn?) was saying because of the noise from the widescreen television which was blaring out some news flash about a major traffic holdup in London. Then the noise ceased. The noise just stopped dead. He meant that he could hear himself breathing, breathing suddenly more heavily.

He realised that the girl at the counter, Dawn, had given the remote control to the new customer and this redheaded babe had switched off the television. She had cut it dead, just like that.

The slight noise from traffic outside and even the odd snatch of conversation from within the store—something about Pot Noodles—confirmed this action. He could have sworn he even heard the tweet of a bird. The everyday noises now permeating the store were disturbing and alien to him. They were not super-market sounds. Somebody somewhere dropped a can. Looking straight down the aisle, the assistant at the cash register lifted her hands in a gesture to him, as if to ask, what else could she have done?

The manager now walked briskly and with a purpose to the top of the store, after once more adjusting his hair and going higher on his heels. As he closed in on her, he realised that she was taller than him.

—Hi, Dawn. Are we all good? he enquired of Dawn.

He was determined to be as nice as possible. He liked this vision even more now that he had her up close. He didn't rec-ognise the scent she was wearing, but he knew it was not cheap.

—Hi, you must be the manager, the tall girl said.

—That's correct. Dawn, put the television back on please.

—I'm afraid the television is going to have to stay off from now on, the girl said without even the hint of a girly twinkle in her eyes of cobalt blue.

—Are you for real!? Dawn, put the television back on, he said to the now-deadpan assistant. —Now, Dawn . . .

Dawn politely pointed out that "Éilis" still had possession of the remote control.

—Well, why did you give it her?

—She asked me for it, sure!

The manager held out his hand, edging closer again towards the girl and the remote in her swan-like hand. He spoke softly, putting his best killer smile on display, conscious of his very breath.

—Look, er . . . Éilis, is it? he asked looking at the shopworker, who nodded affirmation. This was indeed Éilis.

—Éilis, you seem like a nice girl and we don't want any trouble, do we? So just give me back the remote, which is the property of Wakefields, and we'll forget all about it. Eh, what do you say?

—He who controls the remote, controls the people, the girl said.

This nonsense zinged around the manager's head. Confusing because it had a familiar ring to it. He had a big order due in any moment and he did not need this. He was beginning to realise that the poor girl was a looper, a total head-the-ball. What a waste, he thought. Also, he now realised that she was younger than he had first thought, maybe the same age as Dawn. A recent school-leaver, then. A firmer approach was needed. If he could deal with baseball bats he could deal with this.

—Listen, Éilis. If this is a windup, I don't need it on a Monday morning and I certainly—

He was not given the chance to continue.

—Did you ask anyone from round here whether they want to do their shopping with Sky News blasting all over the shop?

—You're serious, aren't you? You are actually serious. Look, you have five fucking seconds to give me back the remote and then I am going to call the Guards.

Dawn, who had moved herself directly into the manager's line of vision, drew a face like a sudden toothache and shook her head firmly at the manager's suggestion.

—Then you are not going to listen, Éilis said, looking at him directly.

For the first time he realised that she wore not an ounce of makeup and that he wanted to kiss her full, red lips, which were the more red because her skin was so pale. Éilis gave the remote back to the assistant, walked out of the store with her high ass and a toss of her mane. After choosing the best spot on the pavement, the flaming Éilis unfolded a rolled-up poster she had been carrying, which bore the legend, both in English and Irish: BOYCOTT THIS SHOP! BAGHCATÁIL AN SIOPA SEO!

The manager could not believe what he was seeing. In fact, he absolutely and utterly could not believe what he was seeing. He turned to the counter assistant who just shrugged her shoulders.

—Who the fuck is this space cadet?

—That's Éilis from the flats, sure. She's a good mate, so mind your tongue. She's no spacer. That girl would buy and sell ya, and you wouldn't even know it. She did her leaving cert when she was fourteen, reads serious books, gave a talk to some professors or something once and then when she was only fifteen . . .

Whilst Dawn carried on with a long list of Éilis's attributes, the manager was distracted by the arrival of a delivery van. In the same instant, he saw that a small crowd was gathering around this Éilis one whom everybody seemed to know.

Already one person, who looked to be just entering the shop, had turned about-face and walked away after having a short conversation with the beauty queen from hell. He ran back to the counter and called the assistant over to him.

—Is she a close friend of yours, Dawn?

—I've just said. That's Éilis. We went to school together, though we both hated it.

—Yeah, but can you see what's going on there! She's telling people not to use the shop!

—It's not my business, really. I'm only here a couple of months, but if you want my advice?

—Yes?

—Turn off the TV. If Éilis tells people not to come into the shop, they won't come in. Like, no one. This place will be a desert by tonight.

—No, you mean it will be deserted . . . Oh fuck it. I can't

believe this is happening to me. What, is it Paddy's Day, Red Nose Day, and April Fool's combined, or what!? Is she some kind of witch?

—That's funny! Some people have called her a witch! But a good witch yer know. A white one. She does healing an' all that. She got rid of me granny's warts. But she's very clever too . . .

The effervescent Dawn took some change from a pre-boycott customer for a newspaper, bread, and beans, but continued her potted biography of Éilis's life in a seamless verbal stream.

—A fluent Irish speaker and some other languages, and in tongues as well. You know that thing that Madonna is into. She should be on the telly herself. Not Madonna, our Éilis. Not Sky News, but. Obviously . . .

The manager was not appreciative of the Dublin wit and found that, in a number of firsts for him this Monday morning, he had completely lost control of a situation. He felt his armpits beginning to sweat. Then the bread delivery man nudged him.

—Do you want this bread or not? I can't be waitin' here all bleedin' day. Oh, and there's no ginger snaps . . . who's the good-lookin' bird anyway . . . is she a pop star or somethin'? Think I saw her on TG4 once. Ye wouldn't mistake her. He nudged the manager again.

Things were made worse when the delivery man then approached this girl Éilis in what seemed to be an attempt to gain an autograph.

The day had seemed like every other day for the manager when he had left his semidetached house in the Pale of Kildare. Now this maniac had turned it into a nightmare. A bad hair day. Time to act. He rushed outside to the small clump of people on the pavement and asked, nay begged, Éilis to put the poster away, as he was sure they could work something out. Then, after dealing with the bread order, he took Éilis into his office and discovered very quickly that if this witch were burned at the stake for a fool they would have gotten wise ashes.

—Do you feel that you are suddenly in a dream? Éilis asked.
—What?
—Sorry, what's your name?

—Francis.

—Francis, I thought so. Francis. Frank, Francis . . . you have a Frank face. Anyway, Francis, when all the hullabaloo started, she laughed, did you feel like you were suddenly in a dream?

—Well, actually, yeah I did. A bad dream though.

The phone rang and to his own astonishment he diverted all calls to the answer machine.

—That's good, said Éilis. When people see and feel a different reality they think they are dreaming, but in fact the dream is just as real. If I never achieve anything else, I've helped you see things differently.

—Well, that's certainly true, Éilis. But why do you have a problem with Sky News, for God's sake?

—Well, firstly, people round here don't want Sky News assaulting them when they are going shopping and they were certainly never asked whether they wanted it. It's too loud. It's basically anti-Palestinian and pushing a new Western crusade for the cause of the petro dollar and the pound, and it has nothing whatever to do with what's going on here in our country. Can you tell me one way, Francis, in which having Sky News on in the shop, or say CNN, enriches the lives of Irish people, particularly poor people?

Francis thought and thought, he puckered his brow with the thinking. This girl was obviously very bright and he did not want to come across as a complete eejit from the sticks. Managers were supposed to be the bright ones. Also, he was shocked to find that Éilis had become sexless, or perhaps just plain serious. Francis jumped in with what he hoped was an intelligent point.

—Well, at least, you know, it tells the news . . . you know, world news, like? Current, you know . . . breaking . . .

His voice trailed off to an insipid throat clearance. He had felt stupid the moment he had said it. It was partly the way Éilis looked at him with that direct gaze which he found kindly but unrelenting. Yet, it was also because he had never been made to think about the likes of Sky News before. At that moment, Dawn came in to tell him that they were very low on Pot Noodle. In assenting to a new order of Pot Noodle, it occurred to Francis that Dawn would make a very good store manager, that she actually cared about feeding the locals. But Éilis brought him back to Sky and rolling news.

—It's a spreading virus, Francis. There's hardly a shop, bank, or pub in Ireland that doesn't have this propaganda screaming out from these huge screens, and it has to stop. It's debasing our own languages. Both of them, English and Irish. The way we talk to each other or don't talk to each other anymore. We can't hear ourselves think. It's not even Worldspeak. It's Transatlanticspeak. It's neither here nor there for us.

—And you're going to stop it? All on your own?

—No, I won't do it on my own. You are going to help me, I know.

—Me!? No way, Éilis. I've got a mortgage and a wife to feed, well, fiancée, which is worse.

—Well, not just you. Lots of people like you. We are a small country and things can change very quickly when people start setting an example. Where did the successful Irish blockade of goods from apartheid South Africa begin?

—I don't know, where?

—In a supermarket just like this one, Francis. Normal people deciding to take a stand. Now you are one concerned person.

—Hold on! Who said I was concerned!? Francis pulled at his tie.

Éilis chuckled.

—Tomorrow morning, after thinking about all this, you will wake up and realise that you have been wasting your life and will sit down and take real stock of things, instead of what you do here. I see you going to Africa where your brother is an aid worker.

—How the f . . . sorry . . . how the hell did you know that? And anyway I was hoping more the Algarve. Partial to snorkelling, believe it or not.

—This is people-snorkelling, then, and even more colourful and rewarding. Word spreads quickly. The poor have not and never will forget the past and that is why they are precious in God's eyes. First Dublin, and then elsewhere. I call it redressive action for a post-colonial reality that's being dressed up by the likes of Sky News and CNN to look like a non-reality. Like we are all in this together, the Brits and the Yanks and then the rest of us in tow against some vague, ill-defined enemy. In other words, anybody who doesn't accept their blinkered monolingual, monocultural worldview. Sorry, I know I'm ranting. Water, please.

Francis looked at Éilis afresh. Really looked at her this time and rose from his seat to put on the coffee maker.

—Do you drink coffee?

—Love coffee, but I'd prefer fair-trade coffee if you have it?

Francis shook his head apologetically.

—You mentioned my brother and God knows that's exactly what he would have said. Not only about the coffee . . . about the way we are going, as well. That's why he got out. He used to really annoy me when he started one of his rants. Sorry, but you were ranting.

—Your brother is right. You should ring him and ring him more often.

—What age are you?

—Sixteen. Soon to be seventeen if I make it that far.

—And at sixteen years of age why should you be bothered about all this crap instead of going out chasing fellas and buying clothes?

—That's what they said to Bernadette Devlin and Joan of Arc, and look what she did for France. Mary Shelley was eighteen when she wrote Frankenstein and she with little schooling. And Antigone . . . she was so young, but asserted her right to a moral law that binds all families.

Francis looked up at the ceiling

—Antigone . . . jeez, I remember seeing that play once when I was at school. But, Éilis. Take some advice from me, kid. I mean, I don't want to come the patronizing adult, but jeez . . . you're way too serious. I had a mate like you once. In fact, him and my brother joined the Labour Party together. Now he has a great job in the City of London. Do you know what I mean? As you get older . . .

Now there was a silence before Éilis spoke again. A look that drilled into Francis's brain. She was almost angry.

—Francis. It's not just me. There are thousands like me. In the Occupy movement. The Green movement. The Language movement. But me? Éilis Devanney? I know that I was placed on this earth to defend the people, so that they don't forget the names for things and to honour the dead. So that they don't forget how to dream. Not dream in a Freudian sense where dreams can be interpreted any way the psychotherapist chooses, but dreams from our myths which come from a past reality and have made us what we are. If we forget our myths we will become strangers, zombies in our own country. All standing and staring at that great Sky on the screen. Do you know Kate Tempest, the poet? Read, or better still, listen to her poem *Brand New Ancients*. I, You, We are the people and we go far, far back . . .

A silence developed in the office. It may have lasted hours or even days. Francis the manager was no longer sure of time. He was cradling his coffee in is hand but he didn't remember pouring it. What he was sure about was that he could have gone on listening to Éilis forever. He also wanted to ask her to write down what she was after saying. But then in his own head he told himself that he didn't want to sound like a prick. But he was now convinced that he was in the presence of an extraordinary person. He awoke from his reverie and realised that asking for a date was out of the question. How did you ask Joan of Arc for a date, for God's sake? There was another slight problem in that he was engaged to be married. Francis tucked his belly in.

—Well, all I can say is fair play to you for trying Éilis but its unstoppable. It's company policy. Not only for this company but for all companies providing a public service, as far as I know. Sky News has to be shown at every Wakefields outlet, Éilis. If I don't show it, I'll get sacked.

—Okay, well we don't want that. You won't be leaving Wakefields just yet, so we are going to have to find a compromise.

To yet more self-disbelief on what was supposed to have been just another mundane Monday morning, Francis the shop manager found himself happily agreeing to remove the television from its prominent position above the main till and place it above the fridge at the back of the store with the sound on mute. If somebody had told him as he left for work in his top-of-the-range Land Cruiser that morning that all this was going to happen he would have laughed and bet his house, with the golf-club membership and fiancée thrown in, that the whole scenario was impossible. Dawn just gave a knowing look and put her thumbs up.

When Francis got home that night, he phoned his brother Shane at the hostel where he worked in Nairobi and told him what had happened. They hadn't spoken for six months.

—Welcome back to reality. What else did she say?

—She told me that I was going to go out there to be with you or help you or something.

—Welcome to Africa.

Once Shane had explained the cheaper concept of phone calls over the internet to Francis, the two brothers spoke for an hour and resolved to keep much better contact from then on. Francis told Shane things he had been wanting to say for a long time, about how much he loved him and missed him; that he respected what he was trying to do out there and had been annoyed at—"all right, very bleedin' jealous of"—his brother's lack of care about "getting on" and making a career for himself. At the end of the conversation, Shane touched on something which had been nagging at Francis all day after Éilis had left the store.

—Do you think you'll see her again, Francie?

—Well, I haven't seen her before in the shop. I'd remember if I did because she is an absolute stunner. Dawn says she shops at weird places that sell brown rice and soya, if she shops at all. She makes her own bread and yogurt, apparently. Why do you ask?

—Next time you see her, tell her to be careful.

—What, d'ye think she'd actually be in physical danger, Shane? Nah . . . no way, bro, I don't think so. If you saw her. She couldn't threaten a fly. And everyone seems to know her.

—Intuition, I suppose, Francie. Bad politicians . . . bad witch doctors. Europe is just as corrupt as Africa and in some ways more dangerous. There's an awful lot of greed back there. Every time I go home I realise that everyone is on the make. The Irish have become totally obsessed with money, only they don't want anyone holding up a big mirror saying: here take a look at yourselves.

—Ah, come on, Shane, things aren't that bad. Not yet anyway.

—No . . . ? Then name me one public figure that you would see as being incorruptible?

—Er . . . well there's . . . hold on, let me think.

Francis thought for a long time and then decided to make a joke out of it as he could not think of anybody.

—Dustin used to be good!

—Who? What party is he in?

—No, I mean Dustin the puppet on the telly.

—So, it's a muppet basically.

—Yeah.

—And will the likes of Dustin save Éilis?

—From what?

—A girl like that could end up in a lot of bother, Francis.

—Why?

—Because she sounds very naive and a bit too clever and lippy. Plus, she can't be bought and she might annoy the wrong people with that crusade of hers. A lot of Dublin is rougher than most parts of Nairobi, and she could easily get put down a hole. I feel safer in Africa, and that's no lie.

—Think that's way over the top, Shane, to be honest.

At this point, when reading Éilis's story once again at home, James Tierney pulled out the next few pages and filed them away. He felt bad about it. As a journalist, he knew that he was engaging in censorship, but he had already decided that he was going to show the document as a whole to Tommy Baker, after making his own copy, but this part he was going to excise. It was nothing like the previous chapter. James wondered whether Éilis herself was a junkie, or maybe a recovering addict? Suddenly she begins writing in a delirium, or stream of consciousness—going on about her parents as devils, that their name wasn't Devanney; there was a Finn and a Séamus and her uncle Antain who had first taught her Irish but had apparently died in a bike crash, which Éilis had predicted.

It was here that the drug dealer Heffernan first made an appearance and could have been very interesting, but then she breaks off into something about a child being harmed and then the white of her arms and how she wanted to bleed from them and fade into transparency, and then about a bird called Morrígan whose stench made her sick. She spat at the bird, raised a razor-sharp letter opener, threw an ancient block of amber. Something about a bouncing ball. Images on the wall. Mad stuff.

But still. He felt this tremendous urge to go and visit her right away. Study her face. See if she was for real, ask her probing questions. Also, he had already heard of these so-called Untouchables she wrote about so vividly.

Three Dolls

THE HEAT WAS not of any Irish season that was ever known, and was unbearable. Initially, the people of Dublin had welcomed the fierce sun with a common dementia, which led them to shed their clothes and expose themselves to the hot elements. Invariably, this led to burned flesh and pre-cancerous boils on skin so fair. Alcoholic and drug-induced anger also.

Warnings from the ancients on doorsteps to cover up were ignored and often not politely. It was cool to be sautéed in sun-oil and to ape their betters in London, California, and the beaches of Benidorm and Ibiza. Deep behind the sunglasses, however, an old, Irish question worried at the psyche: When was it to break? For the Irish could no more do without the rain than the rain the Irish.

Before they were driven indoors and made invisible by the cheek of the youth and the heat from the flagstones on the footpath, the ancients warned that something was wrong, the weather being as it was. Things had not been right since the Yanks started sending those satellites up and people had stopped talking to each other. Worse than that, the old people understood that the Irish love of Irish weather, and thereby the Irish temperament was disappearing in the whitening and anodyne glare of the New Age where was there no craic at all. You switched the telly on early morning and were confronted with people on a stage swearing and cursing each other, always at the top of their voice and always on the brink of violence, talking about "issues" and abuse and sex, casually, serially, always back to sex, and though the people changed, it was the same every day, so you turned to the radio because you were worn out worrying about all those young people, who were only really proclaiming the social disaster that was upon us since they had killed God and His angels and all the glory and mystery that held us together and the scientists laughed, broadcasters winked knowingly at the audience, and the younger populace was appalled to see these old ones giving out about satellites and the death of discourse.

Within the firing kiln of this collective lobotomy, Éilis appeared as an aisling, a vision, a dream, of what had been. A rare and tender flower implausibly alive where its radiant genus had perished under the comet-crashing fireball that was the global culture of morbid product-purchasing and maniacal consumption.

Now sitting on a low brick wall, using an old, hard book cover as a seat pad, her white blouse billowing softly in a breeze that she seemed to have conjured from the thin air, Éilis read from a slim volume. Oblivious to all extraneous interruptions. A gang of workmen who honked at her from a passing van. A man who presumed to comment about her legs. Even the good day of an old lady. A police siren somewhere, an airplane, shouts from the flats. Only when she sensed the arrival of Sinéad and Sinéad's cousin Deirdre did she put the book away. Replete.

This low brick wall had been a constant place for them to meet and be girls in their own right. Away from the tight walls and piss-flooded stairwells of the flats, and with their own code, the subject of boys and not boys, makeup or not makeup, the vagaries of their bodies and the changes, their discussions, their laughs and their carry-on. However, it was not just the far-seeing Éilis who saw that the days of mad craic on the wall, the flouncing and funny stories were drawing to a close. That this was the wall's final summer. All three girls sensed that, come the winter, God bless the winter! they would have made their separate exits from this urban stage and the teenage life that surrounded it. Conscious also of being too old too young.

Across the way from the wall—where once was a small children's park, whose swings had been hacked and assaulted and finally laid low, the other play contraptions fired to death—there was now a wasteland of battered fridges and chairs, cars and boxes, and here a group of youths had the custom of gathering as some kind of weird counterpoint to the female wall. An abandoned leather sofa, their daytime, all-male, and very public throne. Since all of them refused to own a mobile phone, the sofa and their tent was a useful, nay indispensable, rendezvous point. They had washed up here because their group had been evicted from an Occupy site in the centre of Dublin and Star of the Sea flats was one of the few places where a Goth squat would be laughed at, enjoyed, and more or less tolerated. In fact, local youths became, for the most part, quite proud of their tolerant behaviour to these "weirdoes and puffs." Besides, they were clearly anti-authority, so as long as they kept themselves to themselves . . . The Goths' internal rules were made up as they pondered things along. All shades of black were allowed within their dress code, which would always be at least partially covered by the expected long, black coat, also very handy for shoplifting, which in turn was offset by a gaunt white face. Deep red lipstick was also sometimes applied, mostly away from prying eyes and at secret gatherings. No women at all in their public midst. That would have been a complication too far and a danger to the solidarity of their male-Gothic code. Chivalrous, romantic knights of old preferred to yearn, long, and pine, and anyway, the presence of girls would have attracted too many hoods and gougers. Though Goth girls were allowed to visit their squat, they too had to be gone by cockcrow. Romance was a thing to be studied, mulled over, and praised, occasionally grieved over, even acted upon, but should never threaten the integrity of the group or its poetic raison d'être. Ah Keats, Byron and Shelley. Wordsworth also. High art amongst the common man!

One Goth in particular was a poet of note, adored for his odes to Byron, Shelley, Oscar Wilde, and Earl Grey tea. His name was Turlough McKenna, this surname being widespread in his home county of Monaghan. Turlough's country father had thrown him out because he had begun to apply a deep strike of blue to his beautiful mane of black. Worse he had taken to walking the streets of Carrickmacross in a leather jerkin adorned with a flower, tight evening dress trousers, and Chelsea boots. His mother rather adored his rebellion and sent money up to Dublin via a secret channel. This poet had seen Éilis several times in town, at protests, sit-ins, sit-outs, sit-downs, and bank occupations, but she was beyond his ken. He feared her Celtic autism and its dislocation from refined intellect. She was too immediate and terrible and definite and supreme and his brain shook at the thought of approaching her. He did, however, have a more definite eye for Deirdre, whose lustrous skin and full breasts were a wonder to him, pale ambrosia offset by black, Irish hair like his but without the curls; her innocence also—her simplicity and goodness, her obliviousness to the rats and the rat race all around her. He'd had occasion to stand quite close to Deirdre though she may not have been aware of it. She wore no perfume that he could register but her skin scent was pale gorse and slightly astringent. Nor did she smoke. Unlike her fierce friend whom he espied walking with Deirdre to the Snow Queen. Éilis.

From their old-settee redoubt, these long, pale youths also expected an end, a storm to break. A tempest in which their antique, collective umbrella of eccentricity would no longer protect but simply conduct the wrath of the contending elements. All reflection was viewed as suspect, the slow consideration of life a sign of a terminal malady, an affront to the constitution of commercial gain. What profit in ten slothful youths dressing up in a confusion of sexuality and seemingly without productive duties? Yet the Goths knew all this and prided themselves in their stoicism, their preferred form of anti-consumer rebellion. In their slow, aesthetically pleasing suicide pact, they set their faces and waited.

The Tangling of Threads

—SERIOUSLY, DEIRDRE SAID to Sinéad as they drew near to where Éilis sat. —You wouldn't believe the things they throw away. I got this deadly dress out of VDP's the other day. I'm gonna wear it to Siobhán's do. I saw a wedding dress there once. At Vincent de Paul's, I mean, not Siobhán's do . . . because we haven't had Siobhán's do yet . . . I swear, Sinéad . . . don't laugh!

Sinéad, holding her cigarette with a seasoned air as they walked, shook her head and gave Deirdre a look which to the outsider could have passed for contempt.

—I wouldn't get anything from Vincent De Paul, said Sinéad, I'd rather go and rob it. Why should we live on charity?

Deirdre, however, was holding her own conversation and was not listening to Sinéad.

—Get married . . . yeah . . . I don't really mind who I marry as long as he's nice to me. A film, you know, a DVD on a Saturday night . . . DVD and VDP, Sinéad! . . . Me bleedin' life could be sorted moving between the two o' them . . . few cans . . . kids in bed . . . snuggling up.

Through the heat shimmering off the tarmac, Sinéad shot a glance at the boys on the sofa. The drugs bazaar near the arch. The tenements of Star of the Sea flats. Flicks a drop of sweat near her eye.

—Jeez, I want outta this place. There's no way I'm getting married. See getting stuck in a place like this, with screaming kids, trying to bring them up here! So not going to happen, D.

Sinéad then gave Deirdre a playful elbow as they came within earshot of Éilis and she theatrically raised her voice, —Now if I was Éilis and had a fella like Finn on me arm, well, that might be different. How ya, E., what's that you're reading?

—It's about life . . . as usual. It's good, though, makes you think.

—Oh yeah . . . ? What's it called?

—*A Guide for the Perplexed.*

—Per-plex . . . ! Deirdre exclaimed. That was that stuff I was telling you about, Sinéad. The shiny stuff on that dress.

—That's "Lurex" you mean, Deirdre, you dipstick.

Éilis laughed, enjoying the routine from her two bosom friends. One of the joys of her life.

—How d'ye mean life, Éilis? said Sinéad, who drew up near the wall and looked out. She was interested in the book. —Does it tell you your future? What's that eye on the front?

—Well, it's a bit heavy but, yeah I suppose, it does tell you about life and the future. It's not like the clairvoyants we go to, but . . .

—Sure, you're the best clairvoyant around, E., said Deirdre, returning momentarily to the conversation from her ruminations on marriage. —Can you read your own palm?

Éilis smiled with an urgent glint in her eye. Her attempt at another laugh was thrown back at her from the sky.

—This is more important than that, D., it basically tells you to have faith because not everything can be proven scientifically. If you feel it strongly enough, then it's real enough . . . that's faith.

Deirdre began to hum a song and look over at the Goths, who lifted their cups of chamomile tea in salutation.

—Would you not think those eejits would at least take their coats off, said Deirdre. He's not bad, the one with that blue stuff in his hair. I saw him at the welfare last month. Cool guy.

The poet Turlough McKenna beckoned to Deirdre, —Come pay the Goths a visit, moving to the edge of the Gothic circle as he did so, much to the consternation of his morose comrades who wished they had the gumption to do things like that. Deirdre, in turn, moved to leave her friends but was dragged back with some violence by Sinéad who was still crooked in the umbilical cord of her elbow.

—Me ma's always talking about faith, said Sinéad, grimly hanging on every word that Éilis said.

—Well, without faith, said Éilis, we're all up that creek without the paddle basically.

—Big shit . . . Deirdre interjected.

—I think I had it once . . . faith, said Sinéad. Don't know what happened then. I think I just lost hope . . . that something might happen . . . you know . . . something good. Then there's all those disgusting priests.

Sinéad threw away the end of the cigarette.

—You see, Éilis, you've all those things going for you . . . and good luck to ya . . . you deserve every one of them. You're the star of the estate and we're all waiting for you and Finn to go out and conquer the world so that we can ride on your coattails.

Éilis wanted to dissemble. Say it wasn't true. Heart bulging with pride in herself but torn with empathy.

—Me? Éilis Devanney? What do I have going for me? I'm way too serious and miserable to conquer any world. I'd rather stay here and do things. Start a film-and-book club maybe, and oh yeah, guys, wait till you hear the mental thing I did at the supermarket.

But Sinéad ploughed on, her joy and anger flashing like a sword in the intemperate Dublin air, in her clear eyes, her battling intelligence, her fine teeth and fair hair, her mounting despair.

—Éilis Devanney has class written all over her. You could walk straight outta this excuse for a brothel . . . we can't even do that right . . . and straight into the swankiest club in town. I'll tell yer what we'll do for the dare next week.

Deirdre now began to take a real interest again as Sinéad got excited, her voice more animated.

—We'll doll up next week. No wait, the weekend after Siobhán's do, and march up to Connolly's Wine Bar, you know, the one Heffernan runs, and I'm putting her wedding dress on you getting in, and us standing in, well it won't be the cold, but standing like spare fucking dildos at a lesbian love-in. And then Éilis will just wave her wand and we'll get in, I betcha. Connolly's is all for the toffs to score, and we can't get near the door. Of course, if Éilis asks, can we be let in, they'll let us in. That's the truth of it, but I don't mind riding on your magic carpet, Éilis. I'll take whatever gold dust you can fucking sprinkle on me.

The air, the traffic, the street, the Gothic chorus, grew ominously quiet. As if the very dust in the flaky, substandard brick in the walls of the flats was absorbing the import of what had been said, waiting for Éilis to pronounce a decision upon it, until Deirdre broke the spell with her magic wand of innocence.

—It's because of the Irish, she said quietly and seriously.

They all turned—the street, the world, the Morrígan Raven—all turning.

—That's where we went wrong, me and you, Sinéad. Éilis has a different head on her. The Irish puts you there, out away from here. She's in a different place. How do you know when you have faith, Éilis?

The tone of the question came from some place in Deirdre that Sinéad had never heard before.

—Well, Deirdre, you just know it's there. It's like love. No doctor or scientist can show you love . . . you can't see it, it can't be touched, or weighed on a scale, but you know it's there when you have it. Hate is the same, unfortunately.

—What's faith called in Irish? The two girls said this almost simultaneously.

—Faith, said Éilis waiting for the cosmos to regain its shape, and Áine the sun goddess to kiss her brow. The world heaving a sigh of relief for Sinéad's distress, for Éilis's soothing words.

—Faith is supposed to be called *creideamh* in Irish.

Sinéad mouthed the word *creideamh* and squeezed her hand so tightly in trying to will this thing *creideamh* into her very bone and sinew that the still-connected Deirdre gave a yelp.

—But I prefer *muinín* which is like "faith" only it means "trust" as well, said Éilis. Like, would you two ever do me any harm?

Howls of protest now. Sinéad on the verge of tears, and the two girls both hunched down to the floor in front of Éilis like two imploring supplicants paying homage to a deity that had appeared before their disbelieving eyes only to begin to fade from view in a world where miracles were no longer seen or believed.

—Jesus, Éilis, don't ever ask that again, said Deirdre. You could bring on the bad luck.

—Ah, hold your tongue, Deirdre, said Sinéad genuinely angry. Give over with your bad luck.

Sinéad steeled her face and looked at Éilis.

—See, if I thought anyone or anything was going to harm you Éilis . . . but the clank of jaw attempting to mouth the words that were cartwheeling from Sinéad's mind defeated her. She was tongue-thick and her head ached to say the right thing.

—Of course I know that, said Éilis. But that's my point, Sinéad, how do I know it? I only know it in my heart through faith. I don't even need to think it. It just is. Faith, *muinín, creideamh*, and no big man in a white coat can write it down in a book because it's in our hearts.

At that point, a card slipped from Éilis's book and she grabbed at it before anyone else could.

—What's that, E.?

—It's a poem for Finn. It's his birthday today.

—Ah! isn't that lovely, said Deirdre. He'd probably be wasted on the likes of me, but. Even the name . . . Finn!

—Eh, what do ye mean, D., the name Finn? inquired Sinéad. That's his name, sure.

—You know, Finn . . . like a fish . . . Finn and chips.

Éilis covered her mouth trying to suppress her mirth but then quickly slipped card and book into her bag.

Sinéad just looked.

—D. . . . do you know what I am going to tell you . . . you are a certified, one hundred percent nutcase . . . but I love ya, she said, her voice choking in a flood of thought.

—It's all disgraceful and swimmy, like a . . . like em, like a fish! Cod, is it? Finn and codpiece. Where did I hear that once? Codpiece, it reminds me of Finn.

—D. . . . D.! and it's "graceful," not "disgraceful"!

—It's a all kind of upright . . . kinda sticky-uppy name. Like you couldn't imagine a Finn being floppy . . . What's Finn mean in Irish, Éilis?'

—Bright One. He was Fionn Mac Cumhail, the bright hero of legend, brighter even than Cúchullain. He's the head of the Fianna.

Deirdre was devastated. —So it's not a fish at all?

—No, D., it's not, and Finn can't even swim, for God's sake, big and ugly as he is. And I'm going before I crack up!

Sinéad called out to Éilis with a catch in her voice and she blinded by the sun as Éilis walked away.

—Come here, Éilis, we're all invited to Siobhán's rave, the do that I mentioned. It's Siobhán from Drumcondra. You know Siobhán . . . she's having it at De Courcey's . . . the big old house on the hill. Them Goths is doing a music set in one of the rooms. We'll go over together will we . . . ? You know I'll look after you if you go. It's happening at the end of the month, so loads of time, but don't forget it.

There was no better chaperone than the streetwise Sinéad, and Éilis half nodded in acceptance. She called back to the girls across the street on her way to the arch and the entrance to the flats.

—One of these nights that weird Éilis one might bless you all with her presence!

The girls curtsied theatrically.

—And then it's Heffernan's club the week after, don't forget! For the bet! Sinéad called.

The Goths on the derelict sofa sipped their tea, but the poet defied the daytime code by pulling a can of beer from his longcoat.

—That redhead. Éilis she's called . . . reads too much . . . everyday on that wall. And why not in her garret? What is wrong with her bedroom redoubt? It's not good for you . . . all that thinking outside. Takes a certain nuttiness or force of will to shut out the world like that. We should face into it with our insouci-ance. True. She achieves an impossible feat but is up against the wall. If only she would join the Goths. She's a natural Goth, but for her ideas of mad saints, angels and gods.

—She's red as a Celt.

—I'd give the one in the blue cardigan a touch.

—Who, Sinéad? She'd devour you and then spit you out if you touched her clutch.

Turlough the poet swung his coat. Took something from his deep pocket. Three small dolls.

—Three monkeys . . . one, not on this planet; two, not happy and frustrated by thoughts beyond her ken; three, not smart enough but gentle and affectionate and the apple of my Irish eye. But if they're the three monkeys on the wall. We are the ten baboons watching it all.

—Ever the poet, someone said.

Now Turlough Blue Stripe looked where Éilis walked towards the arch of the flats and declaimed to the world with his deep country accent.

—She's for the chop, boys. We're all for the chop, hey! All the thinkers, tinkers, poets, artists. We've nothing to sell but our souls, and our soul food is well past its sell-by date.

Now he stepped forward to a coffee table bizarrely appointed before the decrepit sofa throne.

—But I say she goes first. She's already way out on the narrow ledge.

He placed the three effigies with great care on the oval, glass top of a misshapen and warped table. Two of the female figures remained upright. The cracked and splintered glass patterns configuring the providence of the mute subjects within its realm. The third doll fell over straight away, a dark, angry slash where once was a mouth.

Cave Drawings

ÉILIS WAS STILL laughing at what Deirdre had said and then at Sinéad's looks in response. The pair of them now bickering back there in their most intimate of ways—two parakeets in a cage. As she approached the arch in front of the tenements and the drug pushers, a stir in the air caused her to hesitate. As if she had remembered it before. The memory of it dragging her mind, so that all time became forced to a terrible pinhead, to the very quintessence of an event, the shift of dimensions in a moment, the smell of ferocity, the life-changing seconds. The feel of the ground against her feet and the red smell of the brick almost unbearable to her. The young men, no physical threat to her, were scattered ahead. Two of them dealing with a heroin-scorched wretch in a hoodie and no meat on his bones. Beyond this scene, the arch, then the waiting flats, stairwells, balconies, dark brick. Too close.

Inhabitants of Star of The Sea flats had always called the covered passageway that led into the inner courtyard of the flats "the arch," but it was in fact a murky tunnel that residents always avoided at night. Who would build such a place? Now also during the day because of the presence of the pushers and attendant junkies. There was one other entrance into the flats, via a side lane, and though it meant a longer walk around from Wakefields and the joke of a "park," this diversion was the preferred route for most.

Only the Dempsey family and their large group of relatives would walk past the pushers and through the arch with little care. However, the Dempseys did not live in the flats proper, but in some houses nearby.

Éilis stepped onto the footpath. A Garda car sailed by oblivious, and a cat watched proceedings atop one of the columns that buttressed the railings. Tail flicking. The Untouchables were congregated at the railings, either side of the grey concrete lane that led in to the arch.

Now she was a hind entering a clearing in the wood. Scenting the wind, her front foot lifted. Something was awry. She saw beyond the cloudless, glass ceiling to where fire and ice burned a path through space. What she knew in her heart of hearts, that the chalice of remembrance cannot be taken away.

Mise Éire, mo chlann féin do dhíol a mháthair.

A child's grief sang in the dead air. Some child was going to be harmed in this place. The raven dream had foretold this very thing. Which of these brutalized pushers would deliver the blow? Yet Sinéad gave her hope. Who else? Finn? He would not be there, alas. And yet, his younger brother Séamus would walk the fire. Stand firm in a whirlwind. A dissipating world. It was Séamus who was a *laoch*—a hero. Not Finn. Woe to her.

Uaigneach crann
I lár na coille
Uaigneach file
Thar gach duine

Yes the *crann*, the tree, was lonely in the heart of the forest, but it stood proud and Éilis took strength from it. Seeing also that Séamus was a crann. This vision now possessing her. Turning her world, her world turning. Who else? Father McCartan. Walk the fire for truth. Walk it in utter, ineffable belief and you will feel no pain. Walk on sword blades but float with joy also.

The Untouchables watched her, ill at ease. What was she doing, the nutter? She was talking to herself right in front of them. That fucking Lord of the Rings language again. They saw her crouch near the floor at the foot of the railing in the lane, as if looking for something, or was that a prayer she was saying? One of their number, Darren, went to speak but clenched his mouth at Éilis's intonations.

—Will somebody take this from me? And I will fade into the bend of the arch, the arch of history, and whisper into the ears of the sleeping Fianna. It is too long you sleep and the old ways are gone. *Seasaigí suas a bhuachaillí . . . músclaígí gan mhoill.* There's a child that needs your help.

She moved past the bodies of the youths. A hall of mirrors, where they were to be seen ridiculous in the heat, seeking to exaggerate their physique, their height, their cult of mean. Spitting on the floor, legs astride, arms akimbo. The weird Éilis. Queen Éilis, making bizarre and meaningless their toughness and jutting jaws. Her presence before which they were powerless. But they posed for Éilis and for each other in their sharp jackets and cool gear—the sartorial signs that they were a cut above, the generic hoods and football gear abandoned long ago as they raked in the cash from the middle class. A fashion queue. A rogues gallery for yet another turkey shoot, before new rogues were assembled and shot. She would warn them but they would laugh and unlisten. She put her hand on Darren's shoulder and he so pleased as she made her way onwards.

—Hey, did yez see duh way she came over to me, eh? Ah, don't get bleedin' jealous now, lads.

—She's out of your league, Darren.

Another pusher shook his head.

—She's a nutcase, sure. She should be locked up. Did you see all that carry on . . . smelling the ground, mutterin' to herself and talking Polish or sumtin'. You'd swear she's on the gear except that she would have to get it from us.

—Nah, said Darren. There's something about her, something magical, and yez have to admit dat she's a lovely bit a stuff.

A young man passed by, keeping his head down.

—Any Es, meth, H, blow, whizz? inquired Darren. No? . . . Go round the other way next time then, cunt.

A large, brawny youth emerged from a café across the street— Spanzo by name. Legend had it that he had got his nickname from the time in his early youth when he was always fixing cars and a spanner was never out of his hand. Another rumour was that Jimmy Heffernan had dubbed him Spanzo because he had spanners for brains. The café Spanzo used as his private haunt was also his office, where he could observe the passing trade and hold private conversations with his regular and more lucrative clientele; they, of course, preferring not to have to deal at the arch. So it was that throughout the day, and particularly in the evenings and weekends, a veritable fleet of upmarket cars would arrive and depart from this establishment, which officially was called Mario's Café. However, even more than these lucrative, down-and-dirty sightseers, the dedicated and in-the-know taxi drivers were the heartbeat of the operation—ferrying drugs, prostitutes, and contraband across Dublin on behalf of the Heffernan empire. Naturally, the real café owner—whose name was not Mario took his cut and asked no questions. All the hoods in the area thought this alleged Mario was Italian, when in fact his real name was Abdul and he was from Afghanistan.

Spanzo's hands fell like boulders in easy swings from his rangy shoulders as he loped his way from Mario's Café and across the road to the arch. His head was all of a block and a thick, stubby thatch of dirty-blond hair danced and nodded as he moved. He, easy in the power of his physique and enjoying its continually frightening effect. Spanzo was the more high and mighty after dropping a small amount of speed to accompany his morning whisky coffee. He had heard the remnants of the conversation about Éilis as she disappeared ghost-like across the square beyond the arch, and he spat.

—You keep well away from her, Darren, he said as he puffed his chest out and held court.

—Éilis is gonna go places and not with the likes of us.

—Who, then . . . Jimmy H.?

—You better believe it . . . Jimmy's big into her . . . wants her to be the ace face in his club, thinks she can be a supermodel, a supermodel with brains, he told the Cube. But say fuck all you lot. He's gonna go big with her—press, TV, and a fucking FB page. And there'll be shag-all Mister Bleedin' Super-Clean Finn Dempsey can do about it. But, do you know what I think? She smells like trouble.

—Er, point of order, Spanz? Darren called.

—Wha'? What order, you sap I give d fucking orders round here and don't you forget it.

—Aren't they related anyway through Éilis's ma?

—I wouldn't mind getting a grip of her, said another.

—If I was Jimmy, I'd keep well clear, said Spanzo with venom.

—Wouldn't like to get in a row with the Dempseys all the same, Darren said with feeling. That Séamus is fucking bone hard. He's a kickboxer, and if Finn ever got started . . . The guy is, like, huge.

—Finn would be a one-man army, came a cry.

Spanzo shook his head in bewilderment at the idiocy of his minions. Like, what was he even doing there with them?

—Finn Dempsey is a no-mark, waste-of-space, goody blee- din' two-shoes. Who runs this gaffe? Us or the Dempseys? Who walks round in the proper gear and tells the Guards what's what? The Dempseys dress like culchies and don't even use deodorant. That fuckin' Séamus wears a fuckin' jumper from sheepland or Iceland or whatever the fuck.

Spanzo shook his head again, sucked and tutted, spat again, only loudly this time and then walked off towards the arch itself barging everybody out of the way. He wanted to check one of the stashes in the flats. But then a thought came to him. First dimly, then with ever greater radiance, and as he walked he began to drop fifty-euro bills onto the ground. His dogs closed in as their pack leader walked away, howling, snapping, sweating to dispute the scraps.

Little Dessie Noonan had run after his ball in the tunnel but stopped to look at the glazed tiles in the curved wall of the arch, all cracked and glarred with grease. For in the gloom of brick and plaster, the brown of what used to be tile, he saw cave drawings invoking former deities, the hunt, the dance, the constellations, the spiralling universe and its stars. The child with an angelic face whom Éilis had just minutes before caressed, now chasing his deep-red ball through the arch. The child in his second sight of wonder with no heed to the flutter of money floating around his legs. Bang! The first blow fell. Then little Dessie received another stiff belt across his face from Spanzo for the sin of not moving out of his way in the requisite time. Spanzo's teeth, purposely abandoned to their crooked state, his angry pimples and alcohol breath.

—What are you staring at, you little prick!

The child rubbed his head and could not speak for the gorge of tears, the rush of salt in his nose, and the lump in his throat, for which silence he paid with another clatter.

—Ow! That up on the wall, mistah!

—What on the wall? Go on, fuck off or I'll bite your fucking ear off . . . and spit in the hole.

A stiff kick joyfully administered to the child's backside then the tail-end of foul abuse before Spanzo leered back to his gang rolling his eyes to heaven as if he had just been obliged to swat a troublesome fly. The stash could wait.

As Spanzo retrieved a fluttering fifty-euro note, the child stood in the cool of the arch rubbing his head and inculcating the violence, the cauldron of revenge he would boil throughout his life. His new ball had been kicked away and he couldn't see it anywhere. Hot tears seeped through his fluorescent eyes provoking a fierce need to spill all. The Untouchables watched him in judgement. For the child must not cry. This he now knew.

Here was another moment where James Tierney had laid aside Éilis's urban tale of the flats. He goes to his bag and fishes out a clean notebook. He takes another beer from the fridge, decides he doesn't want it, and takes iced water to the table instead. Wants to endure this story with a clear head. Devour, inculcate, inure himself to it. On the cover of his notebook, he simply writes "Dawn" and then his name and the date. Before working with Tommy Baker, James had eschewed all paper paraphernalia in favour of an electronic notepad that had an inbuilt, high-quality audio recorder. But Tommy Baker had threatened to burn it, throw it out of a window, or failing that, to stamp on it unto death. All things must in the first instance, Baker insisted, be written down with a very good pen or legible pencil. This meant that, when asked to take notes in one of Tommy's interviews,

James had been obliged to revisit the shorthand skills that had lain dormant since journalism college, but he quickly found that he actually preferred writing to digitizing.

Now at the table, he sits, dark head bent over the page, like a young warrior invoking the gods. Enters the fascinating insight and details Éilis has provided. He was sure that the names, for example, were real and would be useful at a later date. Heffernan again, Connolly's club, Spanzo at Mario's Café (would the real owner talk?), a low-level pusher called Darren. Then these Dempseys? And what about "telling the Guards what's what"? Bribes? Heffernan again—nothing really that proved he was a criminal mastermind. No proof in any of this really. But he could breathe its veracity.

The Promise

ÉILIS WATCHED LITTLE Dessie run up the stairwell from her vantage point in the corner of the square. She placed her hands around her face. There were smiling women looking down from the first floor balcony. There was a roaring noise and images of a blade rasping across skin, a deep wound and then blood spurting into her eyes. Now she was standing in front of the women still with her hands over her face. Mary in the dusty heat of Fatima a thrumming whirling Síle na Gig, woad and paint of flower extract, faces crowding in on her. As if wiping away the images from her mind, Éilis brought her hands slowly down from her face to her side and breathed downwards through her nose. Looked calmly at the two women. Smiled.

—Don't be worrying, Nora. Really, I don't mind doing it.

The two women dug each other in the ribs.

—I'll be down later . . . after my dinner.

Nora and Mrs Nolan ran in a panic into Nora's flat. Nora Farrell's home was spotlessly clean yet boasted little by way of decoration apart from religious memorabilia. Above the front door, there was a statue of the Child of Prague. A Bridget's Cross and a Mass card for Nora's late husband were pinned on the living room wall, and a large representation of the Sacred Heart of Jesus stared serenely at the goings-on in the house from its central position above the mantelpiece. In the kitchen, there was a large picture of Pope John Paul, whom Nora had adored, and in the window was a bunch of flowers, which she tried to replace once a week. Mrs Nolan threw herself onto Nora's sofa and lit up a cigarette. This habit was, for Nora Farrell, a heavy cross to bear, but she put up with it, as Mrs Nolan was her only bosom friend now that her husband had passed away.

—Jesus, she should be making millions, that girl. Did you hear that? "Of course I will," says she . . . she knew all along we was going to ask.

Nora was only half listening, already looking round her living room for the small bottle of port she kept for such occasions. It was in the house purely for its reviving and inspirational qualities. She did not like to leave it in open view but would then forget where she had hidden it.

—I'm telling ye she's blessed, Nora said, having found the bottle stashed down the side of the TV armchair, where it was always to be found.

—Sure. Do you remember last year when Philomena's youngest got them warts, and didn't Éilis put her hands on her . . . they disappeared in no time.

—Wait till I tell the others, Mrs Nolan said excitedly.

—Ah now, Mrs Nolan, don't be going and telling everyone. This is a special treat for us. Besides the girl's sensitive, you know, highly strung. She doesn't like a big deal being made of it.

Assenting to this request, Mrs Nolan ran out of the flat, only to run back in again for her glasses. —Don't forget to bring a bottle round with you, Nora Farrell said as Mrs Nolan ran out again. Mrs Nolan always forgot to bring a bottle.

Éilis walked up the stairs towards the third floor. She wondered did people really know what it took out of her to read palms. It was the things that she couldn't bring herself to tell them that wore her down the most. Still, it was a place she wanted to go to. It was a way of sharing things with people. And as far as she knew, there had always been someone in her family that could divine. That was what she had heard from certain old women when she was tiny. Her real family in the Donegal Gaeltacht.

The brightness of Éilis dazzled the gloom around her in the stairwell, which had been built in such a way that it would allow precious little of the sun's light to penetrate its musty confines.

She passed a man on the landing who was pulling some kind of package out the back of his trousers. She shook her head and rounded the corner to the last flight of stairs, closed her eyes as if in pain. There was a hand on her face then an arm around her. Is it me? Leaning against the cold brick, she saw urine and needles. Was there a recognition of the hand holding the knife? Black now, then great blinds of light. A dog slithered away from under her legs. She looked down and saw excrement covered in flies and the stench of it all. She dry-retched and placed her head in her hands and began a prayer. She then rose and went back down the stairs in a series of stumbles past the dizzying graffiti. She had decided not to go home, where no home was, and sought out Father McCartan instead. The Dominican priest was just emerging from the local old peoples' home when he saw Éilis heading towards the parochial house.

—Éilis, *tá mé anseo*! he called in Irish, but she seemed not to hear.

Then Éilis turned to look at him, and in that turn he saw disaster written in the haggard features of his "grace child." He hurried over to her, oblivious to the fact that his rosary beads had fallen in the street.

—Éilis, *an bhfuil tú ceart go leor?*

—Something funny is happening, Father

In the kitchen now, with the kettle placed on a blackened range, the sides and upper frame of which were festooned with vivid icons, a pipe was lit to assist the priest in his deliberations. Priest and acolyte. Éilis was calm and able to eat the fresh rolls and cheese without nausea. No extraneous grief imploding her mind.

Father McCartan stood well over six feet and his broad hands and gentle face spoke of a country upbringing. He always wore a beret, even indoors, claiming that he felt empowered when wearing his favourite headgear. The beret also served a practical purpose in preserving his domed and largely bald head from the elements. He sat back after taking a draw from his pipe as a signal that Éilis should begin.

—I've been having these attacks, Father, *taomanna*, you know?

Father McCartan nodded. Despite his concern for Éilis, he basked in the way she used the tongue so instinctively. Éilis was living proof, as far as he was concerned, that you did not have to come from a native, Irish-speaking area to have the language in your heart and soul, even though her real parents were pure Donegal. (He had still not managed to work out properly how Éilis had been snatched away from there as a baby.) If his theory about Éilis was true, then the Irish language would survive, and with it a set of thought processes which were entirely Gaelic in their origin. The latent language in peoples' hearts, he reasoned, would carry through after centuries of oppression and neglect. Father McCartan puffed on his pipe as he listened to Éilis describe her raven dream and wild knife and "scary blade flashes." The priest watched and waited until she was talked out and becalmed.

Éilis basked in the warmth of a loved kitchen. Incense of pipe; two people, two faith healers, who could communicate without speaking. Sometimes just particular words would be bandied forth and back—like *comhghairdeas, grásta, lúcháir,* and *gliondar*—and the pair of them would sit back and read or listen to the clock tick, the kettle steam. Once, they had spent more than an hour studying the Spanish word *suave* and its affiliation with the Irish word *séimh* and the English word *suave*. This was another reason that Father McCartan's kitchen had always been a refuge for Éilis. There were books there, books in a kitchen, just as there were in the rest of the house. Seemingly thousands of books. Books in six different languages, with a whole wall dedicated to Shakespeare.

The kitchen also reflected Father McCartan's role as a spiritual teacher amongst the people. He, quietly ploughing his own democratic and truly Catholic furrow. The seeds planted there over the years had borne great fruit in the community, where he was loved and revered for his honesty and humility. The local people understood that, for Father McCartan, the centre of Christ's message was love, and that the sharing of resources, the opposite of greed and avarice, was a key part of that love. If the collapse of the Church and the barbed comments and attitudes of his superiors ever depressed him, Father McCartan only had to look at his kitchen wall for his faith to be revived.

Pictures of pensioner outings to Knock and to Lourdes, and cards from local youths in the boxing club with various humorous messages and greetings on them. Now augmented by a group-picture of the Goths, whom Father McCartan laughingly called his new seminarians. Some weeks ago he had got them to sing at Mass, much to the surprise and delight of the local people, who could recognise good singers when they heard them. The fact that the content of the lyrics to their song "Kurt Cobain, No Pain, No Gain" were a mystery to them was largely irrelevant. Éilis had also sung that day, and Father McCartan was under no illusion that it had been his resounding sermon which had inspired the Goths to remain behind and partake of tea and lemonade after Mass was over. Éilis served the tea.

Éilis could hear Mrs O'Grady, the housekeeper, somewhere in the big hall. She would bustle in and out in a pinafore which was always pristine, yet carried a wafted essence of bread and baking powder. Mrs O'Grady would prepare endless rounds of tea and biscuits and cluck around Éilis who was her favourite chick. The housekeeper never shared with Éilis her feelings about Éilis's stepfather, Neville. But the priest was well aware of the charges laid against him and he wondered daily about Éilis's "surrogate" mother Bernice Devanney and exactly how she had extracted Éilis from Donegal.

The priest removed his glasses, inclined his head, looked directly at Éilis and spoke now with the hooded, wisely eyes of authority. She, falling into the visage of his ancient wrinkles. He, aware that she was exhausted. The drag of too bright an intelligence physically draining her, so that only her fierce will was left. The priest also aware of the evil crowding in on the girl.
—*Termon*, he breathed quietly. —Refuge.

—Now Éilis, this is very serious and I want you to do exactly what I say. If you do exactly, and I mean exactly, what I say, we'll be all right.

—Yes, Father.

—Now I'm going to go off and organise a few things today.

We need to get you off on a break to the Gaeltacht again. I'll talk to Jimmy McBride.

—Oh, brilliant.

—Yes, to Donegal with you, for six months, maybe longer.

—Six months! You mean right through the winter? You want to banish a Dublin girl to Donegal for six months! I'll go mad.

—You'll go mad if you don't.

The priest's quiet words almost burst Éilis's eardrums. Echoing far and wide in her inner psyche. This grim countenance was a side to Father McCartan that Éilis had never seen before.

—*Sin go breá . . . Tír Chonaill so.*

—Yes, Éilis, I think you should spend more time there. They are your own people really and Dublin . . . well, Dublin's fine if you can deal with its dark side. But even I find it very wearing sometimes, may God forgive me. But it's my cross and God blessed me with broad shoulders and a stubborn mind!

Éilis got back to the side entrance of the square in the flats just as Finn flashed by on his trail bike and he pulled and skidded to a halt. The zeal of her embrace imparted its own message. There was a heat in Éilis's cheeks which was close to grief.

—Finn! Ah, that's great you're all right. I'm so glad to see ya.

—All right? How d'ye mean "all right," Éilis? Why wouldn't I be all right?

She took the poem from her bag but burst into tears. She placed her hands on Finn's face like some ancient physician who would read the symbols that lay within.

—Jeez, Éilis, slow down . . . what's wrong!? And aren't you going to wish me happy birthday?

But Éilis could only shake her head and gasp for air in between the sobs. People began to emerge from the flats and watch in silence.

—Finn Dempsey, I want you to promise me one thing. One thing only.

—Ah, now if it's about the soccer and the booze-up on Sunday afternoons, Éilis, well . . . for you . . . even that!

But Éilis shook her head, her eyes glistening, as she took another deep breath and tucked in her chin.

—What then?

—Promise me you will never, ever, ever, ever go in that flat up there again. I mean, our house. I mean, my old house.

—Well, seeing as how I'm not exactly a frequent visitor . . .

—Finn!? Please! she stamped.

—Okay! Okay! I will never go in that house again, for fuck's sake.

Then a look of dawning concern passed across Finn's features and a short silence ensued.

—Does this mean the engagement's off? he asked tentatively.

Éilis could give no answer but leaped into Finn's arms and clutched at him with the vigour of death itself.

Tears welled in the eyes of the captivated audience in the floors above, young and old alike. The Untouchables watched from the back of the arch. Some of them began to laugh and mock. Truly, that Éilis one was a nutter, but Darren Bulger turned away to the railings, hiding his face in a newspaper which he pulled from his back pocket. The child who had been Spanzo's victim, little Dessie, ran giggling into his bedroom and retrieved a teddy bear from his bunk bed, ran back out onto the landing, and flung his prized possession over the second-floor balcony. Out of the arms of babes.

As Finn lifted the sobbing Éilis into his arms, Éilis (willed on by the people of her square) laughed through her tears and took the bear to her bosom. She surveyed the flats in streams of water in the heat and the swing of Finn's strength, and a pattern of necessities quickly emerged in her mind. Yes, she knew that Finn would keep his promise and never enter her house again and, therefore, that he was safe from the harm that she was convinced awaited him there. Éilis also knew that she had to leave Dublin for a long time. On this balmy evening, they could walk into town.

Then she would let him go.

He was safe. And all this was good.

Connolly's

NIGHT WAS FALLING as Jimmy Heffernan walked towards his exclusive wine bar down by Dublin's quays. The club was situated on prime real estate near the Custom House on the river Liffey. Heffernan's pace was all wrong for the balmy, night air and the sprinkling of shopping-dazed pedestrians wandering to bus stops or their parked cars. This ethereal man was too quick, too voracious. His pale, angular features dramatized by his short and straight, jet-black hair, marked him out where he walked, sparse and streamlined, all tensile strength, large cheekbones pushing his searching eyes back into his neat skull, drawing his mouth wide and tight. The careful gait of a leopard, his long back slightly arched, and a step that was almost on tiptoes, as if he were stalking the shoppers for strays that might be chased down and devoured. Do not engage his gaze. There were also passing cars and faces to be scanned and studied. The usual precautions, second nature to him, as he stepped in and out of the rising shadows and the cover of buildings. Heffernan stopped a cat's pounce short of his club and was on such a mental and emotional high that he took out a cigar, checked it for lumps and the colour at the ends, then fired up. He felt he was getting very close to her. Also, this was a big, big night at the club. Loads of press, media, salacious stuff lined up for around eleven o'clock—perfect for the next morning's scandal sheets. *He groped her, she spread her legs in her micro-mini to reveal . . . snogged, snagged, snapped, snared by the camera.* All the dickheads buying their Sunday fry and gossip columns for their ersatz lives—some glamour and sheen to brighten their own vague and faded dreams. Heffernan knew that some journalists were bringing Pierce Beaumont, the newspaper columnist and Empire TV star, along that night. Beaumont had been to the club many times before, but this was more of a public thing. A gossip columnist would be there and a photographer from the *Irish Record* ("The Paper of Record," etc.). One of his lieutenants on Dublin's Southside (the Cube, so named because of his square bulk and square head) had been supplying Beaumont's habit for drugs and "dirty" ladies for several years. Now it was time to reel in the investment. Throw it into the larger game, which was to establish Connolly's as a chain across Ireland. Beaumont had no choice but to do a little publicity for club owner and entrepreneur Jimmy Heffernan. The Empire TV star was caught like a rabbit in headlights, except the headlights were the spaced-out lamps in his own head. Sap. The laugh was that Beaumont not only worked as a "face" for Empire Television but also wrote a regular column in the *Record* denouncing the "Crime Lords" and "Gangsters" and calling for a clampdown on drugs.

Heffernan breathed in the cigar smoke, made a mental note, reminding himself to get Paul, his technician, to check, back up, and reset the wall- and keyhole-cameras which were motion-activated and secretly placed in the club's private rooms and VIP lizard lounges. The places where his special guests could properly relax and go with the flow, whatever they wanted, once they had loosened up. He also had cameras and audio equipment in designated rooms in select hotels across town. This was how Pierce Beaumont had been ensnared in the first place—a too-young girl shooting a line as he gave it to her up the back. Sap. No class.

Heffernan watching the evening unfold. The quiet, ancient blue of the Liffey flowing on towards the first sparkling stars in the dark that loomed to the east beyond the harbour. The dazzle of neon and apartment lights from the new town down by the Port Tunnel. Rich velvet of soft Irish air. He in his element, savouring the cigar smoke in his mouth, controlled, not inhaling, civilised, worldly like aged port and Roquefort, a man, nay a modern-day chieftain, who understood the weight of responsibility this title carried.

Cigars were one of the few indulgences he allowed himself. That and a good bottle of wine. Lager really was for louts. He blows his cheeks, throws his head back slightly. When all this was over, he vowed, he would let go a little bit. Go to Cuba, go meet the Mexicans, whom he revered for their severity, the understanding of their profound role as society's purifiers, learn Spanish, learn more about cigars, cuisine, start an exclusive wine cellar, an astounding library with first editions and prints. She would like that. His Queen who would jaw-drop anyone. Anywhere in the world. She was worthy. Some early punters preparing to enter Connolly's. The club just being a stone's throw away from the statue of the great revolutionary himself. Heffernan clicked a smoke ring and laughed out loud, much to the consternation of an old woman who clutched her purse all the tighter as she passed by. Two young hoods walking by also. One tugs the other's elbow and they give Jimmy the thumbs up. He nods slightly, gravely, then dismisses them. Eyes swivelling back to the club. Charlie. That beautiful, white stuff, and wouldn't she look great on a coke high, slightly dishevelled maybe, in a backless dress and sling-back shoes, green her dress would be, hair falling across her face, nudging into his arm for warmth and protection. She is slightly tipsy from the drink. No, he doesn't want that. It's not for that. It's for the look that cannot be bought. No amount of money could buy what she had. He would make her the new Marilyn. No. She was more Ingrid Bergman with a bit of Audrey Hepburn thrown in. Once they were married he would get her to eat a bit more, do her amazingly thick hair differently. Put it up. More sophisticated. Tight diamond or ruby earrings. Nothing big or flash. A sophisticated lady. An Irish Jean Shrimpton. Back at his town-based studio apartment over in Ringsend (his actual home was a huge country stud in Kildare), he would go through his cuttings and albums again. No Internet. His own montages, stills, little notes. Most of all, he loved her intelligence. She was as clever and sharp as he was. Sure, he accepted that he had become obsessed with her. So what? She deserved obsession. The more she played the Ice Queen, a stunning Ice Queen, a deity; the more she turned her face, walked away; the more he laughed, actually was tickled. Was determined to succeed with her. And she did show him little kindnesses. Her face would relent and she would allow him to engage with her. She would emerge from her force field of frost to let him near that warm, beating heart she had for humanity. Jimmy gave one of his rare hearty laughs at this. Anyway, she had no choice because this was his wish. All women were the same in that way. They wanted you to make the effort, for her and only her, praise her, never give up. They wanted to know that you were desperate for them and only them. That they were special beyond measure. All very controlled, and light of touch. Like one of the best fillies in his stable, she shivered when he touched her. They had to feel that there was no one else like them and there really was no one like Éilis. She would see him and his world in a different light. The age difference was actually a plus. He was twenty years ahead of her. Wiser. A wise guy. He smiled at that and blew another ring. And sixteen/seventeen was legal.

Truth was that he preferred the company of men and bodily necessities disgusted him, lowered him to levels beneath him. But she was a rare, rare thing and raised him in the eyes of others. One must possess an exquisite woman so as to step out into his society. This was necessary both for the social etiquette of it and for his own self-image. They all had them. The Colombians, Mexicans, the cream of New York, where he had learned so much. And they weighed your discernment by the women you possessed. She was it.

His cigar had gone out, and just as he fired his Italian designer lighter, the club's head of security, Ned Behan, approached him from across the road. The granite, jutting jaw of Ned. His square head and bright eyes, not dim.

—Jimmy.

—What's the story, Ned? All under control?

—Saw you here, Jimmy. So just wanted to make sure you were okay. Just keeping everything shipshape you know. Keep the Man happy.

Heffernan smiled and expertly flipped a hundred-note from a slim, clipped wad of money in his jacket pocket.

—That's very much appreciated, said Ned, looking directly at Heffernan.

Heffernan looked straight back at his chief goon. Ned was a hard man. Famous in gangster circles for having taken on the Provos and won, probably because he had been a Provo himself before he got sense. He knew where everything was buried and, more importantly, where everybody lived. Ned had also been through a very messy divorce.

—Good man, Ned. Keeping order, that's what I like. A busy man needs order in his busy life.

—Exactly, Jimmy. As a new group of people bustled noisily into the splash of light at the club entrance, Ned glanced back and moved to return to his duties.

—Oh, and, Ned.

—Jimmy?

—That's Damien Kelly over there, isn't it?

—'S'right Jimmy . . . Is there a problem? He's very reliable, picked him from my own karate club. Disciplined. Not a bully or mouth.

—I know he's reliable, Ned, but he seems to be wearing the wrong colour shirt. Dark blue is not turquoise, and turquoise is the rule. No exceptions.

—I'll sort that right away. There's some spares in the storeroom.

—Tell him not to do it again.

—Will do, Jimmy.

—Also, Ned . . .

—Yes, Jimmy?

—I don't mind "Jimmy" from you . . . to all the rest it's Mr Heffernan, okay?

—Gotcha, Jimmy. Mr Heffernan it is . . . for everybody else.

The cool of cigar smoke in his mouth again. Ned was damn

good. In fact, Ned was probably going to have to take over from Spanzo. He'd heard some disturbing things about Spanzo, and he would have to be disciplined and put out to grass, some sprawling estate in West Dublin was good enough for him. Unwashed grass, unwashed hair, bleak estates, rough as get out—what a Neanderthal like that needed. Ned was the right man for executing that personnel change as well. In fact, he saw Ned as maybe running the whole Dublin shebang when he cleared out. Heffernan sensed that Ned knew he might be onto a good thing. The Cube was good for the rest of Leinster. Ned also had good northern connections from his Provo days. The West of Ireland was still a problem though. What to do about the Wild West, where the sophisticated gangster failed to impress, failed to intimidate? He didn't get that. It was no use even talking to the Limerick ones—hit hit, bang bang—endless wars with each other and the cops. No understanding of the social role gangsters played. They would watch *The Godfather, Scarface, Carlito's Blah Blah* over and over again, but only for the gun battles and violence, and completely miss the fine suits, the good living, the respect for the Don and the stability it brought. To be charitable was a big part of it. If he had tried to explain to them that a benevolent gangster was the logical, no, necessary apotheosis of capitalism—ruthless but sophisticated men who ruled by a mixture of terror and largesse . . . because greed and fear were man's basic instincts . . . Well, if he tried to explain that to them, they would just stare blankly, a slight shake of the head maybe, a slackening of the jaw. His intellectual superiority would bewilder them. Which was also good and proper.

Where was he? Ah yes! Limerick and what's-his-name. Heffernan took out a card from his linen jacket. Tommy Baker— "Investigative Journalist." Saw himself as incorruptible, couldn't be bought. He had seen the TV series he had made on the faces behind the lap-dancing game in Limerick and Cork and how some Guards had been involved. It was bang on. He needed to talk to Pierce Beaumont about this Tommy Baker.

Heffernan strolled over to the club after grinding his cigar into the pavement, the way they did it in the noir films that he loved. He acknowledged the respects paid to him by everybody, the quick glances, the heads of the cocktail girls just in the corridor darting upwards, all of them dogging his arrival, straightening hair, checking their cleavage, tightening toes—a flustered Damien Kelly rushing back to his post with his new and correctly coloured shirt and perfectly knotted tie. Jimmy the Man, purifying, terrifying, establishing order.

James Tierney. Still reeling from what he was reading about Pierce Beaumont. Could this be true? Also, was Éilis really aware of what went on in Empire TV? Yet she trusted Tommy Baker?

He blundered into the next section of Éilis's tale where a loose sheet of paper had been taped onto the space between the two paragraphs. Also, the writing was in red ink and blocky. James wondered whether he should remove it, as he had with the previous strange section, and perhaps place it at the end with his own note, but decided instead to make it more secure and leave it where it was. This was Éilis speaking in the third person. Outside of herself. He, wanting to rush to the hospital right that minute. Just to look at her. Tell the nurses to put her in a secure wing. He was convinced he knew what she looked like. A suicide risk?

What she found unbearable, she said, was not the casual cruelty people inflicted upon each other but the masks they wore and the fake characters they snatched from some place in the dark parts of their own psyche. Before violence and rapine, comes the pretence. As if the only thing that was real and true was the list of dissatisfactions they held against the world and each other. This, then, had to be expressed in their characters. Terrible caricatures of their true selves because they could not bear to be fully human, admit that they were vulnerable, weak, flighty, ecstatic at the brush of an angel's wing on their faces, the brilliance of a flower, or the call of a bird in flight, being soothed by waves along the shore or the profound presence of a mountain, that they would want to read or write a book, paint a landscape or exotic figure. Admit to weakness, sensitivities. The chalk and cheese of the personas they projected. The whole mass of humankind playing its part in this charade. People meeting, interacting, intertwining and all aware that other people (more solid, more real people, but also closer to angels and gods) were to be found behind the shell of fake smiles or grimaces, postures and simulation. She desperately wanted to strip all that back so that souls were revealed and were present to each other in the world. So that souls could follow their true path. Their inner call that was only true for them.

My white arms, the soft pulse of my wrist, the perfect state and perfect peace of human death, flowing joyfully then ebbing away. Embraced by the realm of eternal bliss. Take me away from all this.

James wanting to ring the hospital. If indeed she was at the hospital. He couldn't be sure of anything.

Rebel Ireland

—DAMIEN, COME HERE.

—Oh, yes, Jim . . . er . . . Mr Heffernan.

This was more a test of Ned than Damien Kelly, and Jimmy approved of Ned's alacrity in "keeping things in order." Heffernan swung his bouncer around with a natural ease of strength, which belied his very lean frame. Took Damien off balance.

—Let's have a look at ya now. Heffernan made a show of straightening Damien's tie and then slipped a fifty into his inside jacket pocket.

—That's better. Now keep it that way.

—Yes sorr, Mr Heffernan, sorr, said Damien, feigning a country accent and beaming at the tip.

Heffernan knew that Kelly was sensible and a teetotaler, but also a bit dense, fighting-thick, and therefore a perfect foil for the razor-sharp Ned and the indoor security staff. You needed blockheads who actually liked the cold and the rain to stand at the entrance.

When Heffernan had moved far enough into the club so as not to hear anything, Ned Behan hit Damien a ferocious box on the side of the head.

—Don't ever make jokes with Jimmy like that again.

—Jeez, Ned, give over, that was sore! . . . Ah come on, I was only messin'.

—Don't mess with him, Damien. That clatter was for your own good and remember it.

—You're serious aren't ya, Ned? said Damien, rubbing his ear

and glancing around into the club. —Do you know, it's funny
. . . everybody's so scared of him but he doesn't look much. Now
speaking under his breath, —I reckon I could take him, Ned.

—You are a monumental eejit, Damo. Don't kid yourself.
He'd flatten you, or me, with one punch. The guy has amazing
natural strength. He arm-wrestled the Cube with his supposedly
weak arm a few months back, and Jimmy won in seconds. But
that isn't the problem.

Damo shook his head in part disbelief at what he was hearing from the infamous, rock-hard, third-dan black belt and kick
boxer Ned Behan.

—What is, then?

—It's what he knows, Damien. About every one of us. The
man is the Wikipedia of thugs and gangsters and general terror. I
went to school with one of his older brothers. Jimmy comes from
a family of nutters. But he was always the loner you really didn't
mess with. Even his own family are in shock and awe of him. He
wouldn't beat you up. He would blow you up with some small
device he'd put together, or he'd spread a rumour about you. Put
a rat in your bag. He used to correct the teachers in chemistry
and physics classes as well. I'm telling ya, the guy's a genius and
probably a psychopath. I've never seen anything like him and
he scares the shit out of me because he's capable of anything.
A quick death with him would be a mercy. Hannibal fucking
Lecter has nothing on him.

—But can he fight or can he not fight?

As another wave of punters washed up at the club, Ned
Behan looked at Damien Kelly more in pity than exasperation.

—Just do as I say from now on, Damien, and that is not
a request. I pulled a few strings to get you on here and I don't
want you messing this up. This setup is very, very tight and it's a
goldmine and I'm having some of it. So keep that gob under your
nose as buttoned as your from-now-on permanently turquoise
shirt and . . . Ned turned to some celebrity wannabes. —Sorry,
folks, tickets or passes please. And you, sir, you won't get in
wearing those baseball boots, I'm afraid.

—But I'm a radio star!

—Very sorry, Mr Star, but rules are rules. Unless you are on
the VIP list . . . which you are not, because I manage it.

Inside the club, the proprietor of Connolly's gave a simple
nod to the head waiter that he was about to sit and a glass of
finest Pinot Grigio was brought to one of the alcoves, along with
Malmö spring water. The crisp, cool wine cleared his palate of
cigar and he set to thinking again. That guy Tommy Baker, he
had been sniffing round Sherriff Street and the flats for a while.
Let him sniff. Jimmy boy would put the hammer on him at some
point. Give him some rope first. Find out what he had found
out. Baker, he knew, had also been up at Hanlon's Corner. In
fact, all round Stoneybatter, too. Weird when you met people
that weren't interested in money. Just fronted up to him this
Baker had at the launch of an art exhibition in Temple Bar and
asked him to spill the beans when he retired. Made some joke
about "Jimmy Heffernan's philanthropy." As if he knew. They
always had that far-away look in their eye. Éilis was like that.
But then girls were different. Finn Dempsey. He was getting
him offside. Big family, needed managing. Ned would have to
be consulted. The eldest brother, Anto Dempsey, was dangerous and had his own connections. Then there was talk of their
little brother Séamus and a tight crew of kung fu heads he was
supposed to lead, but that was kids' stuff. Spanzo or the Cube
could deal with that.

Connolly's. What a brilliant idea!

Heffernan, this twister and shaper of so many peoples' lives,
raised his glass as if to acknowledge some grinning djinn across
the table from him. A silent homage to his own achievement,
or as if conjuring that spirit to execute his further plans for
his club and for his imminent disappearance. Only saps hung
around when they got to the top in the gangster trade. He had
been raised in the 1980s with songs and stories about James
Connolly all around him. Now he had used it as a niche title,
an approach that no one had even dreamed of. A certified cash
cow for his retirement and the standard of living that was to be
expected. He had got the idea in New York when he was brought
by mobsters to a "Che Guevara" club. If Che Guevara was okay

in Manhattan, well, wasn't one of our own good enough for O'Connell Street and every other Irish town? Maybe not certain parts of Belfast, but apart from that . . . okay, the angry brigade in Sinn Féin weren't happy about it, but so what? They were history anyway. He had put up Connolly flags in the club and pseudo revolutionary posters on the walls, along with reprints of actual Citizen Army volunteers drilling and all that miasma of now-meaningless posturing. Though there were things about the so-called "Fight for Freedom" that he did appreciate. That famous shot of IRA men patrolling Grafton Street was his favourite and had pride of place in a blow-up picture above the main bar. Grim and determined, longcoats trailing in the wind, and the sheen of revolvers and carbines in their hands. Some of the media and marketing heads who used the joint had called the whole concept a stroke of genius. Jimmy had been particularly proud of that. Of course there was always a clever one. A well-known stage and set designer in the club one night had called it history eating itself, becoming parody. No one except Jimmy understood his point. And Jimmy ensured that he never again got within spitting distance of the club. Oh yes. In truth the recalcitrant—re-cal-ci-trant, yeah, that was it—designer deserved a visit, but Jimmy had enough on his plate, and anyway, those days were nearly over.

At the very edge of his peripheral vision, almost smelling him before he saw him, Heffernan saw that his younger brother Seánie had entered the club, all starry-eyed and gormless, like he was bedazzled by the metal blue and glass in the tables. At least his older brothers knew to keep away from him. But Seánie, Seánie. What to do about Seánie? Seánie dwarfed and intimidated by the huge, high wooden panels on the walls, the cushions, the deep bright of the sofas, the massive statues of Larkin, Connolly, and Pearse. He had just never learned how to present himself in public. If Seánie needed lessons in public presentation, then Carmel Daly would have been the ideal teacher and Seánie a very willing pupil, her slave, her plaything, except that Carmel viewed Seánie with obvious and open disgust. There she was, this striking blonde in a keen skirt-suit striding right through the bar just at that moment, turning heads as she went, crossing her legs up on a stool, aware of the effect, super cool. She also knew rightly where Jimmy was. He, in turn, aware that she was waiting for Seánie to be gone before approaching him. A family it was not.

The effect of Carmel's entrance on Seánie was so pronounced that he did not hear his brother calling him above the soft strains of Latino music that was the early evening sound design in the club. Heffernan had taken a slim notepad from his jacket pocket and written numbers on a page. These were a series of codes, which were to be simply handed over along with a package of keys to the Cube on the other side of the city. The keys were in a drawer in the locker room. In his Carmel Daly reverie, Seánie had successfully performed Jimmy's instruction to pocket the note but dropped the keys on his way out of the club. Under baleful and hooded eyes, Heffernan watched his younger brother leave the club and then return for the keys. Carmel reading his mind, leaning her breasts forward as she sipped lime and sparkling water from a straw. Carmel was there. Removing his djinn. Then moving into his personal space.

—So when do we make the move upmarket and get rid of these losers? Carmel giving Heffernan's earlobe a soft nip as he remained staring ahead of himself.

Carmel Daly. Another one that had to be dropped.

Hardball

NIGHTTIME. ÉILIS WAS writing furiously in her hospital bed, pushing her mad hair away from her face, filing it back over her head, tugging at its ends, tearing strips of paper from her notepad and starting again with sighs of frustration, tears, balls of paper on the floor, a nurse coming to the bed placing hands on hips. Quiet, firm words—compressed. The essence of admonishing-nurse words.

—It's two o'clock in the morning, Éilis.

—I know but I have to write this. I've just worked something out.

—Shh, keep your voice down. You're making an awful racket and waking the other patients.

A look—imploring, strained, desperate—the nurse moved to sympathy. Éilis becoming ephemeral —disappearing into the wall with only an appalled face remaining, an open mouth. A gaping verge of something. The nurse taking pulse, mouth temperature, checking her arms, clocking the marks, a chart at the foot of the bed. Wondering if she should be sectioned as her parents had suggested. She would at any rate be moved to another ward the next day and then another hospital, a more secure regime, poor child.

—I'm not supposed to do this, Éilis, but if I pull the curtains round your bed, do you promise to keep mouse-quiet and stop tearing paper up and talking to yourself?

—Yes, promise, but it's Frankie Byrne, I've worked it out and it's Finn's friend Frankie Byrne.

—Shh! Haven't a clue what you are talking about, but I'll give you till three o'clock and then you really must turn in.

In a bright, spacious office that was neither hot nor cold but reasoned, and with an abstract painting up on the wall behind a big desk, a valuable painting with strong lines and vivid colours, three men with comfortable paunches sitting easily atop their groins looked at the pencil-thin Tommy Baker. The man behind the executive desk was Joseph Cullinane, overall head of Empire Television's News, Current Affairs, Documentaries, and Factual Programmes Division. Tommy Baker's ultimate boss.

Cullinane large in bulk but easy with it—a grandee of television. Silver-haired, urbane, high-browed, and proud of his public duties: to entertain, challenge, sometimes amaze the public. There should have been a woman there—Cullinane's understudy and future replacement, Rosie Boylan—but she loathed Tommy Baker and what she called his "male-chauvinist dinosaur attitude to women." So much so that she declined attendance. Baker would go out of his way to open doors for her, call her "love" and generally highlight the shallowness of her obsessions. Her lack of concern for the female cleaning staff, her aspiring middle-classness. The other two men looking across at Baker were Joseph Cullinane's lieutenants—Andrew Mendoza and Diarmuid Farrelly. Mendoza, whose father was from Spain and mother from Larne near Belfast, ran the Current Affairs and Documentary Features Section. Farrelly was head of News Operations.

Mendoza with the face of a wide cat, but tall, rangy, and big-framed, only now beginning to bulk after years of dedicated swimming and running. Strange eye colouring of green and brown. A big, careful cat caught by an exotic strain, a twist in his Presbyterian tail. Mendoza wise before the fact, as if he had watched it from some high vantage point, compassionate eyes below black hair greying at the sides. Then Diarmuid Farrelly.

Tommy Baker's aversion to Diarmuid Farrelly was in direct inverse proportion to his admiration and respect for Cullinane and Mendoza. Farrelly—thin, long face beneath a dark-red beard, like some intemperate medieval Irish earl who had swallowed a pheasant bone, he too a tippler but kept under angry control. Pink blotches breaking through his wiry, russet-ginger beard. Baker once suggesting that he accompany him to an AA meeting, further enraging the animosity between them. Farrelly vainly trying to convince his inner self that his personal dreams and those he had once harboured in the long ago of his passionate youth for the commonwealth of man had been accomplished. Baker was his guilty conscience. His nemesis. Baker who once had a wife who adored him no matter what. Baker, the mirror to his inner child that he wanted to forget. Fucking Tommy Baker who had it all. Fucking Tommy Baker, the perfect romantic alcoholic who never seemed to suffer.

Baker was far away from them on a plush sofa by the wall. Like an ageing rock star discussing one last tour, one final contract. Looking down at his slim tie. Running his fingers up through his slightly thinning mullet haircut. Brushing imaginary specs from his tight designer trousers. The Alvin Stardust of reportage. Had just told the senior management that, because of his "problem with the bottle" he was winding down his career and was going to take early retirement but had a special assignment he wished to complete. His three superiors issued grunts of understanding, mumbled words of support, commiseration, of course, of course, very (cough) sensible hgrrmm! Grown men, intellectuals with good degrees, working in the communications industry for decades but unable to communicate the most basic of emotions to each other. On the part of Andrew Mendoza and Joseph Cullinane, the sympathy was genuine but Tommy Baker knew that Farrelly's sympathy was fake, knew that Farrelly was secretly punching the air at the thought of getting rid of him. Farrelly all choleric, a former socialist, guilt-ridden because he was now a game keeper and not a poacher, hating Tommy Baker all the more because, despite Baker's success, his house in leafy Rathgar, his wine collection, his encyclopedic possession and knowledge of books, despite all this, he had retained his radical edge, his ire for justice, made no apology for his success but still argued for wealth distribution saying, It is not equality of misery we want. And therefore Baker irritated Farrelly more intensely, just as Baker irritated fat bishops and smug politicians. Hated people like Farrelly who chose the slow suicide of cynicism.

And Farrelly glaring at Baker's effortless intellectual prowess, his huge brain behind the once-full but now-withered face, his shrivelled body and those fucking pointed boots. Ha, fucking winkle pickers, he called them, garish waistcoats, vibrant shirts and leather ties, all that ostentation he insisted on wearing, nay flouting. May the bottle kill him. The way Baker looked down his spectacles at people when querying their arguments, even though they normally towered above him like Farrelly did. No, this was an affront to basic etiquette and what was expected of television producers, and to Farrelly, quietly clenching his right fist to celebrate Baker's plans to leave Empire. Baker the last of the visionaries who gave not a fig for viewing figures, audience share, advertising revenue in Empire's part-state, part-commercial arrangement. Not a fig for "growing the trust of the audience," or whatever meaningless, empty and ridiculous PR-speak that was de rigueur at the moment.

Baker who would never be "on message" like the other Empire drones but would always be counter message. And Diarmuid Farrelly hated him the more for this and to hell with his dead wife, which Baker never mentioned the more to evoke sympathy he was sure. Farrelly furious beyond fury with him because he spoke openly about his love affair with alcohol and "gorgeous wines." The chalk and the cheese, the cheese and the worm turning. Baker reminding Farrelly of his former self. Now he was rid of him. But wait . . .

Baker was talking of a new, young prospect coming through, a chip off the old public-broadcasting-ethos block. A visionary. Baker knowing which television buttons to press, to enrage Farrelly's red-faced choler, engage Joseph Cullinane's patrician favours, Mendoza's love of conviction journalism.

—Can I mention my young protégé, James Tierney, and the renewal of his contract?

Farrelly—clenching his teeth, his quivering jawbone visible through his wiry beard—snapped his pencil audibly.

Éilis moves to her third-floor kitchen window where, if she leans across the sink, she can see the Gaelic football pitches and the old indoor handball ally where Finn was playing that evening. She forced to steady her arms on the back rim of the sink, smell of damp, jerry-built walls, mould—the opposite of fragrant flowers, gardens, leafy South Dublin suburbs, butterflies, bees humming in the summer, lunch al fresco on the lawn—these are homes built for the dregs to reinforce their dregdom, so that when they are dragged to the large, spacious courts before the bright, breezy cappuccino bistro, sated barristers and lawyers from the leafy suburbs and the gated 24-hour patrolled communities, these dregs drag the hovels and their notworthiness on their backs. And so forceful is the vertigo that assaults her mind she steps back from the ledge and wills herself to focus on four young men playing a furious handball game. Yes, the flesh is willing but the spirit is weak. Falling through the window, falling, falling, to the grey concrete in the failed hero's sweet relief, aaaahhhh! and in that moment of oblivion the young child after she had reluctantly ceased her caresses and put him down again, not wanting to let little Dessie go ever, ever, ever, and no, it is so unbearable, but I still have four strong sons with shoulders of broad, high cliffs, powerful limbs and powerful hands to work four green fields, and they bouncing off the worn walls in the alley and dancing around each other to get to the ball, like some ancient death dance prior to battle. But one is fey and she can smell his fear, see the firebrand of Iscariot. It is Frankie Byrne who will not look into her eyes.

The shadows thrown, their forms, reminiscent of the shapes and icons the child had seen in the arch by the flats. Spanzo's grinning face and Éilis plummeting to Finn and the game.

Get thee behind me.

The last point in the game. Gameball. The hardball singing from the walls and roof before slamming back into play again on the court. These young men, with Finn Dempsey a giant in their midst. Gameball of hardball. Wearing hard goggles to protect their eyes from the tight and dense sphere, like blow torchers or Mayan Indians grunting incantations. An Irish Haka Maori dance—heads shaking with each fierce belt of the projectile, arms snaking forward, the smack, slap, and zing of the ball around the walls. Other young men and women who had been involved in a previous game staying on to watch when they heard that Finn Dempsey was playing in a doubles match. Finn oblivious to their admiring oohs and aahs as he raced around the alley, always getting the better of his opponents, such was the power and grace in his movements. He finally smashes a volley into the baseline of the front wall which comes back so low and dead that it is an ace in the hole. Gloved and be-sweated hands up in delight after ripping off his goggles. Frankie Byrne high-fiving him. Éilis standing at the Perspex glass at the back of the alley waving her hands and shaking her head and crying, Frankie Byrne! Pressing her face and smearing lips to the window by the sink so that she teeters. Frankie Byrne! But she is not there and nobody is listening and she is falling.

Iscariot

THE STEAM FROM the showers clings to the green walls and the battered lockers where Finn Dempsey changes quickly into jeans and T-shirt, cracking jokes and throwing his ball at the back of Gerry MacDowell's head. Gerry studying Finn admiringly. These bone-hard young men grown up together, rarely fallen out, and with few jealousies between them. Finn would have laughed, and in a rare explosion threatened violence, if somebody were to suggest to him that Frankie Byrne, one of the central characters in their group, would be willing to set Finn up for the Untouchables. Frankie was mad craic. A lunatic and would do anything for you and would never let you down if you were in a tight corner. Back to back or shoulder to shoulder. No way was it Frankie Byrne, and Gerry saw that Finn's frame was filling out. Not one ounce of spare flesh existed on his muscled body. Yet his movements were fluid and athletic. He was lean rather than bulky and yet for all his strength he had never been known to pick a fight. Of all the Dempsey brothers—Anto and Declan (the two older brothers) or Séamus and Denis (the two younger brothers)—Finn was the least likely to lose his cool. Handball, perhaps, or any talk about Éilis were the only things that really got underneath Finn's supple skin. It is true that he had once physically lifted a referee for some bad calls when a match had gone against him. Two of his brothers having to return the referee to terra firma. Finn—an all-Ireland handball champion. Gerry pricks his ears up when Frankie Byrne shouts across to Finn that a good job was coming up in England.

—I'm going back over in around a week's time if you're interested, Finn? said Frankie.

—Yeah? There's another job coming up, Frankie, is there?

—To be honest, Finn, I gave the foreman of the job your mobile number straight off coz he said he was looking for a good ganger man to run a few of the sites. You are the obvious one for that with the size of you and all the concreting you've done. Hope you don't mind?

—Jeez, Frankie, not at all . . . good man. Been no work for ages.

—There's loads o' money in it, Finn, said Frankie.

Finn's warm reaction and he getting so excited about the job, Frankie momentarily forgets that he was being paid to betray his comrade.

—It'll be a laugh too. There's six going from here including meself. Come over, Finn. You should have come the last time. The craic was brilliant.

—I'm going over Finn, said Dermot Lacey.

—You going too, Gerry?

—Ah, there's no way herself would let me go, Finn. Jeez, I wouldn't mind the money tho' . . .

—Yeah, that's the thing. Meself and Éilis are supposed to be saving money for a house . . .

Gerry nodded his understanding. —See, that's the way they get you, women . . . they tie you down.

There was a murmur of agreement from Frankie and Dermot Lacey at this. Finn stands up. There is a huge slam from the door of the locker.

—Come over to ours tomorrow anyway, Frankie, and tell us the craic. *Slán anois.*

—Hey, wait there, Finn, don't forget that your man is going to ring in the morning, so make sure your mobile is on!

Carmel Daly knew Jimmy Heffernan's problem all right. This Éilis one was a Holy Grail. She would always and forever be far more of an untouchable to Jimmy than anything he could ever muscle up on the streets or his weird brain could control. And that Jimmy could not bear. He snapped his fingers and got every-thing. Nearly everything. She had known from the start that it had been a risk getting into bed with Jimmy Heffernan. She all business, a head for figures, good club contacts. The fierce, mer-ciless drive of women to manage, set up home, control, manipu-late, scheme—ruthless to the domestic extreme if needs be. And so what if he was not good looking? The comfort of strangers. A Devil's contract that satisfied them both. He not interested in sex but powerful and a connoisseur of fine things. Quick, silent, in and out. Like those lizard-skin ties he wore. The club taking off and more to come. The prospect of a life of leisure and preening in Marbella. Jet-set shopping to Paris, New York, media stars, VIP lists and waiting areas. The subservience of waiters and concierges. Okay, he was talking of Cancun, what-ever. But little had she believed that the risks she had taken, and the extreme comfort zone she was trying to build for herself and her children with him, would be threatened by what sounded like the last sixteen-year-old virgin in Ireland. A moving statue that everybody worshipped, or so she had heard. Oh yes, don't worry, she had done her homework. Spanzo was a gouger but also a mouth. But it wasn't going to happen, she said to herself. It so wasn't going to happen. Her toothpick stabbing a bright red cherry at the bottom of her glass.

—Yes, Jimmy, it is time to move on, she said. We've got the gear, the brains, the contacts, and we don't have to sit around anymore watching it happen. Are you listening? We've got to get out of that street stuff NOW and go permanently upmarket, into the stratosphere, the blue yonder, and gone out of this for good. Jesus wept! Your brother! He'll land us all in it if we're not care-ful. Let him and Spanzo deal with all the dross. We don't need it.

Heffernan shaking his head slightly. She not understanding that there was violence to be dispensed and scores to be settled, accounts to be reconciled. An immediate threat of terrible but very precise infliction of pain and the fear of pain. The admin-istration of fear. An overhanging pall of subjugation before the big move could be made. No use moving, then having to return to firefight. Anyway, Carmel wasn't going anywhere with him.

She didn't even come near. The Sandymount equivalent of an Essex blonde. Her saving graces being her excellent legal and real estate contacts, her head for figures and her callousness, her utter indifference to the fates of those outside her immediate sphere of concerns. Heffernan shakes his head—women. Ruthless within, brainless without.

Carmel reached her hand out to Heffernan's.

—Talk to the Cube about it and some of the others, Jimmy. It doesn't make sense to keep all this going. It's always going to be more hassle than it's worth. Leave it to Spanzo and the rest of the lowlifes. He's creaming off the top big time anyway. That's what I want to happen. Now, Jimmy. And you promised me when we set up shop together.

She putting her hand out to him. He liked holding hands even though he didn't like undressing or sharing a bed. Fucking weird. And it wasn't that he couldn't do it. Strong as a snake. But whatever. Give me your hand. Yes, he likes my hands.

Heffernan's mind turning, turning, turning, returning, ever turning to Éilis, who was above it all. The ultimate possession. The Koh-i-noor of her species. Heffernan already constructing the pristine bulletproof-glass case in which she would be ensconced. Going away from her to another room, another country even, but always coming back to behold, admire—okay, to worship, venerate. Éilis looking up from reading Nora Farrell's palm. Heffernan taking Carmel's hand. He wanting another cigar, a Bolivar this time, *los belicosos finos*—ah yes . . . bellicose. All that would have to stop. Laying his head back, the crowd all admiring, camera lights popping, controlled and not inhaling, cultured and not brutal in any way. Paparazzi being pushed away. There would be constant talk of them, but their appearances would be few. He would be Howard Hughes to her Irish Greta Garbo. She would approve and deign to take his arm, her full, perfect Celtic breasts, not ponderous cow udders, white orbs in her green dress, nudging against his tautness and filling the cleavage as they popped their lights. So that he was completed and metamorphosed and no longer Jimmy the Psychopath. She was his path to purgation and redemption. His path out of his psychopathy. Only she could complete him, make him whole, because she herself was beyond sex. Only she, he knew, could make him human, because there was no grudge in her and no avarice. Physically and mentally perfect and clean of all sin. A miracle.

—That's what I desperately need now, he breathed hoarsely.

Carmel bending her head, trying to lip-read what Heffernan said. He looking down at her hands but lost in some other space.

—What, Jimmy?

She tried to pull her hand away, but Heffernan's grip was too strong.

—Now, who's this fella that's been chasing you, Mrs Farrell? asked Éilis.

Nora Farrell and Mrs Nolan huddled around Éilis, with Nora's cracked and lined palm lying in the swan's wing that is Éilis's limb. Nora gave a swift and guilty glance at the picture of her husband, Michael, who was dead these ten years.

—Say nothing to Michael, she said fingering her crucifix.

Éilis nodded. Nora continued.

—Sure, he's only a bit o' company . . . he's great for me angina, the doctor says. Makes me relax. Not that there's anything going on, like. I'm trying to pass him on to Mrs Nolan.

—Ah! Me?! Give over, Nora. What would I want with one of them things at my age? I've had enough of fetching and carrying for men.

Éilis studying them both carefully. Weighing the atmosphere. Something not right. Two glasses of brandy and ginger sat near the "patients," whilst Éilis sipped chamomile tea. (She had brought her own supplies.) All three women laughing and deadly serious. What does life hold for me? What does it mean? Have I worked my life to death for these bones? What's in the air around me? Why do I still feel chosen? How can I curse or change my lot? Give us the goodness of this bright child, her natural saintliness, her innocence, so that we might be returned, however momentarily, to our pure state, or essence in which all are equal, rich or poor.

—Anyway, ladies, whatever way it turns out, romance is definitely in the air for one of yez!

Éilis seemed then to choke and shiver on this remark, like a cloud passing over her, a shadow seeking to quench her light. The laughter died and a tension rapidly built in the room. The lighthearted palm-reading becoming a dark séance. She becomes small and highly charged. Arched. Like a cat ready to turn and flee. She looking down at her hand to see Jimmy Heffernan's hand holding a woman's hand. A woman unknown to her. Éilis snaps her hand away from Nora's. Heffernan looking up with a start at Carmel, who was shouting at him.

—Sorry, Nora! Éilis cried.

Nora now old, defensive, flattened against the sofa and fearing the worst of prophecies as Éilis turns to her.

—Nora, you have to be careful who you lend money from.

Mrs Nolan shooting Nora a glance as if to gauge her reaction.

—How do ye mean now, Éilis?

—Nora. You know . . . she said, quietly looking up from Nora's hand. —Go to the Credit Union, see Father McCartan, you don't have to have them on your back. They can't mess you around as long as you're willing to pay something.

Nora laughs bitterly. —I was going to say that you don't know yer man, well, not him exactly, but his cronies, but you probably do.

—Ah, don't worry, Nora, I know him. He's my cousin unfortunately. But it was probably Spanzo, was it?

—No, not him, Éilis. Another young fella who's not from round here. Nice young chap actually. Seemed a bit apologetic. Think he was Darren. See, I was a bit short and got the loan of a hundred but then I had to get a another loan to pay off the first one, but don't you be bothering yourself about them things anyway. You stick with Finn, he's a lovely big fella and you'll be grand.

—I'm going over to see Finn now. He'll be on his way from the handball alley.

Éilis rose to leave too quickly for the likes of her ageing sisters who wanted to delay her departure with conversation.

—God! cried Mrs Nolan. I remember when they played that against the walls outside. Can't do that now with all the dirt hanging around selling drugs and mithering people. The old days have gone for good.

The Contract

TOMMY BAKER ACKNOWLEDGED the greetings of a camera crew as he walked across the Empire TV restaurant. Already craving another alcoholic morning fortifier but not desperate, not yet. If he could just hold out till lunchtime. Talk to his dead wife. Get to an AA meeting. He wryly observing the fashion sense of young Dublin 4 television people: their peacock pantomimes; pert, precocious, self-obsessed young women with skirts outrageously short at ten o'clock in a new day; feminists they claimed, and they already on the mind-numbing conveyor belt for botoxes, infills, outfills, cellular implants, all the contrivances in the struggle to be perennially fifteen. The young, eviscerated TV men making way for them, bowing and scraping. Eunuchs subservient to the faux-female deity that has conquered the media, these men still dressed like the undergraduates they had recently been. All clueless and pompous show—Plato, Ethics, Civics having gone through one ear and out the other. No thoughts of speaking to and for the nation, no ethos of service, viewing only themselves as the nation and talking only amongst themselves of promotions and demotions, who had shagged who, how they could grow the trust of senior producers. Media dilettantes worshipping Narcissus and middle-class mediocrity. Empire TV little more than an extension of the nearest designer shopping mall. Baker aware that to them he is a dinosaur, not even on their radar. Good.

Baker could see James Tierney in the far corner, the young man's broad back almost turned to the crowd and reading voraciously with shoulders hunched furiously, then writing something in a notepad. Baker simply watching him like he was the son he never had. Already proud of him. Startled at all the new discoveries James provided, cognizant of his mannerisms, his approach to the world and the way he challenged it. Baker not jealous of Tierney's physique, rather being proud of it, as if it had flown from his own loins. He would be Chiron to this Achilles, provide him with talismans and magic weaponry, feed him the innards of she-wolves and the flesh of wild boar and lion. Find his one weakness and guard it. This was his overbulging heart.

Approaching Tierney now. And the boy all dark, sober clothing in this otherwise chattering menagerie: a white shirt, strong shoes, a styled but masculine jacket to suit his male frame. His buckler and shield already girded. Three books on the table. One of them an Irish-language textbook. Baker settling into a seat opposite him.

—Morning, young James, brushing up on your Irish I see, *maith an fear*.

—Ah, howya, Tommy. Yes, this Éilis one has Irish so I thought I'd make the effort. It all helps . . . you know yourself. I used to have very good Irish so I should really use it more. Well? Did you read it? It's amazing isn't it?

Baker looking at him. The energy bouncing off the seat, like he would tear down the walls and eat.

—Do you want the good news or the really good news?

—You read her, what shall we call it, essay . . . her report from the front line, and want to make a film about it and I'm going to be the researcher. Happy days. I'll ring her friend Dawn so I can arrange a visit. Actually, I'll do it now if you'll let me use my mobile?

—Ha, ha. Woah there, Jamesie, not so fast. I'll come to that in a moment. He waves to another Empire veteran, sits back. —I browsed through it. I actually remember her, I think, going by what her friend Dawn has told you. Really attractive. In fact shockingly. Stands worryingly close into your personal space. So I don't think I'm wrong. But first about your contract.

—Ah, fuck the contract, Tommy. I'll be all right wherever I am. Are you going to make a film about Heffernan or not?

Tommy Baker weighing his words carefully. Conscious that his incendiary apprentice needed to be coaxed, that his glowering presence, his impatience and West of Ireland, to-Hell-or-Connaught anarchy had to be channelled into fertile zones, translated to positive ions. For the life-or-death game amongst the dark Gods that had to be played.

—James, your career is important. Not just for me and you but for lots of people. In fact, *for* the people, if there are to be any publicly minded tribunes left in this fucking madhouse. It's a long war we are fighting and we have to gather people round us, think strategically. The enemy did that years ago, and this place was hijacked. A few of us veterans feel the same and are working quietly to bring people in. Keep that to yourself. Now, I've swung you a year's contract, and if that's successful, which it will be, then you'll be taken on permanently. There'll be a slight bump in the middle where you'll have to work directly to News instead of us and you'll be under Diarmuid Farrelly, but let me deal with that.

—Diarmuid Farrelly? Diarmuid fucking Farrelly? You're joking? He hates me almost as much as he hates you. And news? I'm not interested in news. I want to make films. Serious in-depth analysis. You agreed with me, remember, Tommy? That's why you took me from sleepy Loughrea. I could have stayed there and become a county hurler instead of a news gopher, and besides—

—James. News is important and it's good to learn the trade. Quick writing and putting packages together. Say you might have to make last-minute changes to a film half an hour before it goes to air. Being able to turn things around quickly is a great skill to have. Now, just trust me and let me guide you through this. Cullinane is on our side on this one, and Mendoza has taken a shine to you: "breath of fresh air," he said.

Tommy Baker chose not to tell his young Achilles that he had already begun his investigations into Jimmy Heffernan long before Éilis's extraordinary manuscript was presented to him. Nor did he admit that he had read it several times and how remarkably accurate it was. But whether it told the future? He doubted.

He refused to believe in shamans: "witchtrickery," Baker called it. The girl must know someone in Empire. The Irish language heads in here feeding her the stuff. Thick as thieves they are those *Gaeilgeoirí*. That was all.

The Finn Trap Closing

FINN WALKING HOME with Dermot Lacey and Frankie Byrne. The three young men heading towards the Wakefields shop. Dawn waving to Finn as they stand near the entrance, kids doing bike wheelies in the road scattering at the approach of deep, reverberating bass and drum sounds, the ground rumbling, a black Mazda sports car flashing by and then pulling up across the street, and Seánie Heffernan putting on a reading light above the passenger seat. Spanzo is seen to dart into a nearby house whose door had been left ajar. Frankie Byrne looking warily over at the car. He tugs lightly at Finn's arm.

—Don't you be getting in a row with him now, Finn. You know who that is, don't you?

—Did I say a word . . . did I? They don't worry me, Frankie.

—Ah, Finn, you know all that talk at Christmas time about a feud starting between the Dempseys and the Untouchables after your Anto broke your man's nose in town. Don't want you getting into bother.

—That's not Jimmy Heffernan there anyway, Frank. That's his younger brother Seánie. Though he's a drug-pushing, wea-selling, little scumbag like his brother.

Frankie wincing at this, and Dermot moving quickly into the shop as Finn showed no care or caution that he might be overheard and laughed out loud. What could they do to him?

—In fact, Frank, the only reason the scumbags at the arch didn't get a kicking as well is because Éilis asked Anto not to be going to war on them. Our Anto was right annoyed because he was out with his wife when they fronted up on him. They were off their heads on something I think. Must have been, to start on our Anto. Even I wouldn't stand a chance with Anto. He's got arms like bulldozers and no fear. But Éilis is related to Heffernan, remember. It was all smoothed over, but they know better than to mess with us.

—True for ya, Finnius. Jeez, I never saw you worry about anything, do you know that? said Frankie, trying to be humorous but almost whispering and glancing nervously once again over the road.

—But all the same, let's move on, eh?

Spanzo's proximity more than anything making Frankie so jumpy. Dermot came out of the shop with sports drinks for everyone, and Finn laughed again as he quenched his thirst and nodded in the direction of the *Dark Star* car.

—The Heffernans don't bother with us. They've more sense.

—Jeez, Finn . . . you wouldn't start a row with the Untouchables? said Dermot. Leave me out of it if you do. I don't want a visit from Spanzo and his gorilla friends and end life as a chopped-up hamburger in one of their dodgy takeaways on Dorset Street, no way man.

The young men laughed at the thought of Dermot as a cheeseburger, but Finn was going to finish his point.

—I wouldn't start a row with them lads. Not because I'm scared of them but because it's a waste of time. If the Untouchables weren't doing all that drugs stuff it would be somebody else. You'd spend all your life in diggin' matches and with a baseball bat or even a gun by the door, and who needs that? Let them and the Guards sort it out. Although sometimes it's hard to tell the difference.

Frankie Byrne disappearing into the shop for no other reason than not to be seen with Finn at that moment. By the time he re-emerges, however, the Mazda had disappeared and they walked to the corner of the next street, which was the turn for Finn's house and the flats further down the road.

—Come over for a drink with us later, Finn, said Dermot. Meself and Frankie will be in Hogan's at half ten. Then God knows what we'll do.

—I'll see what Éilis wants to do. I need a proper drink after whipping yez. I'll ring the brothers and see what they're doing. Then I have to talk to Éilis about London. She's supposed to be going to the Gaeltacht again, so it will probably suit us for a while.

—Is Éilis going to the Gaeltacht? asked Frankie with more urgency in his question than he had intended.

—Take care she doesn't already know about London, Finn . . . she's spooky, that one, the way she knows things, said Dermot.

Finn looking at Dermot with a pained expression. He resenting the jumbo stuff but letting it pass. But Dermot's comments had also upset Frankie. For the first time, it had occurred to him that Éilis might even know that he was being paid good money to set Finn up with a job in England. Get him away. Why did Heffernan want that, really? It had started out as doing a kind of favour for Finn. No harm, really. Now it looked and felt like a kiss of death and thirty pieces of silver thrown in the face of one of his best mates. Frankie wanting to think and put some distance between Finn and his guilty conscience.

—Come over to the house tomorrow, Frankie, said Finn. And don't be worrying, I'll keep my phone on for your man. Thanks again for the leg up.

Ronagh Durkin

A SECRETARY SMILING at James Tierney as he walks down a corridor in the upper echelons of Empire Television, he feeling like a rat in a warren. Not wanting to smile at all. Not wanting to glad-hand Joseph Cullinane, so desperately wanting to sign the contract, yet his body screaming to run away to the West. To wild winds and the lough shore, call of curlews and crunch of shale. The secretary wondering who the hunk with issues was. She would find out, she resolves.

Tierney receives genuine congratulations from Cullinane and encouragement with regard to his career as a television journalist and is in fact moved. Inspired. Feels taller. Not even the signing of his contract in the presence of a Human Resources apparatchik who is all blank eyes and false cheer can now dampen his spirits. Then yet another meeting to go to before heading back to the canteen. At the last meeting, a senior producer in Andrew Mendoza's department assigned him to research a story about fish kills in lakes and rivers in the West of Ireland. He would be going back home.

James goes back to his favourite table in the restaurant, and she tracks him down there. Has seen him there before. Always in that same spot with his broad back to everyone, which tickles her. Heard that he was a moody bastard, arrogant. But also a big heart and loyal. Her name is Ronagh Durkin, born in Dublin but with lineage in County Clare. She watches James Tierney sit down as she waits for her cappuccino. A smile dancing in her smouldering-coal eyes. She straightening her pencil skirt.

Fluffing up her black hair. The black hair of the Armadas, svelte, swarthy skin, and mingling of the gypsy Black Irish, white crystal bracelet dazzling against her dark wrist. Never one to back away from a challenge. In the corridor, she had sensed a half smile as he had turned away from her. Sure also that he was a bit of a bollix, contrary. Yes he had been discussed and pointed out at lunchtime. Her best friend, Úna, telling her that he had trouble written all over his big, cheeky, culchie face. A face and head that cried out for a low-tipped cap to frame his infinite blue eyes.

Trouble? All the better. The urge that women have to change them, to tame them. To be the chosen. To be the She who would harness him, ride and calm his rage, cap his volcano. So she steps into his brace.

—Talk about Mr High and Mighty, said Ronagh as she stood opposite James at the table. Looking down at him, a laugh on her full, red lips, eyes sparkling. —May I?

—What? Oh sure. You were on the corridor this morning. Sorry I was a bit unfriendly. I'm in better form now.

—I'm impressed that you remember.

—Always remember good legs and a bold face.

—No. I mean that you remember you were in bad form. Rude and ignorant actually, ha, ha.

—Ah, come on . . . er, what's your name, sorry?

—Ronagh, Ronagh Durkin? And you are James Tierney. Look, that's my office crowd over there. Do you want to come and join us?

—Ah jeez, Ronagh. Do we have to? Can we not just stay here and flirt. Is this some kind of bet?

—God, you're such a bighead! And so presumptuous! Aw, come on. For the craic, Jamesie. Honest. It's not a bet. Come on.

Ronagh Durkin rising from the seat. Leaning slightly towards him as she stands, her upper shape projecting at him. Now displaying her full figure and swaying slightly as she moves away. Feminine wafts of soft perfume. James Tierney desperately wanting to read Éilis's diary again. Then he had notes for Tommy Baker. Tommy at the AA, or communing with his dead wife. Definitely wobbly that morning he was, Tommy. Understandable really when you think that his wife died in child labour, and the baby, a boy, died with her. Still, given what had happened in his own family and then Tommy's enslavement to the drink— all that vindicated his own decision to be careful. But James is chivalrous to a fault and unable to refuse a woman who made a direct invitation. Anyway, she was nice and soft and looked like she was from the West despite her Dublin accent. Wide face and showing her teeth when she smiled. Not a bit careful or sly. So he gathered up his things and sat down with her amongst her friends and bore the cross of mortification, the knowing glances and invisible nudges around the table, for her sake. Aware that he had pleased her and that some kind of pact had been agreed. James Tierney and Ronagh Durkin. If she could deal with his obsessions. For example, this Éilis story that he'd mentioned ten times already. Also his obviously frequent and urgent need for quiet (would everybody please be quiet, please, while I just think?). It might work. Ronagh leaning into him to pass a remark in a way of offering her thanks. Ronagh annoyed when Úna began describing a drug-related shooting near her house. James showing Úna too much attention. James tickled when she butts in to change the subject. Touched by her want to possess him, claim him. Úna annoyed. Insanely jealous for a moment actually though happily married herself. It might just.

One psychiatrist saying that I need stabilizing. Special care in a secure environment. Now waiting for a second opinion. Me forcing myself to be calm. Doing the breathing exercises that Séamus Dempsey showed me. Now moved into my own room at health-service expense until a decision is made. Me, Éilis Devanney. Her parents wishing to see her and she refusing. Now Dawn comes and she bursts into tears and so do I. Finn standing behind her, awkward, looking away. The faraway stare of incomprehension. Why can't she just snap out of it? Me, Éilis, scooping my notes off the bed and flinging them quickly into her press and walking towards him in my mad nightgown is what Finn sees of me. Psychotherapy next. All he sees is Psycho and wants out.

Where Is She Going?

IT IS A normal thing for two girls to walk across a park. Even a park that resembles a bomb site—shorn and bald grass that not even the mangy, tethered horse will eat because it is strewn with glass and worse. It is normal to see them walk, Sinéad and Deirdre, speaking into each other's face. A laugh, then Sinéad stopping to light a cigarette. But then some of the Goths emerge to watch, and the girls watch the Goths back, and stories are constructed in the minds of all. Deirdre has not yet told Sinéad she was chatting up the Goth with the blue streak. He wonders why, wonders will she ever get beyond her cousin's toughness. Sinéad merely sees the farce of their couch and their sad sack "Occupy" tent and creates more of her story. The one that sees her escaping. The blue-streak Goth ponders the problem of lusting after a she who is *so not a Goth*, as avowed by his fellow Goths. That he as a leader had to set an example.

Dawn walking home from Wakefields to the flats. The Goths not on her radar as they have already been calculated. Calling to Sinéad and Deirdre. Now even less of a normal thing. A triumvirate of worry about Éilis. The blue streak knowing the difference between banter and serious debate. Where had she gone, the poetess, the priestess, the girl far too serious and otherworldly for this place? Pondering. Turning to the table, but she was not there.

—No. She said they want to section her, said Dawn. Cheeks and jaw set firmly. Taller somehow.

—She's gonna have an operation, said Deirdre

—Deirdre. You get sectioned when you are put in the loony bin, and that's what they want to do with Éilis.

—No way. I mean. She is a bit mad but not mad like that.

Dawn and Sinéad looking at Deirdre. Dawn telling Sinéad that she was going to see Father McCartan before her work the next day, and the weather finally beginning to break with a cool wind and the promise of rain. The blue streak wondering why he had plumped for the fluffy, airhead type. Her doe eyes of deep, kindly brown. It was her angora jumpers that did it for him, and the way she shaped them. It was the scent. He had remembered that scent before in some other life. In a bower of trees at dusk, and a woman serving wine from a smoothed decanter of fired clay—long ago she was. Calm, slender wrists and holding his gaze for him. She is unstressed. Undressed. Immediate empathy and want. Some delightful kink in her that needed kinking more to see her true nature. The voluptuous Deirdre who veered from veneer to seer, soothsayer then pure comedy. Easy with herself.

Sinéad shakes her head. —That's a pity because we were going to take her to Siobhán's do in a few weeks. You know, over at the big house in the Grange. Some of the Goths have occupied it. Or part of it. Rattrap it is but should be a laugh. Do her good to let her hair down for a change.

Dawn looks at Sinéad with stony eyes. The eyes of dread wise. She pronounces —You have to be joking, Sinéad. There's no way Éilis can or should go to anything like that. Anyway, she wouldn't want to. And Finn wouldn't let her.

—Well, I just thought it would be good for her. As for Finn. Fuck boring Finn.

—Ah, I like Finn, said Deirdre, still looking over at her favourite Goth.

—Well, I forgot he's supposed to be going to England any-way, said Dawn. I'll see Father McCartan first thing. He needs to tell them about her smack-head parents. Don't start me about them.

The Rearguard

EMPIRE TELEVISION AT night is like a cruise liner at sea. Brilliant. Flashy in its angles. Splendid in its nighttime illumination after the flat mediocrity of the day. Its central arc of lights twinkling and shimmering before fading into evening purple around the lawns and flower beds, the night-velvet foliage and black bark of the tree copses from which might be heard occasional bursts of hubbub from the congregating audiences at the studio entrances where shows were being recorded. Other than that, nothing. The odd bark of a fox perhaps if you were clever enough to judge. Cars passing by on the nearby dual carriageway now the only sound. A holy quiet in the grounds. Sometimes figures could be spied moving behind the blinds in the dimmed brightness of rectangle and square window at the offices. Solitary shadows working late. A more productive time. Time for reflection. Absence of inane, pointless meetings arranged only for egos. Serious note-taking and research. Time also for planning and plotting.

Diarmuid Farrelly sitting at his desk, trying to read a report on social-media trends and their growing impact on news reporting. He casts it aside, gets up from his chair, and paces the room, hands on his hips, head tilted back, thinking. Rosie Boylan was late. But he is still fond of her and feels comfortable with her. They had once had a thing together in the heady days of the Red Flag Party when life was simple and very black and white. Stalinist black and white. We knew better than them. Had them and ran them and they were happy. Everybody was happy. Then it all went wrong in a typically Irish fashion. Comrades walking away. Indiscipline. Doing stupid things. Not being careful enough. Mavericks always mavericks blabbing stuff that was internal. Giving the likes of Tommy Baker a chance. One slit, one opening was all he needed, that fucker. Investigative journalist? No, a shit stirrer that should have been got shot of a long time ago. Didn't see that it was about protecting the citizenry from its own idiocy. Oh no, he cared nothing about the common good. Just rake up dirt, cause a commotion, everybody look at me, clever me. An affront to public service. Well, no way. He, Diarmuid Farrelly, was still there, and others, like Rosie. Where the fuck was she anyway? But he had already forgiven her for the mistake she had made in not attending the meeting that day. It could be sorted still if they concentrated.

In Rosie walked, all business and bustle. She had been thin, back then in the heady days, and big-breasted, a pleasing oval face also. Old warhorses now both. Shorter now she was, and stocky. A thickening setting in, beginning to occlude the difference between bosom and stomach, knee and ankle—all much of a thickness. She all in black but with a dark-purple rose on her dress. Tommy Baker had once called it a boiled rose for a boiled Rosie Boylan. That was back at the start of their now-permanent contretemps. For this very reason, she continued to wear it. It was her black protest dress. The nearest she would now get to a suffragette.

—Sorry I'm late, Diarmuid, had a meeting at the gender-balancing group, good fun actually.

—Well, have you heard about Cullinane's surprise? It would have been good if you had been there.

—You mean about James Tierney's contract? Yes, I heard he got a year, which is a bit excessive.

—A bit excessive? A bit fucking excessive!? It goes right against Empire policy and I sense a conspiracy.

—Oh, for God's sake, Diarmuid!

—No, hear me out, Rosie. In the last year we've had two new researchers who are fascists.

—Diarmuid, they are not fascists. Provos maybe.

—Rosie, that fucker Tierney wears a miraculous medal or

whatever the fuck they call it with its blue string. I can see it under his shirt! He's clearly a green fascist.

—Hold on, Diarmuid. A Catholic medal hardly makes him a fascist, and I think we have—

—Sorry, but I think you're going soft. You're forgetting why we decided to keep them out in the first place. That Empire would be a great bastion against the dark forces that want to drag us back into some Celtic fucking Catholic Stone Age. And we succeeded. Defended the state, stressed our indebtedness to British culture and trade-union history. The hand of friendship. That's what you have forgotten. And now they're sneaking back in. Well, I'm not fucking having that. I didn't work all these years to see—

—Diarmuid. I'll forgive the rant . . . I haven't forgotten. It's just that you are getting very cranky in your old age, if you don't mind me saying. I've asked around and people I trust have told me that he's never so much as mentioned politics or Sinn Féin to anyone. Seems to be more interested in philosophy, which is a bit weird for a young man. Now I know the four new recruits you're talking about. One in radio and the rest on TV side, but only James Tierney has a year contract and the rest of them are on three months. Baker is leaving, and Tierney has to do three months in your department. We are in control of this. So will you just leave it with me? By the time Tierney is with you, Cullinane will be gone.

—All right. Sorry, Rosie. I'm a bit stressed at the minute. That fucker Baker. I could cheerfully strangle him, and of course Tierney idolizes him and follows him round like a lapdog.

—Well, Tierney's getting followed as well by all accounts. He's got all the girls in contracts drooling after him. (Ahh, watch the sting of envy heaving in Diarmuid Farrelly's paunch.) — Well, I wouldn't say, "like bitches in heat," publicly, but you get my drift. Swooning for him anyway, even if he does dress like a farmhand.

—Well, he'll be going back to Bogland after I've finished with him. Since when did Empire have journalists from County Galway?

Starry, Starry Night

FINN GETTING HIS things ready for London. His first items a collection of handballs. There were often good walls on the sites where he could practise and always lads who were handy enough. Three hard balls. Three soft balls. His toolbag and clothes bag ready. He not wanting to admit his relief at going away. All his brothers except Séamus telling him not to go. His mother, Máire, tearful. His father, Gerard, agreeing with Séamus that a man must.

Finn watching Séamus. His younger brother so focussed and already in a career path as a sports and fitness coach. Some sort of socialist also. Kung fu as well. Way too serious, Séamus. Finn loving Séamus. All his brothers, thinking that really Éilis was the sister he never had. Turning off the light in his room and watching the ink of night seeping across the Dublin skyline. It was something he would like to paint one day. The way things flowed, moved and changed, but could be captured if you didn't look at it but felt it. His art teacher had always encouraged him to paint and go to art galleries. Used to say he had a rare talent but that painting might be painful for him and that was why he avoided it. He would pick up a brush and do it someday but then he knew that he would only paint the stars and their ineffable sadness. Van Gogh was his favourite painter because he felt the charged poignancy in the air and Éilis embracing him and that nothing in the essence of the ether could be changed. Something stopping him from going there. To have to face that blank canvas all the time and delve deep to dredge things up, when it was all pointless. But then she was a living star and there she was in front of him. Knowing that, were he to paint Éilis, he would implode in the supernova destruction of his own ennui. His innate lethargy. He could not face that existential change because he felt the pointlessness in his bones. With handball, or work, hard grafting work, he was alive because it was instinct for him. His body on the line. His body he trusted, and no need to worry about it. No need to think. He knew his physical body and it knew him. All those mind games killed him.

Finn sees how the dark of the river Liffey seeped into the sky and smeared the lights from the ships and the houses across the river in Irishtown. Water everywhere, and the stars reflecting mutely on the surface, in the river, the canal locks, the drains, and in her eyes where she approached him from the end of the bridge. Her beauty grasped at his breath and he could not bear it, for it was a thing that he could not deny, and so he turned away from her overwhelming all-too-muchness. Resenting that she spoke Irish to him. Her futile fight. A tiny bird flapping against a vortex.

James Tierney scratching at his thick head of hair. Pushing it back from his forehead. Not wanting to read this, when a woman is suddenly standing before him with a cappuccino in her hand. The good-looking one from that morning. What was she? Ronagh?

The Tears of the Madonna

WHEN THEY APPROACH each other she starts to cry. Finn looks around embarrassed and exasperated. A couple walking by arm in arm and looking at them with a half-interested air. His jaw tightening.

—Éilis, you have to stop all this high-wire shite. Sometimes I think you make things happen by wishing tha— I know he regrets them. The words. As they were spoken. But then blundering on anyway, saying that if I couldn't just snap out of it and accept that life was shit, well then everything would always be up in the air, and she, they, their kids would always be on the edge, and he really wondered at her sanity sometimes.

She cried out in pain and grabbed him as roughly as she could but it was a feather buffeting against a mountain. Then the sobs came again, and he fell into the stars in her eyes and moved to capture them, and oh, she knew, she knew, but it wasn't him, and tore away from him, and he shook his head, he exasperated standing on the bridge, the many bridges, and began to walk more quickly after her, but she ran like the wind and disappeared from the bridge, and some passing boys who mocked until he glared and balled his hammer fists, and they were scared, and Finn Dempsey just exasperated and giving up.

Finn turns to stare. Finn, my disarmed God, turns to stare at the water. Sees a picture there, a revelation that he won't paint because he's scared to. Armless. Disarmed. Salvation can only come when you truly believe. Go seventy thousand fathoms down Then find you can breathe.

Me running weightless with utter loneliness. I drowning in the air for there is no rock there. Her very movements through space, my arms, her face becoming separated from the body—the nocturnal lights around her were all soft colours. Only my face was black and white. Now she was running away from Finn, crying happy birthday as fast as light with objects racing past her. Now so slow that I would never reach where I wanted to go. Then she was in the arch of the stairwell leading to her home. In the kitchen in her house she approached the kettle which I sensed bore a malevolent power. Without moving, it was pulsing, growing ever larger in my vision making her head shake. There was a power in the world which was beyond control and unfathomable. It coursed through everything, and Éilis—me, Éilis—could see it, feel it. Now she saw her own face vaguely in the distance of the square down below. A pipe bomb or something went off somewhere near or was it in her head, this massive rush of air, and my own face right in front of her as she ran. She mouthed a prayer.

Remember, O most loving Virgin Mary, that it is a thing unheard of that anyone who had recourse to your protection . . .

Now, me, Éilis, staring up at the statue of Our Lady in our square. She felt so small. Sensed some kind of collapse. As if it was suspended on a rope, tears flowing from the face of the Madonna.

Cén fáth nach bhfuil duine ar bith sásta éisteacht liom? Maybe you are listening and can't do anything? Is that it? Is that why you shed tears? Me looking up like a child of Fátima.

Finn caught up with Éilis where she knelt in the rain before the statue. He speaks to her and touches her shoulder gently.

—*Éilis,* éirigh leat a stór, gheobhaidh tú do bháis.

But Éilis only had eyes for the Virgin and child and the tears streaming down My Lady's face.

—*Yes, he said. She has finally cracked.*

The Weight of a Pub Clock

HE NEVER MADE it to his AA meeting, Tommy Baker. The draw of the pub he passed on the way being too great. The comfort of it, the solitude and peace. The sense of magic at eleven o'clock in the day, with the dim, suffused light and the quiet of it. The big, white ornamental clock above the bar smiling at him in reverse from the shine of the counter. Backward time. Back to the womb of comfort.

You take out a book and a notepad, and the small scattering of early habitués know to leave you be. The respect for books and learning, the satisfaction they take from your erudition, that you will sit amongst them, the honour bestowed upon their hostelry. A scholar in their midst. One face at the back is familiar in the half-light, and smiles are exchanged and glasses raised before Baker returns to his problem. He needs to work out the problem that is Jimmy Heffernan. It will also be James's problem. Concentration and quiet needed. For beyond the clear facts of crime and corruption there is a deeper question he must understand before he can go further. So he has turned once again to Dostoevsky's *Demons*. His bible for all criminal types.

The red-wine alcohol surge firing through his body like a barium meal of the senses where he visualizes the labyrinth along which his thoughts are leading him. Which character is he, this Heffernan? Verkhovensky? No. Too weak at the end of the day . . . and certainly not Kirillov, who actually commits suicide because he is not God and must taunt, must flaunt, death. Only by dying can Kirillov defeat death but he is driven crazy with this fixation, and Heffernan is not crazy. He is coldly calculating. Heffernan is a leader of men, but he is more than that. What does he want?

Here in the quiet of the alcove, Tommy Baker is an alchemist seeing shapes and portents emerging in the universe of his mind. It is Stavrogin. Dostoevsky's Stavrogin. A demon. Clever, nay brilliant. Ruthless. Charitable also, they say, but wait— would Heffernan marry a cripple and epileptic on a whim? A huge heart? Local boy into huge success? Yes, a huge beating heart there. But it was black poison. Doing great things in the area? Possessing unnatural strength and capable of anything. Yes. Wanting to experience all things, but some weakness there. A weakness stemming from his ultimate need of approval— approval from what or whom? God? Certainly not the world. Not the world, nor the flesh, nor even the Devil.

Tommy Baker pours more wine into his glass. The satisfying richness and glug, glug, glug of claret, its bouquet infusing and enthusing his words so that he writes: *STAVROGIN, Heffernan, elastic intellect, toying with power for the pleasure of it, pondering transformation of humans simply by the bending of his will and power, to discover whether he could create a myth about himself and possibly others—goodness, purity, self-sacrifice, what were these things to him? Things to be manipulated like chess pieces.* But then more wine was poured, and the barman notices that his bottle is empty and after a questioning cock of the head, arrives with a fresh. Now he has it. Baker takes the glass, sits back, savours it, raises his head, and it is as if the whole room, the quiet tables and chairs, the snug of the fitments, the gaunt, stoic men with their backs to him up at the bar, their wasted lives awaiting his judgement as their reversed backs ticked to the minds of their childhood. Then the utter chill in his bones, like an influenza of the soul. For what can we do if we cannot speak of love? Or if love is not enough? He has no love at all, this Heffernan. Even Satan had love. But Heffernan shares with Satan the idea of the "accuser." Yes! That's it . . . Heffernan holds court because he is all powerful and all those human wretches fascinate him and reinforce his power. Baker composing. Tierney reading. Éilis stretching herself so thin. Baker convinced by these words that Stavrogin committed suicide seemingly because of his weight of guilt. His nefarious deeds pressing him down in the end. The flame of human love scorching his heart in the end. Writing indelibly now that Heffernan would never feel this guilt because he was ice, there was ice all about him in the sharp bends of his bones and the cut of his jaw and he must needs snuff the warm flame of purity, the chaste spirit. He could never be scorched. Yes, that was it. Now Baker squirming in his seat, nearly rising to go out and take a cigarette, but no, sit down again and write this God damn it. Because Heffernan neither understood it nor intellectualized it but he could sense the ineffable power and glamour of goodness. Yes, the glamour. That this was the most captivating thing, and he was evil, because this was his choice, to darken the light. If he were allowed. Yes! It was Éilis that he wanted and she was his fixation—his fix! Because he couldn't bear her untouchable distance from him. She had a power he could not touch or corrupt. Éilis lamed him.

Baker half stands up again. Wants to call out but sits again and stares at his notes: *He is Stavrogin's coldly calculating LOGICAL CONCLUSION who has discerned the power that lies in the working class's appreciation and familiarity with violence. With an innate and finely tuned understanding of violence, a finely tuned, rapier mind, and the power to corrupt because of his already obscene wealth, Heffernan could do anything.* The door swung open, and in that shaft of stark light and the darkened female shape, Tommy Baker quailed. For the first time he felt real fear. For he would not leave that place.

It was Eileen Brennan. A personal secretary to one of the main programme executives at Empire, walking in from the bright to the dark just before he ordered his third bottle. Myles Fitzgerald's secretary, becoming smaller as she walked in. Alien to this place, but all her slim, sharp-as-tonic features intact. Bright, inquisitive eyes. She shouldn't be involved in this. His last big hit. His swan song. What was she doing here? Myles was Special Investigations and he would be overseeing any film on Heffernan, but they hadn't got to that stage. Did Eileen have a message? No, she was just walking towards him with a wise look.

Wise, caring eyes with glints of sadness, her car keys in her hand. She shaking her head at the barman's offer. The sidelong glances of the other men. Assuming it was the wife. Tommy rising unsteadily. Old, ingrained instincts making him check for his notes, not to forget his wallet. Not movements purposely done to melt her heart. Simply what he always did. Then he turned at the entrance to go back. For he could not bear to leave that peace, and there was something he needed to write down. That he couldn't do it. He couldn't make that film but he would. She restraining him gently, but he saying, Tea, only tea. So they sat down again and had tea, and he told her his theory. That Jimmy Heffernan was a body snatcher. She absorbing. That he had finally encountered someone who was beyond redemption and didn't want to believe it and tomorrow he would stop for good. She nodding. Tomorrow, I promise. I can't make this film but I will, because I must. For James and for Star of the Sea. For he is far worse than any Devil. He is perfect in his cold malice. And we have created him. Then I'm going to leave, he told her. If I still can.

The Stud

THERE ARE NO overly high, forbidding, blank brick walls here, and the security gates at the main entrance are tastefully dressed with nothing more than thick, dense hedges of verdant green. These have the added benefit of occluding the high-tech surveillance and human-heat-sensing devices from the eyes of those who might take an interest in such things. Similarly, the top of the lengthy enclosing wall that encloses Heffernan Hall is dressed with green foliage that hides the razor wire threaded through its branches and twigs. Careful landscaping ensures that the mansion house itself cannot be seen from the road and there are also heat sensors strategically placed around the estate that trigger zonal cameras and alarms when triggered.

There is an old head gardener. A local man who knows the soil like the grain of his own palm. Loving palms and long, sinewed arms, browned by year after year of outdoor work and peat fertiliser. His flat Donegal cap and hooded eyes have seen things here as he has worked over the years. Things that have surprised, even amazed him. That these could be the new owners of such formerly aristocratic estates. But his love for the grounds and their gardens, in his family for centuries, makes all other questions regarding the powers that be irrelevant. Theirs was never to question what the better-off did. Whether it was the ravishing of servant girls and boys, the visits of degenerate toffs from England, the opium, or carnal orgies in the huts dotted over the estate, the waste of food and the trampling of vegetable beds. Or this new thing in his time with loud Dublin jackeens, roaming

the pathways on quad bikes, shooting at trees, and the residue
and debris of strange powders and burned pipes and tin foil they
left behind after their picnics. He had seen some of their faces in
the newspapers—what was it—the Cube, the Don, the White
Adder, who apparently was an accountant, then of course the
Boss himself. He'd been on the telly shaking hands with that
man Pierce something? Crime lords as new celebrities and were
they really any worse than the old colonial masters?

But Mr Heffernan seemed straight as a die, very clean and
upstanding, was courteous, appreciated his work and paid him
very well, even knew the history of his family in the area and
had great attention to detail. So there was a year-round complement of assorted and vibrant flowers in well-tended beds which
bordered the length of the tree-lined thoroughfare that ran up
to the residence itself. Overseas visitors always expressing genuine delight and appreciation at the way Jimmy Heffernan has
laid out his country spread. For the brash ostentation so typical of the parvenu and nouveau riche was singularly absent
here. The roving business agent, the coke or arms dealer with
his entourage landing in Ireland from Miami or Paris was not
subjected to squirm-inducing cocktail parties on lawns where
awkward women in crushed-linen skirts and streaking fake tans
would stand freezing in the usual, horizontal, drenching rain.
No brash, half-naked morons, all breasts and well-pummelled
thighs, drinking sherry from champagne flutes and calling it
rosé, whilst the host and prospective business partner would
attempt to conceal his low origins by embarrassing attempts at
long words which were mispronounced and often used in the
wrong context, so that the visitors' toes collectively curled in
their patent-leather shoes (the foreigners having better English
than their hosts), and all this to the accompaniment of a string
quartet which played badly because it was frozen and ill at ease,
ventriloquist smiles on their lips as they sawed away in disgust
at themselves and what it had all become, this life.

But Jimmy Heffernan? Why should he make pretensions
about his poor background? He is confidence personified and
knows when to buy and when to sell and the crucial difference

between the two. Says exactly what he wants to say, all of which has already been well considered. Also he knows the importance of Ireland as a discreet bridge to and from Europe and far beyond.

And is it not the rich and powerful that court and curry his favour like wild pigs seeking out the heat and sweet meat of truffles buried in the heart of business transactions and secret deals? Money being the great leveller. The vast amount of money provided by middle class drug habits. The grim accountant that Heffernan can look in the eye without flinching. Business seeking out business. The iron law of trade. As a racehorse owner, he had studied the form of all the other "businessmen" who had been bred and reared in similar circumstances to his own and not one of them had lasted the course. Most of his entrepreneurial peer group from the inner city were either in prison, in exile, or dead. Even those who had seen sense and moved out, usually to Spain, had found they just could not leave the old life behind. Or, the old life came looking for them in the shape of past mistakes, bad grudges, or international judgements. No. Jimmy Heffernan was going to put himself out to grass where he was legally and physically safe and start something new and completely legitimate. A place where he could forge a new empire and Asia was where the new empire was at. Create a home for his wife. If he was going to have a family, he needed to act quickly. He did not want to be an old man without a legacy. Without his own dynasty. Children to study and mould. His own children. Children who not only should be beautiful but should also have beautiful brains. Beautiful Irish brains. Supremely clever Irishness was his selling point. His ruthlessness was nothing special. But the fact that he enjoyed its iconoclastic potential was different to most gangsters. Chic gangsters who loved those Irish actors with their mellifluousness and devil-may-care were attracted to his ice-coolness, his brazenness, his easy assumption of big decisions. Some wanted to give the system the finger, but most simply desired the continuation of fabulous wealth accumulation. But they misunderstood Heffernan.

He, Jimmy Heffernan, wanted to take the system over and

have its minions do his bidding. It was not even having the best of things. It was about commanding respect, even adoration, because he was better than anybody else, cleverer than anybody else, was the Grandmaster Chess of this game. The nice, refined things, even herself, were simply dressage, what was expected at his level, further testimony of his intellect and power. He had already bought out two big-time middlemen by combing through their accounts and compromising them. Another businessman who had often been at Heffernan's stud had refused to hand over his very lucrative and strategically placed haulage company but had soon relented when the Cube visited his haulage yard and explained in a personal and very polite interview the technique he used in forcing billiard balls up the anus of unwise businessmen who refused Jimmy Heffernan. Vaseline ready to go.

Heffernan had a meeting that morning with his accountant, Philip Enderby, whose middle-of-the-range SUV sat outside in uncomfortable comparison with an assortment of Heffernan's vehicles, which shone immaculately in the sweep of pebbled driveway running up to the front entrance of the Heffernan mansion. Heffernan's head mechanic had advised him "not to be letting" the cars sit in the heat and glare of the sun for too long as "they didn't like it," but Heffernan had, nonetheless, ordered them all out that morning just so that he could observe them from his terrace-room reception area. The pizzazz of the Porsche and the retro chic of his customized and ancient Jaguar would provide a welcome diversion for him from the whingeing tones of Philip Enderby, who factored away at a computer set up at a long table at the far end of the room. No e-mails, of course— everything done by ancient fax in the first instance.

Heffernan sitting at the chaise longue at the far end of the large room, so that Enderby had to strain to hear him speak if he lowered his voice. The graceful, elegant, aesthetically pleasing, deep-buttoned, Victorian chaise longue he had simply taken from an antiques dealer who was a cokehead and secret homosexual. Which reminded him that he would have to mention to Ned that one of the "gay ride" boys would need to be activated for a judge who had been "noticed" in that kind of bar recently. A High Court judge d'ye mind. Ned had already moved the hard copies of the photos of all the other judiciary. Heffernan knew this because he had checked—and where had he moved them to? The Law Library via a friendly barrister—ah, priceless. Thin Vermeer of smile, he says. Low smile, slinking slightly into couch and enjoying couch when it is a chaise, and he seeing the judge on playback, or the cop's face when the briefcase is opened classic-style as he had ordered, just like in the films, and the cop's face when all the loot is shown. The endless possibilities opening for him in this dead-end hotel at the dead end of the Dublin quays, and why is the cop important? Because he has the keys, just like a jailer or top house-thief. Or it could be one of his girls from Connolly's opening her legs for twenty grand, and the old man who runs the PC system at the bank. Flash! Bang! Thank you, man—now could you just move this to this? Or Vehicle Licensing, and could you just check out this plate after you rimmed that? Vermeer me away from all this dross and tat.

The interior of the house, first built in the 1700s, was exquisitely decorated. There was a beautiful print—*Girl with a Pearl Earring* by Vermeer—on a wall in the study. Heffernan delighted in telling anyone who cared to listen that Vermeer's real name had been Jan van der Meer van Delft. He also delighted himself privately by endlessly studying the print, preferably at night with just the picture lamp on the wall for illumination. The hurt and vulnerable yet suggestive young woman in the picture could only be Éilis Devanney, and the story of how Vermeer fell in love with his "model" appealed to him immensely. Or at least, it was the story out of many about this entrancing image that he chose to believe. The Vermeer contrasted vividly with the Pop Art in the lounge area and the bathrooms, whilst Chippendale chairs and an ancient harpsichord graced the reception room, which boasted, as its centrepiece, a mounted and enlarged picture of Jimmy Heffernan's family which had been taken near Star of the Sea Flats in the 1970s. Jimmy's great-uncle Cathal was in the picture, and he had actually known James Connolly and had drilled with him in the Irish Citizen Army. It was a source of great pride to Jimmy Heffernan that he was now about to clinch a business deal that would see Connolly's wine bar franchises springing up all over the country and then abroad. There was big, big money in the Irish-rebel myth. Big, big power. Big, big medicine.

Philip Enderby's accountantspeak of words, of profit and deficit and the need, in certain areas, to regroup, retrench, and consolidate seeped softly through the sycamores and the oak trees across the grounds from the house where Jimmy Heffernan deliberated watching the head gardener. Mind plucking at the flowers below and composing stratagems for other and more important meetings that day. She loves me. She loves me not, but that is irrelevant.

This seeming lack of attention on the part of his wealthiest client did not bother the accountant. He had never met anyone with Heffernan's ability to rapidly process several incoming sources of often-complicated data all at the same time. A frightening grasp of things.

Heffernan's thoughts dallied for a while at the stables, where contented horses nuzzled at the best of feed, while the discussion continued as to what stock could be moved where and when. The stock in question was usually a euphemism for either drugs, property, or assets loaned to other end users. Not that the contribution to the Heffernan empire from drugs could be seen anywhere on paper. Heffernan reflected that he was going to miss Connolly, his favourite filly, when he made that jump over the sticks and disappeared. More than anything, Connolly gave him due subservience, whinnied whenever he approached, stamped her feet. Yet disappear he would.

Timing. Timing was everything for Jimmy, and everything in the house and in the conversation between accountant and client was bright and businesslike until Enderby chimed the name of journalist Tommy Baker.

—Tommy Baker? Mr Enderby, what news, prithee, of the scribe Tommy Baker?

—Sorry, Jimmy?

Mr Enderby liked his humour straight up and down, Heffernan mused to himself, and with regards to literary and dramatic allusions, Enderby was more a taxidermist than a thespian.

—I was attempting a Shakespearean vernacular, Philip, which obviously shot straight over your shiny head. A scribe is a writer or journalist, and the journalist in question, Philip my man, is one Tommy Baker.

—Oh, that journo Tommy Baker . . .

—Has he been in touch again? asked Jimmy, his attention now entirely focussed on one thing.

—Been in touch! He's a pain in the Royal Arse, and it worries me that he's so persistent.

—What is there to worry about, Philip? All our business ends are quite proper and aboveboard. Are they not?

Philip laughed because one of his top clients was now in a jokey mood, and he should therefore follow suit.

—Absolutely, Jimmy, but when was it ever a good time to talk to a nosy journalist? He was trying to tell me the other day that you had actually agreed to meet him.

—I have. I am meeting him this evening in Connolly's.

—What the fuck!? Jimmy, I really . . . I mean, without sounding in any way disrespectful of your own abilities . . . like, really, the thing is that . . .

—Come on, Philip, you'll get there.

Philip Enderby cleared his throat and his eyes dilated.

—Well, Jimmy, I must stress, as your businesses adviser, that you do not attend any such meeting unless I am present, and probably Carmel as well.

—Insist, not stress.

—Sorry?

—You meant, Philip, to say "insist" that I do not attend, but the stress got to you. You're probably stressed. Tell me what he asked you about?

—I just don't think, Jimmy . . . and if my name was mentioned, well . . . Eh? . . . What he asked me about? Well, just what kind of person you were, how long I had represented you. I mean, I would hardly call it representing . . .

—Philip, shut up and listen. How much do you earn in

fees from me? No, don't look up at the ceiling or at your tie. Thirty thousand pieces, Philip. Now, do you understand the word sphincter, Philip?

—Sphincter? Yes, they are those statues near the pyramids in Egypt. No?

Heffernan let this ridiculous mistake go for the moment, as he wanted to land another, even bigger bombshell into Mr Enderby's lap. He was, he told his accountant, going to register a new property in his own name. The accountant was aghast at this.

—Ah, for fu . . . Look, Jimmy, he said, nearly raising his voice. The whole point of putting your real estate in the names of your relatives was to avoid any sourcing of income directly back to you. If you get lifted by the Guards or customs and revenue, they'll start looking at your finances!

Heffernan turned away to the window to look at the grounds and lifted an internal house phone to have the cars, apart from his jeep, moved to the garages.

—Sometimes you don't listen good Philip. Don't worry about the revenue or the Guards. They are in my pocket. Not I theirs. No, this one is going to be in my name. Yes, you can move them in now, Gerard. Think that MG could do with a respray. What do you think? No, Mr Enderby, this will not be in my name. It will be our name, and it has to be up front and legit, because we have to have somewhere to live other than this place.

—"Our" name?

—Yes, but don't worry, this will be our little beach hut off Africa. Well, when I say little . . .

—"Our" beach hut. Jimmy . . . ?

—Yes, Mr Enderby. I'm getting married.

Philip Enderby's hands folded in shock, and more for effect than anything else, Heffernan stifled a giggle in response to his accountant's visage, his glassy, bald blankness of noncomprehension. Heffernan then flicked at some imaginary dust on the chaise longue.

—Right, whose names then? Your own and Carmel's?

—No, not Carmel. Éilis. Her name is Éilis

Philip's mouth went dry.

—Who's Éilis? I don't think . . .

Heffernan waved away Enderby's clear nonplusment. There were many things he had not told his accountant. His Swiss bank deposits, for example, had filled up with revenue from cocaine consignments, and the cash earned was cleaned up there for onward depositing via bogus transport franchises recording freightage that never happened, and companies purchasing equipment for resale that never actually existed, all of which would have been news to Philip Enderby. Of course, Heffernan was also aware that Enderby was hotly in love with Carmel Daly and was a panicker and a waffler. The two of them, Carmel and Philip, had also tried manipulating his businesses into particular deals linked to friends of theirs, kitchen installations, transport fleets, and so on. Never mind. Heffernan jumped quickly from the chaise longue and swept his jacket up as he did so. At the door he turned and fixed a cold stare on his accountant. His official, upfront accountant. Face to face with Enderby quivering slightly and wanting to run from the cobra's stare—way out of his depth and flailing inwardly.

—I want the whole Connolly thing tied up this week. If the two outstanding sites push for the extra five percent, give it to them. No more than five though, and ring that guy in Sligo and tell him the answer is yes.

Heffernan deactivated a small feng shui fountain on his desk and grabbed his car button and keys, which were adjacent to it. He then deactivated the alarm on his jeep through the window of the room. An unlikely vehicle for a drugs mogul, but then it was armour-plated and had secret compartments. A jeep more the better for carrying the weight.

Heffernan turns to look at his soon-to-be-former accountant.

—When you get a minute, Google the word *sphincter*, because yours is beginning to smell.

The accountant waited, waited, waited. Checked all the windows repeatedly and then checked with the mechanic that Darth Vader was gone. Then he gave Heffernan the finger and roared fuck you fuck you for twenty minutes.

This is me (Éilis) sitting in front of the passive-aggressive psychoanalyst. She has the smile of a killer white. Looks to kill. Clothes to die for. Mind closed to every option other than the prognosis she has stitched up. She could almost be grunge, but so carefully arranged that lack of care—a downbeat jumper, gelled-up punk hair, one dangling earring. Sharp as thin, she is. Smiling now, asks me how I've been. Why the anger? Did I feel that the world was ganging up on me? Laughs when I say it is political and philosophical. Nothing political, she says, about slashing my arms and breasts. About trying to jump from three storeys up. Talk to me about your parents again. When your mother's sister took you away, and you so young when you were swapped, describe the anger you feel about that. I'm not angry about that, I'm angry about the banks. Miss Psycho laughs, leans back, places her hands together in the mantis position and purses her lips. I've got a right one here, she saying. A psycho gravy train for life in Killiney.

This is my sixth.

—You're angry about the banks?

—Yes, where do you live?

—Éilis, no need for the aggression, I'm trying to help. If you like, we can come back—

—No, I'm fine. But seriously, Gemma. Your name IS Gemma?

—Yes, but I prefer Doctor, if you don't mind. Keeps the distance, you know. A professional detachment. We are both in a safe space here.

—You have to be distant, Gemma, but you want me to disembowel myself in front of you? Answer the question please, Doctor Gemma. Where do you live?

—Well yes actually I do live in Killiney, but look, in these sessions I ask a series of questions to help you, and your responses—

—No, you ask a series of questions so that I don't have a chance to ask you anything. It's a power thing, and you . . . You are supposed to be in charge. I am disempowered and subjugated. Are you in therapy as well?

—Éilis, can you promise to listen just for a moment? Éilis, this is not a game. You've been self-harming and apparently tried to kill yourself. The punctures in your arms. Some of them are fresh. Then

there was this rape incident. Now, we are specially trained over many years to help people in those situations.

—*Are you in therapy, Gemma? . . . Sorry, Doctor Gemma . . .*

—*Well, we are all . . . we have to subject ourselves to therapy so as to develop.*

—*So it's a continuum.*

—*What?*

—*A vicious circle . . . therapy. It solves nothing.*

—*Éilis. You need to understand that we are doing these evaluations so as to see if we can avoid treating you in a more secure environment? So it's in your interests to cooperate. We don't want you locked up, do we?*

—*It's in my interests to jump out of a window. But sure. I'll play your game if you will answer one more question.*

—*Hah! oh well . . . go on? (Leans back.)*

—*Have you read Dostoevsky?*

—*Of course I've read Dostoevsky. All psychoanalysts read Dostoevsky.*

—*Then why have you never asked me about civic grief? Is it not blindingly obvious that I'm suffering from civic grief?*

Civic Grief

THERE IS A knocking. There is always a knocking at the Star of the Sea flats. It cannot be the police for they have no presence here, other than an infrequent invasion to make an infrequent arrest. There is a knocking and banging so that the people become inured to it. Deliberate deafness that is a joy to them. So that they don't hear the row on the stairwell; not the window going in across the way; not the skanger looking for his night score in the middle of the day. Knock, knock, bang, bang, crash, what was that flash? quiet now again for ten minutes. The whole estate quiet and braced. The whole estate built and abandoned for just this.

Spanzo didn't bother with a polite cough, a rap, or even a hard knock, and never he would. Just kicked the door in to admit the electrician, because these hook-up things had to be done quick and right if they were done at all. The door going in for the effect, because the door would be fixed no sweat, Mrs Farrell, and I'll get on to it right now, but there was just that question of the outstanding debt, and the fact that you'll never clear the interest.

Take this as a happy alternative that suits everybody.

Nora Farrell not even protesting as Spanzo brushes past her in the hall, and he already talking to some carpenter on the throwaway mobile, and a little man with a toolbag following him. A little man who won't look at her and politely declines a cup of tea because the electric will be off for a while. Little man, head down, eyes staring into the distance of wires and circuits in the flats. Anything to keep himself sane.

The banging, the banging, and Spanzo explaining that what he calls his crash pad next door will only be used over the weekend, and the electricity supply will be paid by Nora Farrell until such point that her debt was cleared. Nora Farrell nodding and saying of course she understood, and how terrible she felt at not paying it back straightway, and yes about thirty a week was fine. And yes, she would tell the Corpo carpenter that there had been a break-in, and no, of course not a word about the hooked-up meter, and no, not even Mrs Nolan would she tell, and how did he know about Mrs Nolan? His first grin. This very big man with the terrible teeth. The green film of teeth and the breath of him.

The Tide Turns

Tommy baker walking around the area near Star of the Sea flats. He was never taken for a cop, nor a social worker, nor the man who comes to tell you politely that you are behind on your dodgy, installed kitchen payments—the man who appears about a fortnight before the heavies. He was no pervert either. The kids in the backstreets could never work him out, because he looked them in the eye with a face that had suffered, eyes that had a laugh in them also, a bit of craic, and not trying to hide something. Didn't look like he had a fat wallet either.

First he walked over to the Goths who emerged from their Occupy tent and offered him herbal tea from a cracked cup and leaflets about global warming, the European Central Bank, and mortgage foreclosures, but he had read them all anyway. He told them the truth, which was that he was from Empire Television and that he was thinking about making a film about the area. Some of the Goths were offended that he was not specifically interested in them, but he showed enough interest in their views for them to engage, explain why they had been chased from the centre of town, what they meant by Gothism. Soon a bit of a row erupted when Baker told them that turning their backs on society was a dead end. They hadn't expected criticism and polemic. Journalists were not usually that straight. Always cagey about offering their own opinions, but not this one. However, ripping up cozy assumptions and asking awkward questions was a central part of Baker's DNA.

One said Gothism is way of life. Not a fashion trend.

Baker tells them that was exactly what he said in his days as a hippie, when they, too, really believed they could change the world.

—Yeah, but that was, like, in prehistoric times? We have the Internet now? said another Goth who could have been mistaken for a girl, and Baker—noting that Irish English was turning into one long, rising, American-English interrogative at the end of every sentence—turned to the Ladyboy.

—Yes, it was a long time ago, but just like you, we believed that we would turn everything upside down and create a new world. But in our case we thought hippiedom, by that I suppose I mean free love and so-called soft drugs, would be the magic potion that freed up everybody's mind, but they tamed us and turned it into a marketing thing. Hippies for profit. They did the same with punk. They've done the same with Gothism, though I must say some of its radical strands, like yourselves, have surprised me with their longevity. You might outlast the Teddy Boys.

—The what? said one

Baker is now shocked because a tall Goth stands up and begins quoting Shelley and Keats at him and reduces this erudite TV journalist to a mute state by asking him had he ever read *The Cenci*. —It is a key text for us, he says. Beatrice. A brave girl who stands up to the system and incestual rape. Corrupt popes and aristocrats, and the intelligentsia bought off and cowed. Sound familiar?

—It is indeed familiar, says Tommy. And I must admit, to my eternal shame, that I have never read it.

—Well, what, then, is your answer, Mr Empire? asks a spikey youth.

Tommy Baker fumbling slightly. —Well, my answer is, young man, that you can't get round the need to build bridges with people who don't have alternative lifestyles, and—

—We sing at the local church every week, said the boy with the blue stripe in his hair as he emerged from the tent, a mug of tea in his hand. —Even though God for us is more Ian Curtis and Kurt Cobain than Father Christmas. We're more Nirvana than Paradise freaks.

Tommy Baker sitting on the outside sofa that was now more a collection of planks and cardboard than an actual sofa. At first he is leaning forward, tense, defensive, wanting to argue, wanting the surge of alcohol, but gradually the listening becomes more important than the craving. These young people thinking deeply, deeply affecting him, deeply releasing his innate humility. That journalists usually did the opposite of what they are supposed to do, which is to listen. These youths should, he thought, be eulogized and honoured for their idealism. They are in it for the long haul. One is the son of a banker, another one's uncle is a company director in a multinational company; but no, they've seen through it all. Which insight he now imparted to the increasingly silent youths who nodded as he pronounced cynicism to be the greatest sin and that journalists and politicians were the greatest offenders in this regard. Baker holding his thin hand up, and they all seeing his weakness for the first time. The shakes on him. Then he told them of his love of jazz, Chet Baker, Miles Davis. Lonely sounds often, haunting, dare he say Gothic? Also, that a researcher called James Tierney would call to see them and that it would be great to make a film about them if they could agree on certain things. He now apologizes more fully for being arrogant and not, indeed, listening to them properly.

When he gets up to leave, his insides screaming for a drink to augment the buzz of the discussion, Turlough McKenna, the blue-striped boy, pulls at his arm.

—Any chance of a quiet word, Tommy?

—Sure, my car's just parked a bit towards town. Safer there.

—No, your car is being watched. I'll meet you at Heuston Station in half an hour, okay?

—Well, I was hoping to see Father McCartan, but I can rearrange that.

Turlough McKenna is already sat at one of the tables by the window of the railway station café when Tommy Baker walked in. He is already drinking tea, so Tommy must go up to the counter and order. The counter is too close to the bar. He forces himself

to go back to Turlough, to sit and squeeze his knees. The bright
Turlough looks up.

—Can I get you a coffee? Something stronger?

—Jesus, no. I'm a terrible alcoholic. (He gulps for air.) —
Trying to stay off it. Talk to me quickly.

—Ah, sorry. Wish I could help, really . . . really . . . Well,
there's some serious shit going on at Star of the Sea, and you
would need to be careful, that's really what I wanted to warn you
about. There's this girl called Éilis Devanney . . .

HR Positive

THE OFFICE USED to be called Personnel, but now Personnel is looking after human resources and is therefore HR. Like most employees in Europe, the staff at Empire are human resources—they are HR positive until they lose their contracts and become HR negative. James Tierney does not know whether it is best to be Positive or Negative. Diarmuid Farrelly had called him into his office that morning to icily congratulate him on his contract, remind him that he was still wet behind the ears, and in general attempt to belittle him, before telling him that he wanted to bring his time spent in the News Department forward, "to quicken the very necessary learning process." Eyes meeting across the room. Tierney's fiery blue softening to a resolute gaze and an imperceptible nod. So be it. Tierney resolving that he would be an HR positive in Empire for as long as he possibly could if only to spite this bitter, curdled hypocrite before him, who obviously was once a radical journalist before some lure, some bribe, some payoff he did not yet understand had led him to calcify, turn to stone, a rigor mortis of both his intellect and principles. Why does Farrelly shun empathy? Tierney intuiting that it has something to do with a rejection of God and the afterlife, or at least the wonder of existence. Farrelly pulling his paunch in, standing on toes slightly, trying to be taller. Farrelly trying to conceal the venom in his eyes with a glint of bonhomie. Trying to remember that he is in charge, trying to ignore the challenge of strident, pulsating youth, trying to forget how he himself had once been. What makes this bastard so fucking cocky? As if contracts and the status of Empire can come and go, but he will always be so. And a culchie to boot with his big leather boots—well, I'll be booting him back to the bog. Fucking carrot crunching Catholic.

Now to Personnel. Tierney walking to Personnel. There was always an atmosphere of sex in Personnel. A man walking into the main office with its ranks of girls swivelling to reveal thigh and swing of breast and wafts of perfume would either wither and shrink or bulge into testosterone and become too loud. But Ronagh had noticed that James just walked right in like he didn't give a one God damn. Back in the days of pencil skirts and tight blouses it was more understated. But then as now, now in HR, women dressed for each other in the first instance, as a statement of what they were to each other. Confident of their breasts, or legs, their big hair, their flamboyance, the gifts from men that they had acquired, the expense of shoe and stocking, the gay male icons or film stars over whom they could drool. Pictures of adored children also, which were never joked about but cooed and ahhhed. And then the serious discussions about a film, a book, mothers, nurseries, or bus services, where they planned to parade, to flaunt, to lunch that day. Then about boys and men and the difference between them. The fact that size mattered, then giggles about lengths of feet and disasters they had known, outgrown, become bitter about.

The letter Úna was waving at Ronagh in breach of all rules was the one that acknowledged James Tierney's one-year contract and pointed various pension and staff benefits, particularly were he to be kept on as an Empire employee for a second contract term as continuous service starting from the date of this present contract.

Not only is James a hunk, he is an employable hunk. He is confirmed as HR positive. So Ronagh rings the scheduler in Current Affairs to see if James is doing runner that day. This is confirmed, so she sashays down to the canteen, knowing he will be there, the swing of her skirt pleasing her. There in the corner reading a book. She sits across from him at a certain distance so he would have to turn to see her. Knows to wait until he has finished his page, to be in his direct line of sight when he looks

up and round slightly. How can he be a brooding hunk and a
bookworm? Something serious there. She is sure that he will
come over when he closes his book, and so he does. He is easy
with her, and his big hand touches her shoulder when he returns
back with coffee, sweet manly man. Úna and the others know
to stay away when they arrive for three o'clock sugar boosts.
Ronagh says to James that if he is not going to invite her out,
then she would have to do it for them. He laughs. Bright wide
smile of teeth to die for, and you so wholesomely, cleanly manly
man. Pick me up please and swing me just because you can.

—Okay, Ronagh. Let's go to the pictures on Friday.

—But it's Wednesday today and I would need a new frock.

—You need a new frock to go to the flicks?

—Flicks? Haven't heard that in years. You are such a cute
culchie.

—Less of the culchie, Mrs Jackeen.

—Ah, so you won't have culchie, but no objection to cute.

—I know I'm cute.

She laughs and draws closer to him. Tells him that she can
go see a film Saturday, and was delighted he wanted to take her.
There was a new Leonardo DiCaprio film.

—No, it's *Battle of Algiers*.

—What? A war film! No way, Jamesie! I'm not going out on
a Saturday night to watch a war film.

—Firstly, it's not actually a straightforward war film. It's a
classic anticolonial tract, a revolutionary tour de force, a thought
and mood piece, and second of all, that's the film I'm going to
see this weekend. Sorry, forgot, did you want a bun or are you
fake dieting like the rest of them?

She looks at him and realises that it is not aggression. It is
some kind of innate serenity and singlemindedness that will
cause bother further down the track, a track that will be a steep
learning curve for her. Cling she will. Strange also that he didn't
drink much. Though he might take a glass of wine at their meal,
he said. The odd cold beer. So she fingered a curl of her dark,
dark hair at the side of her face and smiled at him.

—Well then, she said, as James Tierney rose to get the buns.

Pipe Dreams

FATHER MCCARTAN'S HOUSEKEEPER, Rose O'Grady (Mrs O'Grady to the local populace), led Tommy Baker into the priest's study and the moment she went off to find the priest, Baker's fluttering heart and legs were becalmed by the quiet, the wise icons that had seen it all before and passed no judgement, just finding the soul of the observer in their soothing empathy. Just looking at them, Baker felt some call of ancient wisdom to be at peace. Like he was floating beyond himself. He sat in a magnificently comfortable chair that was almost round and sumptuously cushioned in cardinal red. Deep buttons. But then he got up to inspect some of the reams of books on the dark, grand oaken shelves. The call of alcohol a distant yet persistent drumbeat in his lightening bones, so that he could not quite feel his feet.

Away out of the room, he could hear a deep voice bidding farewell to someone—that someone obviously being a local youth who said something about a stairs, or stairwell, and then "clean up." Footsteps approaching as Baker lifts *In the Skin of a Lion* by the Sri Lankan writer Michael Ondaatje.

—Ah, you enjoy Mr Ondaatje, said the big, bluff priest as he darkened the room and held out his huge hand

—Hello, Father. (Baker struggled to conceal his shock at the size of the man.) —No, I was actually surprised to see him on your shelves because I hated the film. Talk about playing to your audience.

—The film? Oh, *The English Patient*! No, the film is nothing on the book, and anyway, you can't understand *The English*

119

Patient unless you read the book you have in your hand. Ah yes. The wonderful, wonderful *Skin of a Lion*, which could be about this place just as much as the former slums of Toronto. Would you smoke a pipe?

—A pipe?

—Yes, your hands are quivering slightly and a pipe might help.

—It's the drink, I'm afraid, Father. My God, I suppose I would smoke a pipe? Haven't smoked a pipe for years.

The priest studying the man as he fetched his tobacco particulars from his press. Deep, wounding sorrow at the suffering of feeble humanity—the wish to alleviate, to empathize, to uplift. His essence of priest embracing the man, this small, brilliantly gleaming gem of a man before him with eyes of fire, like a glittering dwarf. Father McCartan with a true priest's warmth and compassion.

—If you have an addiction, which we all have, addictions I mean, God bless us. Well then, you have to do two things, and the first immediate thing is to fight the bigger, more damaging addiction with a smaller addiction.

—That's an interesting line for a priest: feed your addictive side. And what's the second thing?

—Well, we have no choice but to start with the human condition, Tommy. It is Tommy, isn't it? And unfortunately we humans become addicted to things. Here, light that up. The question of addiction is not that you are addicted but how much damage is it doing both to yourself, your family or loved ones, and to wider society. Then the second thing is the deeper thing. What is making you so unsettled that you want to disappear into an alcohol, drugs, or say gambling—oblivion.

—Hmm, that's amazing. I've not smoked a pipe in years. Sorry, go on. I'm about to cough.

—Well, let's say that when your craving for drink reaches a crescendo, what's wrong with reaching for a pipe? Especially given that a lot of the background to addiction is that it's about not only calming or transporting ourselves but also needing to have something physically to do.

—My God, it's a wonderful crutch. So we all need crutches and shouldn't apologise for it?

—Yes, a few crutches and a bit of God in our lives. But what did you want to see me about Tommy?

Me, Éilis, in my room waiting for his arrival. He is a grinning puppeteer with all those marionettes. It is the scheming that he likes, the pulling of all those strings. Matching the patterns in his head. Every soul accounted for, every move boxed off, like some gigantic watch whose workings only he can see. Oh, evil, fairy-tale watchmaker. At school he used to dismantle watches, they say. Every soul except his own and there deep down something stirring. He never wanted to look into his own mechanics, for he suspects it goes beyond all computation. He trades on man's weakness so must not ponder his own. Must reject the possibility. I sense his approach and will be glad of it, as it may avert the disaster. There are things he cannot grasp and this stings him. Places where his aura cannot pass, his demonic side becomes nullified, disarmed. Empathy. He cannot bear the thought of empathy but is utterly drawn to it. Like a tortured zombie perennially seeking the warmth he would shun. Hates it therefore. Sees the threat in honesty. If a man admits that he has sinned, bears the humanity of his heart, begs for forgiveness. Prostrates himself before his own humanity and the marvel of exis-tence then rises to live on. That is enough and it is good. Then he cannot be controlled, be bribed, blackmailed, usurped. Thus in his very debasement and scourged state, the thousand fathoms of his despair, he is a prince, for he cannot be twisted from Grace. Confess, confess, confess to someone, even the sky or rolling tides. For with this, this coming clean, is the liberation that sets you free. Means you cannot be bought. This, Jimmy Heffernan knows. He is the dark. I am the light. Amen.

Éilis the Vamp

JIMMY HEFFERNAN BOMBING his way to the flats. Bombing, speeding, breaking lights, cutting up drivers, availing of lanes forbidden, sailing, breezing in the bus lane. Music thumping, fist clenching, jaw jutting. He is untouchable. Parks in his usual spot and his young "valets" are already there. Guarding, cherishing it for the Man and his huge reward. Police look away, parking wardens know not to dally. He briskly walking to the flats, below Our Lady's outstretched arms. The flats as tight as a bodhrán. The slightest touch of rumour hits off a series of notes of deep and resonant discord. Talk of young Séamus Dempsey having confronted a dealer. Put him to flight. In every home, in every landing, there was talk of something about to blow, but nobody quite knowing. The sickness descending after the hot weather. The dangerous anger of the Dempseys, the scorn of the Scumbags, the police informers, the clogged drains, and the rats by the overflowing bins, and the litter warden, and his van riddled by some strung out kid, some shot-up kid with the gun that he robbed, for which he will now be shot. The worming riddle of life in Star of the Sea.

Éilis had moved her sewing machine many months ago from the kitchen to her bedroom. Her last redoubt. She needed it for her escape hatch. Her bitch vamp also. She has sewed and mended, ripped and torn and shortened for his visit. Smokes a cigarette, which she hasn't done since she was twelve or thirteen. Sends a text to Dawn saying that she will be staying with her that night, which is a conceit between the two of them as she will be staying in the room above the Wakefields shop—deletes text, turns off phone, and places it in slim shoulder bag containing purse, clean knickers, T-shirt, and pumps. Thrrrrrrrrrrrum. Thrrrrrrrrrrrum. Judiciously placed patches to put on her oh-so-tight skirt. After her shower. In the mirror. She looks at her sixteen years and smiles. Then she assembles for a new frieze. Her recently serrated whole being zipped crazy-fashion back together again, back within her tapestry. Time and skin heal. Yes, she can see the joins and the overall pattern. Glad about Finn's departure to England. Lightheaded. She kneels on the floor of her room and places an upside-down glass on her floor. Through the wafer-thin plaster and concrete she can hear Neville Devanney coughing in his chair. Her mother, Bernice, busying about the room, putting more briquettes in the fire. Éilis looking sideways at her full-length mirror and wiggling her ass. A sex-bitch warrior she now is. Head up so that she can weigh her red beehive crown of glory, her tresses falling to her pale and not yet full breasts, the small, delicate mole she has darkened for effect. Suggestion of nipple. If you look further down. Now she crawls doggy-fashion in her snagged fishnet tights to the mirror and pouts, stands up, straightens her green, fake velvet skirt, and adjusts her pale-blue chiffon choker. Pout again and kiss. No makeup but a base layer of cream to accentuate her pale, ethereal pallidness, and then the ruby lipstick. Put on girly bomber jacket. He is dead in her palm. She will not be his Laura Palmer. With this she will lay the evil troll low. Let the comatose Fianna sleep on. No time to wait anymore. She picking these threads to her satisfaction when a wind—no, not a wind, a *síobán sí*, a mere zephyr—blown through her mind's attic window by some spirit is too cold. Jimmy Heffernan here. She throws long, long lengths of bedsheet out of her window then checks her secret hide out on the landing. Arranges the curtain up in the dark of the last shelf in the clothes press. Has already checked several times that she can curl there. The Velcro already in place. They in their panic of rush will already be looking beyond it. They, he, are grave robbers, but she will snatch her own body. She is the Rapunzel who didn't wait for a Prince, outfoxed the evil puzzle. And there was the drag of the tide, the inexorable swirl of time, which she knew was now upon her. Now was the time to be the calm at the centre of the vortex. Lie curled in her womb. Trust. Because teenagers are brave and foolhardy to the point of wreck. She laughs at that. She spinning her bottle, showing off her great legs in those dirty tights. Her fuck-me high heels. Confuse, infuriate. For Éilis Devanney is the future, not the likes of Jimmy Heffernan, and if she had been chosen to raise her people's standard like St Joan of France or Gráinne Uí Mháille out in Clew Bay or Eibhlín Dhubh Ní Chonaill beating in the proud heart of Munster, then so be it. Ah, the relief as Heffernan enters her domain. Bang goes the door. For this was the beginning of the end of her torment. When he goes into the living room, the small, pokey living room, he too tall so he must stoop his pinhead with his bizarre, ranging, looming presence, she kneels yet again, glass in hand, to listen. Never would he come near her again.

The Fire That Cleanses

HEFFERNAN PUSHING AT the door to the Devanney sitting room. Neville and Bernice both turning, looking, mouths dropping. He registers their look of shock, but his mind is with his accountant, Philip Enderby—when was there ever a good time to talk to a journalist? Heffernan then dismissing his own slight calibrations of concern. Who could hurt him in the space he was in? What could someone like Tommy Baker do to him? No, Tommy Baker was going to be useful for Jimmy Heffernan, that was all. He proffers the expensive bottle of champagne like some talisman of new times as he enters the stunned room.

—Neville, Bernice, get your glad rags on! We're going out!

—On a Wednesday night, Jimmy?! his aunt Bernice cries out in delight.

Éilis hears Neville's voice above the background inanities of an afternoon TV chat show.

—Er . . . things are a bit tight, Jimmy.

—Nev, this is Mr Heffernan you are talking to, and this is a family thing, and all this is on me? We're celebrating.

—Oh right!? What's to celebrate, Jimmy? asked Neville, a hint of caution in his voice.

—Ah, yez know me. I've always lots to celebrate. I have a little idea I want to talk to you about, Neville. It could work out great. For both of us. Anyway more of that later. Come on! Yeah! On the town! We'll go for a few drinks, have a meal, and then maybe go to my club for a nightcap. Well, you can drink your fill. I'll be a bit more careful as usual. Glass of chilled wine as we talk shop. Maybe Éilis? Is she . . . ? Is Éilis around?

Heffernan places a thick clip of money on the low coffee table in the centre of the room and time is sucked in and compressed and Neville will not look. No, he will not directly look at this money, the myriad notes that would bulge his wallet, for fear that it would not be there if he looked directly at it. So he shoots sidelong glances . . . so many notes that he could paper his room with them, and they so fine, and he will not look, but he knows each type of clip and what they hold and calculates as he stares into the fire that there is at least ten grand, ten thousand fucking euro, and he squeezes his thighs in delight, and his thin face puckers to an involuntary smile, and he pushing his thin strands of hair back across his thin pate, his leather-brown skin darkened by the flames. Say nothing and wait. Say nothing and wait. Payday. Payday. Bingo! Bingo! Bingo! Tango! Romeo! and fucking Juliet! What's this all about? Jimmy and Éilis? Well, well. Gift!

—She's up in her room, Jimmy, said Bernice as she walked almost backwards with a beaming face ready to call Éilis downstairs, and she opening the door leading into the hall, but then standing back into the sitting room as if beaten with a baseball bat of incomprehension. Her mouth a round O of shock. Éilis descending the stairs.

Now Heffernan's mobile phone is felt to vibrate. He swings away from Neville and Bernice, leaving himself facing the mirror above the fire. What? What? All they could hear was a deathly whisper as Heffernan looks to the floor, studying a speck on his shoe. Yet Éilis coming through the door could hear every word of the conversation. Heffernan's obscenities about talking business over a mobile. The fear in Seánie Heffernan's voice. Éilis stands there, lurched against the door. Her front leg pushed apart. A cigarette lolling at her mouth as Neville swings round from the fire and Heffernan speaks down to the floor still. Now he speaks of Éilis as he switches off his phone and begins to look up to the mirror.

—I'm surprised she's here at all. She's usually knocking

around with that bleedin' no-hoper Finn Demp . . . Heffernan now looking at the mirror again and sees all his finest computations arraigned there before him like some perfect, inverted perversion of all he had. Never would he. The desecration of his grand and beautiful. Never.

—No, no . . . fucking no! That's all wrong. That cannot be. It has to be done the right way or it won't . . .

For once he is left speechless and disarmed. Pushes roughly past Éilis at the door. Then turns back. Grabs her shoulders. She all insolence, twists away and walks into the centre of the room. Lifts the wad of money. Heffernan watching from the door. And he will not look at her legs. His voice low and feral.

—Neville, you better sort this out. If you and she know what's good for you. All of you. This can either be really, really good, or it can be very, very bad for you. For all of you.

The door leading out onto the public balcony outside bangs shut and Neville stands up, takes a step towards Éilis, removing his belt as he does so, and she moves to the fire with the clip of money. Neville's eyes widening in comprehension, apprehension, time suspension. Bernice says —Éilis, don't even think about it.

Éilis holding the money near the fire turns to both of them as Neville takes a faltering step. She says, —It doesn't matter what he wants, and you two are far worse than him. You should be ashamed of yourselves. This is the end of it.

Neville steps closer.

—Éilis if you so much as fucking—

—But you will have to face that evil someday. So I pity you both and your black hearts. Sell your own daughter. Or should I say stepdaughter.

With that she threw the money into the fire, and Bernice shrieked a Jesus, no, and Neville made a grab, but Éilis then amazingly did not run but stepped forward, shoved Neville Devanney backwards with surprising force, and delivered a ringing slap to his face as he fell into the chair. She gone before he could recover, and now he is burning his hand trying to retrieve the money, Bernice screaming and trying to push him away to get the blazing money with the fire tongs, they both falling, and

Bernice sobbing, and Neville staring nonplussed at the flames, too late, too late, and then staggering up, staring at his blackened fingers, then turning to chase but falling over the coffee table, then turning back to the burning, quickly cindering wad and his stupid wife throwing a jug full of water over it, from the kitchen it was, well, really a scullery, and this finally releasing his voice that was heard all around Star of the Sea, the *fuck* and *bitch* and she was *dead* when he . . . and his disbelief at being slapped, and he running up the stairs and bursting into her bedroom only to see the room empty and feel the cool breeze and the window wide open and off its retainer bar, and he rushing there, looking down, and the flowing sheets, and he sure he sees that hellbitch at the bottom. Because at the bottom is a smashed doll with mouth agape—ah, Jesus!

Running out of the room. Into their bedroom and the box-room. Neville tearing open the clothes press, darting his head inside, but nothing there, then in any fucking room. Now running down the stairs letting out great AAARGH, AAARGHs, and Bernice after him, she saying, What? what? what? where the fuck is she? what? what?

—The fucking crazy bitch. That's what. Crazy bitch is going to have us all jailed because if she's not fucking dead already I'm going to kill her.

Éilis curled in a ball up on the top shelf of the clothes press behind her black curtain, heart banging against the wooden slats, waiting for the angry, anguished voices to fade before slipping out onto the public landing and exiting the flats from the opposite stairwell. Nobody saw her. Never was that Éilis. Never-never-neverland that could never have been, but it was the people insisted anyway, because that is the truth they wanted, and the myth of Éilis's leap was born, and only the Goth sees, and he smiling, breathing, turning away and smiling and breathing cooly again, and glad to be alive to see it. *Out of my league. Total respect to the girl. The autistic, self-creationary artist. She is walking art.* Then confusion and the fire brigade arriving and the legend of the money beginning, and never did Turlough McKenna say what it was that launched a thousand poems in his heart and gave him hope in the stars and the nonsensical. A hero to match Shelley. Also knowing why he had fallen so far for dizzy Deirdre. Because for her all fairy tales were real in the innocence of her heart. Only faith can conjure a leap. Can spring belief.

The Cure of Metaphysical Discourse

No THOUGHT NOW of alcohol. Tommy Baker riveted to his chair in confessional discourse with this priest, but the priest is perhaps even more open than he is, freely discussing his love for his housekeeper and how this is an open secret in the parish.

—Sorry, Father, you are saying that yourself and Mrs O'Grady effectively live as man and wife and everybody knows about it?

—Well, she was never "Mrs" O'Grady. That's just a generic Mrs, but yes, she is very close to being a Mrs McCartan.

—And the Church has no problem with that?

—What can the Bishop do? After all that has happened. Is he going to cause a huge row and defrock a, if I may say so, hard-working and very popular priest because he's in love with a woman? Anyway, the hierarchy knows that the days of celibacy are coming to an end—in the very near future it will be voluntary, which is how it should be. Slowly, frustratingly slowly, the Church is going back to the place it should never have left.

—Which is where?

—*Pobal Dé.*

Father McCartan stood up to expend his restless energy as the light began to fall across the room, exclaiming that if the Church was going to abandon a place like Star of the Sea then it wasn't a Church of God, the poor or penniless, of Jesus anyway—it wasn't worth a single candle in other words.

—With respect, Father, a lot of people would say that the Church is a dead-and-buried body in this country after all the scandals and awful abuse cases.

130

—Yes, the Rome hierarchy opted for Satan, not Jesus.

—I'm sorry?

—No, the Irish Church is alive and well. The Rome mafia will have to collapse for us to see a real rebirth, but that's no bad thing. But just like the Russian peoples, I think the Irish have to have some form of collective spirituality in their lives and the message of Jesus really is the only way, regardless of evil, child-abusing priests and arrogant Bishops who act more like pompous fat cats than servants of Christ, the carpenter's son.

—You say the message of Jesus is the only way? What message?

—That we either love each other with true love and empathy and see the divine in every human face, or we are doomed. We will be reduced to feral animals, which of course is the final logic of atheism.

—I wanted to ask about this young lady Éilis, Father.

The priest stopped his pacing up and down the floor of his study and returned to his chair.

—Éilis Devanney. Our precious flower? What about her. How do you know about Éilis? She's been through an awful time and I'm getting her offside to the Gaeltacht. To get her some peace. That's a precious soul that needs peace and a refuge from anxiety. She's also extremely bright and needs peace to read and study, feed her mind. The kind of peace working-class kids never get. I would ask you respectfully to stay away from Éilis.

—I actually met her without knowing who she was some time ago. But then she, or rather a friend of hers, handed in a document to my researcher at Empire Television, James Tierney. A good lad, James, and I'm sure you will meet him somewhere along this path.

—And what is it, Tommy? This document. What does it say?

James Tierney had gone back to his apartment to check again, but everything stopped there where Éilis had seemingly fled from her home. Or did she in fact jump? He felt an urgent need to know more about this event. Wait a minute. Maybe it wasn't an "event." Maybe it didn't happen at all. What if this whole fucking thing was just the ravings of a madwoman? He needed to know where Tommy Baker actually was. He needed to discuss the stuff in this diary, because he was heading off to Portumna on the Sunday and wanted to be clear about what it was they had in their hands. He would have gone to the West earlier in the weekend, but now he was roped into this film thing with Ronagh at the start of the weekend and he had to check his list of interviewees and places to visit before heading off. Now he relents. Ronagh was nice and he was full of anticipation, which he straightaway cooled because it was also a pain in the ass when all these thing were happening. He rings Dawn and she says she's wrecked from the shop and the manager Francis was AWOL, and no, she still hadn't met this fucking Tommy Baker, and no, she didn't want to talk about Éilis, and could he ring again in the morning when she was in better form—CLICK.

The Hidden Eye

THE UNTOUCHABLES WERE standing in their usual spot within the arch as Heffernan's jeep crawled the kerb alongside the railings which dressed either side of the front arch of the flats. Darren Bulger was the first one to see Heffernan and alert the rest to his arrival. He was also the first one to see Neville and Bernice Devanney in the back of Heffernan's jeep. Never in his young life had he felt such a crushing blow to a hope he had secretly cherished. The hopeless hope that Éilis Devanney was somehow going to save them all. It was now clear to Darren that Spanzo had been correct in his prediction. Heffernan had moved in on Éilis, and Jimmy Heffernan always got what he wanted. Like always. End of story. Darren Bulger had never felt so angry and disgusted before. For all his young man's fantasies, Darren knew that he had no chance of wooing Éilis Devanney himself, but the way she had always looked out for him and made him feel special, regardless of what he ever did, regardless of the crime, never mind he was a scumbag, had bound him to her in an unspoken oath of allegiance. Darren looked at Heffernan, at Spanzo who was walking across the road from his café, at his fellow pushers and their death masks, and he swore a solemn oath that he would make his life good in honour of Éilis, extract some kind of vengeance, he knew not what, on Heffernan and his abuse of her. Heffernan was not even fit to lick her spit, never mind ride her, which was obviously what was now going to happen.

It was not the first time Heffernan's own personal jeep had

been seen in the flats, but the event was rare enough to spark everybody's attention. Heffernan called Spanzo over to him as he stopped the jeep parallel with the arch. Spanzo swaggered around to the driver's window of the jeep trying to look less subservient than the rest, and he pushing his broad chest out as he went to emphasize his special relationship with Dublin's Ace Face. He unaware of Heffernan's seething anger.

—What's the story, Spanzo?

—Good. Yeah, Jimmy. Spanzo sniffed and looked away as if Heffernan's appearance was a slight intrusion on a busy man's time. —Cool. Things is busy, he said as he shot a quick glance at Éilis's parents in the back seat.

—Yeah!? . . . excellent! said Heffernan.

With this, Heffernan coils an apparently friendly arm around the brawny youth and brings his face close to his own with the lazy, relaxed strength of a boa constrictor. The driver side of the jeep bows and curtsies slightly with the torsion of it all, as if in deference to its owner's power and purpose, allowing Heffernan to pull Spanzo's head across the window frame and partly into the jeep's interior. Now holding Spanzo by the hair, Heffernan pushed the window button so that Spanzo's head became trapped inside the jeep whilst the rest of his body remained outside on the pavement. Heffernan's demeanour gave nothing away, but Spanzo knew better than to struggle. He simply put his hand across his throat as the window closed so as to save his windpipe. Heffernan blasted up the music in the jeep. A sound which alerted the Goths to this theatre of potential violence. They melted away into the sunny afternoon haze, not wishing to be a witness to anything. Heffernan leaning closely to Spanzo so that he could whisper his words.

—Do you know what, hog features? You are costing me money. I'm down about fifteen percent on this patch, not just this patch, the whole of this fucking area in the last six months.

—Jimmy, I swear on the life of my children!

Heffernan hit Spanzo a playful slap and studied the frieze of faces within the arch. This whole drama was partly for their benefit. Yet one face was missing. Darren Bulger. Where was

Darren Bulger? A Garda car went by, and Heffernan turned and looked, and then waved to the driver.

Neville Devanney was sheepish and cowed in the back of the jeep. Spanzo had always frightened the life out of him, and he had always made sure to keep to the safe side of him. Yet his wife, Bernice, Heffernan's aunt, was enjoying the whole thing immensely. Spanzo had given her cheek on occasions and it was good that he was now being instructed in the reality of his situation. As Heffernan watched Darren Bulger's back moving away from the arch in the direction of the park, he released Spanzo's head and pulled his clip book from his pocket.

—Nah, relax, Spanzo. You're being smart. You probably deserve it.

—Fuck, Jimmy, you had me worried there.

—Spanzo, come here to me. You know very well that if Jimmy Heffernan was seriously pissed with you, you wouldn't even see it coming. At least you're showing a bit of . . . eh . . . Do you understand the word *initiative*?

—Yeah, 'course. Is that the interest they put on top? Spanzo asked as he extracted his head and straightened his shock of hair and his slightly ruffled designer shirt. Too thick to be embarrassed.

Heffernan enjoyed this faux pas and laughed, bending to whisper again to Spanzo in an almost sexually suggestive way, but his voice still thick with the anger of Éilis.

—Just don't ever be greedy, that's all I ask. Get too bleedin' greedy and my A-team will be round with the chainsaw. By the way, I want you to go over to Paris in around a fortnight's time.

—Yeah!?

—I'll be down tomorrow to explain. I'm looking for a dress.

—Me bollix.

—No, seriously, a dress, and a few other things. It's a shame I won't be there when customs stop you and all they find is a dress. So everything is okay around here?

—Safe, sweet. Yeah. Why what's up? If it's that Séamus Dempsey thing don't worry about it. He'll get what's coming.

—No, not that. Or not just that. Just a rumour I heard today from our wonderful police service. Someone snooping round. It's probably nothing. You can handle it anyway. Listen, I'm gone. We're celebrating.

Heffernan gave Spanzo a handshake and a high five, which again was more for his foot soldiers than anything else.

Tommy Baker's cameraman turned away from the net curtain at the window which overlooked the arch from across the street.

—What you reckon is going on down there, Sitric? the sound recordist asked. "Sitric" was Sitric Cunningham, a veteran Empire cameraman, and his interlocutor and long-term filmmaking partner was Alan Magilligan.

Sitric lit up another cigarette, even though he knew this caused great annoyance to Alan. Lighting up partly because this caused great annoyance to Alan.

No more action on the streets, so Sitric, in his laconic way, was able to consider Alan's question at length for at least ten minutes. An air of satisfaction after inhaling the first heavy drag of nicotine into his lungs.

—Heffernan's making a show of himself, Alan. That's what's happening. Don't know why he would do that. We'd need to talk to Tommy, but it's obviously some kind of show. Gorillas marking out territory or something.

Sitric, who like his four other siblings had been named after one of the ancient kings of Dublin, reached for another recording disc from his bag.

—Looks like we've got him, that Heffernan fella, with this stuff, Alan said as he took the cans away from his ears and moved as far away from the smoke as possible.

—Why do you say that? Sitric asked, already knowing the answer.

—Well, he obviously knows them, Sitric, those pushers I mean, and is on speaking terms with them, and then he goes and puts a headlock on your man Spanner.

—Spanzo.

—Spanzo, then. Is that not good proof?

—It's good general footage all right, Alan, but it wouldn't stand up in court. The light's starting to drop a little now. Any sound?

Alan's response was a shake of the head.

—No, we're not getting anything, Sitric, he said glumly. We need to get closer to them. Preferably someone wearing a personal mike and a recorder. Where's Tommy Baker anyway? He was supposed to be here hours ago.

—I'll give you two guesses, Al.

Police Inquiries

IT WAS MRS GRADY who had answered the bell when the Garda called inquiring of Éilis Devanney's whereabouts. He was brought into the priest's study and then explained to Father McCartan that the police had received word of some sort of commotion. Father McCartan leaned forward slightly in his seat and asked the Garda why he was looking for a girl of sixteen who was probably just out with friends. The Garda looked directly back at the priest without flinching and said that this didn't seem to be a run-of-the-mill teenager. Looking at his notes and then firmly back at Father McCartan he mentioned self-harm, anorexia, possible hysteria and mental instability.

—Was it Jimmy Heffernan, by any chance, Garda, that sent you round to me?

Again the Garda held the priest's gaze.

—It was Éilis's parents, Father McCartan, that lodged a missing-person request at the station.

—And are you aware of the fact that they are drug abusers?

—Well, you'd need to speak to the community liaison officer for this area, but we would have a general concern for the family's well-being. An unstable, dysfunctional family and a young, vulnerable girl whom we'd—

—And what section of the Garda Síochána are you from?

—Sorry? Oh, me. Crime Branch.

—So we have a serious-crimes officer looking for a sixteen-year-old girl, do we?

—Are you aware of Éilis Devanney's whereabouts, Father McCartan?

—With God as my judge, officer, I'm not, but with God as my judge, if I did know where Éilis was, I doubt very much whether I'd share that information with you.

Now the police officer finally did colour and rose abruptly to leave just as Mrs O Grady came in with tea. The priest called him back as he made to exit through the door with a short, gruff *good luck, then.*

—Sorry, Garda, I didn't catch your full name and rank?

—Carberry, Father. Detective Sergeant Fintan Carberry.

—Hmm. A detective sergeant? I'll be contacting your commander in the morning.

—By all means do, Father. Our only concern is for the welfare of the apparently missing child.

With the officer gone, the priest and housekeeper looked at each other. Dawn was the one who would know where Éilis was, they both knew. Father McCartan took his tea and then rang one of his counterparts in the Donegal Gaeltacht to stress that Éilis being settled in the Gaeltacht should be kept as low-key as possible. He also told his fellow priest that he personally would drive Éilis to the Gaeltacht the following day. After that he quickly put on his coat and went over to Dawn's house. Here he learned that the same police officer had already been there looking for Éilis. The priest wrote out a message in his notebook: *Where is Éilis?* Dawn wrote two words on the back of it, walked to the priest, and opened the note fully: *Upstairs, Wakefields.* She then walked to the peat-briquette fire, which was always on the go in her cold-as-damp house. She stood there looking at the note for a second and threw it into the flames. All burning. There are those who will face the flames and those who will not.

—Flame, you are my friend, Dawn said. Burn, you bastards. Burn, the lot of them.

The Box of Pandora

FRIDAY NIGHT AND still Tommy Baker had not been in touch and was not answering his e-mails, and James Tierney cursed him from a height. He looked across at Éilis's diary, and no, he would not read it again. He picked up his big book. He always kept a big novel in his courier bag, a book he could lose himself in—this one was Thomas Hardy's *Tess of the d'Urbervilles*—but he turned away from it, then thought about his book of short stories *as Gaeilge*, but no, not that. Then a brilliant idea. A genius idea! Sitric Cunningham. Yes, Sitric would know where Tommy was at!

He browsed to Sitric on his phone. Picked up the house landline and punched his free hand in the air when the ringtone was answered within seconds. Sitric's unmistakeable drawling.

—Yes, Sitric here? But the rest was drowned out by the surge of a noisy bar.

—Sitric, it's James here.

—Hello? Oh, hi James, see your name there. House phone. What are you doing ringing . . . young lad like you . . .

—Hello, Sitric, are you still there? Silence and James's grip tightening around the phone. Now he comes back.

—Sorry, very noisy in here. I'm in Keogh's, let me go outside. More silence and then waves of noise. James eating his jawbone as he waited.

—Now, James. Sorry about that. What's up?

—Sitric, where the fuck is Tommy?

—Tommy? Ha, ha, you've a lot to learn.

—Yeah, yeah, but just tell me where he is.

—Tommy is, or was . . . hold on a second . . . sorry, do you have a light there? Silence again and then a *thanks* and *no problem* and *yes*, I tried those electric vapour ones, and then Sitric is quite clearly there but not saying anything. James slumps into his chair at the kitchen table.

—Sitric, what are you doing?

—Sorry, James. Just lighting a cigarette. Tommy should be back at his house by now, but I'd leave until the morning if I were you.

—Is he in a bad state?

—Well, this is fuckin' amazing, but he's been sober all day. Told me he hasn't touched a drop for two and half days. There's a big downside though.

—Tell me quick.

—He's started smoking a bloody pipe.

—Sorry, Sitric, I'm not in the mood for jokes. I'm off to the West on Sunday and really need to speak to Tommy.

—No joke, James, he really is smoking a pipe, but he's spent all last night and today reading some diary. Only came in when we finished filming for the day.

—Filming? Filming what?

—Don't want to say over this. But you know. To do with the diary. Tommy got pictures and names from somewhere yesterday and pulled us off a news story to go down there. Diarmuid Farrelly is bulling about it, ha, ha! Ah! Dear Tommy is priceless.

—Down where, for fuck's sake? Where's down there?

—The arch. I'm gone.

—Sitric, hold on. Were you filming at the fucking flats today and nobody told me? Hello, Sitric, Sitric, fucking answer me.

Just silence, so James slams the phone down but it didn't slam hard enough for his liking so he slammed it again, but far too violently this time and the receiver end suffered a fatal crack.

When Ronagh picked up the phone the following night after

waltzing gaily into James's apartment at half past two in the morning, she turned to him, her lilac, open coat with the soft lining flaring as she did so.

—Temper, temper, Jamesie, she half pouted, shaking her head, hair falling forward, and brandishing the broken end of the phone, smiling admonishingly.

James stopped midstride, glowered at the phone, threw his coat onto the sofa, and marched towards the bathroom.

—Where are you going?

—To clean my teeth. Is there a problem?

—Are you not going to show me round. Give me the tour?

—No.

Ronagh raised her voice as her man disappeared into the bathroom. She was still tickled by the state of the phone.

—I liked the film more than I thought I would. We shall discuss this in the morning.

She heard a gargling noise, then James popped his head out of the bathroom. A faux-quizzical look on his face.

—What makes you think you can stay here?

—Do you always clean your teeth before you make mad, passionate love to a lady?

—What lady is this now?

At half past four Ronagh woke up, as the drought in her mouth from too much white wine and Prosecco had disturbed her sufficiently to realise that James was not in bed beside her. Eyes still closed, her hand reached out to confirm the space where he should have been. Man space. A large depression. Long he is with a powerful head. Always blessed with superb hearing, she thought she heard the rustle of paper, or was it the brief sound of running water coming from the breakfast bar without?

He was sat at the table writing a note to Tommy Baker. So engrossed was he that he didn't see her standing at the alcove leading to the bedrooms. In a retrospective act of modesty, given the physical urgency of their lovemaking, she had thrown on the long winter coat found in his press. He was simply wearing a white vest and boxer shorts, and she knew him to be a god. The sinews of his right arm flexing fluidly as he wrote. The weight and depth of his dark hair pulling his head toward the table. Feet and thighs constantly in motion. Then he looking up to think of some point. Regal jaw like pure iron and eyes of blue fire. Like his children to come. She didn't know how, but he spoke at her without lifting his head. How knowing that she was there.

—Sorry, Ronagh, but I have to write this because he may just miss it. It's this . . . well, I won't say his name.

James opened his left arm to her, and she sat on his knee as he turned his notebook over. Then he lifted her and spun her like a feather, and she knew that he was half-mad and extraordinary and thrilled at the thought that he had fallen for her.

When she woke again at midday, she was once more conscious of his absence but already knew that he was gone. The place was dead without his presence. Ronagh Durkin lying back where his pillow should have been, remembering him saying that he didn't like pillows. Stretching her legs and conscious of his shape inside and around her. His stamp. That he was at ease with himself like no man she had ever met. Where was he? Never did she think he was serious that he would go to Galway that day and leave. Why could he not do that work from here? A quick zip into town for brunch and Bloody Mary cure. Bloody Mary. The pangs of annoyance at him.

She got up expecting a note, but nothing. She slamming the kettle into place and her low lip fattening as it always did in her annoyance. Hating the quiet. Going to the bread bin and then opening the fridge for milk, seeing all the good food and thinking that he was very self-sufficient, and annoyed at that, too, and there it was, the note. The note and the flower he had bought from that Rumanian who was a familiar face around town. But Jamesie knew him and knew his name, and gave him five euro, and she had forgotten the flower.

Ronagh. It takes something for me not to want to go home across the Shannon. I'd set up two meetings for today that I couldn't change and it's an early start for filming tomorrow. Really enjoyed the whole night and

I mean that. I'll give you a shout later, see if you're
okay. There's pasta there that was only made yesterday.
Is bean álainn thú
xx
Jamesie

She felt stupid at the tears in her eyes. Already knew her mascara was spoiled. Sits down at the table. Then douses her face with water at the sink. Laughs at the carry-on of him when he lifted her. Sniffs. Sniffs more and must spit in the toilet. Eats her toast and reads the note again and again. Bewildered by his mix of boyish recklessness and towering sense of gravity. Like everything mattered and was vital, every point he made and every second he breathed, and do not turn your head away or move away from him when conversing, and she now doubting if she could live with it. The fucking arrogance of it. His fire would consume her and she would be reduced to ashes. Rises from the chair, dresses, and begins to explore. The scarcity of his wardrobe. Two white shirts and a blue one. He was wearing the blue one when she saw him first. Two pairs of trousers and two of jeans. One pair of jeans faded to nothing. Barbells and assorted weights on the floor. Now she walks back to the other bedroom and sees the wardrobe. Of course. The rest is here. NO! Opens the press to see a mountain of books. Many of them carrying note markers in their pages. Tolstoy, Dickens, Patricia Highsmith and all those Ripley books. Then books in Irish, Seosamh Mac Grianna and Ó Conaire. She had read Ó Conaire's short stories herself whilst at school in Ennis and had enjoyed them. Now she lifts Hemingway in both English and Spanish—*Por quién doblan las campanas.* Gabriel García Márquez as well. *Cien años de soledad.* Never could she keep up. But he had told her in their entwining that she knew many things he didn't. What things? What bloody things could she know that he didn't? They both fitting like tongue and groove, and she arching back at the wardrobe doors and taking his manhood once again in her closed eyes and the hard reality of it, her need to channel it, ride it, tame it to her will, but he pressing her into the bed and holding her neck, and was it him that was moaning or this growl she had never heard coming from deep inside herself? like meeting something all-powerful that was more a memory than a new thing, and he waiting for her until she seized him. When she had risen to find him at the table writing, dizzy with her lightness of being, she saw her long scratch on his right arm and small bruising from her ecstatic thumb and fingers on his left bicep. Saw also that he accepted this as a fact like the scratches on his back. How she was the She-Devil who would cap his fire and emotions in their bed struggle. They were wonderful.

Now she moves back to his room and feels guilty for opening the drawers to his dresser, and in the second one down finds a picture. James standing in a balmy, evening country with a hot babe with flaming-red hair and freckles, and she lifted it to throw it through the window or smash it. Never would she have hair like that. Never a body like that. Why had he hidden it? Why had he ridden it? Why was it there? God damn you to hellfire for all eternity, James Tierney. You are fucking toast!

This is me, Éilis. I am supposed to be in a hospital ward, but really I'm in the flat up above Wakefields waiting for Dawn to open up the shutters, and this was my dream.

I'm back in the house I've left forever but should be on the way to Donegal and the whole world is looking for me, but my normally acute hearing does not at first pick up the sounds of footsteps on the stairs. A great fright in my heart. Someone, a stranger, was outside my bedroom door. Hurry softly to the locked door.

—Hello. Who's there?

Me wanting my voice to be strong and forceful, but tremors betraying me, my knees buckling as I try to speak into the quiet. Tentative but more insistent knocking from without. Taking my very breath in hand, swinging the door open.

—Are you okay, Éilis?

—Darren Bulger! Ye scared the bejasus out of me, and you're white as a sheet! Come on down with me and get a cup of tea!

When I wake again, Dawn has opened the shop, brings tea and biscuits and tells me that Darren Bulger wants to talk to me in secret.

Heffernan Slips Up

JIMMY HEFFERNAN'S ARMOUR-PLATED jeep was now in a very different world from the drug arch and Star of the Sea flats as it nosed its way into a reserved space in the private car park beneath Connolly's nightclub. The car park was a major plus point for celebrities who wished to grace Connolly's with their presence. There was always a complement of staff waiting down there, ready to attend to their every need. Prying reporters or photographers were unable to witness any indiscretions that might be committed, various states of inebriation, chemical changes in the conditions of one's body or mind, or changes in the usual romantic partner. The very meat and drink of tabloid revelation. These images were, though, of course, recorded in minute detail by a battery of high-definition colour cameras placed in a wide range of vantage points.

Éilis's confused parents spilled out from the vehicle into the echoing vault which was all white walls, columns, statues, porticos. They could not understand why Heffernan was still entertaining them and anyway were momentarily stunned by what they saw around them. How could you have what seemed to be like a posh hotel reception area in a basement car park? Top-hatted flunkies opening their door, their smiles seemingly genuine. However, the effects of a second bottle of champagne, which had been consumed in the jeep, soon had them chattering and laughing again, and they paid little more attention to questions of décor or architecture. Jimmy Heffernan, however, was in a different frame of mind. He had only taken a sip of champagne to humour them and had brusquely refused any encouragement to take more. He mentally preparing for a severe upward shift in the gears of his operation.

He had burned the notes he'd written down at his desk at six o'clock that morning but their content was emblazoned across his rapid thought processes. However, something Heffernan had seen in the basement car park had also excited his thoughts, not least because he owned the same sort of car. An old MG midget car was parked in a bay along the opposite wall. Heffernan had never seen this car before and was certain that he knew the make of every car which might appear in what he called his "honey trap." How had this person wangled his way down there? For the first time, Heffernan wondered whether his fixation with Éilis—no, he would not call it a fixation—his pursuit of Éilis had seriously made him take his eye off the business ball. Maybe Carmel had a point? he muttered to himself, as he turned to Éilis's parents and an image of Éilis sitting on her bed came unbidden into his mind. A thought process that surprised him, but nonetheless he chose to wallow in it for a moment. He knew what he wanted to do with Éilis and he would still require her parents' support to make it happen. He was still going to marry her and she was still going to be the star of Connolly's. The specially composed and designed image would be the first thing that patrons saw as they entered the otherwise darkened corridor that led them into his chain of nightclubs. She all dazzling bright in her vivid, green dress, soft flesh, and red hair as the punters moved into Heffernan's dream world. The marriage would take a bit more managing, but he had seen it done before. In New York, even an instance of it in Dublin. In many ways that kind of marriage would suit him better, given the way he was. The utter attraction of an almost-perfect female like that, the lines of it, the aura of it, and then the utter repulsion of the deed that was required to sire children. The requirement to sully such icons of taste. The better consummated if she were comatose, drugged up. His fantasy doll. That weird bitch would learn.

In the meantime, he had already ensured that a counter-rumour to the one about money being burned had been circulated around Star of the Sea flats. It hadn't been money at all that was burned. It was just airline tickets to Spain for his aunt, and that mad Éilis had refused to go. Stamped her foot, screamed, and finally threw the tickets into the fire. Then she had tried to jump through the window and Jimmy Heffernan had saved her. A newspaper article would appear in the tabloid *Dublin Tribune* referring to the incident and rumours about Heffernan's heroics. Heffernan would refuse to either confirm or deny the story.

Affecting an air of bonhomie, Heffernan ushered Neville and Bernice Devanney into the private cloakroom in the basement of the club.

—Folks, welcome to Connolly's Wine Bar and Bistro. Consider yourselves permanent members as from tonight, and that is a privilege some people would die for.

Then Heffernan pressed something into Neville's hand. And he would not look. No, he would not look, but his legs thrilled with the feeling of that hard wad in his hand. So all had not been lost in that astounding blaze.

The bouncers at the downstairs entrance to the club showing Heffernan the respect he expected, and he called one of them to him and whispered something in his ear.

Two young blond women then appeared to relieve Bernice and Neville of their coats and accompany them upstairs to their reserved table. Heffernan informed Éilis's parents that he had some business to attend to and that he would rejoin them within the hour.

—If you need anything, anything at all, just ask Amanda here and she'll sort you out. Amanda is your escort for tonight. It's all on the house.

Everything was soft from where Neville Devanney was looking. He had never seen the beauty in Éilis that everybody always raved about to him, but he had to accept that this amazing turn of events showed that there was something in what people said. He felt like he had won the lotto. What was Dublin's, no Ireland's, smartest crook up to? The bubbles from yet another bottle of champagne which had been carried to their table. Though he could not resist asking for a pint of Guinness. A man had to have a pint. The lights. The fancy clientele. Celebrities with their air-kissing and their carry-on. The breasts and legs of the girls who swanned and sallied around the customers. Bernice Devanney was equally impressed with the setup, but she wondered at the mood change she had observed in her nephew Jimmy. That mask that had come upon him was the Heffernan mask. There was one thing Bernice Devanney was sure about, she was going to enjoy the champagne while it lasted because she was equally sure that the whole thing between Jimmy Heffernan and Éilis would end in tears, and Jimmy Heffernan was not one to be shedding tears. That little bitch Éilis would not get away with spiting Jimmy like that. In the weeks that followed she heard on the Star of the Sea jungle drums the story of what Jimmy had been up to round the flats. People looking for Éilis and not finding her, the rumour that it wasn't money at all that had gone in the fire, a rumour she was only too happy to confirm, the newspaper articles—Jimmy the Robin Hood figure. But what was most intriguing was when she met Nora Farrell on the landing and her praising Jimmy, and it was "God bless your Jimmy" and she always knew he would come good. Nora telling a story of Jimmy paying her a visit, all largesse in his gingham shirt and tailored slacks, reassuring Nora Farrell, pressing crisp notes in her hand, and not a word, and there you go, Nora, and a bit for yourself, and that will sort it, but we'll keep the flat next door to you coz it's handy, so not a word, and Nora Farrell closing the door and blessing that good Jimmy Heffernan and kneeling on the carpet in the living room, her arm on the sofa for support because her knees were shot with all that cleaning, and tears of relief, and thanking her dead husband up on the wall and all the angels and saints and you, my brothers and sisters, to pray for me to the Lord our God, who she thought had disappeared, and Nora Farrell shucking her slippers and scooting as quick as she could hobble down the urine-stained stairs to Dawn at Wakefields for a bottle of white wine and some ginger snaps. Now she had some craic for Mrs Nolan.

Now what did their Jimmy want that flat for, Bernice Devanney asked herself as she raised her hand for more champagne.

Back down in the basement, Heffernan did not have long to wait for head doorman Ned Behan to arrive from the floor area upstairs. Heffernan observed that Ned looked more than a little flustered, which was not like him.

—What's wrong, Ned?

—Well, first off, I presume it's about the car, Jimmy?

—His name is Tommy, isn't it?

—'That's right. Tommy Baker. Is he cool? Heard the name before. Empire TV?

—Yes, Ned. He's fine. Sorry, that was my fault. I should have warned you. Did he have a car-park fob and club-membership card?

—'S'right. One of the Connolly Citizens Gold Card ones. Kevin down below here stopped him and copied to me. I mean, we've never seen him before, but it all seemed to be okay. He said he was meeting up with Pierce Beaumont. And then, as you know, Chantelle, the lead singer with Flame, is due in tonight to do the photo shoot with Pierce, so there's even more scumbag photographers knockin' around than is usual. Telephoto lenses and all that, so I just decided to get him in as quickly as possible. I wasn't sure what the story was. He didn't look right tho'. Not Connolly Citizen Gold Card material anyway?

—No, you did right, Ned. Where is he?

—He's in one of the alcoves eating a steak. The only trouble is, Jimmy. I mean. Is this guy a nut or what?

—He may well be. He could be useful to us though, Ned, so don't be going heavy on him. Not yet anyway. What is he doing?

—He's got no respect, Jimmy! I mean. An arrogant little fucker. The way he talks. Then didn't he pull out a pipe?! And I swear he was going to light it up. A fucking pipe in Connolly's, and not even in the coke den. Sorry. Private leisure area. Anyway, I spoke fairly severely to him about not lighting up. Then he goes, "Sorry, Ned." Like he knows me?

—That would be from your days as a freedom fighter, Ned.

Heffernan reached for his clip book and extracted some hundred-euro notes.

—You did absolutely the right thing, Ned, so don't worry. Here, this is for yourself.

—Good man, Jimmy. It's appreciated, as I am sure you know.

—Just make sure you mark his face for future reference.

—When you say mark, Jimmy?

—No, I mean remember him again.

—Well, it's not hard. He's struggling to make it over five foot.

—Bring him up to my office, Ned, when he's finished eating. Is he drinking?

—No. Just tap water and lemon. That's it. Wouldn't even take the designer water, which is free to celebs. Saw the shake in his hand. Must be a dipso is he?

—Okay. Look, I've some calls to make, Ned, I'll give you the nod if I need that backstair-exit routine. Do you get me? With the photographer waiting outside the backstairs entrance. Get him to kick some trash around as well. Just around the door.

—Not a problem. Any breakages?

—Just one arm and the alcohol rap will do.

Heffernan turned to go to the lift which would take him to his office, but Ned called him back.

—Er, there was something else, Jimmy.

—What?

In that simple act of turning and the poised and darting rapidity of its execution, Ned Behan understood why Jimmy Heffernan was so dangerous.

—What "something else," Ned?

—Well, Carmel has been on the phone all day looking for you and she was very . . .

—Persistent?

—Er, yeah, very persistent. Said you were supposed to have been in earlier on, and . . . well, I have a job to do here, Jimmy, but at the same time she is your . . . I mean you and her . . .

The rest of the words died in Ned Behan's swiftly parched mouth, throat, gullet, chest of welling regret at what had just passed his lips.

—That is most unfortunate. Unfortunate for Carmel. If she

comes in tonight, let her know that I am in a meeting and ask her to wait in the office by the kitchen. We don't want any scenes and I've some rather shocking pictures to show her.

—Right you are, boss.

The Empire Celebrity

TOMMY BAKER ATE his steak and salad with a gusto he had forgotten was possible. He was enjoying this. Watched the paparazzi shoot with Pierce Beaumont going on the funk/hip-hop dance floor. Pierce doing his poses with the fabulous singer. How he loved it all, this A-face celebrity. Standing up, extending his long frame and *artiste manqué* of hair, pushing it back, smiling, joking about some politician. The rock star Chantelle disappears with her entourage and Baker makes his move. One photographer retreated to the bar, hopped onto a stool, flashed his press card, and drank a soda and lime. He also kept his jacket on, as per Tommy Baker's instructions. The photographer was a great admirer of Baker's work, and Baker likewise had a great understanding that this "snapper's" shots were very often magnificently composed, and he had even used some of his stills in his films for Empire. What the photographer didn't understand was that Tommy had given him strict orders not to take any pictures but just to raise his camera if and when a club bouncer should arrive at Pierce Beaumont's table. Just to lift the camera and adopt the pose to shoot, he had said. The photographer watched as Baker moved his small frame from the alcove to the main seating area of plush, almost-circular sofas that ringed the dance floor. The music was now playing louder as more punters arrived in the club. No, Heffernan insisted they be called "guests."

Baker now standing at Pierce Beaumont's table.

—Do you not get tired of all this celebrity malarkey, Pierce?

—What? Good God, Tommy Baker, what are you doing in here? Sit down, man. I've drinks on the way.

—Well, Pierce, I'm trying to be good at the moment.

—Oh, for God's sake, man, get a drink. We're a long time dead.

—No, really I won't. I'm on my way out actually.

—Well, I'll be gone soon as well. Just a few snifters. You know, yourself.

Baker sat down beside his Empire TV colleague, at the edge of the sofa with his back turned to the rest of the room, so that he could speak more confidentially.

—You seem to get snapped a lot in this place?

—Eh? How d'ye mean?

—Well, I'm not a tabloid man, but I seem to see you splashed in Connolly's quite often.

—Yes, I do regular promotions here. What's wrong with that?

—What's wrong with it is that you are the public face of Empire Television, a public-service broadcaster.

—Oh, here we go. With motions of his left hand, Beaumont shooed the two young and nubile women sitting near him to the far side of the sofa as he turned fully to face Tommy Baker.

—Do you know what, Baker? You were always a po-faced, holier-than-thou, fucking know-all. I promote lots of Irish businesses. This one's no different.

—Pierce, you know very well you are promoting a drug lord and probably the most dangerous gangster in Ireland.

Pierce Beaumont leaned into Baker's face at this point.

—Listen, fucking Mister Goody Two-Shoes. Sure, Jimmy Heffernan comes from the wrong side of the tracks and has had to fight his way to the top. But he's totally legit now. Look at this place. It's fabulous. The best of design, and do you know what? Sex on a plate as well. That's your problem at heart isn't it, Mister Boring Socialist. You just can't stand all glamour and pizzazz, and you won't see a scumbag or gangster in this place. Jimmy Heffernan deserves praise, not to be pilloried.

—Pierce. Deep down I think you are a decent person, and I—

—Don't you patronize me, you little fucker. I'll chew you and spit you out.

Beaumont's raised voice attracted the attention of other club-goers, and a bouncer at one of the main exits from the dance floor spoke into his wrist. Ned Behan, meanwhile, had received an order to bring Tommy Baker up to Jimmy Heffernan's private office. By now, Beaumont's voice was clearly audible alongside the music.

—Do you know what your trouble is, Baker. Eh? It's jealousy. Knee-high to a pint bottle and soooo not glamorous. You see all this glitz, people having a good time, watch all the high life, the bling, the babes, and yes, the bloody drugs as well, and you curse your luck that you can't be part of it. That's why you are a shrivelled little Provo, a bitter little communist. All you need is your fucking little Chairman Mao book.

Baker dipped his head. —Pierce, listen to me.

Pierce Beaumont saw the serious intent in Baker's eyes and calmed his rant. Baker put his small left hand on Beaumont's wrist.

—Get out and make a clean breast of it while there's still time.

Ned Behan now strode across the dance floor and placed his massive hand on Tommy Baker's shoulder, but as he did so, Ned's ever-alert peripheral vision noticed the photographer stepping over with his camera raised. Baker turned to face Ned Behan.

—Hello, Ned. I'm just leaving.

—It's Mr Behan to you, sir.

Baker's photographer friend knew enough to step between the bouncer and the departing Tommy Baker. Ned Behan was well aware that he could hardly drag Tommy Baker over to the elevator and up to Heffernan's private office. He was also aware that the younger punters would have been filming the scene, ready to post it on YouTube if anything controversial happened with Pierce Beaumont in attendance.

Once outside, Baker immediately lit his pipe and sucked on it for dear life. Air wheezing through the tube.

—Didn't know you smoked a pipe, Tommy.

—I don't. A priest put me onto it.

—A priest?

—Long story. Look, thanks for hanging around, Ciarán.

—No problem, and come here. I know I was a bit bold, but I took shots of the whole scene. You know me, Tom. The girls at the bar just thought I was with Pierce Beaumont. Got a good one of the gorilla as he was walking over to you.

—You beauty. Send them on to me, will you.

—Will, of course. Don't mind me asking, but that was a bit of a row you two were having. You and Piercey boy?

—Yes, another long story. Why don't we meet next week and I'll explain as much as I can. I might have an interesting assignment for you very shortly.

—I am your man. Love the smoke-and-mirrors stuff and the whiff of danger.

—Don't be talking. More than a whiff.

When Ciarán the photographer turned a corner down the street, Tommy Baker switched on his mobile and rang the AA telling them that his car had broken down and was stuck in a basement garage. This not only reminded him that he had not been to his AA meeting (his other AA), it also reminded him that the adrenaline of the last few hours or so had made him completely forget about his need for alcohol. Baker sucked furiously on his pipe and made to ring his wife. Then he remembered she was in heaven. Ten messages appeared from James Tierney as he looked at the phone screen. He smiled.

Flight

FATHER MCCARTAN HAD thought very deeply about the visit from the Garda officer. He knew it was not right, but he also knew he had to play a clever game, nothing rash. The priority was to get Éilis out of harm's way. However, someone within the police force had decided to start searching for Éilis. How strange. People from Star of the Sea could disappear for months, years, be dead, without the authorities even lifting a finger in response.

As a priest he tried to avoid politics but found that he was more and more dragged into the political sphere because of his commitment to the poor. For a long time now he had been complaining at a local level about the blind eye being turned to criminality and drug dealing, with his local congregation telling him that the Garda Crime Branch allowed the Untouchables free rein because they were being used as informers—the eyes and ears of the police in the local area. Privately, some of the community liaison police officers had admitted they had been told to go easy on the Untouchables because they were being used for a "higher purpose" by Crime Branch. But then, there were good people in the police as well. The superintendent for the district for example, and he now knew what he was going to do.

When the battered old Vincent de Paul van turned up outside the charity shop next door to Wakefields, nobody in Star of the Sea flats would have blinked an eyelid. Not the drug dealers, not the addicts, not the cops, not the postman, all of whom had been told to keep an eye out for Éilis. Perhaps, a younger element might have noted that Turlough the Goth was the driver, but then the Goths had taken to doing things for Father McCartan. That was the way he roped you in. Then two other Goths got out of the back doors of the van and produced a wheeled-goods trolley with which they wheeled a large box into the Vincent de Paul store. Another box was then wheeled into the store. All this activity was perfectly normal except that when the two Goths wheeled a third box out of the shop and manhandled it into the van, this box contained Éilis Devanney.

When, the previous evening, the Éilis situation had been explained to Turlough McKenna and two of his most trusted Goths (a fellow poet and a motorbike mechanic) by Father McCartan, there was no need for further background explanations. The wider game was understood. This girl Éilis was in some kind of trouble with the Untouchables and it was obvious that the priest didn't want to go to the cops. Nuff said. Never would this be spoken of. It being a service to Shelley and Byron, to Romance, the high ideal, Bill Hicks, Raymond Carver, and Kurt Cobain. This mission for the Church was in other words a privilege and what the Church should have been doing all along. It was now a proper Church. A Goth Church. Alleluia.

Once the Vincent de Paul van had left the church grounds Father McCartan made two pre-planned calls. One to the Garda superintendent and the other to his great friend and local Teachta Dála Terence Gregory.

Terence Gregory walked up the steps to the local Garda station as he had done countless times before. He never drove a car and, as a point of principle, always walked about his inner-city constituency. Always available to the people he served. The people who had elected him to Parliament, or *Dáil*, as it is called in the Irish. Gregory was just over average height but gave an impression of being taller still because of his confident bearing and a sense that his clear blue eyes and fine brow looked beyond what was directly in front of him. Also because he was slim to the point of thin. A thinness accentuating his sharp intellect. Indeed a formidable intellect and also one that would not play the normal verbal games played in polite circles. He detested the banks and expressed understanding of those who would rob them. He described business moguls as robber barons living on disgusting wealth made off the backs of working people. Gregory was also brave. He had no compunction in confronting the drug dealers in his area but his ire was directed far more at the drug barons and their middle-class support structure than at the street pushers. Indeed he had named Jimmy Heffernan in a parliamentary committee that called for a different approach to drug dealing. It was not a drug war that was needed but a social war against the corruption that drugs had engendered. The James Bond intrigues of secret-police drug units and their network of informers inevitably led to deals being done and a blind eye being turned to serious crimes. In fact, a blurring of what should be a clear line between police officer and criminal. These words and sentiments had been widely reported in the press and neither Jimmy Heffernan nor the drug-squad officers had been impressed. However, there was little that they could do. If any harm or disturbance happened to Terence Gregory, the whole of the inner city would have risen up. Such was his stature. A really authentic Untouchable.

Once inside the Garda station, Terence Gregory saw the officer behind the protective glass screen stand to attention slightly and he was immediately let through to a reception room for visitors. There he asked to see the head of Crime Branch, which again raised the officer's brow, but he firmly and professionally confirmed that he would "ring upstairs."

Meanwhile, Father McCartan had made his second call—to his friend the police inspector. As soon as he hung up, the priest, with Éilis Devanney safely in his car, immediately hit the motorway road going north. In his call to the police inspector, he had asked why Crime Branch was taking an interest in Éilis Devanney when she was in fact a social services problem. If problem she was. He therefore asked the inspector to pop in to see the head of Crime Branch sometime that morning and assure him that Éilis was safe and well. He was more than happy to liase with social services regarding Éilis and explain the situation.

Father McCartan was of course aware that the inspector, whom he had phoned at home, would call in to Crime Branch as soon as he got to the station.

So it was that the station inspector knocked and walked into the head of Crime Branch just as he and Terence Gregory were in the middle of a clearly rather tense discussion. A discussion that had started with Terence Gregory asking why the almost paramilitary Crime Branch was taking an interest in a sixteen-year-old girl from Star of the Sea flats. Had they not better things to be doing?

The conversation between Terence Gregory and head of Crime Branch Derek Nally had run thus:

—Who is this girl, Terence?

—Her name is Éilis Devanney and what disturbs me about this case is that she is a cousin of Scumbag Number One Jimmy Heffernan.

The mention of Heffernan's name brought a charge into the atmosphere in the room. The head of Crime Branch stood up and walked to his window before turning to Gregory with a look that bordered on supplication, an appeal to be heard.

—Look, Terry, we've known each other a long while and I'm aware of your allegations against Heffernan . . . I mean, there is no doubt that he is, or was, a bad bastard, and we watch him like a hawk, but, if I may say completely privately, in recent times we've received important help from him that has led to a number of drug seizures, arrests, and lengthy prison sentences.

—Ah come on, Derek, it's clear what he's up to. He's using the Garda Síochána to marginalise the opposition. How much have you seized from his so-called Untouchables at Star of the Sea?

—Well, that stuff's fairly petty really, we have—

—Petty? Petty? Those fuckers terrorise the people on that estate.

It was at that point that the inspector had walked in.

—Morning, gentlemen. I think freshly brewed coffee and some pastries in my office might be a good idea. Step this way, please.

Séamus Dempsey (But Not Yet)

IN THE INITIALLY tense meeting between Terence Gregory and the two senior policemen, it was Gregory who did most to defuse the tension. The longer he could spin the meeting out, the further Father McCartan and this Éilis girl would be away from Dublin. Besides, Gregory reasoned, he would get more useful information about Heffernan if he avoided confrontation.

Father McCartan and Éilis Devanney, meanwhile, trundled their long way to Gaoth Dobhair in the priest's ageing Citroën Deux Cheavaux. As Father McCartan vainly tried to waft his pipe smoke through the open window of the car, Éilis joked that there was more smoke coming from his pipe than from the car's exhaust. The joking, however, soon stopped once Éilis began to tell Father McCartan about Jimmy Heffernan's approaches to her. Including the last one and the burning of the money.

Éilis then asked for the priest to hear her confession, in which she told him all of her thoughts regarding Finn and his brother Séamus. Once Éilis had finished her confession, the priest asked for permission to play some Gregorian chant music in the car and to reflect on her beautiful honesty before a fellow human being and before God.

No more was said between the pair until Father McCartan pulled into a hotel just outside of Monaghan town and declared gratitude to God, all the angels and saints, and big, fat, blessed Buddha that lunchtime was upon them. Once the main meal had been despatched and tea was ordered, Father McCartan offered his thoughts and advice to Éilis.

161

—For a start, Éilis, I would not mention Jimmy Heffernan's behaviour to Finn when you write, text, or mail to him, or whatever it is you young people do this weather. There is absolutely no point upsetting him. Nor should you mention it to Séamus. We have got you out of the situation now and will let the hare sit.

—Yes, Father, and I'm never going back there. It's such a relief to be out of that place. I should have done it a year ago or more, but then it broke my heart to leave my room, my mates at the wall. Even those mad Goths. Then Dawn would often stay with me and always watched me. Finn and Uncle Antain were always very close to me there in that room. All those things.

Tears now, and the priest saying that grieving was good and necessary.

—This is a big change in your life now that you have finally flown the nest. Now, with regard to what you told me about Séamus. Once again I would advise caution. If you want my full and frank opinion, where I am confessing my feelings under your oath of secrecy, then I think you and Séamus would be better suited.

Éilis's eyes widened at Father McCartan's statement and she nodded almost imperceptibly to encourage him to go on.

—But. And there is always a *but* I suppose . . .

Éilis was ready to jump at the priest and wring the words from his heart, given that he was so long in joining one sentence to another.

—Sorry, Éilis, I know you are impatient to know my thoughts and you've hardly discussed this with anyone else. I feel strange though . . .

—Father, just tell me.

—Yes, I feel strange even talking about it. I mean, I love Finn and have watched him grow up. And you must understand. I'm not your parent.

—Father.

—I mean. I don't want you to do anything hasty.

—Father McCartan.

—Can we go outside? That's one of the great things about this unseasonable weather. We can spend more time *amuigh faoin speir.*

Éilis forbore Father McCartan's procrastinations with good grace as they moved down the main thoroughfare in the hotel. More waiting and fidgeting until he had lit up a pipe in the gardens at the back.

—You see, Éilis, part of the problem is that priests are never supposed to talk about relationships with our people. We learn the rules of the Church and that's it. We are emotional cripples most of us, and that's why we can't deal with proper human contact. What a crowd we are. We deserve all the criticism.

—Father McCartan, if you don't tell me your thoughts about Séamus right now I think I am going to faint with the waiting.

—What?! Right, then! Well, Séamus is far better suited to you for a number of reasons, but not yet.

—Why not yet?

—He has to work out his anger, Éilis. He is a very, very angry and passionate young man and in this he is the total opposite of Finn. I know he has struck up a relationship with those Chinese fellows who do all that, what's this you call it? Sounds like one of those dinners you can order from the Summer Palace. One of my guilty pleasures.

—He practises Wing Chun with them.

—That's it. What a name, eh?! Well, I've seen him become more controlled and calmer since he started training with them. At least now his anger and aggression has a focus. But. There is always a *but.*

—Father.

—Yes, I know, Éilis, but I was really only musing upon how fascinating it is that in a way it doesn't really matter who we marry at the end of the day as long as the commitment is there. Or more accurately, the level of commitment, passion, and respect that both partners require. You won't get all that with Finn quite frankly, but you will get it with Séamus, eventually.

—When? When is eventually?

—*Tá fhios agat an abairt, tá an fhirinne searbh ach tá sé fíor?*

—Of course I know that saying. The truth has a bitter taste but it is true all the same.

—Well, Séamus will be ready when he finally accepts that there's nothing we can do about the likes of Jimmy Heffernan. Just like the poor, it seems that gangsters and evil souls will always be with us.

A fire erupted in Éilis's cheeks and her vehement response to what the priest had said about Séamus took even herself by surprise.

—So the answer is to abandon Dublin and hand it over to them. The *Gaill*, the foreigners. No, not the foreigners. The zombies, the ghouls. The ones who spread the canker, *an galar, an saint*. Father, God forgive me, but if that is what you are suggesting then I am with Séamus: *Céad faoin gcéad! Go nithe na péisteoga iad*, may the worms eat them. The fuckers. Oh Jesus, sorry, Father!

The priest laughed behind his eyes at the curse, then clearly began weighing whether he should tell Éilis something. A quick glance at her. Staring at the road. At the heavens. The girl needed encouragement and there was no harm.

—Éilis, *éist liom a stór*. I can tell you something now because you will be in Donegal and away from the mess we are in in our parish. A TV documentary is going to be made about the flats and the drug pushers and Jimmy Heffernan's connections to them behind the scenes. It's all been very secretive and I know very little about everything that's going to be in it. But they must be very serious, because they've been getting our local TD Terence Gregory to find out things for them.

—Oh my God. Are you in it, Father?

—I am. I am in it and so is Finn's father.

—Why did they not ask me to say something?

—I talked to the producer about that. His name is Tommy. And I asked him not to approach you. Or rather, we asked him. Hold on, Éilis. I can see that you're angry, but now, after this episode with Heffernan, perhaps you can understand why we did all this behind your back, and indeed behind Finn's back.

Silence now, and Éilis incensed that she, as the one who had approached Tommy Baker, had been excluded.

—Éilis, first of all there is your age. And then people could have used your medical records . . .

—So you're all saying I'm a cracker factory? Father, you may let me out of the car here. Dawn believes in me.

—Éilis, you know I don't think that, but there's a big tactical game to be played here. Jimmy Heffernan is more powerful than even you realise, and that is my point about Séamus.

—Father, I am not going to Donegal while all this craic is going on!

—Éilis, Donegal is the safest place for you and Donegal is where you are going. When all this settles down and we are all a bit clearer about how it's going to turn out, I'm certain you'll get your chance. Absolutely certain. *Tiocfaidh do lá.*

—Why are you certain?

—Well. Because . . . well . . .

The priest pulled into the hard shoulder on the dual carriageway just before Letterkenny, hazard lights flashing, and he stopping his pipe. Éilis just looked ahead and waited. After what seemed an age, he told her that the journal she had sent in to Tommy Baker had caused great excitement to both Baker himself and his young researcher, who was called James. Feature film material they had said. So hair-raising and unbelievable in parts that it held the ring of truth. Beautifully composed they had said, if rather frantic in parts.

Then the priest drove on. On past Letterkenny and into the wild mountains of Northwest Donegal—*Sleibhte Dhoire Bheatha.* When Éilis saw Muckish and Errigal mountains, she was, just as the priest had intended, suddenly proud and confident of who she was and what she wanted. Proud of her impassioned journal. Proud to be acknowledged as a writer.

Into the Gaeltacht they went, and Éilis Devanney happy with it. Now let things go the way they will, she said.

A Death Warrant

JAMES TIERNEY WAS in great form altogether. His research in County Galway had got him very close to identifying several unscrupulous characters and one factory that were dumping waste, including animal waste and fertiliser, into Galway's ancient waterways. Also, and even closer to his heart, on his return from the West, Tommy Baker had instructed him to go to his favourite pasta restaurant for lunch and he would be informed of all the developments. Just as close, perhaps, he admitted to himself that he badly wanted to see Ronagh again, missed her aura, her scent, the look of her. Her eyes looking at him across the table. But there were things Tommy Baker was not going to tell him, and then Ronagh.

He saw her in the canteen and laughed to himself, she was in his seat, far from her workmates. But Ronagh gave him nothing more than a perfunctory wave and began to inspect her nails as he tried to ask her did she want a bun. What was up? Had they gone too far on a first date? But then, she was if anything more eager than him. He sits in front of her and sees her brain willing her eyes to remain impassive. He spoke first and without waiting.

—What?

—What "what"?

—Well, you're not exactly—

—What or who is this, Ronagh said as she looked down to her bag and pulled a picture from the front zip pocket.

—That's my ex and do you mind telling me why you were rooting through my things?

—Don't avoid the issue, James.

—There is no issue to avoid.

Ronagh raised her voice more than she intended.

—Well, why did you keep it a secret!

—Shh, Ronagh. Come on, let's go outside.

Outside but not far enough for Tierney, she turns to confront him. Straight-backed, arms folded. He conscious that the whole canteen could see them through the glass windows.

—Who is she?

—I'll tell you when you give me my photo back.

—Here. Tell me who she is.

—Have I asked you about your previouses, exes, slip ups, one night stands?

—Tell me who she is.

—Her name's Carina. She's half-Irish, half-Spanish and I met her at a film shoot when I was doing my training. We did a modelling agency.

—And you did the model. Had to be you of course. What was it, a porno movie?

—Ah, come on. Anyway, she's not a model. She's a dancer. Modern dance. She—

—I knew it, an *artiste* with a stunning body. And how am I supposed to compete?

—Ronagh, you're being irrational. We split six months ago. Let's sit down over on that bench. She was an axe merchant. Or more accurately a scissors merchant, and I have the scars to prove it, as you may have noticed.

—I thought they were just football or hurling scars, Jamesie. You are from Galway after all.

Her use of "Jamesie," the softening of her body, the relenting, the letting go of the envy, visible in her aura as her ache sought to meld with his because she had missed him frantically. The soft fold of her blouse beneath the jacket fluttering in the slight breeze as they walked. She searching and seeing in his eyes the truth of that same want.

When they sat down on the bench, Ronagh demanded that he destroy, shred, or incinerate the picture of this "fucking

Carina one." But he refused and said that he and his past, such as it was, came as a job lot and could not be divorced. He immediately regretted the word "divorce." She looked away from him at the staff parking lot and then looked back at him to find his vast gaze was upon her so that she fell into the blue of it and what was it about men from west of the Shannon and their true manliness, the simplicity of it and its firm resolution? The wise vision of it that made Dublin shrink by comparison.

His hand was on her lap.

Tommy Baker was just driving through the Empire complex and saw James and Ronagh, obviously intimate in their movements back to the canteen, shoulder gracing shoulder. He had known Ronagh long, long, and wondered if her sometime tough headstrongness was the best for his protégé, who was a God but with the Achilles heel of innocence, an oversensitive heart. Oversensitive and too soft for these times. Too innocent and romantic. All the reasons why he loved the boy-god and why Ronagh might crush him.

Baker didn't go into his office but made straight for the IT department, where a small, wiry youth stood up when he poked his head in the door. Once outside, the youth pulled, with a look of triumph, a black button from a brown envelope. This was Stephen Ross. Not only a computer genius but also a truly wired electrician.

—Get wardrobe to put the rest of them onto your jacket, Tommy.

—How do you activate it?

—Squeeze it at the sides in a pincer movement, like this. With thumb and forefinger.

Baker held the button aloft to inspect it. His manner dubious, unconvinced.

—And what way does it record, Stephen. I mean, where the bloody hell is the sound and picture going?

Stephen gave a slight shake of head.

—Look, there's no point explaining, but it's basically a stripped-down tablet using two chips. Here, I won't actually do it, but this is the movement. You'll get about an hour's worth of sound and video out of it. Bring it back to me for conversion.

—Great, I'll get Bernie in wardrobe to put matching ones on.

—She's waiting for you, Tommy. 'Twas herself gave me this button. Bit wider and deeper than a normal one, but not so's you'd notice.

—Right, I'm off for lunch with Mr Tierney. Anything else?

—Go get the bastard, whoever it is. That one in Limerick worked a treat.

Tommy Baker walking to the restaurant in Donnybrook village. Blessing himself at the church and blessing the youth who were far more angry at the state of things than was reported. Than he'd even given them credit for. Bless their fervency, dreams, will to do good; their need for visions and all the angels and saints and their brothers and sisters and their hatred of world poverty, the utter fakeness of celebrity and flaky wannabes; and their desire to engage in ferocious battles for their ideals. Their scorning of death. Their unknowledge and belittling of death. Their belief in themselves. Oh, to be young again. Oh, to be not an alcoholic, driven to distraction.

Once at the PastaBasta restaurant, Baker finally told James that Éilis Devanney was being spirited away to the Donegal Gaeltacht but he asked him to do a strange thing. For Baker asked him to take out his mobile phone from his courier bag and ring him there and then.

—Ring you, Tommy? Even though you're sitting right in front of me?

—Yes, I want you to ring me right now and express your surprise that Éilis Devanney has not been moved to Donegal at all but actually to a care home for young offenders in Wicklow. Be sure to mention that this care home is just outside Gorey.

Taking his phone out of his bag, James asked why he wanted him to do this.

—Because, James, if I were Jimmy Heffernan, I would have someone monitoring my calls.

Three days after this fake phone call, Neville and Bernice

Devanney, travelling in style in a plush taxi, arrived in Gorey, County Wicklow, and sought directions from a local shop owner for the young people's care home just outside the village. The shop owner shook his head as they left his premises. Wondering at their murdering of the English language. Their lack of class. Their white trash.

What Father McCartan hadn't told Éilis was that Tommy Baker had talked about interviewing some young people in the film and this included a group of young martial artists who were trying to keep young people away from the drug scene. One of this group was Finn's brother Séamus Dempscy. Two weeks on from Éilis Devanney's move to Donegal, Baker and his crew had begun using the local handball alley to conduct interviews. It was a secure place and far enough away from Star of The Sea to min-imise the awareness of the Untouchables. But on this day, there was an interview from one of those very Untouchables. Darren Bulger had decided to press a detonator button on Heffernan's Star of the Sea operation. All for the love and honour of Éilis.

Darren had wanted to go to Éilis but she had disappeared, so he approached Dawn and told her that he wanted to spill Spanzo's beans. Maybe to the priest or Terence Gregory. But Dawn says leave it with me, Darren, and say nothing to anyone till you hear from me. She now had a direct line to Tommy Baker's secretary.

Tommy Baker looked out from the van as they made their way to the handball alley and a possibly crucial interview with Darren Bulger. He had lost count of the number of times he had been in this situation and for each occasion his craving for alcohol had grown stronger. Irish courage to soothe his ragged nerves. To salve his conscience at the thought that he was simply using another human being for his own ends. And for what? So that he could make a television programme that most people would just ignore. A programme that would almost certainly put this Darren in mortal danger and probably his crew and all his other interviewees as well. At least James Tierney was out of harm's way at that moment, with filming for the polluted-waterways story out in Galway East. Safe for the moment, and James raging that he did not have a more hands-on role in the Heffernan film.

Baker reached instinctively for his cigarettes in his pocket and then reminded himself that he had just given up smoking and drinking. If he drank, he smoked, simple as that, and cigarettes seemed to pull him right back into the vortex. So the two had to be abandoned in tandem. Where were his cigarettes anyway? Damn. He reached down into his shoulder bag and took out his pipe to suck on. Whistling sounds began to emanate from the tube, and cameraman Sitric Cunningham and sound-recordist Alan Magilligan gave each other a look.

In truth, Tommy Baker knew that he was not going to go dry forever. He was determined, however, to stay sober until the film about Heffernan was made. This he could do and was determined to do. Gazing out of the window, he realised that he saw God in a speck of cloud in the blue sky and in the almost-white palm of a very black woman who was leading her equally black child along the road. Maybe the Heffernan story was the thing he had needed all along. A call to wake up. But to what? A flash of intuition told him that if he could truly embrace the passion of Éilis Devanney, her fully understandable madness perhaps? and the quiet, persistent, stubborn-as-get-out fire of James Tierney, he might, after all, retire and die a happy man and finally give his wife some kind of peace. The Goths had certainly given him hope.

Or were his recriminations really a call to put his hands up and stop? To say that he just did not cut the mustard any-more? Then Jimmy Heffernan's face came into his mind and all thoughts of stopping what he was doing were banished as the anger rose inside him again. No. He did not have any damn philosophy of life like those two remarkable young people had, and the Goths for that matter. But he damn well knew that he was there to stop bullies and demagogues in their tracks.

The conversation between Sitric and Alan had faded to silence whilst Baker ruminated on the interview to come and on the actual worth of his own contribution to the "cause." The cause being?

—What's my purpose in life, Sitric? Baker asked.

—Your purpose? Your purpose is to annoy people, Tommy.

—So that's it. I just annoy people.

—Well, you annoy me constantly. But no, seriously, not just any people, Tommy. You're one of the few journalists left in Ireland who has remembered the golden rule.

—Remind me again, Sitric, about that golden rule. I'm getting desperate here.

Sitric looked back at Tommy Baker from the driver's seat and understood at once that his favourite producer was going through agonies that perhaps only Christ himself would really understand. He checked his inside-lane mirror and then pulled into a lay-by opposite Glasnevin Cemetery. He had driven up through Phibsborough whilst waiting for Baker to tell him where they were going. Alan, who had been running through his equipment, checking his batteries and generally preparing for the coming interview was shocked that his long-time partner had pulled the van over to the side simply because he had something to say. This was not like Sitric.

—I think I want to record this, Sitric.

—Record away, Alan. The camera's on.

—Hang on . . . let me just check something. Okay, rolling.

—The golden rule, Tommy, is that we annoy the rich and the powerful. Doing films about social-welfare fraud and dodgy, secondhand car dealers and ignoring the real shysters out there is not only lazy journalism and going for the easy targets, it's pure cowardice. And you, Tommy Baker, are not a coward. It's the reason why they sleep comfortably on their fat heads in their fat beds while you live on the edge. You're a mate, Tommy, and a brilliant filmmaker and what I'm saying to you won't help you in what you're going to go through over the next few days and weeks. Cold turkey is cold turkey and only you know whether you can really face it and come out the other end still sane and still sober. But I am going to tell you something now, Tommy. You are not the only one that is sick.

—Do you not think I know that, Sitric.

—Shut up, Tommy, and listen to me will ya?

—Sorry?

—I am sick. Sitric Cunningham is sick. Sick of doing yet another reality show that is about anything but reality. Sick of doing yet another fucking home-improvement show for all those middle-class zombies who can't think beyond the next curtain rail and round-the-clock security. Sick of doing shows that are ten years out of date in Britain and America. Like we are some backwater for all their dross. Because that's what we are. And you, Tommy Baker, are one of the few people who make it worth going into Empire in the morning. You know why? Because you actually care and make me care and you actually instinctively know where the bleeding heart of this fucked up country is. Do you not think meself and Alan have discussed how dangerous all this might be? Tommy, we'll go to the wall with you on this one as long as you don't start backsliding on us. Now, let's go and fucking nail Jimmy fucking Heffernan and those fuckers in polite society who seem to be protecting and encouraging him.

Baker could not speak. He simply reached his free hand across to the driver's seat and gripped Sitric's left arm as hard as he could.

—Sorry, Alan, I can't reach you back there.

Alan didn't say anything in response but he lifted the empty wrapping of a Mars Bar from the pocket of his jacket which had been left hanging in the van.

—Sitric. Did you eat my fucking Mars Bar?

Darren Bulger was standing in the middle of the handball court when Tommy Baker walked in. Darren's rangy and underfed physical shape was exaggerated by his pale and forlorn facial features, which radiated a sickly glow in the half-light of the court. Lank blond hair, thin hopeless mouth with cracked teeth, but a glint in his blue eyes of something that was promised him once. Some kind of sturdiness in his long bowlegs also. Like he could have been a dancer. Some lingering rhythm there anyway. Some inner spring and toughness.

Séamus Dempsey was engaged in repeatedly slamming a hardball at the front wall of the alley and returning it back to the wall as it rebounded towards him. The expert sound recordist in Alan wanted to record the eerie sound of the ball in the empty hall but he knew that this might identify where the interview had been conducted were it to be used in the subsequent film. It seemed, however, that Séamus Dempsey had already interpreted his thoughts. Séamus walked towards Alan from the front of the court as Tommy Baker moved over to Darren to introduce himself.

—Do you want to take some of this handball stuff, Alan? My friend Chang is coming soon and you can take a bit of the game as well. I'll put on the lights, will I?

—Well if that's all right with Tommy, but there are not that many handball alleys left in Dublin and Heffernan might . . .

—It's too late to be worrying about Heffernan. When the film goes out, he'll know where to find us. His problem is that we know where to find him.

Not stupid, Alan took an inward whistle at Séamus's cockiness. Séamus then nodded across to Tommy Baker as Sitric joined the conversation. Baker and Darren Bulger had withdrawn themselves to the back of the court, where they held a whispered conversation, the sibilants of which carried across the cool dark air like the prayers of ancient monks in some secret monastery in the long ago.

—Is your man all right? asked Séamus.

—Ah, don't worry about Tommy, said Sitric. He's off the booze and the fags and had a rough night. As for the lights, Séamus, I would leave them off.

Never had Sitric nor Alan heard such an interview. For the first time, they felt they understood the world of the drug pusher. For the first time ever, they digested the fact that drug pushers are normal people and that at least some of them worried about their kids, their souls, made choices, felt bad, were tormented by what they did and the harm it caused not only to other people but also to themselves.

For the first time, also, they understood how absolutely ruthless Jimmy Heffernan actually was.

Another surprise for the film crew was that Darren Bulger's interview was going to be a face-on-camera interview. Sitric

brought in his lights from the van and Tommy Baker explained
to everyone that he was going to arrange for protective custody
for Darren and that the interview would be far more powerful
if the subject could actually be seen. Once you started using
masks, image or sound distortion, you lost audience confidence.

All the people standing in the ball alley had the sense of
something significant happening, including Séamus Dempsey's
friend Chang, who asked permission to sit and listen to what
was being said.

—Do you mind if Chang is present during the interview,
Darren? Tommy Baker asked.

—What? Mr Kung Fu? No, I don't mind. If Séamus says he's
cool, that's fine by me.

—Oh, you know him already?

—I know not to mess with him and that none of his crowd
do drugs. Not like some of their crowd round Parnell Square
who are working for Heffernan now. Can we get this over with,
Tommy?

—Okay. Are we rolling, lads?

Sitric and Alan each gave a thumbs up.

—Why are you doing this interview, Darren?

—I am doing it for Éilis Devanney and a little fella called
Dessie who none of youse would know. Jeez, lads. Is there any
water?

Séamus Dempsey ran into the changing room and fished a
bottle of water from his sports bag.

Tommy Baker looked across at his prize interviewee and saw
that he was already in danger of both physically and metaphor-
ically drying up. An interview device occurred to him which he
had used before where the interviewee was particularly nervous.
This calming device consisted of placing someone with whom
the interviewee was familiar behind him, and slightly to his side,
so that the interviewee felt that they were having a conversation
with someone they knew rather than a strange television character. For this reason, when Séamus returned with the water
for Darren, Tommy Baker invited him to draw up a chair just
slightly behind his own.

—Cheers, Séamus, said Darren. Me throat's like a matchbox and that light is very hard.

Darren seemed to look around at the handball alley for the first time and he studied the earnest faces of those who surrounded him.

—If I get outta this alive, I wouldn't mind giving this handball carry-on a bit of a lash. Get fit. Live a bit.

Tommy Baker began the interview again.

—Darren, could you explain what you mean when you say you are doing this interview for someone called Éilis, and little Dessie?

—Well. Do you see . . . Éilis. Don't be saying this to Finn now, Séamus, coz he'll be after me as well. But I always had a thing about Éilis. Like, you ask anyone in the flats, they'll say the same. She's just a great girl. I mean she's more holy than all of them put together, and when I saw her no-good, lowlife, scumbag parents running around with your man, I just thought, that's it. I mean. I'm lowlife meself. But that's it. I've had enough. Éilis doesn't deserve that. I've been trying to get outta this hole I'm in for a while. I might not have all the brains in the world but I know what's right and what's wrong. I'm in rehab at the minute and me counsellor she's really good and I suppose she's got me thinking about Éilis and all the others in the flats. Ermm . . . Is that okay? It all sounds shite doesn't it?

—No, Gameball Darren, your doing brilliant, Séamus called from behind Tommy Baker.

Baker now realised the connection between Heffernan and Éilis and the significance of Heffernan's connection to her parents. Without even looking around at Séamus Dempsey, Tommy Baker could feel that Darren Bulger's references to Éilis had affected him. Baker also reflected that it had perhaps been a mistake to leave this girl Éilis out of the cast list. The priest had been very insistent that she should not be approached, but he made a mental note to raise the issue again. James Tierney had been right also.

—What about little Dessie? Tell us about him, Darren.

—This is a little chiseller called Dessie Noonan. Well Spanzo hit him a few hard digs some weeks back. I mean this is little Dessie, yeah? He's just six years of age. Well, I was totally disgusted and him throwing notes around like he was at a wedding. What do you call that stuff again, Séamus?

—Confetti, it's called, Darren.

—Yeah, Spanzo was throwing money around like confetti. Well, what with a lot of other things. I am just sick of them and sick of it. Am I allowed to smoke?

Tommy Baker turned to Séamus who nodded his assent whilst Baker laughed to himself at the irony of a drug pusher asking for permission to smoke whilst he had banned himself from doing the very same thing. Séamus Dempsey called out to Darren that nobody had ever been allowed to smoke on the actual court before.

—That's another thing not to be telling our Finn, Darren.

Darren held up his newly lit cigarette towards the direction of the camera.

—Do you see that, boys. That is the real gateway drug. That's how most kids get hooked.

—What about alcohol then, Darren?

Tommy Baker felt that he had shown too much eagerness with this question, but then it was not only pushers who were paranoid.

—Nah, Tommy. I tell ya, it's the fags that get kids dragged in. First off. I'm pushing for a good few years now and I have yet to meet a non-smoker who uses stuff. In this rehab I'm in, we talked about it and the counsellor agrees wit me. That's why this smoking ban is brilliant for the kids. The new ones coming through I mean.

—You seem to get on well with your counsellor, Darren?

—Ah, Claire? Actually she's called Claire Geoghan Smith and she's really la-di-da and when I met her I'm like, hello, who's this English bird? But she's been great for me. I mean, she found out from an old probation officer that I used to be good at the drums, and guess what? Didn't she get some rich fella down in Wicklow to pay for lessons for me. I just love drumming and I was fairly good when I was a kid. Séamus would tell ya. If I keep clean for six months, Claire's gonna get me an old drum set.

—Are you totally off them?

—Off the drugs? Well, I kinda have a handle on them now. I don't do crack anymore or Horse. Well, maybe now and then. Just take blow really and maybe the odd E. Am I allowed to say that?

Darren Bulger could see that Séamus Dempsey was shaking his head in exasperation and incomprehension, and nodded.

—It's hard for you to understand, Séamus and I have said the same thing to Éilis. You're going to go to university, Séamus, and Éilis . . . I mean Éilis is a star. She can do whatever she wants in the whole world, but see the likes a me. Where else can I get that kind a money? And the money's like unbelievable if you are with the right crew. And we are the Untouchables. Do yez know what I'm saying? The money and the crew and all that. It's all part of it. The likes of the Dempseys, they're big families. Who've I got? Me Ma. Da fucked off years ago. A couple of no-good uncles. Don't put that on the telly, okay? About me uncles. Can't believe I'm gonna be on the telly, but fuck it. Better to go out with a bang and a bit a pride in meself. Reckon I'll go straight to heaven. And I'm ready for it. Got me old miraculous medal on again in case I meet herself.

—What about Jimmy Heffernan? Tommy Baker intervened.

—What about him?

—Are you scared of him?

—He's the most frightening man or thing I have ever met. Bar nobody. And don't you go messing with him, Séamus . . . Finn maybe. But Heffernan doesn't do digging matches anymore. He doesn't need to. He's got the whole town in his pocket and when he wants something done in this town . . . Well, this town jumps, including the Guards.

—So, really. You are a dead man walking? Baker asked.

Timing was everything.

—Like I say, this is for Éilis. I can't read bewks all that well, like the Dempseys can, but I can read people and I know what Heffernan is at with Éilis.

Tommy Baker offered a prayer to the gods every time Darren mentioned the name Heffernan as this made it much easier to tell the story when the film about Heffernan was finally put together.

—And what is Heffernan to you?

—Jimmy Heffernan is not human, he's a machine.

Darren visibly began to relax as he warmed to his subject. He lit another cigarette, blew out the smoke, and sat back in his chair.

—Heffernan looks at people and things, sort of, like, what they can do for him. He would treat Éilis like he treats his horses. He would ride her until she wouldn't ride no more and then he'd just put her down. Sorry, don't put that on the telly, lads, either. I mean, that would be desperate for Éilis. Sorry, Séamus.

Darren Bulger's continued references to Éilis had wound Séamus Dempsey's emotions into a tight ball. With horrific clarity, he realised that Darren Bulger had shown more concern for Éilis than either he or his brother Finn had shown towards her. What was Finn doing going to London anyway? Darren gave another fascinating insight into the world of the Untouchables, seemingly oblivious to his capacity to shock.

—I don't want Éilis ending up like your man from that building firm. The one who was kept down a drain.

Tommy Baker's face lit up at this piece of information which was news to him.

—I thought that was supposed to be republicans who did that?

—Ah, me bollix, Tommy. They always say that. That was us. Sure, wasn't it me who had to feed him.

Tommy Baker looking at Darren, and no craving for alcohol at all, only a burning desire to tell the world about the real Jimmy Heffernan.

—Who was this man, Darren? The one you had to feed.

—Heffernan has gangs of workmen on his books. Poles, Latvians, all that. Not Nigerians. He won't let anyone in the firm deal with Nigerians. If you do, you are out big time.

—And what about this builder? This man you had to feed?

—What? Oh yeah. Well, basically he refused to take one a these gangs on. You know, under the table. Spanzo, and I think the Cube, went to see him and another one of the lads, but this guy is one of them huge redneck fuckers. Sorry. You know, one a them mountain men from up the hills. So he was a bit of a handful apparently before they got him tied up.

Facts from the case came back to Séamus Dempsey at that point and he realised the importance of the fact that Darren Bulger was explaining what really happened on camera and he called across to Darren as Tommy Baker made to ask another question.

—I remember that now, Darren. Jeez, they kept him naked down a drain near Croke Park.

—'S'right. In fairness, we gave him water everyday and a blanket at night. All that other stuff about him getting raped and injected wit heroin is a load of bull.

—So it was yourself that had to feed him, Darren? Tommy Baker asked.

—Well, Heffernan himself gave me the instructions because he knows all kinds a shit about food and chemicals.

—What instructions did Heffernan give you? And in your answer can you say, "Jimmy Heffernan told me"?

—Well, I was told.

—No, Darren, you're supposed to say Jimmy's name at the start, Séamus Dempsey explained.

—Oh yeah. Well Jimmy Heffernan gave me this thing, like a small glass thing and I had to put this thing into his mouth every morning and every evening and squeeze the rubber bit. That's probably where the stuff about heroin came from. But it was vitamins as far as I know. I still have the glass.

—Vitamins? asked Tommy Baker.

—Yeah, I mean he was there for nearly a week and Heffernan didn't want him dying on us or anything. Your man was brought out everyday and asked whether he had changed his mind. I think Heffernan enjoyed it, torturing him, like.

—How d'ye mean, Darren?

—Well, you work it out, Tommy. Heffernan could have got him to change his mind really quickly if he'd a wanted to. Making an example, he was. But he likes that stuff too. Here,

I'm gonna have another smoke if that's okay? And some water, please? All this talking.

Once Darren Bulger had begun another cigarette and drunk two glasses of water, he explained how Jimmy Heffernan ran many of the large building sites in Dublin.

—It isn't just the labour. He also makes sure he gets the cleaning contracts, and listen to this, he puts cameras in the penthouse suites. Or that's what I've heard.

Tommy Baker glanced at Sitric at this point and his favourite cameraman raised his head from the lens and widened his eyes as a signal of appreciation of what was going into the camera. Darren was on a roll now and would not have stopped even if he had been asked.

—Heffernan takes pictures and recordings of everyone. Or usually he gets someone else to do it. The guy is a genius. He is ten steps ahead. He got great stuff on one of those girl-band singers last year out of that new hotel on the quays. She was shagging three in a bed. Now she owes him one and has to sing at all these new Connolly's clubs that are going to open up.

Darren stopped speaking for a moment to take another drink of water and became conscious of the dead silence in the court and the echo of his own cough. Tommy Baker chose the moment to lean forward and get some more context for his interview.

—What happened to the builder in the end, Darren? Baker asked in the manner of a dog worrying at a bone.

—Well, everybody knows that he released and that the ransom money was recovered but that was all a . . . what do you call it?

—A red herring, a cover for something else, Baker volunteered.

—That's right it was a cover for something else. The man finally gave in when Heffernan showed him some stuff about one of his daughters. One that lives in London. I don't know what it was, but he agreed to take on dem Latvians and give Heffernan a cut on the other jobs on the site. Getting the money back was all over the news, but Heffernan arranged that to cover up the fact that he had your man in his pocket. "Super Goordee and

Empire TV" and all that bollix. Goordee is deh police, Tommy.
That's my point. Heffernan is like a cat playing wit' a mouse. Not
only that. Every other builder got the message as well.

—And what is the message?

—The message is, if Jimmy Heffernan wants something, you
better give it him, because if he can't hurt you he'll hurt your
family, your friends, your cat, your dog. It's like that fella who's
running Wakefields, you know, the one down near the flats.
He's told Spanzo he's not paying the money anymore and he's
got some gorillas in from the north to watch his shop. The plan
is to burn his house and his girlfriend or wife or whatever . . .
hold on, dry as a bone.

—What about the girlfriend?

—The plan is to throw acid over her. He's supposed to be
going off to Africa or something. The Cube's mob have been
listening to his phone.

—Tell the viewers a bit more about this guy called Spanzo,
Darren.

—Spanzo? Spanzo is pure dirt. Heffernan really showed his
true colours putting him in charge of things down here. And the
biggest laugh is that Spanzo is ripping him big time. Running
his own operation from the Italian caff across from the arch. The
real owner, he's called Gatano, or something, which is Italian
obviously. We call him Guitar Boy. Well, he knows but there's
not much he can do right now. He's told me he's going back to
Sicily because Dublin's got too dangerous. Gone mad for drugs
and he doesn't feel safe and he's right. You should see all these
southsiders piling over to get their gear there. I mean nobody
even pretends anymore. Used to be that they would be careful.
You know, park their car near Connolly Station and use a local to
make the approach or even do courier which is how I started with
a DJ from Sandymount and I was only twelve then. I couldn't
believe the money, man. But now they just drive up in their jeeps
and what have ya. If they really hit the snobs over the drugs, the
country would collapse. You should get your cameras on them.
Anyway, Spanzo knows he can do what he wants in that area
around the flats.

—Anyone watching this and listening to you is going to say that you're mad to go on camera and tell us these things?

—Well, like I say, I'm sticking up for Éilis and for little Dessie. It gives me a kind of power over them, if you know what I mean. But come here to me. I am gonna tell ya. Do yez think any of us are gonna get outta this movie alive? No way, man. Let's get this straight. Anyone involved in this, even if it's only making the tea, is going to get a visit. A serious visit. I mean. I have my reasons. But you lot. You're fucking mad to be doing this, in my opinion. My life is over either way. I'm totally bollixed. But youse have good jobs, nice homes . . . why would yer be doin' this?

At that moment, the mobile phone which was in Darren's coat pocket made a quick rapping sound and Darren lifted the receiver to his ear and then made a knifing sign to Tommy Baker.

—Howya, Spanz, wots d'story, bud? said Darren into the phone, winking over at Séamus Dempsey.

When the interview was over, Tommy Baker reviewed his notes, which included a memo to contact Father McCartan urgently about the manager at Wakefields. Baker also gave instructions to Darren about making contact with him shortly before the film was due to be broadcast and that under no circumstances should anyone be told that he had done the interview. A stricture which included Darren's drug counsellor He should also continue his activities at the arch and just try to be as normal as possible.

—No problem, Tommy, it was actually easier than I thought.

—Really, why is that?

—Well, I expected some kinda Henry type. You know, a stuck up southsider, but then you walked in. I mean to be honest, I thought you were a caretaker in this gaff, and you look like you had a late night last night. That made things easier.

—It's an ill wind.

—Ya wha'?

—It's an expression, you know. It would be a bad wind that didn't help at least one person, even if it's annoying everybody else. In this case me.

—Oh yeah, right . . . course.

Doomed as he felt he was, Darren Bulger refused Tommy Baker's urgent advice that he leave in the crew van instead of just walking home. Like he wanted what he knew was coming to happen quickly. Happy that he had left a bomb under Heffernan's empire.

And so it seemed to be in his crossed stars that as he left the vicinity of the handball alley, a car passed by which was being driven by none other than Frankie Byrne, who was returning from an errand for his mother. He'd promised his mother that he would pick up some of the heavy shopping, like spuds and washing powder, before going to London that weekend with Finn Dempsey. Frankie drove up the road, then turned the car at a junction. Waited for one minute, which he knew by counting sixty to himself out loud, and then drove the car back up the road he had just come from. There he definitely saw Darren Bulger. This time fishing for change as he entered a phone box. Frankie slowing to watch what Darren was doing then getting a start when a motorist beeped from behind. Frankie zooming off. His brain in overdrive.

Frankie got to wondering why Darren Bulger was anywhere near St Uinsionn's handball alley. The more Frankie wondered, the more Jimmy Heffernan's words came back to him about ready cash being always available if Frankie could tell him anything at all about what the Dempseys were up to. Lights, the new iPhone, some good Charlie in London in a high-class swingers or lap place. All danced into his mind.

Anything at all, Heffernan had said, even if he thought it was useless information. Frankie had been amazed on opening a bulky envelope, which had been given to him by Spanzo after his help over Finn, to find that it contained one thousand euros in hundred-euro notes. Spanzo was a person who made him physically sick with fear but the thrill of the money and being somehow involved in a secret intrigue more than compensated for the extreme angst of having to deal with Spanzo. When Frankie got back to his house, he walked over to Mario's Café and was told that Spanzo was in the upstairs dining area. He ascended the stairs and as quickly as possible told Spanzo that Jimmy Heffernan might want to ring him about something.

—What's it about, Frankie?

Frankie Byrne was already on his way down the stairs and called back that he just needed a word with Jimmy. Frankie was so eager to get out of the café that he bumped into the edge of a table, sending cups, cutlery and a salt cellar crashing to the floor.

The Waking West

JAMES TIERNEY HEARS it in his half waking. The weight and massiveness of the West. Atlas carrying the mighty and profound mountains, the soaring stacks and the pounding waves. The wide Shannon pushing the world forward. Turning in his hotel bed and scenting the rushing peaty-brown water of the Lower Corrib, the salmon races, vital, vibrant, deeply felt water crashing, cascading down through the Galway City rapids, below the bridge, and past the Spanish Arch, rushing out to meet Galway Bay and the mute, ephemeral swans holding watch on the other bank in that half-light which transforms grass to purple and overpurple, the swans to Children of Lir.

Flaccid Dublin with its flat accent and the pathetic trickle that is Dublin's river and the men in their nonbelief and nonamaze, turned into themselves facing the pond of the Irish Sea, only a fool's leap to England, the land where cynicism is an art form. Dreary Dublin of Lilliput.

James Tierney lying in his bed thinking. It is six o'clock in the morning and he is wide awake thinking. His usual dawn-breaking circumstance, but well rested, not needing sleep, just needing to think. He doesn't want to be in Dublin, but needs Dublin, and Dublin needs him. He could have gone home to Loughrea for this filming trip but preferred a hotel in Athlone. Space to think, to read, to ponder. His work on the water-pollution story in the West was almost complete, but Andrew Mendoza wanted one more silage story, and he had found a great one up near

Headford. But that wasn't what he was thinking about. He was thinking about Éilis and Tommy Baker. No not even that.

The old man he had met. The kindly old man telling of the clearing of the village like it was a natural event. A thing natural to Ireland and all the Famine souls walking for all eternity. In from Connemara, from Clare and Tipperary, to join hands with Galway East and Offaly, Roscommon and Mayo and on and on into the future and no one would speak, became tongue-tied because of it, lost their language and points of reference, dropping in the ditches and eating the tough grasses of all the depopulated land, till their bowels distended and the yellow shit ran from them into pools of dysentery in a land where fish still swam, deer were stalked, and grain was sent to England. Why were there no films about Galway East?

Tommy Baker had said that the Éilis story was too early for him but it was neither too early nor too late. Being a hurler from Loughrea, where your head was stitched at the side of the pitch and the biggest battle you would ever face was the head-to-head against New Inn, An Cnoc Breac, Knockbrack—Jimmy Heffernan was child's play.

But I want the job because I want books. Dublin means a proper desk and the wherewithal to release the souls from the torment. With each prayer, poem, film, book, one more set free from purgatory, the purgatory of silence and shame and I want Ronagh. Want Ronagh to be with me on this Odyssey. Because she is soft and gentle and he needed her urgently now. And here was the difference between him and Tommy Baker. Tommy wanted to expose hypocrisy from wherever it came, but it was no freedom crusade. Yet for James Tierney all is political. He didn't want to expose fat cats and drug barons, he wanted to tear their houses down, purge the land, the flaccid, impotent, and defructed soil of the mind so that they could all think and speak again. Remember what they had forgotten. No use carrying that news back to yourself. Carry the good news to the good people. For the sake of that old man.

Éilis Gone

JIMMY HEFFERNAN QUIETLY replaces the shortwave receiver into its container and sits back in his chair. The plush chair that swivels and sits high and from which he doth pronounce *ex cathedra*. The news about Darren Bulger does not surprise him. He had seen the gap.

Well, Darren knew the rules when he joined up and now Darren was going to have to pay the exit fee. Frankie would have to go as well. Just in case. Heffernan clacks his pearl-white teeth with his pen. It was time to begin pulling his strings at Empire Television. Pierce Beaumont needed to be brought into the fray. The process of tidying things up before his departure was pleasing to him. He would call Tommy Baker again. Baker, he knew, would be expecting it.

Heffernan then walked into his study and looked at his Vermeer. No. He would not think of her, but he would think of the image. The ideal of her, which he could still have. All the press, all the world and the gangsters of New York bowled over by it. His Donna, all that *bella figura*. The conjured image. No, she could not hide from what was expected of her. What he needed. The image. His cachet. The only thing that made him big.

Finn Dempsey laughed and shrugged his big shoulders and told his parents that he would ring Éilis later in the day. Finn's brother Séamus muttered darkly into his cornflakes and Finn threw a handball at Séamus's head which he caught without even looking up from his breakfast bowl.

—That Kwai Chang or whatever it's called has definitely speeded up your reactions, our Séamus, fair play to ya.

—Wing Chun. And you watch now, Finn. When you come back from London, I'll play you a challenge match at the alley and whip your ass.

Finn Dempsey sighed theatrically.

—Dream on, Séamus. Dream on.

Finn's mother entered the living room with porridge for the younger children and a cooked breakfast for Finn.

—Have you started getting your things ready for Saturday, Finn?

—Yeah, and it's a real bummer. I started packing early because meself and Éilis were supposed to be going for a meal tomorrow night and I'm coaching some young fellas on Friday morning. Me last few days in Dublin and now she's up in the Gaeltacht.

Mary Dempsey ruffled Finn's hair and then pulled his ear.

—Well, the first thing you do is give Éilis a ring and tell her you'll be over to see her when you get your first free weekend.

—Well, what we'll do is, Ma . . . Éilis comes up to Dublin all excited to see me and then we go and get that Chinese in the Palace that we had promised ourselves, and while I am saying that, Ma . . . sure, me and Éilis may as well shack up seein' as how . . .

Finn Dempsey never got any further with his scandalous suggestion as his mother gave him another far less playful tug of the hair. And, as is the way with younger children who delight in hearing anything to do with matters of romance or chocolate, Denis and Roisín drew in their breath whilst they waited to see what they would hear next.

—What's "shack up," Mammy? asked Denis, his mouth the shape of awe.

—Hold your tongue, Denis, and finish your porridge, and Finn, you can forget about coming here whenever it is you get some leave from work. You'll need to go and see Éilis.

—Yeah and Éilis can come to Dublin. She'll be only too delighted to get away from the torture of living down there in the middle of nowhere.

—Finn, Éilis can't be coming up and down to Dublin all the time. The arrangement is, according to Father McCartan, that she stays up there full-time on account of her nerves. Living in them flats. I don't know. Would slaughter anyone's nerves.

—Ah, Ma, would you stop with her nerves, you have obviously never done that trip to Gweedore. It's a horror movie. So I'm supposed to get off a plane after weeks of hard graft and then get on a bus. You get to Letterkenny and you think you're finally making progress, but no, after Letterkenny there's another hour and a half of misery because this luxury coach has to go all round the coastline of the second biggest county in Ireland! I don't think so.

—Well it's about time you learned to drive, Finn.

—I would, Séamus interjected.

He looked directly into Finn's eyes and then his face began to colour like a temperature.

—You would what, Séamus?

—What I mean is, Finn, if I had a girl like Éilis, I would walk to Donegal to see her. *Tá tú leisciúil.*

—*Níl mé leisciúil ar bhealach ar bith*, Séamus. It's just Donegal. I mean the Gaeltacht. It's not like Ireland at all.

Mrs Dempsey put her head slightly to one side and her hand to her face. Always a sign that she was going to say something heartfelt.

—Finn, if your father could hear you. It's lucky he's at work. That's where he learned his Irish, in Donegal, and we used to go there every year when we were first married.

—Ma, I know it's got a lot of meaning for you and Da, but there where Éilis is they're still pretending Irish is a living language when in truth it's dead as a dodo.

Only Mrs Dempsey saw how her son Séamus's brow knitted and darkened at Finn's words. Jaw flinching like some shark she never knew existed.

—*Níl an Ghaeilge marbh*, Finn. It's not dead, said Séamus.

—Séamie, the language is dead. And the sooner we all understand that the better. It's a waste of time and money. Irish is gone for good and we all have to get over it.

Séamus rose from the table without saying another word and his breakfast half-eaten. A silence then emerged between Finn and his mother

—Ma, our Séamus. He's just way too serious for his own good. Everything's life and death to him.

—Yes, and your father and I have spoken to him about that, but there's the opposite problem with you.

—Me? I don't have any problems. I'm a happy person. You know that.

—Finn. You very often give the impression of just not being bothered. I mean, there's Éilis gone off to Donegal and you've barely mentioned it.

—To be honest we're taking a bit of a break from each other. Éilis has issues. As we both know.

—Jesus, would you listen to the man of the world! The way kids talk about so-called relationships these days, as if they're all experts.

—Mother. I'm not a kid. I'm eighteen years of age and do you know what? I can't wait to get away from Ireland. Get a bit of work. Have a laugh. Do normal things. Ireland is a head wreck of a place.

Heffernan parks his jeep in the basement car park at Connolly's Wine Bar. A flunky offers him one of the hot towels that were kept permanently in his private downstairs bathroom area. But he doesn't hear anything. Heffernan then asks what the flunky wanted and takes the towel perfunctorily—masks his face in the damp heat, but no relief. All he feels, sees is his walk over to a payphone where he called Éilis's home. Bernice Devanney answering the phone.

—*She is not here, Jimmy.*

—*Did she stay at the Dempseys?*

—*Well, she wouldn't normally. And Jimmy, all her things have gone.*

—*What do you mean her things have gone?*

—*Well, her room has been cleared out. Don't know who did that. We must have been asleep. Somebody saw them weirdos hanging around as well. Them ones in long coats. I've tried the Devanneys,*

*but they moved from Gweedore to Letterkenny years ago. So there's
no guarantee that's where she is . . . Hello? Hello, Jimmy?*

*Heffernan holding the hot towel to his face to mask his grinding
cheekbones and white hot anger. The flunky taking two paces back
and waiting.*

When two of the Cube's henchmen picked Darren Bulger up, he
made not even a pretence at resistance. Smiled simply. Then simply asked for a cigarette, for which cheek he was smacked across
the mouth with a knuckle-duster. He was taken to a disused
warehouse on the South Circular Road. Constant noise of traffic.
Constant building noises from a site next door. Cock sucker.

Tables Turning, Turning Walls, Stairs Revolving

LEGALLY, TOMMY BAKER was obliged to approach Jimmy Heffernan, or his representatives, and offer him a chance to respond to the accusations that were being made in his film by the likes of Father McCartan, Terence Gregory, and far more explosively by Darren Bulger. But then, the rules stated that if there were an overwhelming case for subterfuge, where the alleged crimes being investigated were so great, all such niceties could be dispensed with. But this derogation from accepted journalistic practise usually only applied to stories of national or international importance—the running of government and so on.

Tommy Baker did both a sensible and a stupid thing at one and the same time. He privately approached Joseph Cullinane to ask for permission to secretly film Heffernan in his office, which he knew would probably happen upstairs in the rooms above the Connolly's nightclub. Cullinane was aware of Baker's investigation, partly because he had already approved secret filming at the arch near Star of the Sea flats. Cullinane signed the form for the secret filming of Heffernan after first speaking to Andrew Mendoza. He, grave in voice and manner when advising Tommy to tread with great care.

But uncare is what Tommy does next. Tommy Baker does not tell anyone that he was set to meet Heffernan on his own at an appointed hour that very night. So nobody knows where Baker is bound. Not only on his own, launched way out into uncharted space, but also carrying a recording device concealed behind a fake button on his jacket. Heffernan had rung Tommy several

times, telling him straight out that he knew what he was up to
and that it was probably best if they had a chat before Tommy
did anything "foolish or rash," something he might live to regret,
and no, that wasn't a physical threat. Would Jimmy Heffernan
be so foolish as to issue physical threats? he asked Tommy.

On the third phone call, Baker accepted the challenge. Daniel
in the lions' den. Baker's calculation was that Heffernan would
not dare to physically hurt him. Heffernan said that he would
be told the precise time of the meeting very shortly.

Some need of Baker's to personally confront Heffernan. To
look him in the eye and let him know that the whole world was
not in his pocket—that there would always be guardians of pro-
bity and justice. That, for Tommy Baker, was the inviolate com-
pact that journalism had with society. To overcome personal fear
to confront an untruth that had become hard currency. Within
an hour he learned that the meeting was set for seven p.m. That
was the hard fact of the matter.

Jimmy Heffernan's office was on the fifth and top floor of
the Edwardian building in which Connolly's bar was housed.
Heffernan's first action on locking the door leading onto the
outside corridor with a remote control was to go to a safe-deposit
box which was disguised as a light fitting on a wall. Here, he
extracted a folder containing pictures with text captions at the
bottom. Then he closed the heavy door of the safe, drilling the
safety-code dial around to a neutral position. This special safe
was only one feature of an office that owed more to the designs
of a government-style emergency-planning room than a working
office. A room of war. The walls of the office were soundproofed
and contained interior blast shields. There was only one way into
the office, via the armour-plated front door, but there were two
exit doors from the office. One of the exit doors led to the roof
and a helipad via a specially constructed double-lock stair-and-
trapdoor arrangement. The other exit door led onto an emergency evacuation stairwell, which again was completely separate
from the main building.

The office was also remarkable in the fact that there were

no personal computers or telephones to be seen there. Jimmy Heffernan had learned the Mafia rule that these things were sources of entrapment rather than a means of communication. The office, however, was tastefully decorated with pooled lighting, substantial dark-oak bookshelves and, once again, a special print of Vermeer's *The Lacemaker* dominating the wall opposite Heffernan's desk. What he loved was her sheer concentration, her lack of fear, her assumption that she had all the time in the world. A pure heart and soul, a lissom face, finger dexterity and grace. How to keep all that precious but also possess it?

Heffernan moved to his huge desk of black teak, studied the pictures in the folder he had taken from the safe again, and then put them in a drawer. He leaned back in his pilot's chair and closed his eyes, pondering his approach to Baker. No use being coy with him, that wouldn't work, but at the same time don't be too heavy. He might just bite without any coercion whatsoever. What was it again Ziti had said?

—*Listen up, Jimmy. You're a smart guy. Listen to your friend, tu amici. A made guy.*

Z. Z. "Ziti" Falcone.

—*Once you have a secure system in place, Jimmy, you can start to relax. Be polite to people. Dress and eat well. Take in the shows and the theatre. Be seen and liked by the media. Get a nice wife and treat your kids good. Don't take things so personal. You Irish take things so personal. It's not a murder business. It's a cultural and social business. Wise Guys have to take their social responsibilities seriously if they want to prosper and do good deeds.*

The intercom light on Heffernan's desk flashed and he drew the top drawer of the desk, which contained a flat screen showing the movements of people in the corridor outside the office. Heffernan pressed the buzzer that allowed Ned Mulligan and Tommy Baker into the office by deactivating the lock on the security door. Behind Baker's back, Ned gave Heffernan a thumbs-up sign. Ned also brandished a pipe and shook his head behind Baker's back.

—Well, Tommy, I hope you enjoyed the steak. And nice try with the pipe.

As Heffernan rose to shake Tommy Baker's hands, he placed

the envelope containing the pictures back into the folder and handed them to Ned Mulligan.

—I think she's waiting for these, Ned.

—She's just arrived, Jimmy. I'll give them to her right away.

Heffernan pulled a black chair on silver castors up to his desk and motioned for Tommy Baker to be seated.

—This is some place here, Jimmy. I'm impressed. Well, the setup impresses me. I'm about as keen on the name as James Connolly himself would have been.

Jimmy Heffernan surveyed the man in front of him and realised for the first time that Baker's state of health was actually very poor. His face was blotched with the overindulgence of red wine. He showed a vivid facial colouring which was enhanced by an unnaturally white pallor, like set wax. There was also a slight shake in Baker's hands.

—I know, Jimmy, I'm like death warmed up. I'm the dead man walking, I'd say I have five years left, if God spares me that long.

Heffernan realised that Baker's first words were not a fake show of bravado, or warm-up banter for the serious discussion to come. Baker spoke the words he wanted to speak because he had no fear. Or rather, he had conquered his fears. His quick assessment was that something had happened in Tommy Baker's life which had left him reckless, heedless of his own safety. His wife's death in labour perhaps, or his only son's death immediately after. Heffernan looked directly into Tommy Baker's blue eyes where no shake or infirmity could be detected. Tommy Baker looked directly back at Heffernan. Neither man averted his gaze because they were both looking at something beyond the physical object which was before them. Two sorcerers already locked in a metaphysical battle for superiority

—I've got six months to a year before the damage I'm doing to my liver becomes irreversible. My doctor has told me to stop drinking and smoking, and to move to somewhere warm so that I can dry out in a pleasant atmosphere. But sure, where's the craic in the sun and sand without the sangria? At least I'd be able to smoke though. This smoking ban is killing me.

—I hear you were up in Manor Street a fortnight ago, Heffernan said.

—That's right, I was asking some of your old boxing partners what you were like as a child.

—And what was I like?

—Hungry.

—Hungry or angry?

—No, hungry. If you had have been angry you would have been closer to James Connolly than you are now.

—And where am I now?

—I'd say you have made your money, discovered the finer things in life and you want out before the whole thing collapses on you. You are one of the most intelligent criminals I've ever studied.

Not even Jimmy Heffernan could help an intake of breath. It had been a long time since he had been called a criminal.

Tommy Baker involuntarily reached for the cigarettes in his jacket pocket as he sensed that the jousting was about to ensue. Jimmy Heffernan understood Baker's body language and handed him some prize snuff from a side drawer, which contained an assortment of perfumes and tobaccos from around the world. Baker offered a Buddhist salutation in gratitude and inhaled the snuff deeply into his lungs.

—Don't you take notes? Heffernan asked.

—That's what that nice man Mr Behan asked me when he frisked me. I can understand him taking the car-park pass from me, Jimmy, but it wasn't very nice of him to relieve me of my pipe as well. Although this snuff more than makes up for it. As for taking notes, I suppose I'm about as keen on paperwork as you are by the looks of your desk. What have you got for me?

Heffernan looked at Tommy Baker for a length of time that was longer than the journalist was comfortable with. Then he spoke.

—Intelligence appeals to me. It appeals to my better intelligence. It wasn't very intelligent to pull that stroke with the car and annoying Pierce Beaumont, because it annoyed me, and that shows a fault in your analysis of me. Bad move, Tommy. But you can start making up for it now by showing your intelligent side again.

Heffernan then produced another folder from a drawer in the desk. He held the folder across the desk in front of Baker's field of vision.

—I want you to think, Tommy, after I have shown you these. Meeting me has already placed certain obligations upon you. You sought me out and that was a life-changing decision on your part. Of course you knew that anyway. What you have is a need to look the adversary in the eye. The fearless journalist who believes in his noble role as the last defender of the people when everybody else is cowering in fear. It's time now to move on from there.

Baker inhaled more snuff.

—I'm not a man of the people, Jimmy. I just hate hypocrisy from whatever place it arises and especially amongst the rich and powerful like you. That's how I view our role as journalists. Yes, I take risks with many people whom, as you put it Jimmy, I "seek out." As for fearless. I am not without fear. The fact is, your capacity for completely studied generosity and blithe terror petrifies me. But yes, to answer your point, Jimmy. I am known for going into areas where many other journalists can't, or won't, go. That's why you entertained me in the first place. Without wanting to sound too lofty about it, I am one of the few journalists who is willing to stand up to the Power. That thing that the Yanks call the "Man." You are the new Power.

—I think what I have, Heffernan said before correcting himself. The story I want told, can suit both our purposes. You are leaving Ireland in the summer according to my sources and you are looking for a suitable swansong. I think this is it.

Heffernan withdrew a plastic zipper bag containing photographs with typed cards attached to them which identified the persons who appeared in the photographs. Tommy Baker whistled as he studied people whom he knew to be senior police officers and legal dignitaries in various apparently compromising sexual situations with young women and men.

—Why are you showing me these?

—Because I want you to put them on the television.

—Well, it's strong stuff all right, but I am not a sex-lies-and-videotape kind of journalist, which you know from asking around about me. I need something meatier, really.

—I know that, and I can provide that meat.

—How's that? asked Baker, genuinely intrigued.

—I'll give you two people to interview who can reveal things about these gentlemen and their activities in the '70s and '80s. It will make the Donegal Gardaí scandal look like the six o'clock Angelus by comparison.

—Are you talking about what I think you are talking about?

—Heroin.

—Now I am very, very interested.

—Do you know about the Littlejohns? asked Heffernan.

—The two brothers who were spies working for the Brits in the '70s? They robbed banks and worked with certain members of the Garda Síochána to get information on republicans.

—Very good, said Heffernan, but there is a lot more to it than that. I have a tape recording of a senior Garda telling an equally senior colleague about how a gang connected to the Littlejohns brought top-class heroin into the country in the 1970s. This stuff was the business and it was being sold for a song. And that guy there, the one on top of the young man, is one of the Gardaí who helped them to bring it in.

—Two questions. Number one, is at least one of the people that is ready to do an interview describing these events actually a decoy for you? Number two, are you going to give me a copy of the tape of the conversation between the two Guards so that I can analyse it myself?

—Don't start getting ahead of yourself, Tommy. All these things will become clear as long as you agree to my basic approach.

—Which is?

—That there will be no mention of Jimmy Heffernan, and no profile of anyone like Jimmy Heffernan in this film. In other words, that you make a film that solely concentrates on this gang of Garda perverts here in Dublin and their link to bringing this stuff in.

Heffernan pushed the packet of snuff across the table to Tommy Baker and smiled.

—Have some more snuff, Thomas.

—Thanks. So what's in it for you? It can't be your social conscience, because you don't have one.

—See that Garda in the picture there who happens to have a thing about hot young redheads. Girls and boys I mean. Well, he personally went out of his way to block my first big loan from a bank. And this judge with the young fella, he made a big point of embarrassing me at a business function.

—So this is revenge.

—I'm from Buckingham Street and I've fought my way up. They didn't need to do what they did and the only reason they acted like that was because of who I was and where I'm from. End of story.

Baker inhaled more snuff and looked at the books on the shelves and the Vermeer print on the wall. A silence emerged between the pair whilst Baker considered the implications that any deal with Heffernan might have. He was truly excited by the pictures. He had done deals with criminals before but not when the stakes in the gamble were as big as this. It was not quite the story he had set out to do but that kind of thing happened very often. Baker pondered the rumours he had heard about how and why top-grade heroin had come into Dublin in huge amounts from the mid-1970s onwards, but he had never heard it explained, as it were, from the mouth of the Horse.

—I've just noticed that there are no clocks in this room and that this place is probably soundproofed. The sound is all muffled, dead, said Baker, who wished to explore Heffernan a bit more before coming to a decision.

Heffernan ignored the remark.

—It's no skin off my nose, Tommy. I reckoned you might have the balls to do it but I can go elsewhere with it.

—Let me think for a minute, Jimmy. This is a big one.

Heffernan rose from his chair and pushed a button on the

wall to his left and behind his desk. Seconds later, the button began to flash and Heffernan opened a panel on the wall to reveal a dumbwaiter loaded with drinks.

—Now there's a sight for sore eyes, said Baker, are you trying to soften me up?

—I can soften you up anytime I want, Tommy. No, I'm just killing time while I wait for your move. Have your drink and then this meeting is over because I've other more important things to attend to.

—Okay, fair enough. I am willing to enter into a devil's pact with you, Jimmy, on two conditions.

—Which are?

—One, that it is understood that I have no final guarantee that Empire will be happy to show this film. Those nice Dublin 4 executives love salving their middle-class consciences by doing social commentary programmes. It's a bit like pottering about in their gardens in Killiney. They get their hands dirty and break the odd fingernail, but having a go at the Brits they will not do too readily.

—This film will not be about having a go at the Brits. What I want is for those four Gardaí to be shown up for what they have always been. Leave the Provo spiel out of it. That kind of stuff really irritates me. So basically, you can give me no guarantee.

At this point a light began to flash on a panel on Heffernan's desk and he asked to be excused for a moment. Once outside his office, Heffernan pressed a red button on a wall intercom and Ned Behan's voice was heard in the speaker.

—Jimmy, Carmel got the package. Would you mind telling me what was in it because it got some reaction, I can tell ya.

—Where is she now?

—She ran out through the kitchen into the back where the lads have a smoke and someone opened the back gate. She was very distressed by all accounts.

—Strange how women get all wound up at the sight of blood.

—What was in the package, Jimmy? I'd love to know.

—Just Mr Bulger sucking some cock. His own. By the way, Ned.

—Jimmy?

—That thing needs fixing on the stairs.

—Right you are, Jimmy. When?

—About half an hour I'd say. How are the Devanneys.

—Well, himself is half-asleep but she's not missing much.

—It's in the blood, Ned. Remember what I said before.

—I know. Tell her nothing.

Heffernan re-entered his office and Tommy Baker sought to reassure him about the chances of a film being broadcast.

—I can assure you that this stuff is potentially so powerful that they would have to broadcast it. If they refused, there would be a major scandal.

Heffernan poured out a straight Jack Daniel's and placed a bottle of Heineken alongside it.

—What's the second condition? There were two conditions?

Baker winced at the pleasure of his first shot of soft Tennessee fire. It helped to digest the fact that there would be no meeting of minds between himself and Jimmy Heffernan. The fact that he was in serious danger. He raised his glass to Heffernan.

—You are a good listener and you, too, have been doing your homework. Touché.

—Come on, Tommy, don't patronise me. It's Jimmy Heffernan you're talking to now, not some lap-dancing-club owner. You drink in Slattery's in Ranelagh. You start particularly early on Thursdays and Fridays and you stagger home around half one in the morning. Your house is not alarmed and you usually leave the back window open. You must have changed your car recently because you usually drive a mini.

—That MG belonged to my dead wife, God rest her.

—And she was a midget too, and that's why she died in the labour ward delivering your one and only child. Tight bellies, eh. They cause havoc.

Baker felt the earth move and sway beneath him and it was all he could do to stop himself pitching forward onto the floor.

—Do you know, I was prepared for a cut-and-thrust debate about drugs and alcohol. Questions about why and how you started and about this new industry which has you as its head hydra in Ireland and is completely unstoppable. The whole thing fascinates me. But really, I don't give a damn about that. Do you know what I want to know?

—Yes, I do. You are going to ask me something about my feelings. Or lack of feelings.

—At what point exactly did you become so besotted with Éilis Devanney that it began to affect your judgement? Your Empire, even?

Never. Never would Heffernan have believed it. That he would feel a blow like that. A blow he never for a second saw coming.

Baker poured his beer into a glass as Heffernan rose from his desk like a quietly raging lion and began to circle around Baker with his hands in his pockets. The two-tone cut of Heffernan's suit caught the soft light from the wall lighting, and Baker misread his mood for a moment.

—Imagine that power, Mr Investigative Journalist. To be able to decide everything there is to decide about a human being. Does he or she eat or not eat? Sleep or not sleep? Live or not live? I chose to take life on, you have given up. You are a loser and I am a winner.

—And this is what you call winning? Let me tell you something, Mr Heffernan. In our younger days when you and I were growing up, there was a hard man in every pub. Okay, it was a rough kind of justice, but these champions amongst men sorted things out and were usually fair. There are no hard men anymore. The packs of hyenas that you have sent out across this city in their thousands have dragged them down one by one. They are hyenas and you are no more than chief dog.

Standing directly behind Tommy Baker at this point, Heffernan performed facial exercises and stretched at his ease and then began to clap sarcastically as he returned to his desk. Baker continued his tirade regardless of this.

—Now there's a Spanzo in every pub, on every street corner and every estate in the inner city. And you are responsible for that.

Well done, Mister Cool, Suave, and Sophisticated.

Heffernan placed his head to one side and looked at Baker in the manner of a bored Caesar.

—You have a death wish don't you? Heffernan said.

—Not just yet.

—Do you understand that you will make the film I want you to make or you won't be making any film at all? You are way out of your depth.

Heffernan watched the anger rising in Tommy Baker's demeanour and this amused him. He looked briskly at his watch like a psychiatrist wishing to be rid of a bothersome patient.

—Consider this meeting over and good luck, Mr Baker, because you are going to need it.

—You are a body snatcher and Éilis is the real target, not me.

Heffernan's countenance darkened to the colour of black blood at this remark.

—It's no good, is it? Unless you bend me to your will. Unless you break me. Well, I can tell you for nothing that I am so broken already that I cannot break anymore and that is your big problem. Bad move, Jimmy boy.

Baker wanted to spit the remains of the snuff in his mouth onto the floor, but this great urge was countermanded by an even greater urge to stay alive. For he saw that Heffernan was white with anger. The door on the side of the room farthest away from the front door gave an ominous click. Tommy Baker bolted the last of the Jack Daniel's down his throat and stood up, preferring to meet what was coming next head-on. At the very least, he knew he would not be leaving the building the way he came in. His hope was that he would still be able to drive his beloved MG out of Connolly's underground car park.

Baker's voice shook as he spoke.

—There will always be someone out there who will stand up to evil Jimmy, and you are evil. You will get what's coming to you.

Heffernan rose now and motioned for Baker to move towards the side door. There was no urgency in his voice when he spoke.

—You are a stupid, stupid man. I offered you something on a plate but you are a like an old wreck that got left behind when the world moved on. Now you face extinction. Drugs, crime, corruption, they are here to stay. Get over it. Is it not better that someone like me is running the show?

—If anything happens to me, or the people in my film. I have another film all ready to run. I really enjoyed putting it together and my friends are going to put it on the internet for me. It's all about you.

Heffernan shoved Baker through the door where a pair of large hands grabbed his small frame from behind. There were at least two men in the passage other than Heffernan, Baker was sure of this.

—This man is gagging for a drink, boys, and he is very partial to Jack Daniel's. Are they ready down below?

—Just waiting for the shout, Mr Heffernan.

Heffernan stepped into the half-light which spilled from the door leading back into his office, so that one side of his face was visible to Tommy Baker and the rest was completely black.

—This is lesson number one, Mr Baker. If you learn your lesson and understand that I run this town then you might just survive long enough to get the fuck out of this town. There won't be another lesson. The next step for you is the real snuff movie.

Everything went black as the door eased back into place with a quiet hiss. Baker then found himself being bodily lifted then sailing through the air down a dark stairwell until he was slammed onto the floor with a force that drove every breath of air from his body. He was then held down over some kind of sheet and the neck of a bottle was forced into his mouth. He writhed and tried to kick but it was no good. There was a ton weight on his ribs and chest and he felt something give and there was a loud crack. He gagged as what he judged subsequently to have been half a bottle of Jack Daniel's was poured into his throat. His great fear was that he was going to drown but the hands which were holding on to him allowed him the odd gasp of air before he passed out. His arm and collarbone were broken in the fall that resulted from his being thrown again. This time, down the last flight of concrete stairs. His ribs on his right side had been crushed by a knee that had eighteen stone of weight behind it. What Baker didn't know was that he was then thrown like a rag doll into a van and transported to a side lane running off Pearse Street, where two prostitutes had been told to look after him.

Baker woke up in a cold of vomit, his face and hair in a pool of mire. Two women standing over him. One half-dressed. They tried to lift him to his feet and Baker was aware of flashes from a camera.

—Are you some kind of celebrity? one of the girls enquired of him. Are you looking for more business, love? As more flashes happened, two Garda officers hove into view.

—Am I being arrested? Baker asked as he bent over in pain and got sick again.

The bigger of the two Gardaí stood back from him and turned his face away in disgust. Both were wearing blue protective surgical gloves

—No you are not being arrested but you probably should be. We got reports from a bar round the corner that you had been ejected for being drunk and trying to light a fag on the premises.

—Is that true?

The smaller police officer took a firm hold of Baker's damaged arm at that point and Baker shrieked in pain.

The Garda shoved Baker away from him.

—Jesus, how much have you had today? You are stinking with it!

—Guard, my name is Tommy Baker. I work for Empire Television and I badly need an ambulance. I think my arm and collarbone are broken, as well as my ribs. Ah, Jesus.

Baker used his good arm to check whether he still had the snuff that Heffernan had given to him. Then he remembered the camera on his jacket. He said a prayer to St. Jude that there was usable footage in the camera. Then he passed out again, but not before thanking God that he no wife had. Not in this life anyway.

After being patched up and arm-slung at the hospital, Tommy Baker used his free hand and arm to sift through the debris of what was once his favourite room in his house in Ranelagh. He had lived there for nearly twenty years. The residual throbbing pain in his upper arm was as nothing to the pain caused by looking at the destruction of his home. His study had always been a place of calm and reflection for him. He even imagined that he craved the drink less whilst working or reading there. There were papers and old video cassettes strewn everywhere, all apparently stamped on or hammered to smithereens. All his paintings and works of art had been torn, slashed, or smashed. The thieves had obviously been looking for one particular thing and had left a trail of deliberate destruction as they moved from room to room. There was a smell like petrol that seemed to come from an attempt to set fire to the carpet, which was scorched and blackened around his free-standing lamp. Jimmy Heffernan obviously now knew that their meeting had been recorded.

Baker scanned the shelves of his prized book collection; row upon row of books gathered together after years of collecting, reading, digesting. At least they were untouched. He had laughed and cried with them and had drunk gallons of lovely wines in their company. Many of them had been bought whilst he had been abroad on holiday with Susan, his deceased wife. He felt a pang of pain and longing for a fortifying glass of blood-dark Shiraz and wondered when and where he would drink again. He had lost another friend, temporarily at least. He was amazed that his withdrawal symptoms were not far worse, but then he also knew that it was the imminent danger and his fierce desire to bring down Jimmy Heffernan that were keeping him on the straight line. But what about after that? One day at a time. These thoughts reminded him that he was supposed to call his day counsellor at John of Gods and arrange a counselling session.

He offered a silent prayer in gratitude that there was no trace in his study of the red dye which had been thrown about the rest of the house. The fools had obviously believed that his kitchen implements, family photos, top-of-the-range television, and expensive audio equipment were more precious to him than his books. This meant that Heffernan himself had not been here to supervise the destruction. He would have known. Baker tried to remember the name of Heffernan's sidekick who owned a wine bar in nearby Rathmines as he picked one of Fyodor Dostoevsky's works down from a shelf. The "Cube," that was it. A big, fat bear of a man. The type of character who would grace the pages of a novel by Dostoevsky.

As he moved into the kitchen, Baker imagined the Cube dressed in Russian Cossack gear, all greasy stubble, watching one of his staff doling kvass out of a tank from where he sat at a table drinking vodka and occasionally consulting a ledger book to check the loan payments that were due for collection. It was the Cube's underlings who had done this. Fortunately for Baker's frame of mind, the only damage to his much-loved coffee cafetière and espresso set was a trace of red dye, but otherwise they stood unbowed amongst the carnage in the kitchen. Baker refused all thoughts of looking at his wine rack whilst quickly downing one strong espresso and taking the next one back into his study.

Once back in the study, he brought the Dostoevsky book to his desk and browsed through the pages, some of which he had underlined lightly with a pencil. As he settled to read, he wondered about the possible return of Heffernan's hoodlums, but dismissed the thought. They would wait until the Guards had completed their futile exercise in note-taking before doing something else. The next time, they would come straight for him. A car or house alarm was blaring somewhere in the distance. The sound of modern Ireland. He rose, closed the door to the study, and opened the window to his garden, where a convocation of birds twittered over the stale bread he had thrown onto the grass. His thoughts returned to the Cube and Dostoevsky as a text message flashed on his mobile. A message from Sitric to tell him that the button had worked. Good vision and audio for the most part. Baker smiled grimly and switched the phone off so that he could concentrate on his book. Yes Heffernan almost certainly would see this same message, but the footage was home and dry. He had done good. The coming battle with his bosses at Empire could wait until the afternoon. Everything was all right and was not all right.

In fairness to Dostoevsky, Baker mused, the Cube would have been presented in a very rounded way, and not just because of the expanse of his girth. Fyodor Dostoevsky was always scrupulously generous to his characters, no matter how badly they behaved. He almost always tried to give a background to their actions so that they could achieve at least a modicum of sympathy from the reader. That kvass seller and Cube look-alike, say, would have been shown to have come from a desperately poor background and committed fratricide, but only to protect his mother from an assault by one of his drunken brothers. Dostoevsky's gift was to present an incredible panoply of characters nearly all of whom had at least some redeeming features, and it was they and their souls which suffered most from their own actions. The book in Baker's hand, *The House of the Dead*, which Dostoevsky wrote following his experiences in a Siberian prison camp, offered some perfect examples of this. He turned to a page where one of his favourite passages from Dostoevsky was underlined and immediately thought of Jimmy Heffernan. The passage literally wrestled with a bloodthirsty tiger. A tyrant who became an executioner, inured to the taste of blood and the infliction of pain on his fellow humans. A tyrant, furthermore, whom society celebrated and worshipped. What was the effect on the tyrant himself and on society?

There are people like tigers, who thirst for blood to lick. Whoever has once experienced this power, this unlimited mastery over the body, blood, and spirit of another human being, his brother according to the law of Christ; whoever has experienced this control and this complete freedom to degrade, in the most humiliating fashion, another creature made in God's image, will quite unconsciously lose control of his own feelings . . . What is more, the example, the possibility of such intransigence has a contagious effect upon the whole of society: such power is a temptation.

It seemed to Tommy Baker that Dostoevsky believed that, under certain circumstances which were peculiar to each individual, all human beings were capable of becoming tyrants and that these individuals would pay a price for their actions, just as society would pay a price for its adoration of them. This was something he, too, accepted. Jimmy Heffernan would pay a price, somewhere, someday, for his actions, even though he himself would laugh at the idea. Irish society, Baker had decided, was already paying a price for applauding and cheering its very executioner.

He got up from his chair and watched the birds in the garden cheerfully disputing what little bread was left on the ground. He left the study and put just enough water into a shallow plastic bowl so that the birds could stand in the bowl with ease. As he took the bowl to the garden he realised to his utter joy that his free hand was not shaking. He left the bowl under his study window and retreated to his room of books to watch the sparrows and tits nervously inspecting the bowl of water and the area around it for any sign of humans or cats. Finally, after many dashes, squabbles, and panics, the first bird hopped into the water.

Baker returned the Dostoevsky book to its place on the shelf and went back to the window, scaring the birds away as he did so. He wondered what he himself believed and resolved to commit his thoughts to paper during his convalescence from the drink, which he suddenly euphorically hoped would last the rest of his life. He lifted a landscape print by Cézanne, *Mont Sainte-Victoire*, from the floor where it lay in a forlorn state. The frame was broken and shards of glass had scratched the picture. The glass had been driven into the picture by a boot which had left the imprint of a sole on it. He made a mental note to alert the Guards to this fact and then carefully removed the remnants of the picture from its frame. He and his wife had often visited the area around Mont Sainte-Victoire, and Cézanne was one of the artists who most inspired him to carry on. What about writers? What about the beliefs of writers? Dostoevsky believed that an overarching spiritual framework, obviously Russian Orthodox in his case, was necessary for man to able to live with his fellow man. Left to simple economic materialism, humankind would degenerate and succumb to its myriad forms of inherent weaknesses—of the Flesh, the World, or the Devil. Here Dostoevsky had not only flashed a warning message to the world of the totalitarianism that was to come, but also to the world's rich elite that they could not continue to tyrannise and exploit the poor with impunity. Ibsen would probably point to the hypocrisy that lay behind the bourgeois mask and call for utter honesty in all human relations, an impossible task. What about James Joyce? Joyce had thrown his hands up with the Irish after offering them a perfect model for modern relationships and reconciliation in Leopold and Molly Bloom. He withdrew his genius from the stage in a fit of pique and retreated from the people into the land of *Finnegans Wake*. A process continued by Beckett who contrived to set riddles on almost blank canvases seen through revolving doors.

Baker threw his summer jacket over his shoulder and packed a small bag of clothes and an even smaller bag of books. Waves of pain now. His choice of books was important as he realised that he would probably never see his house again.

The books he chose to have with him were Dostoevsky's *Brothers Karamazov*, Shakespeare's *Hamlet*, and Homer's *Wrath of Achilles: The Iliad*. All three books sought to engage with their audience, to tell them a wonderful story which displayed life in all its tragedy and glory, and yet at the same time sought to raise the most fundamental of human questions; how families might live together, how war might be avoided, and the simple beauty that life presented to us everyday if we only cared to look.

As Tommy Baker walked out of his home for the last time, he noted to himself that few writers, and certainly not many average documentary makers, had ever managed to change the course of history. Writers were about as influential as soccer players in that regard. However, if one person had been moved to tears when looking at, say, a still life by Cézanne, or after reading a poem by W. B. Yeats, or maybe roaring in laughter because of the wit of Myles na gCopaleen, well, that work had shifted the very heavens for the good. Tommy Baker wanted just one person, just one viewer, to change his or her mind about the likes of Jimmy Heffernan and the spectre of amoral greed that was stalking the land. Encouraged by these thoughts, he caught a taxi to Empire Television and on the way there resolved to do an interview with Éilis Devanney. All roads in the story about the flats and Jimmy Heffernan seemed to lead to Éilis's door. She was the light, Heffernan the dark. There was no point in scruples anymore. All the forces for good had to be brought into play.

Gemma is her name. My psychotherapist. Jemima actually. Goes with Killiney. There's been some switch in her though. A change that made her a different person. Just a person. Think she worked out that I wasn't self-harming before. She's smart. I'll give her that. And must have gone home and worked some of it out for herself, seeing as I won't engage with them. Reassure them. Make them think they make a difference. Ease their consciences at the money, kudos, and status they have. She's dying to know about Heffernan. But I'll deal with that.

—Éilis, can you tell me about that photo of you and this Jimmy Heffernan person?

—He's my cousin and asked me to show up. That's it.

—But you were in the newspapers. Standing next to him.

—Blank.

—Were you on drugs at the time?

—Blank.

—Were you paid for the, ahm, "appearance"?

—No. He was.

—Heh, heh. He was?

—Yes, my cousin Jimmy.

—Éilis, why did you leave Donegal? after all we did to set up the move, arrange new counselling, etc. Father McCartan, the Gardaí, everybody pulled strings.

—Blank.

—Éilis. We . . .We've no choice now but to commit. Get you better We can't have you slashing your wrists. You're clearly also a danger to others.

—What stage are you at in your own therapy, Jemima?

Some Kind of Valediction

AFTER THE INEVITABLE tabloid stories about Tommy Baker (or about "veteran Empire journalist's shocking descent into the gutter" as it was described, he all "drunk, dishevelled, and consorting with prostitutes"), and following a long conversation between Baker and Joseph Cullinane, Empire Television had decided to refrain from issuing a statement on the affair. Hoping the issue would just be faded away by other sensations involving much bigger celebrities in the 24/7 rolling sensation train that passed for journalism. However, Empire's board of governors had asked to be briefed on the issue, and it was clear to all that it was going to need "managing." There was also a strengthening view at board level that Cullinane's imminent retirement couldn't come too soon. Cullinane, it was being whispered, was too soft, not suited to these cutting, thrusting times, and the much more "hardball" Diarmuid Farrelly was viewed as favourite to replace him.

No surprise, then, that Baker's arrival back at Empire two days after his "downfall" caused a stir. Phones were lifted on sight of him in the canteen, heads dipped to consort, people moved to windows to watch his progress from the canteen to senior-management offices. Clearly a broken man, pronounced the shaking, pitying heads.

James Tierney, meanwhile, had instructed Ronagh Durkin to have her friends right across Empire contact her the moment any of them saw Tommy, and then for her to ring him, as Baker had clearly abandoned his mobile phone. This was not, James said, a polite request but a strict order, as he needed a serious conversation with Tommy Baker before he disappeared on him again. So Ronagh had laughed, told James he tickled her with his seriousness, but promised the Great Master that she would do his bidding.

Tommy Baker on his way to a meeting with Myles Fitzgerald in the Special Investigations offices. Walking, limping, feeling ridiculous, a gimp struggling down the long first-floor corridor which housed various technical areas and also Empire TV's News and Current Affairs department. Special Investigations at the far end. Hating his sling, himself, his existence, searching vainly for his inveterate stubbornness. Trying to get angry with Heffernan again, but failing. Then thinking of the circling vultures like Diarmuid Farrelly, Rosie Boylan, Pierce Beaumont, all the ones who wanted to turn Empire into one long lifestyle show with news as an afterthought, all soundbites and PR driven. So that they themselves would never feel challenged or remember the conscience they once had. A private-broadcast station serving the Dublin 4 of the vapidly decorated middle-class mind. Feels his anger returning with grim satisfaction.

From the opposite end of the fully carpeted corridor, Baker sees a fellow producer/director, as they liked to call themselves at Empire. Baker had never worked directly with this person but they had both worked for Empire for many years. Under his flopping front curl of hair, Baker watched the man's body language as they slowly approached each other. The man seemed to see something tremendously interesting in the thread of the brown carpet. There was also apparently a fly buzzing at his head. Or at least this was his demeanour as he constantly followed the flight of something in the airspace immediately above him. A grown-up, educated person busying himself with any number of distractions in order to avoid having to look at a colleague. You would want to look at a colleague if he were in the state Baker was in. But no.

Baker born and reared in the Coombe. Here it had been, and still was, the norm to offer a greeting when meeting another person on the street. Regardless of whether the people involved knew each other or not. Now Baker is angry.

—Hello, Brian.

—Oh, Tommy! Hi there. How are you? Still causing trouble, I hear.

—Well, isn't that what we get paid so well for, Brian?

Producer/Director Brian had already moved a yard away from Baker and was forced to make a half-turn as he laughed somewhat nervously at Baker's remark.

—Ha, ha, Tommy. You'll never change.

Swinging his head slowly round, Baker stopped and thought. Wanted to smoke, drink, think. Be positive. Don't give in. Not to cowardice. Not to Heffernan infecting society with goons on street corners, every town and street with hoodlums ready to do his bidding, goons in businesses and in the very echelons of the state.

He pushes on. Has to admit that Myles Fitzgerald, the executive producer of Special Investigations at Empire, could not have been classed as having the same attributes as the new male producers, like air-head Brian. Fitzgerald was too long in the tooth, and too independently minded, to be lumped in with a group he himself had described as a bunch of male eunuchs. Fitzgerald, however, had always had a turbulent and fractious relationship with him. A Fine Gael man through and through, saved by basic decency and a commitment to old-fashioned journalism. Stop, drink-think again. Starting to forget his ailments. Anger buzzing now at what Heffernan had said about his wife, Gráinne, and their child. Their child. Their poor child. Who should have survived. If only he had survived—little Lorcan. Gráinne had always loved that name. If Lorcan had only.

Myles Fitzgerald had some important decisions to make regarding Baker's film about Jimmy Heffernan. At the meeting which was just about due to start, Baker was going to request an extra fortnight's filming to cover the new and explosive narrative provided by Darren Bulger. He also wanted permission to take the film crew to Gaoth Dobhair in order to do an interview with

Éilis Devanney. James Tierney had been right all along. Baker
was just about to enter Fitzgerald's private office, where the meeting was scheduled to take place, when Fitzgerald popped his
head out of the general meeting room and called out to him.

—Ah, Baker. Late as usual. We're having a prior-meeting
meeting. Get yourself in here.

Tommy Baker did not appreciate being addressed as Baker. It
was obvious that Fitzgerald was behaving with a somewhat justi-
fied anger about the pictures which had been splashed across the
tabloids. But then, Baker had a better case for grievance over the
fact that Fitzgerald had said that he was late. He took the e-mail
from his jacket pocket which contained the details of the meeting. This had been sent to him by Eileen Brennan, Fitzgerald's
personal secretary, and someone whom Tommy trusted and
indeed had come to love somehow. In fact, there had been a
time after his wife's death in that long, lonely, long ago when it
seemed that he and Eileen might become attached, but the booze
had put an end to that. The booze. The recklessness. His leap into
save-the-world, firefighting oblivion and all the candles burned
at both ends till only his stumps were left. Recklessness like he
wanted to die and take everyone and everything with him. But
then that day Eileen came to collect him in the pub. How did
that happen? How was Eileen in that pub? So early in the day?
He had never asked. Drove him home. Even ordered a pizza for
him and watched him eat a slice. Didn't try to take two. Wolfed
three. Hovered, hoovered, fussed.

Eileen Brennan's e-mail confirmed Baker's own view that he
was actually twenty minutes early for the meeting. He pushed at
the door which had been partially closed by his retreating boss.

Up to that point, Baker had not worried about what others
would think of his physical appearance. His arm in a sling, his
unkempt clothes and unshaven visage. He was Tommy Baker
after all. He stepped into the room and was confronted by a
number of faces he wasn't expecting to see. This was to have been
a private meeting between himself and Myles Fitzgerald. Yet there
were also two senior producers present and Pierce Beaumont.

—What's this? Baker said. A lynch mob?

The first face Baker actually focussed on was that of Eileen, who shook her head almost imperceptibly. Don't lose it, Tommy, she seemed to be saying. This gave him hope and strength, but his legs were weak, and for the first time since waking up at the hospital, he felt that he would gladly take a drink and not regret it one bit, a really stiff drink, a double of something, and more doubles and just keep on drinking. Just let go of the whole thing. Let it slide to fuck. Eileen looking down at the notepad on her knee. Long legs in fitted trousers. Slim, a light grace about her fine lines. Something Viking about her and her blond hair pushed back behind her ears and over her neckline, accentuating the light blue of her eyes. Something far away. Like a piece of sky he could cling onto. Skywoman.

Myles Fitzgerald speaks as Baker walks over for water.

—Thank you for gracing us with your presence, Tommy, he said, barely containing the hint of exasperation in his voice.

There was a smatter of laughter from the two producers present but Baker's confidante, Eileen, openly flaunted her defiance of Fitzgerald's jibe, fetching her favourite producer a drink of water and providing him with a pen and new notepad. Eileen had devoted all her working life to television and had once confided to Tommy Baker that she was desperate to have a child. At thirty-seven years of age, her time had almost run out.

Baker's now-urgent longing for alcohol had vanished the moment Fitzgerald made his snide remark. He was once again ready for a fight. Mood swings of confidence. His refound combativeness battering him that there was a war still to be won with Jimmy Heffernan. Probably the last war he would ever cover. Focussed. Head up.

Baker took a seat up near the head of the table, almost alongside Myles Fitzgerald, and he theatrically turning his seat with his free hand to face the room. An action which caused more smiles and a grimace from Pierce Beaumont. Pierce throwing his head back now. Staring at the ceiling and blowing air from puffed, rounded cheeks. Tapping his boots together.

—C'mon, Tommy, Fitzgerald said. Let's not turn this into a circus.

—Well, you were doing a fairly good impression of being a clown just a moment ago, Myles. I am not, repeat, not, late for this meeting.

There was just silence at this. All waiting now.

Though Baker's voice was slightly shaky, the strength had returned to his legs. He opened the notepad which had been given to him by Eileen. At the front, there was a note in short-hand which asked him to look in the back of the notepad. Again the writing was Eileen's own.

—Baker, are you with us?

—Sorry?! Oh yes, sorry, Myles. What were you saying?

—I was saying that I had called this special meeting because as you know we've announced a new programme strand for the late autumn. All right, November. I want to make sure this Heffernan film is watertight before, number one, allowing more filming, and two, making it our big splash as our first film to launch the series. We'll discuss the finer details of things on our own but I think it's time to let the more senior people know what's going on. Or at least what the plan *had* been. We're a bit up the air now, aren't we?

With Eileen Brennan taking the minutes, Myles Fitzgerald shook a thought from his head and went on to describe the corporate thinking behind the new investigation series planned for later that year, basically investigating more financial stories than they had previously done. One of the producers asked a question about programme turnaround time, and Baker looked in the back of his notepad as nonchalantly as he possibly could. Here, there was a note written in Eileen's incredibly neat handwriting.

I got your car back. I love you.
Marry me for God's sake and drive me off somewhere.
I'm sick of this and you don't need it anymore. You're beat
on your feet and you've nothing to prove to anyone.
Anywhere will do as long as it's hot!
Love E.

—And how do you respond to that Tommy? Myles Fitzgerald asked him, his tone still piqued.

—What? Well, yes, I will. Of course. Should have thought it myself.

—Sorry? Baker, what the hell are you talking about? You come in late. Cause yet another scene and then can't even have the decency to answer my question. A question that has been on everybody's lips. How can we possibly have you making this film when you've been the subject of such lurid headlines?

Baker was still in shock from what he had seen in the notebook but felt a surge of elation pass through his body. His legs zoomed under the table.

—Sorry, Myles. I've had a rough day or two. And, by the way, for the second time, I am not late. I arrived five minutes early for the meeting.

—Yes, but I arranged this new emergency pre-meeting meeting yesterday, partly at Pierce's request. And sent you a mail last night.

Baker looked directly at Pierce Beaumont, who held his gaze for a second before looking away.

—I was in hospital yesterday morning, hence the sling. I then went to John of God's to seek support, yet again, for alcohol addiction, in the afternoon. All this not long after doing one of the most amazing interviews I've ever had the privilege to carry out. After some persuasion, I managed to get admitted to John of God's for one night. You don't want to know what last night was like. Those people are saints. I'm now going to attend daily meetings, although for safety reasons I'm going to have to vary the time and place. My counsellor, who has known me and my problem for years, has agreed to this, even though I sometimes drive him to despair and beyond. And this morning, I returned early to my home to find the place ransacked.

Baker savoured the effect—of what was a news story that would never be aired. His brutal honesty. There could not have been a better way to swing the meeting, this show trial, in his favour. A grilling of Baker in his own department had been

expected in the aftermath of the newspaper coverage and the
messages of annoyance issued internally from his senior management. Baker spoke up again.

—It's unheard of for me, or indeed any of the remaining
old-fashioned journalists in this place, to talk openly about the
investigations in which they are actively involved. The pictures
in the papers, however, do require an explanation, especially for
you, Myles, as well as Andrew Mendoza, and the DG most of
all, who has to carry the can for these things. Now I've talked
to Cullinane and I think he has accepted my explanation. But
I'm going to break with investigative protocol and explain the
background to the pictures and the surrounding publicity to
those gathered here as well. There's another reason why I can
speak more freely about my investigations in this case, and I'll
come to that in a moment.

—On Wednesday night, Baker continued, I conducted what
was billed as a pen-and-paper interview with Jimmy Heffernan
at his nightclub near O'Connell Street. I secretly recorded this
interview. This had to be authorised beforehand in the usual way,
but foolishly, I admit, I had not alerted anyone when I was given
a time and a place by someone who just walked up to me in the
street. At the interview, Heffernan made me a proposal. An offer
of highly confidential information in return for his effectively
having editorial control over the film I'm making about him. I
did consider his offer. If you knew the type of information he
was offering me, I think most of you would have thought twice.
But at the end of the day, I refused it. His goons then physically
threw me out of the club via a back staircase. Before they did
that, however, they forcibly poured what I estimate to be a half
bottle of Jack Daniel's down my throat. You are welcome to
inspect the pictures of the bruises in my upper mouth. Heffernan
had some of his press photographer friends on standby at a place
some distance from his club, and that was what you saw in the
newspapers.

At this point, Pierce Beaumont, the senior crime correspondent at Empire, rose noisily from his seat.

—Does anyone else feel like me? That we don't have to sit

here and listen to this melodramatic crap from this . . . this dinosaur? Houses get broken into and ransacked every day of the week. This is Dublin, for God's sake. We can't just make a link between that and Jimmy Heffernan just because Baker's fevered mind does so. My sources in Crime Branch tell me that Heffernan is a reformed character . . . Guys, we have to be really fucking careful here. Not least because, and I hope I can say this, Tommy has clearly broken out again and is unstable. I'm sorry, Tommy, but it has to be said. You've a problem with Jimmy Heffernan, but it's more to do with problems in your life than anything Heffernan has been up to. It's pure jealousy. The little-man syndrome. Is Empire going to base its journalism on that? I don't think so. Heffernan owns the half of Ireland by now and could destroy us with a click of his fingers if we are not totally rock solid—and clearly our famous investigative producer is anything but rock solid.

Tommy Baker counted three beats before breaking the silence that was emerging in the room, but was aware that Eileen Brennan was staring at Beaumont. Her face terrible and drawn past her cheekbones with anger.

—Pierce, you and your ilk are not in charge of Empire yet, and until that awful day dawns, we will proceed on the basis of public-service broadcasting. Public-service broadcasting is the opposite of where you want to take it. Though I admit, we seem to be moving rapidly in that direction: a place where crime cor-respondents, or so as not to personalise it, say social-affairs or business commentators, become celebrities and get snapped at what once were called "discos," before they join political parties or company boards and then go back to being celebrity talking heads again. Specifically where those pictures of me were con-cerned, public-service broadcasting also requires a modicum of intelligence. Requires us to look beyond trashy tabloids to establish the underlying context of things, find out what really happened. It's called old-fashioned journalism. All is not always what it seems and it's our job, our Hippocratic oath, to reveal underlying truths. That's what this Heffernan film will do.

Pierce Beaumont made to interrupt, but Baker cut him off.

—I have only one more thing to add, Pierce, so your, ahem, crusade against crime won't be delayed much longer. This film about Heffernan will be my last film for Empire, as senior management already knows. Then I'll start looking after myself. And who knows, I might even get married again. If I can find someone who will have me.

Baker avoided looking over at Eileen but already knew that her face was as red as a rose. She flashing a shy smile before bending her head back down into her large Empire diary. The better to conceal her blushes. Her white teeth.

The two producers present, both keen to move things on from the awkwardness of the moment, began to ask questions about the secret filming and whether the material was broadcastable, but Myles Fitzgerald told them that transferring the material would take the rest of the day. However, he said that the techies had confirmed there was footage and, much to Pierce Beaumont's disgust, he told them that Empire felt Tommy Baker had made a good case for a film about Heffernan, and the secret filming down by the arch had already produced some interesting corroborative material. The new footage taken from Baker's jacket would confirm, or disprove, Baker's story about the secret interview with Heffernan—if it was at least audible, and better still with pictures. Fitzgerald then scolded Baker for not telling senior management of his intentions and whereabouts on that evening, but a warmth had returned to his voice. Respect, also. He then dismissed the producers and invited Baker into his private office.

Just as Baker made to enter Fitzgerald's office, Eileen rushed up behind him and gave his free arm an affectionate pinch before she rushed off again. On entering, Baker was surprised and concerned to see Pierce Beaumont already sat in a chair with every apparent intention of being present at this meeting also.

—Sorry, Tommy, I should explain that Pierce is here because of the recent change in Empire policy.

—Which is?

—Well, from now on, all the senior correspondents in their respective fields of expertise are to have an input into the more, shall we say, combustible programmes that Empire is seeking to put on air. It's a good safety net in my opinion.

Baker was stunned at this turn of events and needed a moment to decide whether to reveal what he knew about Beaumont's personal relationship with Jimmy Heffernan.

—Let me make one thing clear. Pierce Beaumont will not see one frame of this film before it is broadcast.

—Oh for God's sake, Tommy. Stop being so bloody precious, said Fitzgerald with genuine anger. Do you doubt my commitment to broadcasting this story?

—No Myles, I don't.

—And do you doubt my willingness to fight for it upstairs with the executives?

—Myles, you may be a Blueshirt, and I know I annoy you intensely when I make comments like that, but if I didn't think you were a decent journalist I wouldn't be in this room now.

—Well, for once in your life, put down your broken lance, Mr bloody Don Quixote, and listen to me. I've already gained an assurance from Pierce that he will not be involved in editing the film, but I do think he should see the film before it goes to air.

—Has Pierce told you that he has a personal relationship with Jimmy Heffernan?

Pierce Beaumont launched himself out of his chair. For a second it looked like he might move to strike his diminutive adversary, but he threw his hands up and walked to the window. He then took to shaking his head in a great play of exasperation.

Tommy Baker continued in a steady voice.

—Pierce Beaumont is on the VIP list and is a private member of Jimmy Heffernan's club. Has he told you that, Myles?

—No, he has not told me that, Tommy, and if that's true, that clearly makes him unsuitable as a kind of third eye for this particular film.

—In fact, Myles, he launched what passes for a pop singer there not so long ago and I have the pictures to prove it.

At that point, Pierce Beaumont really did explode. Eileen Brennan outside straining her ears to get what was being said.

—What is your problem, Baker! Eh?! Eh?! No, don't reply

to that question, because I can provide a better answer. It's pure jealousy. You are jealous because the old way of doing things is dead and gone. Spending months, even years, on a story and then just ending up with a bottle of smoke. No personality to the stories. No personal witness from the reporter and then this constant Brit and celebrity bashing. Talk about fucking dinosaur. That's your style Baker and it's way past its sell by date. I'll make two further points.

Here Beaumont, his nostrils flaring, swallowed some water from a glass, took some deep breaths, pushed his long hands through his mane of hair, and then continued.

—Number one, Jimmy Heffernan does not own Connolly's and all the signs are that he is simply a very successful business-man. He came up the hard way. So what? Good luck to him. Number two, how dare you impugn my integrity by suggesting that I am not fit to view the film and comment upon it. I am senior crime correspondent here and don't you forget it. You are in a new ballgame now, Baker, so it's just as well you are getting out before you have no choice in the matter.

Baker bit his tongue to prevent himself blurting more dirt about Pierce Beaumont and his cocaine habit, which was fed by Heffernan's lieutenant, the Cube. He knew, and could see, that Beaumont's comments about Baker having to get out had annoyed Myles Fitzgerald intensely. Fitzgerald was the old-style patrician journalist in chief; he still wore a garter on his arm, had been grey at his temples since ever Baker had known him, and if anyone was getting fired, then it would be he, Myles Fitzgerald, who would be doing the firing. Myles tightened his mouth, clenched his fists, pushed his seat back, and made to speak, but Baker rose from his chair to stifle this.

Baker needed time to think. He needed a cigarette and a drink. No, he wanted desperately to get away from all this and go off somewhere with Eileen. Lovely Eileen. Stepping up to Fitzgerald's desk, he poured a glass of water from a jug and drank his fill. He took a quick decision not to say any more about what he knew but rather to push the button's that would arouse Myles Fitzgerald's concerns.

—Pierce, be reasonable. Your relationship with Jimmy Heffernan precludes you from viewing the film.

—I do not have—

—Let me finish, Pierce, I didn't interrupt you, so don't interrupt me. Use your brains. If you're saying that Heffernan is simply a businessman who came up the hard way and good luck to him, then you've clearly already made your mind up about Heffernan. As regards lengthy investigations and the lack of what you call personalities, it's true that I come from a different background to you. You came across to current affairs from light entertainment and good luck to you, as you would say. We now, for good or ill, have the phenomenon of celebrity current-affairs reporters and you are one of them. My view is that the importance of the celebrity has now taken over from the story itself. The world of light entertainment is a world away from the drug gangs in the type of places where I grew up, and it may well be that you don't accept the seriousness of the situation in the same way that I do. After all, I come from the Coombe, you come from Foxrock.

To Myles Fitzgerald's ears, what Tommy Baker had to say sounded eminently reasonable. Myles had always been wary of celebrity reporters. Also, whilst there were few things on which Fitzgerald and Baker could agree completely, one of those things was the grave threat posed to Irish society by the drugs trade. That the main thing fuelling gang and gun violence and the growing acceptance of criminal violence was drugs. He also shared Baker's unpopular view that middle-class Ireland actually financially shored up the drugs trade by secretly partaking of illegal drugs in very large numbers. Fitzgerald was about to congratulate Baker on the conciliatory tone of his arguments and draw the meeting to a close, when Pierce Beaumont released a verbal barrage of abuse at Baker. Fitzgerald being unaware of just how sensitive Beaumont was to the subtle depth charges Baker had laid in the wake of his ostensibly reasonable comments.

—Don't you start that fucking Foxrock crap with me Baker. I know what's going on in the streets far better than you. That's precisely why I frequent Connolly's and other such places so that I can see and hear what's going on. Half the fucking police department are there as well for exactly the same reasons. We meet, yes, God forbid, socialise, and chew the sordid fat, swap notes, make deals. That's the way it works in the twenty-first century. As for the so-called drugs crisis. What a laugh coming from a self-confessed alcoholic! In fact, one of the most notorious dipsos ever to work, if that's the right word, in Empire. Drink, Mr Holier but Drunker Than Thou, has done more damage to Irish society than cocaine will ever do. Besides which, nobody has better contacts with Crime Branch than I do, and they say the opposite to what you say about Heffernan.

Myles Fitzgerald reached into a drawer and pulled a cigarette from a pack. Of course, he couldn't smoke it inside the building anymore, but he liked to run it between his fingers when any of his journalists were having a serious debate, something he enjoyed and liked to encourage. But Pierce Beaumont was preparing for an imminent departure from his office. Fitzgerald called him back.

—Pierce, do relax, please. You've made an important point and I want to hear Tommy's response to it. Pierce Beaumont had no choice but to sit down again.

Fitzgerald nodded his large head of wiry hair as encouragement for Tommy Baker to begin making his point, but just as Baker was about to speak, the office door was opened and Eileen walked in carrying a tray of coffee and biscuits. It was all Tommy Baker could do to stop himself from jumping up and planting a kiss on her forehead. This manoeuvre would have required Baker's going on tiptoes as Eileen was several inches taller than he. Eileen placed two sugars into his coffee and brought this and a small plate of biscuits over to where Baker sat with his back to the wall.

—For God's sake, Eileen, what is it about Baker that has women fetching and carrying for him, eh? What am I doing wrong?

—Ah, Myles, we all just want to take him home, clean him up, and look after him.

—Uhm, so if I, if I may say so, Tommy . . . if I don't wash

for a week, and go on a bloody monumental bender, I might get the same treatment. The women will be flocking to pick me up from the gutter, take me home with them, and give me a bath, will they?

—I'm afraid it doesn't work quite like that, Myles, Eileen said as she made to leave the room.

—What's the damn secret then?

—It's all in the eyes, Myles. The searching little-boy eyes. And the eyes are made in heaven.

—I think I want to be sick, said Pierce Beaumont. However, he was reluctant to annoy Myles Fitzgerald by insisting on leaving the meeting. Fitzgerald still had plenty of clout with the board of governors and was not a man to pick a fight with. Beaumont, therefore, kept his counsel and decided to spend the rest of this waste of his time by imagining the changes that would be made once he was safely ensconced in Fitzgerald's office. One thing that Beaumont would ensure was that his personal secretary would be under twenty-five, nubile, and good for a laugh. So very not an Eileen. She had to be called Sherelle or something tacky and faux—one needed one's diversions working at such a fever pitch. What was this fucker Baker doing?

Tommy Baker eyed Beaumont from beyond the rim of his coffee cup. His counsellor had told him that he could drink all the coffee he wanted during the next few difficult months. Eat bananas also. The caffeine, the biscuits, and Eileen's words, all were sources of motivation and fortification.

—Pierce, that shibboleth about alcohol abuse being the same as drug abuse is just an excuse for people who don't want to look at the truth. It's a red herring. A false comparison. Let me explain by way—

—Tommy, I'm trying to be patient here. Go to any A and E department at a hospital on a Friday night and—

—Sorry, Pierce, are you actually incapable of debating anything in a reasoned manner You've made a valid point about alcohol abuse. Are you actually able to listen to my response?

Pierce Beaumont shot a look of sheer loathing at Baker as he slumped back in his chair with a sigh.

—Proceed.

—Thank you, Pierce. Now there is one simple phenomenon which disproves everything that what I call the new drugs brigade has to say about alcohol abuse being just as bad as drug abuse. That phenomenon, Pierce, comes from a time that you may not even remember. It's a metaphor. The beautiful metaphor of the open door.

—What?

—Where I grew up in the Coombe, every door in the street was left unlocked, very often so that a neighbour who might need something could just go in and take it. There were no alarms on doors. There were absolutely no locks, no security measures, no hurleys or bats left behind doors just in case there was a knock in the night. And yet, alcohol abuse was a big problem in our area. So why did people feel so safe despite the alcohol problem? I'll tell you why. Alcohol, especially in a culture like ours, is primarily a social tool. A way of coming together. Okay fine, particular groups like the young who want to experiment, or alcoholics like myself, go too far and abuse alcohol, but largely the Irish do not drink so as to be, as they say, "out of their minds." They drink to socialise, to talk, to meet. Look, for example, how many phrases we have, especially in Irish, about drink and the social context of drink. Now look at the impact of drugs. Go to the North Circular Road, the South Circular Road, parts of Tallaght and Clondalkin, and look at the multitudes of youths who are old before their time. Go to Wood Quay and the Boardwalk on the Liffey and see the poor devils fighting each other and roaring their despair at the world. What would the Vikings, who built a harbour there and who were renowned for their love of the drink, have made of them? Zombies with yellowed and ashen faces, walking the streets, moving from score to score, from methadone scheme to methadone scheme, from mugging to break in to car theft and much worse. But the zombies are not the real problem. They are the spreading rash, the visible festering sores of a disease that proliferates through greed. It's the massive amounts of money that's driving this problem, not the drugs. Lying behind these visible sores, within the body of the problem, are the pushers and dealers and behind them partly invisible drug lords like Heffernan. They were never going to be content with just selling drugs. They are hooded, ruthless, have money and judges to burn, and are completely without pity. And look at the very young boys who follow them, dress like them, put their hoods up on sweltering days like this, want to be like them. Of course they want to be like them. Maximum respect! Look at all this and then tell me that alcohol and drugs are the same. The middle classes meanwhile not only turn a blind eye but actually encourage them. Go to any private backroom at any nightclub, Connolly's included, and you will see the sons and daughters of the rich and powerful as they highball on Es, cocaine, and champagne. Now here's the rub, you drop a cocaine or even a heroin problem into Foxrock or Sandymount and watch how the middle classes rally round to help one of their own get back on track. They have money, they have influence, they have power and they have friends in high places. You inject a huge amount of heroin, and subsequently cocaine, into a mass of poverty, people already struggling on the margins and all the social problems linked to that, and watch a crime wave, an anti-community time-bomb supernova explode. Poor people once had nothing but were still proud communities even with alcohol abuse. Drugs destroy community. All the addicts of hallucinatory drugs that I have ever spoken to, or interviewed, and who come from poor areas have described more or less the same experience on first trying heroin. "It blew my mind," they all say. Did a pint of Guinness ever blow somebody's mind? Did ten pints of Guinness ever blow somebody's mind and transport them to a place where a completely new reality was revealed to them? A reality which would take over their lives and render all other social interactions as nothing? Did alcohol take them to that place where they will rob, mug, give sex, betray their children, anything, to get the wherewithal to get back to that mind-blowing state? That is the difference between alcohol and drug addiction.

Baker took a large gulp of his coffee which was now almost cold. He had no idea how long he had been speaking or where the stream of words had come from. He didn't want to say this to Pierce Beaumont but he felt that in verbally working out his position, he too had had an out of body experience. He was exhausted and could not go on. Yet there was an uncertainty as to whether he had finished speaking. Baker looked at Pierce Beaumont. His eyes had the sheen of sheer terror in them. Probably, Baker decided, because he wondered what he was going to say next about backrooms in clubs, about judges and corruption. Myles Fitzgerald was leaning forward on his desk, his cigarette now firmly clenched between his teeth. He looked for all the world like a huge bust of poured bronze. All three momentarily frozen in a *tableau vivant*.

Éilis Devanney prays for Tommy Baker as she instructs a group of young girls in the art of machine sewing, needlework, and embroidery. Éilis sitting back in her chair and the backrest slip, slipping away. The earth revolving and she falling though space. Back in her room in her old house. She laid out on her bed. Stone cold. The iron cold of spilled blood as it seeps away to infinity. Across her bed. Blood of innocence whose pulse is ever fainter. For who will protect the innocents now that the high kings and queens of Ireland have turned to dust? Writhing in despair in the bone dry earth at the death of Ireland's glory. Her mediocrity. Glóir na hÉireann cá bhfuil tú?

—Oh Dia ár sábháil! An bhfuil tú i gceart a mháistreás?

—An bhfaighidh mé uisce duit, bhfuil tú i gceart a mháistreás?

Éilis heard and saw the children speaking to her, asking her if she was all right, but she could not speak back in any tongue. She felt for her tongue. To see if it was in her mouth, which of course it was. She shook her head as if to shake off a fly that was buzzing there.

—Anois cén áit a raibh muid a phaistí?

Éilis sitting up, taking up her needle and thread. She would show the children her embroidery. To reassure them. And she drove the needle into her finger until blood seeped across her Celtic angel and she felt no pain.

—*Say the thing about selfishness, Tommy Baker. Abair é nuair atá deis agat.*

Some of Éilis's pupils began to whimper softly in fright. Éilis had

turned ghostly white and even before she fell to the floor again, one
of the young students had run down to the secretary's office crying
that the young class-help Éilis had had a taom chroí.

Tommy Baker swallowed the rest of his coffee in one gulp.

—I'll finish on this point, and it is the most important point.
I am now officially a recovering alcoholic. If I break out, as
you put it, Pierce, and can't afford the price of a pint, I will
lend money from family and friends until they get fed up with
that and then I might start begging and, on occasion, stealing
for the price of a pint. God between me and that. What I will
not do is go and attack tourists, or old ladies, or my next-door
neighbours so that I can fuel my habit. Why? Because, unlike
alcohol, the sale of hallucinatory narcotics is based on encouraging a desperate selfishness. It is a completely privatised experience. The perfect drug scene for rampant twenty-first-century
Irish capitalism, where the view is encouraged that everybody
has the right to do what they want, when they want. From the
addict, all the way up to the drugs baron, who in our case is
Jimmy Heffernan. All transactions are based on this one overarching principle—there is no such thing as Irish society, only
individuals who must be allowed to do what they want. It's as if
we've collectively sat down and asked ourselves what is the worst
thing we can come up with. The thing that will bring us to our
knees. Make bad good. Turn collective memory into amnesia.
Turn brother against brother, citizen against citizen. And what
we came up with was hard drugs and the vast, vast amounts of
money and greed that go with them. Amounts of money that
would turn the head of a saint. I'd say we have twenty years
before we pass the point of no return. I more than likely won't
be around to see the final victory or defeat, but if I can nail this
bastard Heffernan, I will have left my mark on the battlefield,
and a battle is what it's going to be.

Tommy Baker sat back in his chair exhausted. He wanted
to go on but did not have the energy to do so. There was a
moment's silence in the office as, once again, nobody was quite
sure whether Baker had finished speaking. Tommy Baker, whose

pallor had changed from blotchy red to pure white. Baker lifted his free hand to Eileen, who had come bustling through the door, but then everything began to swim in front of his eyes and he felt completely weightless. Wanted to vomit.

Eileen lifted Baker's hand at the same time as the paramedic lifted Éilis's hand in the ambulance on the long and bumpy drive to Letterkenny Hospital. The paramedic's opinion was the girl had had some kind of fit. He checked her breathing, BP, and heart rate again, and wiped some dried blood from her nose. He then moved to examine her tongue for signs of biting when the girl Éilis opened her eyes. He startled.

—Éilis, isn't it?

—*Cá bhfuil mé?*

—Sorry, no Irish, especially not Donegal Irish, love.

—*Tá tart an domhan orm. Ahh tabhair dom braon uisce.*

—I haven't a clue what you are saying. Now stop messing and speak English.

Éilis gripped the man's hand.

—*Tart orm, tart.*

The paramedic called to the driver. —Charlie, what does *tart* mean in Irish? We've got one of the diehards here. She's refusing to speak the Queen's.

—Okay, I'll put a call into base. What's the word again?

—I think she's saying tart. Tart.

—Tart? What kind of a word is that? Ha, she'd make a good looking tart, your one.

—She's a stunner all right.

The paramedic noticed that there was a light flashing in the young woman's bag. Obviously a mobile phone whose ringtone had been switched off. He picked the phone out of the bag and saw that the name Finn was flashing on the screen.

—Hello?

—Hello? Éilis?

—Sorry, Finn is it?

—That's right. I'm Éilis's boyfriend.

—Finn, there's no need to worry, but Éilis is in an ambulance and she's on the way to Letterkenny Hospital. No. No. She's fine, breathing normal now, heartbeat, everything's fine. She just seems to have had some kind of fit. Finn, does Éilis suffer from epilepsy?

—Not that I know of. No. But maybe.

—Does she regularly get fits or seizures?

—Well, she is very highly strung, but no, not actual fits. I wouldn't call them fits. Can I talk to her?

—Wait till we do some further tests at the hospital, Finn. I'd say she'll be grand in a while. It's this heat. It's killing everybody. She just needs to take it easy for a few days. I'd say they'll keep her in for observation.

—Okay, I'll call Letterkenny later. Thanks.

—Oh, and Finn, do you speak Irish?

—I do. Yes.

—Ah good, what does *tart* mean?

—*Tart* is thirst. She must be thirsty.

The paramedic looked down at Éilis and saw that she was shaking uncontrollably and was sheet white.

—*Tá mé conáilte. Conáilte.*

—Hold on, Finn, she's saying something else.

The paramedic held Éilis's phone near to her mouth as she spoke very quietly.

—*Sioctha go smior ionam. Sioctha go smior ionam.*

—What's she saying, Finn?

—She's saying she's freezing. Hello? Hello?

The White Line Crossed

SPANZO STANDING AT customs in Orly Airport, Paris. Red faced, flustered. Out of his comfort space. Unable to strike out at the laughing customs man holding the dress up high. An emerald-green dress. Spanzo too thick to get someone else to do it. Just as Heffernan had predicted. James Tierney spending Saturday afternoon rereading Éilis's diary, constructing a chronology of short biographies of all named. Ignoring Ronagh's phone calls until she arrives at his doorstep in high dudgeon. James pulling at his hair. Who is it that's lying stabbed on the bed? What is that Morrígan—Mór-Ríoghain—or whatever? Was she not some banshee or war goddess? Where's my Irish dictionary? Ronagh throwing fresh bread and hummus onto the table. Sweet tomatoes also. Standing now with arms akimbo.

The dress. Ah yes, the dress. Simply because his will would be done till kingdom come. Heffernan had lined up the best pop video and art director in Europe. Rehearsals had already been carried out with stand-ins. Also, he had sent across instructions to his people in London that Frankie Byrne would be going to a different construction site in the middle of the following week. The photo shoot outside his club the following Saturday and the pictures that would hit the Sunday tabloids and gossip columns. Jimmy Heffernan the stud. Jimmy Heffernan the man about town. Jimmy Heffernan, man of style and substance. Jimmy Heffernan, the man with an Überbabe on his arm. Once Éilis had fulfilled this function, she would no longer be of any use to him. Spanzo could have her, whatever.

234

Heffernan's accountant, Philip Enderby, called him on the business phone to confirm the business tie-up for two Connolly's franchises in Galway and Sligo. Enderby also confirmed a business lunch at Leopardstown racecourse for the next day. As Enderby droned on, Heffernan busied his mind with the task of extracting Éilis Devanney from Donegal and thought he saw a way in which it could be done. If this simple way did not work, she would simply have to be abducted. Either way, she would be in that dress outside his club on Saturday evening.

—Hello, Jimmy?

—Sorry, Mr Enderby, what were you saying?

—I was asking about Carmel, Jimmy. She seems to have just disappeared.

—She resigned from the company on Wednesday night, Philip. Or at least that's what I was told. Other than that, I know nothing.

—God! I am shocked, I have to say.

—Women. Mr Enderby. They are so fickle, one finds.

Enderby chuckled. —I suppose you're right, Jimmy.

—One more thing, Philip.

—Yes.

—Make sure and let me know if that guy Tommy Baker calls or contacts you.

—Yes, you've told me a couple of times. Is there a problem?

—No problem at all.

Heffernan had one more task before jumping into his Jacuzzi. He needed to contact Pierce Beaumont as a matter of urgency, so as to arrange a meeting for later that evening. The Cube, Beaumont's regular drugs supplier, could get the message to him. Within ten minutes, Beaumont had agreed to be at Connolly's Wine Bar at 10 p.m. for a chat. In his vainglory, it never occurred to Beaumont that Jimmy Heffernan's reasons for wanting to speak to him were not because Heffernan wanted to curry the favour of Ireland's most famous reporter. The truth was that Heffernan wanted to know what the chances were of Tommy Baker's film about him being broadcast. A worrying thought had just occurred to him about his chat with Baker. Better to establish Baker's physical whereabouts as soon as possible.

Pierce Beaumont arrived at Connolly's accompanied by an entourage of bright young women, all spangled and tanned, who were accompanied by gangly young men in designer scruffiness, boating shoes, and open-neck shirts. Beaumont led his boisterous circus into the celebrity area, where photographers were on hand to record his entrance. A gossip columnist approached Beaumont with due deference and begged a few words. Empire's star reporter, who was already slightly high after doing a line of coke at home, began his spiel even before the columnist could pose a question.

—Yes, I think the whole Connolly's thing is so fantastic. I mean, we are talking history, yeah, our own history, but the surroundings are chic and elegant. I mean, I walk in here, and I'm like, you know, blown away by it all. It's great to see that there's going to be more of them across the country. Oh, sorry, there's Melanie . . . Hi, Melanie. You look fantastic, babe!

A minor singing celebrity, whose left breast fell out of her dress and the cameras popping as she reached across to air kiss with Pierce Beaumont, screamed her delight at meeting him again so soon and begged him to come along to her gig in Camden Street the following night.

—You don't have to listen, Pierce, just show your face.

—All right, Mels, I'll see what I can do. Hey, come along to the private area later. Just tell the bouncer that I invited you.

Beaumont then pulled Melanie gently back to him, partly to get another view of her breasts and partly to whisper in her ear.

—We're going to have some fun, darlin'. You know. Do a few lines and maybe spin the champagne bottle like last year.

Melanie gave a low whoop and skipped across to her friends. Beaumont turned back to the gossip columnist.

—Sorry about that. Where were we?

The gossip columnist began to frame a question regarding sales of Beaumont's forthcoming book about the Dublin underworld but did not get a chance to put the question because Ned Behan's huge frame suddenly loomed over the table and requested a word in private with "Mr Beaumont."

Beaumont raised his eyebrows apologetically and the columnist gave an understanding thumbs up.

It was usual for Beaumont and Heffernan to meet behind a heavily curtained alcove at the side of the nightclub, with a dedicated waiter hovering out of earshot beyond the curtain. This time, however, Ned Behan led him out of the club area and into a staff corridor which boasted some nice Impressionist prints and a lift. Beaumont tried to make small talk with his burly escort but the usually talkative Ned was taciturn and noncommittal, regardless of whether Beaumont chose the weather as a topic of conversation, or Heffernan's mood. Ned's demeanour unsettled Beaumont, but this concern was nothing to the discomfort he felt on seeing the Cube—whose real name was Vincent Duffy, he remembered—sitting on a sofa in the large room to which he was brought. The Cube grinned, patted his thigh, and tapped his foot where he sat

—Mr Duffy, I thought I said there was to be no physical contact. In fact, I made that a sacrosanct rule for our, ehm, mutual arrangement.

The Cube laughed and turned to Jimmy Heffernan who was sat behind his large desk.

—What's sacrosin, Jimmy? Dat something you put in your coffee?

Heffernan smiled the smile of a shark that is no smile at all and placed a remote control into a groove in the desk as he motioned Beaumont to a chair facing him.

—How's Imogene, Pierce?

—Imogene's fine. She's in Paris at the moment looking at paintings for the hotel chain she works for. Look, I really don't think that the Cube should—

—And how's Michelle?

—Michelle?

—Your ex-nanny Michelle. The woman who nearly had your name all over a certain Sunday paper last week.

—The bitch! Are you sure about that, Jimmy?

—It was me who got the story pulled, Mr Beaumont.

—What story? There was, and is, no story.

Beaumont looking about him. The stony-faced Ned Behan standing by the door, hands relaxed but hanging down. "The Cube" Duffy with a rueful grin on his face. As if he knew what embarrassment was. Heffernan simply staring at him, making no reply to Beaumont's protestations but lifting the remote control from his desk and pressing a button.

The room gradually went dark and a screen appeared on the far wall from behind a set of sliding curtains. Slightly grainy video images could then be seen. Images which showed Pierce Beaumont taking some kind of slim metal pipe from a lozenge-shaped box and then using the pipe to inhale a line of bright-white powder from a table. Phosphorous. Illicit. In the black and faded white of everything. Beaumont's mouth dropped open at what was presented before him. His legs gripped to the chair in icy fear. The potential damage to his career.

It occurred to Jimmy Heffernan that this kind of scene was the thing that gave him most pleasure in his life. To be, to really be, in the world, was to be in the dead-calm centre of another human being's maelstrom of emotions. To watch. To watch and wait. To smell the fear and panic which seized the victim. To hold the balance of things and then to make the move. To calm the storm with the wave of a hand, or to release the genie in all its destructive power. Where would he get this natural high in the Pacific? A female voice on the film soundtrack. This was Michelle, Beaumont's au pair. Her voice was distant but still audible. She pulling him back to her. The legs of people sitting in chairs could be seen. It was obviously a late-night party in a hotel. Michelle's soft whispering felt, rather than heard, in the gap across Heffernan's office.

—Pierce, don't do that here, in front of everyone, you're mad!

—Relax, Michelle baby . . . you're too paranoid about these things. I mean, they're not going to arrest me. I mean *moi*? Mr Anti-Crime 9-9-9. The Garda Síochána know where I'm coming from. Hey! trust me on crime. But let Piercey baby have a good time! That's my motto. I just invented that. Smart, eh?

Applause and a couple of whoops could be heard on the soundtrack but the lights went on again in the room and the sound faded as Heffernan placed the remote control back into its place on the desk. Heffernan looked at the broadcasting star with a pretence at pity. The Cube had vanished from the room somehow.

—Yes, very smart, Pierce. Now can we forget that bullshit about there not being a story. That nearly broke last week, including the stuff with Michelle later on. Nice girl. Seems very straight and obviously believed you when you said you were going to leave Imogene.

—That's the hotel near Ballsbridge isn't it, Jimmy. How the fuck is that on film?

—Yes. But that's irrelevant where you are concerned. All our private rooms, in all the clubs and hotels in which we have an interest, are wired for sound and vision. And let's face it, you've done some damage in all of them. It gives me hours of fun. In fact it's my favourite pastime after the gee-gees. But don't worry about Michelle. Not a bad-looking chick. Great ass. Wouldn't be my type though. But then I tend to be a bit choosier. Ah, come on. What's with the shock-and-awe face, Pierce? Nobody needs to know anything, as long as you actually start being smart, instead of talking about it.

Pierce Beaumont was still not sure whether this was all a game on Heffernan's part, but he recognised how quickly he was sobering up. He decided to play a slightly humorous card, but a card containing something of a threat in its delivery.

—Look, Jimmy, if we want this fruitful relationship to continue, we are going to have to stop this James Bond crap. I need room to be the celeb I am. My being a celeb and a face about town helps you, does it not? Local boy made very good, mates with all the celebs, etc.

—Where is the fruit in this relationship, Pierce? Heffernan asked.

—Ah come on, Jimmy, we are both playing a game. You give me stuff and I give you stuff. You scratch mine and I scratch yours. That's the way celebrity journalism works.

—Pierce, you put on the television what I want you to put on the television, that's the sum total of the relationship. Now tell me about this morning's meeting.

—Well, there's not much to say, really.

—Did you see the film about me?

—Jimmy, what the hell's got into you? First off. There's no film. Not yet, anyway. But I can't divulge things like that. It would be the end of me.

—Really? Two months ago, you gave one of the Cube's, ahm, assistants shall we call him, Tommy Baker's private address and phone number.

—Well, I'd just had a row with Baker the day before and, I mean . . . what are you driving at? That I'd want something to happen to Baker? Well, that's an absolute no-no. No way, Jimmy, and I wouldn't dream—

—You mean the row about you and other senior Empire staff having private dinners at the British Embassy?

—Exactly, Baker is such a Provo! We have meals at lots of embassies. Hold on a minute, is this meeting being recorded?

Beaumont rose from his chair and attempted to kick it over, but without success. Wrestled with it somewhat, much to the bemusement of Heffernan and his men.

—It is, isn't it?! It's being fucking recorded! I have to get out of here. You'll be sorry for this, Jimmy Heffernan. You forget who's in charge here. I made you, don't forget. You can't take on a whole national broadcasting company. Next week I'm going to give Tommy Baker all my stuff on your companies and your empire. Then you'll see who actually has the biggest desk in this little arrangement, which up until now has suited me, right.? Now I might have to change my mind, and God help you then.

By now Beaumont was leaning over Heffernan's desk and almost spitting into his face, but when he tried to rise from the desk, he found that he was being restrained from behind by very strong hands. His head stuck. Head prone. Heffernan lit his Italian lighter and set the flame to maximum and brought the fire very close to Beaumont's face, at which point Beaumont let out a soft whimper and closed his eyes. Once again the room was plunged into darkness. There was silence for a while and then Beaumont, eyes shut, thought he could smell cigar smoke. Still he kept them shut. This was not happening to him. No way was it happening to him. The babes downstairs. His entourage. All waiting for him. Pierce Beaumont aware that Heffernan was now standing near him. The goons still holding him in weird situ. Head over the desk.

—Now Mr Anti-Crime 9-9-9. Do you understand what pain is? Pain is interesting. It's an interesting test of a person's character. I'm not talking about pains like headaches or a cut. Even a deep cut. I mean pain that is so bad that you want to die rather than still feeling that pain. But we've discovered, once again, just recently in fact, that the body can withstand an awful lot of physical pain. An awful lot. Before giving in. Or say, the pain of losing those dear to you. Do you know, Pierce. You really should watch that youngest child of yours and that blue blanket she drags round with her. Child could suffocate very easily. Has it with her in that Paris hotel.

Beaumont looked slowly upwards. Heffernan then placed the lighter flame directly under his nose. Beaumont began to cry immediately. Heffernan then gave a nod to the two men standing behind Beaumont to stand back. A chair was placed behind Beaumont and he slumped into it and placed his head into his hands.

—Do you know what I like most about Tommy Baker, Pierce? Baker understands that life is not a game. I like that. He thinks. Fundamentally thinks about everything that he does, because everything in his life, every step he takes has a significance. Therefore he is vital. He follows the advice of Thomas Aquinas, as I have seen from his bookshelves. The boys here didn't understand my need to see his bookshelves. Or my refusal to allow them to destroy them. Sacrosanct indeed. Pierce. All important decisions in life must be contemplated at length and the various options considered. Now here is the rub, and this is what I love about Aquinas, once this process has been completed the thinker is duty-bound—duty-bound, mind—to follow the conviction of his final decision. You, Mr Beaumont, are no Thomas Aquinas and you are not even a poor man's Tommy Baker. He is not without fear, Baker, but once he decides, after great deliberation, to go down a certain path he confronts his fear. Nor does he take things personally. Baker thinks big-brain things. You know, systems. Global movements and man's position within them. He's entering his pain-time as a stoic would. I like that. I admire people who can stare pain in the face. You, Pierce, are no Tommy Baker because pain has never figured in your life. You are completely without principle, apart from one. And that one principle is self-aggrandisement. You are every, shall we say, "crime lord's" dream.

Again there was a pause, and again Beaumont felt cigar smoke all about him.

—Baker would have made a great businessman, but unfortunately he doesn't believe in the business. It's doubly unfortunate for Baker because he's clever enough to know that there is nothing but the business anymore. We so-called crime lords are simply the merchant buccaneers of the new age. Now, the men standing behind you don't have a clue what I'm on about. If I ask them whether they have ever heard of Aquinas, they'll tell me that he plays soccer for Boca Juniors or something ridiculous. Yet despite their lack of intellect they are very important people, and I pay them more, far more, than my top chefs or hotel managers. Why? Because, Pierce, these good men are the enforcers for our new age, just like the company detectives of old, and their job is quite simply to inflict pain. They are the bottom line upon which everything else is built. No different from a modern, aggressively expanding state army when you think about it. Ah yes. Pain. State-inflicted pain. Or Connolly's franchise–inflicted pain. Not much difference really.

Pierce Beaumont shook his head in the darkness and felt Heffernan's hand on his shoulder but he could not bring himself to look up at him.

—Pain is nothing personal, either. It's just an instrument, Pierce. A couple of years ago, when you first approached me, I happily took on certain obligations on your behalf because it suited my purpose. At that moment you also became obliged to me. Now those obligations you have may, or may not, involve you or your loved ones having to suffer pain. That is my decision and mine alone. But you can affect that decision by the things you do and say. Let us say, the way you observe, or don't observe, the pact you have entered into with me.

A black tray was placed by unseen hands onto Heffernan's desk. Two white stripes of powder seemed to almost dance off the tray's surface. Heffernan placed a metal tube into Beaumont's hands and then guided the TV celebrity's head to the stripes on the tray.

—Now before you leave, you're going to tell me exactly what happened at your meeting and what you can do to get Baker's film stopped.

Beaumont inhaled the white powder through the tube and then sat back in his chair with a sigh of relief and capitulation.

—Okay. I'll contact the board of governors in private next week and tell them of my concerns about the film. That's usually been enough in the past.

—That's exactly what needs to be done, Pierce. It's amazing how Charlie really gets the brain into gear. And where is Baker at the moment?

There is a pause. Beaumont head back. As if playing for time where no time was. As if he still had a choice.

—Jimmy. If I tell you where Baker is, I want your personal word that nothing would ever happen. Not only to Baker but to my children. A sob catching Beaumont's throat at this.

—Now who in their right mind would harm a child?

Beaumont snorted the second white line of cocaine and sat back again.

—Okay. He's staying overnight at John of God's, the alcoholics rehabilitation centre, or stress or whatever it is. But you'll need to hurry because he's moving to somewhere else very soon according to what I've been told. Spain. He's retiring. Look, I presume you just want to scare him. I don't want anything serious happening to him.

Silence. Just silence at this. Pierce Beaumont terrified to tell Heffernan about Baker's secret camera but terrified not to. Heffernan sitting at his desk again. Praying mantis in a pool of light. As if reading his mind.

—Did Baker have a hidden camera on his person?

—Jimmy, I want your guarantee—

—Answer the fucking question, you prick.

—Yes.

E Fada for Éire

THE SAME WEEKEND that the stark reality of ultra-real current affairs washed over Pierce Beaumont like an ice bath, like a thousand million needle scratches—the spread of fear in his skin, the canker he had consumed and could never rid—the Sweeney family picked Éilis up from Letterkenny Hospital. Finn Dempsey had phoned Éilis to ask whether he should call the whole job off and go to Gaoth Dobhair to be with her, but Éilis had got extremely upset at this suggestion. So upset in fact that Finn had to promise that he would see the job out. Éilis did not tell Finn what she had dreamed in the ambulance. So many things she would not, could not, tell him. Especially now. It all dead and gone and never would. The slight heave of her chest and wry smiles that only children recognise.

As long as he stayed away.

As the car radio blared out the news that the hot weather was once again to break the following weekend, Éilis closed her eyes, happy in the knowledge that Finn Dempsey was not in the country. The Sweeneys had asked the hospital to keep Éilis in for observation, but Éilis did not want this and, besides, there were no beds available for non-emergency patients. She had always loved the final leg of the car journey to Gaoth Dobhair, the turn onto the long challenging bog road with Muckish and the quartzite cone of Errigal in the distance. Beyond that the glistening sea by which we all once lived, should live still. That faraway once—when there were no roads in Ireland, only boats. The grandeur and remoteness of it all never failed to calm her

245

soul. She opened her small travel bag and placed her hand on her piece of amber and then fell into a profound and peaceful sleep. The Sweeneys maintained a careful silence for the whole journey back to Gaoth Dobhair, apart from observing to each other that Éilis had got her colour back. Here for good.

As the car entered the driveway of the Sweeney home looking out over Gola Island and the Atlantic beyond, Éilis woke knowing that there was a visitor waiting for her there. Father McCartan jumped down the front-door steps to greet them all, and Séamus Dempsey's beaming smile lit up the porch as he followed the priest out to the car. A bit reticent, he. But pleased despite himself. Grinning forehead and happy hands. Like the elations of the small white clouds. Blue-of-contentment skies. Heat and air and scents of something like sun cream and ice cream and the thrill of bees.

Éilis ran towards them and hugged each of them in turn with a fierceness that took both visitors aback. Tears spilling and a red laughing mouth of white teeth. The lightness of glistening happy eyes. Her being ephemeral. Nonexistent but with the nearness and power of gods.

Once inside the kitchen, where the range was still burning despite the heat, Éilis was eager to discover what had happened in her absence from Dublin.

—Well, our big news, Éilis, is that the producer of the film about Heffernan wants to come to Gaoth Dobhair and interview you.

—So it's still going ahead then, Father. Only a little bird told me differently.

—Well, Mr Baker rang me this morning to discuss an interview with you to be done, if we agree, that is, on Friday morning of next week and, overall, he was in flying form. He said Darren's interview—

—Darren! Darren Bulger! Oh my God, so Darren finally woke up. I prayed and prayed and dreamed for him.

—So your little birds haven't told you all the news, Éilis, ha, ha. No, Darren's interview is apparently compelling stuff, Séamus was at it. Baker said that it had made all the difference with his immediate boss after some bad publicity about Mr Baker.

—What bad publicity?

—Well, he does have a drink problem and he was pictured lying in the street and apparently the worse for wear. In town somewhere.

—Was it near Connolly's?

—But you know these celebrity stories.

—But was it near Connolly's?

The priest turned to Séamus Dempsey. He wolfhound lean. Gleam of eye. Not moving but prowling the room. Thinking, ruminating. Eyes brightening when regarding Éilis, frowning also. He turns to the priest with a decision. She must know everything, she must be in his circle. His cycle of life.

—It wasn't that far from Connolly's, Father, so Éilis is not far wrong, I'd say.

—He'll have to be very careful now, though. If Spanzo and all that crowd find out. But he'll be fine if he's with the Church.

—Who, Éilis. The producer? Tommy Baker?

—No, Darren, I mean. Well, both of them.

—Well, we can tell you more about that after you have had a rest.

—No, tell me now. I have had enough rest.

—*Bhuel, cad faoi ag dul síos ar an trá, Éilis. Is féidir linn labhairt le chéile thíos annsan.*

—Okay, great, Father. We can go to the beach, but please tell me about Darren. *Anois a hathair.* Sorry . . . if you don't mind.

The priest lowered his voice and drew closer to Éilis so as to be able to whisper the news about Darren to her.

—We are helping him to move to Belgium next week, as the film will probably be broadcast two weeks after your interview. Most of the film has already been put together.

—Why Belgium? He doesn't know anyone in Belgium.

—Well, I've a brother who is priest there, Cormac. He's a fully trained mechanic and he's going to train Darren as a mechanic. All at Empire's expense! And you never know, we might make a priest out of Darren yet. From pusher to priest! Now isn't that some craic!

—But where is he now. I mean right fucking now, Father. God forgive me.

—He rang the rectory from a call box straight after the interview and said he'd be back in touch. It's fine, Éilis. All fine.

Only Séamus saying nothing and that nothing is nothing good. Occluded eyes refusing suddenly to engage. Éilis straightening her hands down by her side. Palms down.

—Then he's the first one of us to go.

The priest bemused. Suddenly sure Éilis was right. Few words were spoken on the way to Cúl Buí beach.

Silence on the beach. Éilis standing by rocks and water crouches. Hugs herself. Séamus Dempsey walks and places a hand on her shoulder. Éilis, standing, turning, and placing both her hands on his shoulders. Stand there now and say nothing. Look not into eyes but the undiscoverable, nonexistent existing place where souls communicate. Talk now to break the spell. To let go. They walk back to the troubled priest who smiles as they come on, Éilis taking Séamus's arm. Éilis picking up her voice to include Father McCartan as he moved away to lift his bag.

—Séamus, did you see Finn off?

—We did. It was ourselves who drove him to the airport. His form wasn't great, to be honest. I suppose you getting sick and all.

Séamus Dempsey produced a towel and swimming trunks from a waterproof bag in what looked like a small kit bag like a sailor's. He definite of purpose. Éilis sat by the rocks that gave some shade and turned away to look at the sea and Father McCartan took steps down to the shore to inspect what he pretended was a crab. Shocked by his naivety. That Éilis already knew. He needing to be off. Alone. To pray.

Without ceremony, Séamus Dempsey walked to the water's edge, blessed himself, and dived in.

This gave Éilis and Father McCartan ample opportunity to discuss family matters and her recent fit. What the doctor at the hospital had called an apparent panic attack. Éilis had noticed that Séamus Dempsey's once lithe but skinny frame was beginning to fill out and that his very short hair suited the strong bone structure of his face. Up until recently, Séamus had worn his dark-russet helmet quite long down his neck and over his ears. Unlike his brother Finn, who boasted a thatch of curly reddish-brown hair but kept it short and tidy, modelled and controlled. Séamus's hair was straight except for a wave that ran through it like the tide. With his deep-flaming hair, very pale skin, freckles, and blue eyes, he had looked for all the world like a young Celtic street waif. Now, though, he looked more like a Celtic monk, although a monk with the beginnings of a very powerful physique. Éilis looked at Séamus again as he stroked effortlessly through the waters off Cúl Buí, and as he turned over a wave, she felt her eyes were deceiving her. She stood up quickly and looked again. Séamus's torso, chest, and back were covered in marks.

—Is it the tattoos? asked the priest, who was belatedly reading his morning prayers but couldn't settle to them. Glad anyway of the diversion.

—Jesus. Sorry, Father. Séamus has got tattoos!

Father McCartan sighed and put away his breviary.

—His mother is fit to be tied. She's not speaking to him. She's nearly not speaking to me.

—How long has he had those?

—Well, he tells me about a year. But he says that they're not for show but just for himself. He went to some chap in Cork who is supposed to be a Druid or something, God help us.

—Muirís Ó Súilleabháin?

—The very man. His mother has banned him from having anything to do with this Ó Súilleabháin but that won't stop Séamus. Apparently, Muirís leads an army of youths around Munster like the pied piper. I'd very much like to meet him. I've read his poetry in Irish. It all seems quite harmless to me though. They all have to learn a musical instrument, write poetry, and learn about the old gods. Maybe I am in the wrong job, Éilis.

—Ah no, Father, you are doing a great job. But I don't get it. Why hasn't he shown them to me before now?

The priest gave something of a cough.

—Well even through all this heat, he's kept himself covered

up. He is incredibly disciplined. Actually worryingly so for a young man. But on Thursday, the day after the interview with Darren, he apparently walked into the living room half-naked, I mean, with just a towel from his waist down after a shower and, well, you can imagine what Mary said.

—And Mary blames Tony.

—And Mary blames his father, Tony, Anthony she calls him now, as women tend to do when they get annoyed with their spouses. Use the formal names of their husbands, I mean.

—But you can't blame the father, in fairness.

—Well, Mary says "Anthony" filled his head full of Cú Chulainn, the Fianna, and Oisín. She's not speaking to him, either.

—Who? Cú Chulainn?

—No, Tony.

—What are they anyway, the tattoos, Father?

—They're actually very artistic. I said this to Mary because she came to speak to me about it, her being a woman from the country. But I'm afraid that I made things even worse by pointing out that the Celts had a tradition of painting their bodies with woad.

—I can see he has a flower or something on his back.

—No, if you see it close up, it's a representation of Oisín. He has a running wolfhound on his midriff and just above his heart. Well, on his heart . . . there's . . . It's a, what would you call it?

—What does he have on his heart?

—He. Well, it's just an *E*, with a fada. E fada. *É tá fhios agat.*

—What does that stand for?

—He says it stands for Éire.

When Séamus came in from the sea, he carried with him the cool and freshness of the Atlantic. The priest threw him the towel from his kit bag and then an awkward silence descended between the three, as the less that was said about Séamus's tattoos, the more it was obvious that was a topic of great interest. In fact, the most obvious topic, given that it was standing right in front of them. Éilis put on her sunglasses and lay back on her towel. The heat in the sand and the sea air along with the excitement of the day and the much-welcome visit from her dearest friends eased a contentment into Éilis's very bones and she began to fall over into a semisleep. As she closed her eyes to the rush and flow of the tide, she remembered that it was on this very beach that she had found her amber. The beach where Séamus Dempsey now appeared to her, for the first time as a man. Éilis knew this because she realised that as she had followed Séamus's course in the water that he made her feel like a woman. Her heart had leaped when he had climbed up the small stack out from the shore and the water washing all around it and he waving and grinning with a smile to kill for and she wanted to swim out to him so that they could frolic like *rónta*, seals. Then they would swim away to one of the deserted islands where there was only the call of birds in the cliffs, the rhythm of life and tides and peace. Séamus doing handstands and cartwheels along the tide and not a bother to him. É for Éilis written in the sand and the clouds to prove that dreams are real.

—*Éirigh leat, a thaisce*, Séamus said, now standing above her.

—Oh, Séamus, *thit mé i mo choladh*.

—Sleep! On a day like today. No way, girl.

Éilis held out her hand for Séamus to pull her up which he did only to then pick her up in his arms with surprising ease and run with her in his arms straight back into the sea. The shrieks of Éilis's laughter echoed across the bay where Mac Fheilimidh flashed a smile as his men pulled in the herring, on and on to Árainn Mhór where a troupe of players thrashed their fiddles with furious delight on the quay, and back to the mountains again, where local people swore they saw Muckish take a "bucklep" in the sunshine. Grass waving in the soft breeze along the dunes. Their laughter echoing along an empty beach. He lifted her up and she drenched and exhilarated and she pushing him over a wave then looking around to see Father McCartan disappearing over the dunes, the marram grass, the *Dúiche* that had fed the cattle, hid guns, wrecked ships, observed drowning men and crashed boats, beached whales, illicit affairs, eagles, herons, incipient romances, accidents of romances, and fierce love also. Love so fierce and pure it was mute and celibate. Séamus running back to her now with his towel. A large T-shirt also, and jeans, for herself. No embarrassment or shame at all as she dried and dressed.

Séamus placing his palm on the side of Éilis's face, which dripped salt water and was cool with excitement. Both of them out of breath from pure laughter and the surge of a riot of sea ions and love.

—Oh, Séamus! *Is fada an lá go raibh mé stiúgtha ghaire mar sin!*

—*An bhfanfá liom?* he asked abruptly.

—*Cad é?*

—*Fán liom go dtí go bhfuil mé réidh duit. An bhfanfá?*

—*D'fhanfainn cinnte a Shéamuis,* but we have to tell Finn.

—Well, it's partly for Finn's sake we have to wait. But there are other things. Anyway, Finn would just laugh at his little brother. Wait two years for me. There's things I have to do, Éilis. *Tá go leor rudaí le foghlaim agam.* We're setting up new things about the language and about our culture. You know, me and lots of others. But there's nobody like you and never will be again. So if you'll wait for me.

—Feck this waiting around, Séamus Dempsey. *Tá mise ag iarraidh bheith páirteach chomh maith!* And maybe yez can learn a few things from me, don't forget.

Éilis now took Séamus's head in her hands and kissed him gently on the lips. It took a while for Séamus to compose himself after receiving his first real kiss from Éilis Devanney. Something he had dreamed of for so long. He half turned away. No fake coyness, Éilis knew. She surprised at his reticence. His certain endearing shyness. But then he looking up suddenly determined.

—That's my point, Éilis. I don't know an awful lot about anything. You are way ahead of me. Out of my league, sure. But we want you to be our spokesman person, or whatever.

—Who's we?

—Well, where we are we've called ourselves the Sons of Oisín, but the two Goths involved say they don't like that.

—Those Goths, eh! Who'd have thought it.

—The Sons of Shelley they're saying. Hah, no chance, man.

It's *Athbheochan* in other parts of the country, he says, but is drowned by her laughter.

Séamus waiting for Éilis to stop laughing. Beginning to laugh himself but also looking at the fall of her hair across her pale shoulder. The fine hairs on the nape of her neck, golden in the sunshine. She bending her head down in convulsions. He had never seen the nape of her neck. Would she just stay like that forever and her face slowly rising and they could turn to sand and be monuments to some great thing as yet undefined until the sea came as the sea must, perhaps at her bidding, and they would meld with the ocean, the world, the ether, and the universe because nothing this strong can die, though form might change.

—So we don't have a name, Éilis, but we've been doing things. Small things.

—Like what?

—Much as the same as in Munster. You've heard about Muirís Ó Súilleabháin. History stuff and culture, but also language. Don't start laughing again, but that Goth called Turlough, the culchie. He gave a brilliant talk about Oscar Wilde. But we also do combat training. The ones in the inner circle. The core cadre.

—What do you need that for?

—*Go hiomlán faoi rún.* We're going to clear them from the streets, Éilis. Starting off with places like Star of the Sea and then spreading all over the country.

—Séamus, *níos lú foréigin de dhíth*, not more of it

—Violence? Nobody wants violence. No. We want to try alternative ways like street festivals and things but we're going to need to be able to defend ourselves. I've heard you say in the past that we need the Fianna back. Well, this is something like it, hopefully.

—Yes, but I meant more as a spiritual, holy thing. A new consciousness amongst the people.

—*Táimid ag ceol an phoirt céanna*, Éilis, but there is one problem that needs fixing before we can start changing people's minds at street level.

—I already know what you're going to say and it's giving me shivers because I see nothing but *raic agus achrann*. Can we go walk the shore for a while?

Linking arms and walking slowly feet half in and half out of the tide. Séamus Dempsey explained how the Untouchables had to be humiliated.

—Yes, I know. I understand, Éilis said gravely.

—And do you know why?

—Yes, because of the children. The ones growing up who are so warped by it all they actually manage to see something glamorous in an eejit like Spanzo. It's their only way of earning money and status. I'm are aware of that.

Éilis pulling Séamus round. Looking into him.

—But it can never stop there. It will always spiral and you can't control it. Best to let the Guards and city council, Father McCartan, Sinn Féin, and all the rest of them. Let them deal with it, Séamie. We'll do the cultural stuff.

—The trouble is we can't trust the Guards, Éilis, and political parties are shite. Just in it for votes, then they disappear for years till the next vote.

A raised voice now off somewhere above and smiles as Father McCartan reappeared at the head of the dunes and waved to them to come up for dinner and they raced hand in hand along the shore until Éilis tripped Séamus from behind because she could no longer keep up with him. Or perhaps he dragged his feet at the end. Waiting for her to make the move.

The Laugh of Finn

IN THE EVENING, Father McCartan phoned Empire Television with a message for Tommy Baker confirming that Éilis was happy to do an interview that day week. To the priest's surprise, he received a call straight back on his mobile from Tommy Baker who was delighted at the news.

—My God, Tommy, you are working on a Saturday evening.

—One of the pleasures of the job, Father. I have to get a draft programme script ready for the lawyers for Monday, and anyway it seems that I am safer here.

—Safer, what do you mean?

—Last night at around eleven o'clock some men walked into John of God's looking for me. Mr Heffernan's goons, I suppose. Empire has put me in a special office with round-the-clock security.

—Oh dear. Should I tell Séamus?

—Well, it's as well to be clear with everyone about the danger from Heffernan, but I think they are all aware of that. Anyway, I won't say much more whilst you are on that thing.

—What thing?

—Your mobile, Father. You may as well be talking straight to Mr Heffernan himself.

The priest looked at his mobile phone in horror and threw it down onto the Sweeneys' kitchen table as if it had suddenly contracted a plague.

—Hello, Father? Hello?

This is Spanzo back from France. The front door he pushes at in Star of the Sea flats. Weird because it's open, though the flat's been empty for weeks. Éilis's parents' flat. They've fucked off to Spain. So Jimmy gave them money, did he? Spanzo needs space. Jimbo's eye off the ball, so he expands his flop-pad empire. Few mattresses, few underage Romanian girls, geebags, smackheads, but very popular with a certain class of Dub for some reason. Good stash for the stuff as well. His own stuff he was bringing in. Put a few of the handy lads in here at night to look after things—good kickback for them. Peace of mind for him. This is what Jimmy should have kept doing instead of getting big ideas. Some kind of change going on with some of the Guards. That guy Gregory turning up at the arch. Time to be less visible for a while. Fuck Heffernan anyway. Spanzo punching the door of a kitchen cupboard till it disintegrates. Spanzo's the Man now. Spanzo grins. Gave that cupboard a right dig.

—Oh yes, Tommy, sorry, I threw the phone away. Yes, say nothing. That's the thing, but where are you going to stay? I mean actually live. Oh, sorry, there I go on again.

　　—Well, I've moved somewhere just outside of Dublin. I doubt whether even Jimmy Heffernan could find the place. How's Séamus?

　　—Well, by the Holy Name, I think I can safely say that he is in love!

　　—Ha, ha, I can't recommend it highly enough. Anyone I know? Hello? Father, I've lost you again.

This new world of cautious telephone conversations and second-guessing all actions was a new thing for Father McCartan, and he did not like the effect it all had on his natural exuberance. He had been on the verge of mentioning the seemingly growing affinity between Éilis and Séamus. He stood up from his chair and stared at his mobile phone until he was absolutely sure that he had turned it off. Looked at it. Turned it on again to make sure he could turn it off. Watched the light dying. His cheeks were burning and he walked out into the warm early evening air, which was cooled by a soft Atlantic breeze. He stopped his pipe and stood under a salt wind–blasted pine tree at the side of the front lawn. After a few minutes some of the older Sweeney children and their friends emerged from the back of the house. They were all dressed up in the gaudy yet shy way of country youths, and the priest marvelled at their quick-fire Donegal Irish. Just at the gate they waved to him before heading up the road to a teenage disco, as they still called it.

After bidding the youths a good evening, Father McCartan sat on the wall next to the tree and searched his soul for answers to his many troubling questions. Had it been simple vanity on his part that motivated his desire to help make a film about Heffernan and his henchmen? Jesus above, where was Darren Bulger? He had vivid memories of trying to help Darren's mother off heroin, but she had killed herself with it in the end.

Had his priestly vanity now placed people in danger? Was it going to place Éilis in more danger? He had talked at length with Tony Dempsey and a group of parents from the flats who were all adamant that what was going on at the arch and other places needed to be exposed. He certainly agreed with them and maybe this really was the best way. He had tried to interest local journalists in the story several times, but, to a man, they had said that the story was too big for them, or simply that they were too scared. Would Heffernan come after him? He drew an extra-strong suck on his brier and was content in the knowledge that he personally had the fortitude to face whatever was before him. The true place of the Church was amongst its people, he mused, not in ornate and desolate palaces far removed from its flock. And if giving moral and spiritual leadership had its dangers then it was only the same danger that his people were threatened with every day. Besides, after the way the Church in Ireland had desecrated its own altar with its arrogance and abuse, was it not time for its humble priests to begin to make sacrifices of atonement. To begin the work of banishing the Evil which had been allowed to flourish unchallenged?

Father McCartan rose from the wall, knocked his pipe against its ancient stone and walked out from beneath the tree where *An Seisreach*, the Plough, loomed above him in its majesty. The Plough, a symbol used by the *Gaeil*, to celebrate the worker and peasant, playwright and poet. A symbol that always gave him great hope. A constellation that in its soaring journey across the heavens always said so much to him. He took in great gulps of sea air and his prayers seemed to be answered by the sound of hearty laughter coming from somewhere in the house. He walked closer, head slightly cocked, to the side of the house and realised that the laughter was coming from Éilis's room. A guitar was occasionally strummed—Éilis was very good on the guitar—and then there would be another peal of laughter. This time Séamus Dempsey could be heard saying something about notes sounding the same. Then there was more laughter as Séamus tried to sing the note. Éilis was teaching Séamus how to play the guitar.

The priest turned away, no longer wishing to pry and not wishing to be seen to be prying. He had been invited by the man of the house to join him in a few rounds of cards at a neighbour's house and perhaps a drop of whisky and water. He spent the rest of an enjoyable evening in the company of what he termed "his people." He came away from the cards table ten euro to the good, something which pleased him immensely. It was around one o'clock in the morning by the time he got back to the Sweeney household. There had been great craic and conversation on the neighbours' doorstep and a final *leathchinn* to be had before coming home. On the way to his room, Father McCartan noticed that Éilis's door on the ground floor was slightly ajar. This was unusual, as Éilis had told him that she had taken to locking her door at night. The priest hesitated. Should he look in quickly to see that all was well? He did so, because he knew that he would never sleep, or forgive himself, unless he did. In the weak light of a waning moon, he could see that Éilis was fast asleep. At the foot of Éilis's bed, meanwhile, he saw that Séamus was ensconced in some kind of moleskin sleeping bag which had been laid on top of a canvas mat. Séamus had also laid out some kind of white banner with letters in black but they were too small for the priest to read. —*Cú* Éilis, the priest breathed to himself. Éilis now had her own wolfhound. He said a silent prayer over both their heads and sprinkled holy water before Éilis's door, which he had taken from the small font at the front door.

—May God bless the Queen of the *Gaeil* and those who revere her, he said. Father McCartan then slept a wondrous sleep, certain in the knowledge that his prayers would be answered.

Early on Monday morning Séamus Dempsey returned to Dublin with Father McCartan, but not before he had promised Éilis to be back in two week's time. He had a handball tournament in Waterford the next weekend and he was going to stay there and link up with some young people in the county who had also joined up to Muirís Ó Súilleabháin's organisation—*Athbheochan*. Éilis had told Séamus that she would write something for the group's magazine about her ideas for placing pickets on supermarkets and banks that were busy broadcasting what she called globalisation propaganda, day in, day out. It would be a good way, she said, of preparing for her television interview with Tommy Baker, as there were some wider points she wanted to make about what was happening in her community.

Séamus gave not one squat about community just at that second. His thoughts were only of Éilis as he watched the mountains of Donegal disappear behind him. With each brook and boreen that was passed, he felt that he was slowly being dismembered. Mile after mile was put behind them as, first, regal Errigal and then Muckish Mountain faded and then dissolved into a blue morning haze before disappearing altogether as Father McCartan's car turned off the mountain road and into civilisation. Séamus wanted to be in Dublin the moment there was no more physical trace of the Gaeltacht and was tortured by the bald fact that he had another five hours of travelling in front of him. He cursed Father McCartan's jalopy, which seemed to have gone so fast over the mountains but now inched along at the pace of a tortoise. Cursed it for its slowness and also for its direction of travel. This tortured youth absentmindedly pulled a wide green hairband from his pocket, which Éilis had given him that morning, and to his delight he found a note held by a smaller band. It slipped off and fell onto the floor of the car.

A Shéamais a ghrá. Na bí thíos agus tú ag imeacht.

Ná déan dearmad go bhfuil mo lámh ort agus go bhfanfaidh mé leat go deo. Tusa mo laoch Tusa mo anam chara.

PS—I rang Finn as I knew he was starting work early. It's funny, he says that there is nothing for them to do. Anyways, it turns out you were right, Séamus! I told Finn that I thought I was falling in love with his little brother and he dropped the phone with laughter.

Séamus read and reread the note until his eyes were sore with the reading of it. Then, at an appropriate moment where fields stretched all about the road from Letterkenny to Strabane, he asked the priest whether he minded stopping the car. As soon as the car had been pulled into the hard shoulder and was stationary, Father McCartan beheld the spectacle of a young man whom he thought he knew very well, Séamus Dempsey, running up the curved stem of a large tree, issuing a blood-curdling roar from one of its branches and then leaping to the ground from said branch and proceeding to deliver a series of flying kicks and somersaults through the air. Séamus then adopted a seated position and began to stare into the distance for such a length of time that the priest began to worry that someone else had had a seizure. When Séamus returned to the car, Father McCartan had smoked two pipes and drunk a full bottle of water.

—I am only going to ask one thing, Séamus.

—Yes, Father.

—Was it good news or bad news?

—Ah, Father McCartan, it was the best news of all.

—That was my question. Now comes the inevitable lecture, Séamus. Well, what I mean is that when this happens in close-knit families, which is very rare, but when it does . . . You know . . . I think that what I am trying to say is . . . God help me, I am not very good at this.

—Ah, Father, don't be worrying. Meself and Éilis were talking about it last night. *Tá gach rud cool.* There's no point making a big fuss about it until I get me exam results and see where I'll go to uni. Éilis is talking about staying in Gaoth Dobhair, so I could go to college in Derry. We'll see.

Father McCartan nodded furiously at this fountain of good sense, as he tried to stop his pipe afresh and drive the car all at the same time. He driving with his big knee to Séamus's alarm. The priest wished to encourage caution upon Séamus and Éilis, given that he felt partly responsible for creating this new situation.

—*Ná bí buartha a Athair.* We are not about to run into the house announcing that Éilis is pregnant with my child or anything.

—Jesus, Séamus, don't even mention the word pregnant! the priest cried as he struggled to maintain control of his vehicle, such was his shock. His hands now firmly on the wheel.

—No, Séamus, my advice is to let the hare sit. Your mother is from the country and what with the tattoos and now this.

—Ah no, there's no point saying anything to me mam for a good while, but Finn knows about it.

At this the priest went white.

—What do you mean Finn knows about it?

Séamus looked down at Éilis's note to check once again that he had read everything correctly.

—Éilis phoned Finn this morning before breakfast and kind of mentioned that we were, eh, you know, Father . . . ehm, falling in love, I suppose.

—And Finn just laughed, I take it.

—Exactly, Father, Finn just laughed. Sure our Finn will be laughing at his own funeral. Or that is what me granny used to say, *Dia go deo lei.*

—Séamus. I hope Finn is still laughing if you two do get hitched. Oh Lord. I feel like a concerned parent.

—A concerned Father. Yes, said Séamus.

The Drain of Life

On WEDNESDAY MORNING of the following week, Philip Enderby, who had worked for Jimmy Heffernan as his financial adviser for the best part of ten years, received a short note and a cheque in the post. The note was from Jimmy Heffernan's new financial advisers, who were, he saw, based in Switzerland, and who advised him of the fact that he was no longer representing Heffernan's financial interests. The cheque contained the correct amount owing to Enderby, down to the last cent, for the work that he had carried out during that financial year. A terse line at the bottom of the note reminded Enderby of his continued obligations as regards client confidentiality and gave contact details for any "mutual issues arising in this regard." Tears welling in his eyes, Enderby phoned Heffernan's country pile seeking some kind of explanation. At the third almost frantic attempt, Arthur, the head gardener, came to the phone.

—Ah, Philip, it's yourself. What can I do you for?

At the sound of the gardener's voice, Enderby tried to compose himself and reestablish the professional status quo.

—Arthur, where the hell's the secretary? And it's Mr Enderby to you.

—All paid up, Philip.

—Sorry?

—We are all paid up. Well, Jimmy says I can stay in the Lodge until this new crowd move in, and, well, I met them yesterday and they will obviously need a gardener so . . .

—Arthur, what the hell's fuck are you talking about?

—Did you not know, Phil? Arthur said with a deep relish that only a man of the soil can muster. The house is sold. Mr Heffernan has already moved out. All he took was a painting and his aftershave as he said himself . . . ha, ha. Bit ironic when you think about it.

—What?

—Well, that I should be the only one that keeps his job.

—How long have you known about this, Arthur?

—Well, Mr Heffernan warned me at the Christmas, but there was to be no fuss, he said. Not a word to anyone or I'll chop your dick off, says he. But I must say he gave us all a great send-off, what with that singer being here. What's this you call her now?

—Oh, of course, the party. I couldn't make it. Too much work on, said Enderby, lying to save his face.

—Well, the food was lovely and she loves Pierce Beaumont the missus does.

For a moment, and for the cause of simple burning revenge, Philip Enderby considered breaching his client's confidentiality, his oath of *Omerta* given freely to Jimmy Heffernan, but he knew that there would be far more pain than gain in this option. His penchant for long weekends in Amsterdam, which Heffernan had funded and encouraged, were not something he wanted divulged to anybody else within his profession, nor to his wife and children. Enderby tried to ring Heffernan on the encrypted shortwave business phone, but, as he expected, the service had been cancelled. A half an hour later he received the first call from former business partners enquiring as to why Enderby was no longer representing Heffernan's financial interests. Was there a problem?

Enderby leaned forward on his desk and pushed his spectacles up onto his domed forehead. A thin streak of perspiration marked the track of his glasses to his bald crown and his shirt was warm and damp at the base of his spine. He was in trouble. He had been borrowing money and licence for years on the basis of his relationship with Heffernan. Worse than that, he had promised business deals to certain people, which were now not going to happen. Drinks contracts. Catering. People who were not to be trifled with. People who would not hesitate to do him harm were they to find out that he no longer enjoyed the patronage and protection of the most powerful criminal in Ireland. Some words that his granny used to speak arose from some distant corner of his subconscious—*As you live your life you dread your neighbour.* There and then, he took the decision to emigrate as soon and as anonymously as possible. The day would therefore be spent withdrawing money from secret bank accounts.

The next day, Jimmy Heffernan met with Ned Behan and the Cube on a yacht at a secret location on the coast of West Cork. Both the Cube and Behan were aware that Heffernan was preparing to sail to somewhere in the Mediterranean that weekend. They had both been given the names of the accountants who would be handling all further business questions relating to the nightclubs and wine bars they were running. The changeover was a clear signal that bar and restaurant facilities were now to be run as completely aboveboard business enterprises. Both the Cube and Ned Behan were excited at the prospect of getting their hands on the very lucrative reins of power. Ned Behan suddenly found himself having a shared role, along with a finance adviser and promotions executive, in the running of Connolly's Wine Bars, with two hundred and fifty employees across the country at his disposal, not to mention the ancillary staff. He had come a long way from being an officer in the IRA's internal security unit. Neither the Cube nor Behan would know the identity of Heffernan's business liaison adviser—a Tex-Mex finance executive who was already a legend on Wall Street.

—Ned, make sure you run a personal check on all the new staff that have come in within the last three months. In all the new outlets.

—I've already done that, Jimmy.

—How are you enjoying your newfound power and wealth?

—Well, it's a bit like being back in the RA, except that I get to keep some of the takings and can afford to buy a nice house.

This point appealed to Heffernan enormously and he sat back in his chair exhaling cigar smoke to enjoy the moment. However, he quickly returned to much graver matters. Turning to Vincent "the Cube" Duffy, he spoke in a slightly raised and excited tone.

—Now, about the cleanup. Is London going ahead, Vincent?

—Well, I got a nod from the bookies an hour ago that the going was good. I'll check back later but it seems to have happened. Race over for Frankie.

—And Ned, what about that hole we needed to fill?

—All good, Jimmy. Done and dusted.

—Good, excellent. Let's celebrate boys!

Ned Behan, in his fresh role as an executive, made bold to inform Heffernan that his decision not to go to war with the Dempseys was the correct one.

Heffernan rose from the table to fetch champagne from a large fridge.

—Yes, Ned. They all knock lumps out of each other down at the arch for as long as they want and smash each other's houses up. Let Spanzo attract all that heat. Now, I'll be up in Dublin for the last time on Saturday evening. That's what the photo shoot is all about at the bar, Ned. That reminds me, I've to deal with a Garda, a detective, who stopped me as I was driving into the club and gave me a load of lip.

—Okay, boss, said Ned Behan cheerily.

—He's based in Dublin and I've found out he's related to the housekeeper at St Bridget's. So a culchie obviously. Big ginger cunt. Redneck. He needs a lesson in Dublin manners.

Finn Dempsey returned from his lunch break and noticed that Frankie Byrne was not careering around on a dumper truck as he had taken to doing. It took a couple of hours for Finn to really start wondering where Frankie had got to. He had run off the site that morning saying that he had to send something from the post office. Then Finn had been distracted by a job that was going on at a neighbouring site which was getting a big delivery of concrete slabs and they had discovered that Finn was a very good banksman. When he had returned from the job to his own site, he went down to the rest of the Irish gang who had started the job with him, but nobody had a clue where Frankie had gone. When Frankie had not returned to his digs in the evening, Finn became concerned enough to ring home to Dublin to enquire whether his wife, Nuala, had heard from him that day. He then rang Éilis in Gaoth Dobhair, who was short with him and told him to contact the police straightaway. Éilis back in weirdland, he said to himself.

—The cops. No I am not doing that, Éilis, Frankie will be raging if I do that because I think he's, you know. Well, I know he is. You know, Éilis.

—*Abair i nGaeilge é*, Finn.

—*Tá sé ag déanamh an double, so ní bheith sé ag iarraidh aon fiosrú ó na gardaí.*

—Finn, you have to call the cops. Something has happened to Frankie Byrne. This is the start of the trouble.

—Éilis, *sin tú arís*, starting that craic. Every time something happens it's the end of the bleedin' world. Frankie could be anywhere. He could have met a girl. He could have got a notion to head off somewhere because he can't walk for cash in his pockets and all you can say is . . . Hello? Hello, Éilis, *an bhfuil tú fós ann?*

Finn Dempsey waited for another minute for Éilis to return to the phone, but she never did. She never did. No, she never did.

He went into the locker room on the building site, lifted his coat, his handballs, and his tools, and walked off the site. Dermot Lacey, his best friend from his school days, saw the look on Finn Dempsey's face and ran to collect his own jacket.

—I take it there'll be no more work for us today, Finnius.

—Do you know what, Dermot? There'll be no more work done today and when that Frankie Byrne finally shows up he's dead meat. He's putting everyone at home into a blind panic.

—So, what now?

—I'm going to get cleaned up and then walk into the first bar that hits me.

—Will I run back and tell the others?

—No. Text them later and tell them we'll be in the Old Bell in Kilburn at seven.

Spanzo walking up the stairwell to Nora Farrell's flat, bumping into the walls. Annoyed. His brain trying to work it out. Why was he even doing this? The sooner Jimmy got offside the better. Goes to bang on the door then minds that Jimmy said nice and easy. Sticks a grand in your pocket—nice and easy, Spanzo. So he taps and eventually the old bat opens up, eyes him, wonders about releasing her chain but then relents. He walks in doing nothing. Everything okay, Mrs Farrell? Just looking after you, like. Next door was a bit noisy the other night? I'll have a word. There'll be nobody here this weekend anyway. Haven't seen that Éilis girl around, no? Oh that's right, she's off to Donegal. Bit strange, what with her boyfriend Finn back and all that. No he's definitely back. Saw him meself. I know, I know, Mrs London mustn't agree with him, or maybe he's lovesick. Eh? No thanks, Mrs, no tea. Head off now.

Spanzo appearing on the landing is shot by Dessie Noonan's toy gun two storeys up. One in the head and one in the heart to finish him like in the game. Like in his mind, replaying the moment. Like the football highlights he could pick with his ma's remote.

Spanzo bouldering across the flats wondering what the fuck that was all about and what the fuck Jimmy. Not understanding, and never will, that this was Jimmy Heffernan at his best.

The Morrígan

JAMES TIERNEY HAD a day off as he had been flat-out helping with final fact-checking for his river-pollution story. The film was all but ready and was waiting for clearance from Empire's lawyers. Ronagh had rung him to ask where he was and news of a day off led her to invite herself round in the afternoon, which invitation he refused saying he had stuff to read and didn't even get to saying things to write as she had slammed the phone down. He went for a run, did weights for half an hour, cleaning his mind of all thought and herself raising the idea of marriage, then took a long bath. After that he picked up Éilis's diary and started to piece things together again. The ripped-out sections. There was something in the pages he had torn out—as if there was something growing there. Tommy Baker in some sort of retreat. He blowing his cheeks, setting his shoulders to take the load. Ronagh would have to learn. The pages of the diary. There was something there in all that delirium. Maybe he should ring Ronagh. No, don't. Concentrate, God damn.

Early on Friday morning. Éilis Devanney opening her eyes and realising that this was her last day in Gaoth Dobhair for the time being. Finn. Something urgent about Finn. She'd have to ring. Make sure he was staying away. As long as he stayed away from that flat he was safe. She knew that. She would have to persuade him. Apologise for the way she was, also. That things had changed. That she couldn't change. Did not even want to change. Did not want to fall asleep like he had done, in some way. Even the thought was a betrayal, but it was there nonetheless. Now all she wished for him was to be happy. Happy and alive.

She rose and walked to the window. The bus to Dublin was at seven. House, Donegal quiet. Clouds in the sky. Serious Irish clouds at three or four levels of existence. The first real clouds for weeks and weeks. They had an angry sheen at the rim and a darkness in their heart. Higher above them again was a black speck that would hover and then circle on some blast of air. Not a *Spioróg* or *Iolar*, that.

Éilis took her piece of amber from the dresser and held it aloft with her pale long arms at the window. The see-through drape of her sleeve. The white translucence of her face and arms, which were disembodied by the low light of the bedroom. Separated limbs and flesh softened by an ochre wash in the light refracted from her touchstone. Like some Celtic mime from ancient times. She'd no need to look out of the window to know that the black speck had vanished. She placed her amber on the window ledge and switched on her mobile phone, which buzzed to signal that she had messages.

She was surprised and upset that there was no message from Finn. Surprised also that she was so upset. But she saw that Séamus had left a message to tell her that he was in Waterford and that he would call her over the weekend. It was a revelation to Éilis that she could be both so elated and depressed at one and the same time. A message from Dawn saying that she'd heard Finn was back. Ah. So that's why he hadn't been in touch. Mind made up.

Éilis packed her slim bag. In the kitchen now and eat this banana. Slice of brown bread. Enjoy this banana, yes, lovely. Now the yoghurt. Good, Éilis. Iron now. The bus is at seven so plenty of time because now my mobile will . . . Never mind, it was only half six.

It will. Because this person was not calm. The person who would ring. So it must be that man from Empire.

When it did, it was indeed the television producer Tommy Baker who wished to inform her that he would not be doing the interview with her, which had been planned for five o'clock that day.

—I know. This is the start of the end and we all have to be very careful and strong.

—Sorry?

—The raven is back. That's a bad sign. I need to talk to you personally. I can help you in ways you don't understand. You need to be rebirthed in water.

—Oh right! God I'm not sure what to say . . . Look, Éilis. Is there a landline there that I can use to talk to you? I've something urgent I need to tell you.

Éilis gave Tommy Baker the Sweeney number and ran to bring the phone and its extension cable into the quiet of the kitchen. Baker rang seconds afterwards.

—Are you sitting down, Éilis? You might need to sit down. Only . . .

—Never mind. Is it about Darren or Frankie Byrne?

—It's about Darren. Who's Frankie Byrne?

—We knew Darren was gone. What exactly happened to Darren?

—I'm afraid the Guards have received a tip off that Darren's body has been found somewhere. They're not releasing details yet but . . .

Éilis knew that Baker's remark about not knowing the details was a lie. She gripped the floor with her toes, and the edge of the table with her free hand, to prevent herself falling over.

—He was down a drain or some kind of sewer, she said but the producer was not listening.

—Obviously, this has changed the story significantly. Right now, I have a very important meeting to prepare for. When it's over, at around four o'clock, I'd say, I'll ring you back. Or try.

—You need to meet me at some point. Don't forget. Éilis demurred from telling the producer that she was on her way to Dublin.

—Right. Look, leave a message with James Tierney, my researcher. Dawn knows him.

—I know who James Tierney is.

—Right, bye, Éilis.

—Tommy.

—Yes?

—Are you okay?

—What? Oh yes, fine, as always. Why do you ask?

—Only your voice is shaking.

Darren Bulger

ÉILIS'S EYES INVOKED silence in the room. In the house. In the skies beyond Bloody Foreland. So profound is the passing on of one single being. No wakes in Dublin anymore. But they would talk again, she and Darren. The other side of that great leap he had already made. He was a hero of the Gael because he rose above himself, embraced goodness, laughed at death. Her hand gentle around her amber. The amber that was left in her room with a note telling Mrs Sweeney that Finn was back in Dublin and that she was going to see him. She would go and see Father McCartan as soon as she arrived. Mrs Sweeney shaking her head a few hours later, but informing the authorities was the last thing she would do. Better for the priest to deal with it.

Tommy Baker's rising need for a drink to sustain his forward motion. His thoughts to think. Fishing furiously for his pipe. Eileen gone. Busy studio day she had. Messages of positivity everywhere in her apartment. "One hour at a time." "Every hour is one more hour on the road to freedom." He smoked a pipe and drank water to fill his stomach. Lie down. Listen to Mozart. That's it. Tried to plan for the meeting with Myles Fitzgerald but just felt pathetic. Concentrate on Pierce Beaumont. Yes, that's better. Why had he not interviewed that young girl by now? Extraordinary. But also highly weird. James was right. He'd better ring James.

Baker was expecting at the least irritability and also extreme concern from James Tierney when they met in the pasta restaurant down the road from Empire. After all, there were many things James had not been told. But the young journalist was simply grave and focussed. Himself the son of an alcoholic. Was that why? Baker on edge of his own thoughts. James speaks.

—I was kind of expecting something like Darren Bulger to happen, Tommy. Amazing there's not been more in the media about it.

—Well, I've my own theory about the media silence, but what d'you mean you were expecting it?

—Well, he was obviously a weak link. That scene where Éilis describes him at the arch.

—Jesus, James. You have to stop treating that document as a factual record. She's a gifted girl but a strange girl too. She may actually have a screw loose. I mean, really. This morning, she talked to me like she was my doctor or something.

—Well maybe she could . . .

—Could what?

James Tierney deciding to change the subject in the silence that quickly emerged in Tommy Baker's alcoholic writhing. James telling Baker how he's become enthused by the polluted-rivers story and by the filmmaking process generally. Choosing to say nothing about Ronagh.

—Have to say, Tommy, you were right to keep me and that Éilis story at arm's length.

—Éilis story? Why do you call it that? Heffernan story you mean, surely?

—Well, I'm a bit out of what you've recorded and been told, but it seems to me it all circles round Éilis Devanney. Have you seen her parents, by the way?

—Father McCartan tells me they've upped sticks to Spain, James. But of course she seems to have two sets of parents, at least. And her real parents are called Devanney from Donegal but related to these jackeen yahoos via the woman. What's this you call her? I still don't really get it. Or do I even care? Christ, I need a drink. Sorry.

—Hang in there if you can. My mother beat it but it took a lot of help and support.

—I'm going to contact my counsellor right away but he has
to come to me now and I have to ring a third party. A bloody
go between for security. Pain in the arse. I'm going to go outside
to smoke this pipe.

Now highly wary, Tommy Baker asked permission to use
the back of the premises rather than smoking at the front of the
building. He unaware that Heffernan had ordered that Baker
should be left alone. That the Baker problem had been "sorted."

A more steady and rueful Tommy Baker quietly informed
James Tierney that he had moved all the master rushes (actually
disks but Baker refused to use the term) to a safe place and that
all his programme notes were also in a secure place.

—I didn't know we were allowed to take personal possession
of recorded footage, Tommy?

—We're not. Full stop. All the footage in the hopefully secure
edit suite has been copied from my slash our masters. It's a sack-
able offence in Empire, but I'm fucked if the likes of Diarmuid
Farrelly and Pierce Beaumont and whoever is looking after them
upstairs are going to have those tapes.

—Wow. High stakes.

—James.

—Tommy?

—Well. It's just that you might have to take all this over.
You're the only one I'd trust with that footage. Well, Sitric and
Alan, sure, but they're not us. Not journalists. You may have to
take possession of it.

—Me? Tommy, I'm not sure that's a good idea. I've no pull
in Empire. The opposite in fact. Might be better if I keep my
head down? I mean, of course I'll do it. I don't give a fuck about
Empire Corporate. But I might be of some use in there and . . .

—I just don't know what's going to happen at this meeting.
If I fall off the edge, which may well happen, Eileen will come
to you with instructions.

—Tommy, can we go back to this Éilis and her diary?

—For Christ's sake, James. Would you shut the fuck up about
that bloody diary. You're like a cracked record for God's sake. She's
nothing compared to what I'm going through. Have gone through.

James Tierney watched Baker walk away. Wondering why he had always to deal with alcoholics in his life. Heart breaking for the man also. His designer pipe jeans dropping off him and the jacket with no shoulders to fit around. Hanging. Quiffed greying hair hanging. Hanging in there for grim life.

Still and all. He would go back to that diary and those excised sections. In all their rambling confusion there was some truth hidden there. Something he had overlooked. He was sure.

Tommy Baker wanted to ring Father McCartan to find out more about this person called Frankie Byrne, but he didn't have time as he needed to review the rough-cut version of his film about Heffernan and badly needed to see his counsellor before his meeting with senior staff from Empire Television. He grabbed a sandwich at lunchtime from the snack bar but could not eat it. In fact, the first bite made him nauseous. He rang Eileen even though he knew she was busy with a studio recording that day. He needed to tell her that he badly needed a drink. Nothing. Still killing time before the start of the meeting with his counsel-lor, he almost walked out of the Empire complex but was saved by the sight of James Tierney. Just the sight of him striding back to work. The wonder of his purpose. The vision and confidence in his stride. Big deep breaths, Tommy. One more hour. Then his counsellor arrived at the back of Empire's parking lot and calmed him further.

Baker went to the toilet before the meeting with Myles Fitzgerald, This was a habit he'd developed over many years of attending such events. When he sat down to empty his bow-els, his phone flashed a message. He didn't recognise the num-ber from whence the message came. He guessed it came from one of those throwaway phones. It gloatingly confirmed what he already knew about Darren Bulger's awful fate. As soon as he walked into the boardroom, Baker understood that his film about Jimmy Heffernan was in deep trouble. Not just from the imminent implosion of his own defences but by the cut of Pierce Beaumont's controlled, beaming face. By the fact that his editor, Myles Fitzgerald, had been joined by two board members and also that Diarmuid Farrelly was there and Joe Cullinane was not. Diarmuid Farrelly. All solemn and pleased. And Myles would not look at him. No he would not. By the fact that Myles's hair was pushed up onto his forehead. By Myles's ashen face and by the fact that what he, Tommy Baker, desperately, desperately was going to do was to drink and fuck all else. Did nobody understand? Where was Eileen right now? Somebody was addressing him but he just wanted to go home. But where was home? He could not do this anymore. The Darren Bulger thing had genuinely scared him and now he just wanted to keep living. It was all too big. Eileen had promised to pick him up at tea time if he had finished and she was sure the meeting would go well. Still ignoring whoever it was that was talking to him, he placed a picture of Darren Bulger in front of everyone who was at the meeting. Baker then walked to the door and turned to those present in the room.

—Meet Darren Bulger, gentlemen. He was found down a manhole early this morning with his tongue cut out and his penis in his mouth. They can't move him yet because they have been told there's some sort of device under his body. You don't need to tell me your decision about my film. Nor do you need me to tell you who was responsible for this atrocity. Presumably you will conclude that what has happened to Darren Bulger has nothing to do with the fact that he recently did an interview for us naming Jimmy Heffernan as a killer, drugs baron, and extortionist. Hopefully, the Garda Síochána will take a different view.

—Sit down, Tommy, and enough of the melodrama, somebody said.

Ignoring this jibe, Baker turned to his soon-to-be-former boss, Myles Fitzgerald.

—Myles, I'd already cancelled this afternoon's interview and the flight to Gweedore. As from this moment, please consider me no longer a part of this wonderful crusading organisation. Baker not even trying to hide the quiver in his standing leg. Myles Fitzgerald himself in extreme discomfort speaking to him.

—Tommy we are not cancelling the film but we need to be very careful. Need to discuss what we're getting into and whether it's worth the grief. I mean what hard proof do we actually have against Heffernan apart from the fact that his bouncers ejected you from his club? That secret film tells us nothing without corroborative evidence. Okay, he seems to admit having illegally obtained footage for the purposes of extortion but we can't be sure that's not him just boasting. Heffernan has millions and could clean us out if we get this wrong. Damn it. And I haven't seen that poor young man's interview yet because you've—

—Worth the grief, Myles? Worth the fucking grief?

Tommy Baker turned his back.

Baker closed the door to the senior exec. room and his veteran career, thus muffling the sound of an ironic handclap by an individual in the room. He staggered into the bathroom across the corridor and knelt into a toilet bowl, got violently sick, and then came a tsunami of tears from some part of his head and stomach, which tightened and retched with each fresh squall. This man in the tight cubicle that was closing in on him, crushing him, let me die now, give me a knife or rope, PLEASE, FOR GOD'S SAKE!

He didn't know how long he was there. Heard a being walk in, walk out, but he didn't care. Tears, just tears and sobs. Sobs for Darren Bulger, sobs for his name and career, sobs for this thing that he couldn't fight, sobs for his unbelief and unamaze. That he could not believe so effortlessly and superbly in the way that James did. His patheticness. That nothing could be changed. He writhing in his cynicism and not wanting it but wanting to drag James Tierney down to his despair because nothing was worth it, and not wanting James to have the pain of that discovery. The crash that would come.

Now quiet. The smell of toilet cleaner and puke clearing the bile in his nose. Blood drops in the bowl. Can breathe now and look at my watch. Three o'clock. Yes, I've made it to three o'clock!

The man stands up in his Resurrection, suddenly understanding Christ's Passion. His weeping for the world. The joy of rebirth because nothing dies, though the flesh is weak. Holy,

Holy, Holy Lord. God of power and might. Heaven and Earth are full of your glory. Hosanna in the highest and utter glorious weakness that can be put right. If he just could love. Effortlessly like James did. Believe effortlessly like James did. So easy it was absurd. There in the absurd it is. The simple ridiculous impossible ease of it. It's beyond reason that I can find happiness somewhere so why try to reason, for fuck's sake? Tommy standing at the mirror at the washbasin being lifted by the absurd idea that no sane argument could save him. Just sheer belief without proof. Now hands on the countertop running along the washbasins he starts to laugh out loud. Yes, laughing to himself. Looking at himself in all his ridiculousness and suddenly strong. Careless of the man walking behind him, he straightens up, throws water over his face and walks out of the bathroom. He now knows what he has to do. He can do this but will need to mind himself.

Andrew Mendoza was in a meeting with the head of Empire's marketing and research. The latter saying something about audience satisfaction and peaks and troughs when Tommy Baker marched in without a by-your-leave and having simply ignored Mendoza's secretary when she had inquired of his purpose. At first Mendoza assumed that Baker was drunk but there were no alcohol, or indeed cigarette, fumes and Baker had been down to makeup to get freshened up. A hint of pipe maybe? Surely not? Mendoza gave an appealing look to the marketing guy and he stood up with a sigh.

The pair spent an hour together and the fruit of their meeting was that they would reconvene that evening at Joseph Cullinane's home in the Wicklow Hills. Even though Cullinane was not yet aware of this occasion.

With some initial annoyance Cullinane cancelled his bridge evening and sat down to listen to what Baker and Mendoza had to say. He was also shown the secret film recording of the conversation between Tommy Baker and Jimmy Heffernan. As Cullinane pointed out, even though he was retiring, and even though Myles Fitzgerald—"who still has my confidence, gentlemen"—was not technically obliged to show footage or raise issues with him, protocol demanded that he be shown the footage, and why was he not? Possibly someone from the board of governors had leaned on him. So who was that? He would make discreet inquiries. So, for all these reasons, Baker had done the right thing. What the hell was Myles Fitzgerald playing at really? Baker suddenly wanting to cry with joy. Yes, yes that was it.

As a clock gong somewhere in Cullinane's spacious house bonged midnight, Cullinane shook hands on an agreement to the effect that not only would all efforts be made to show the film on Heffernan at some stage in the future, but that, before Cullinane retired in two months' time, James Tierney would be given a permanent staff job at Empire on the basis of a glowing report and recommendation from Andrew Mendoza, backed up by his signature. The two veteran Empire executives bade a quite emotional farewell to Tommy Baker, who was nothing physically anymore. Nothing except inner willpower.

Eileen Brennan opening her front door with a resigned air at two in the morning. She determined, waiting for the lies, deceits, forcefully upbeat, eyes wide, skin drawn to pallid, scared evanescence, she ready for Tommy Baker pouring himself through the door, half-cut, met a friend, he had bad news, had to commiserate, few pints, but Tommy Baker sucking a mint and smiling exhaustedly.

—Get your bags packed. We're going to Gerona in the morning.

—Jesus, why. Have they tracked you down to here?

—No. I'm just loving myself and loving you.

By the time she had brought decaffeinated tea and biscuits into her—no, their—bedroom, Tommy Baker was asleep fully clothed on top of the bed. Eileen Brennan packing quickly. Going whilst the going was good.

As a middle-aged man who had sat down beside her tried to engage her in genuine, friendly bus conversation, Éilis watched the vast expanse of bog and mountain slip away. She'd received a number of texts from Deirdre and Sinéad about the party in Drumcondra. She would go, she decided. A last swansong for the girls from the wall. She sounded the depths of her feelings and premonitions but could find no threat there. The main thing was to talk to Finn.

Then she turned to chat to the man who asked her whether the language would die, or would some remnant of it cling to these remote areas and these strange mountain and bog people. It was, he told her, some kind of enchanting elf land—a doomed Tolkien myth. Ravendell. But Éilis told him there were young people all over the country and especially in the towns who would not let it die.

Éilis made to switch off her phone as the bus neared Strabane and the Six Counties that made up Northern Ireland—as she hated the welcome-to-another-country texts from her service provider—but just as she made to push the off button she saw a text from Deirdre. It was to remind her that the Goths were playing a set at the party that night and her culchie hunk would be there, so Éilis could meet him. She then said that someone had seen Finn knocking around.

The man next to me talking to me. Me keeping my phone on and ringing Finn but no answer. What was he doing back in Dublin? How had Frankie Byrne got him back? It must have been Frankie Byrne. Finn won't break his promise to me, but I have to tell him that it's best for him to get away anyway. Séamus. Titfidh sé amach lena dhearthair. And, no, I don't know why Irish disappeared so quickly in Kerry or what Dangle is Dingle this minute. Jesus, man. Bí i do thost sa tsioc—shut the fuck up.

Getting Down and Dirty

ALMOST AS SOON as the workman had manoeuvred the skip into position and departed, Spanzo's three henchmen heaved the mattress through the bedroom window that was three storeys above. Éilis's old flat. Part of the window and its frame cracked as they bent the mattress down to get it through the opening. The mattress had been badly soiled when one of the customers had got violently sick halfway through fucking a young Romanian girl who was also having a period. Other dregs and detritus from this shebeen-cum-whorehouse were launched from the window as well. A smashed coffee table, a broken lampstand and drugs paraphernalia stashed into a pillow case. Though the window faced out onto the road running by the estate and not the inner square, news of the skip and its contents spread across Star of the Sea flats as quick as a virus.

Nobody saw or heard anything.

The most intelligent of the three, Ronan by name, realised that they would have to get replacements for the soiled items and walked across the square, through the arch, to Spanzo's office. To his relief Ronan found that Spanzo was in good form. There was a "bird" sitting opposite him who was a cracker and clearly one of them toffs from South Dublin. She trying to talk the talk. Dressed down. Crumpled skin, pants, and boots. Hair pushed back and a tail through a grunge baseball cap. Crumpled T-shirt sticking through her stained running jacket. I'll give you crumpled. Give you more than crumpled ya girl. Obviously arranging a regular coke deal. —Good stuff, Spanz, for top-table people, yah?

Spanzo reeling off a wad of notes. —Sure, Ronan take care
of it. The girl obviously part disgusted, part thrilled by Spanzo,
his brutality, BO, and bad teeth, and this huge guy Ronan and
his big fists and oversize leather jacket and his Northside accent
and her witnessing a real live gangster transaction with all the
gestures and mean looks. The nearest she would get to her own
Tarantino movie. Frissons of ersatz violence: broken noses, spit
and scarred faces up-close, the talk that was more a patois, only
bits of which she could understand. "Mars Bars," Spanzo had
called the ugly, thick, pink, raised lines running like strips of
suddenly congealed sorbet down one side of Ronan's pudgy but
otherwise handsome face. As Ronan strode his bulk out of the
room with his mattress cash, Spanzo explained to Sally that his
nickname was Glass Features. Sally nodded and laughed, narrowed her eyes, shook her tits slightly, proactively, because of
her ennui and trite lifestyle and the girls' meeting at the Frascati
Centre and flirting on girly nights out and sleek cars, Bono and
Bob Geldof and I've broken my Ray Bans again and botox,
uplifts, and parings, and nothing really meaning like this meant.
Nothing at the depths. Something real real. She laughed at Glass
Features but had no clue. Then she paid the money.

It was midday when the bus from Gaoth Dobhair arrived in
Dublin. The air was a lot cooler and the wind blowing up
O'Connell Street from the river Liffey carried the sense of
burned salt and commotion. Éilis didn't want to go to the
Dempsey household, as she would have had to lie to them once
they started asking questions. She needed to speak with Finn in
private. And anyway, the buzz of Dublin was all about. Tourists
posing for pictures by the Needle and the statue of Big Jim
Larkin. She wandered up Henry Street enjoying the Dublin banter as people passed her by. She even treated herself to a glass
of wine in the Italian Quarter down by the Liffey—turning
away from the window so as not to see the Boardwalk junkies occasionally filing past. A Dostoevsky novel on her eBook
reader but choosing *Pride and Prejudice*—sure, a novel of manners from the English gentry, but funny and upright in its own

way. Jeez, time to have a laugh for a change. Then on to Grafton Street to browse in Hodges Figgis and try on makeup in Brown Thomas. Prayers then, and candles in the oasis of calm that is St Theresa's Carmelite Church. St Theresa of Avila and Discalced Monks. St Theresa not only a mystic but a renouncer of property and wealth—a defeater of death itself. Éilis in her other home. Dublin. It embraced her and loved her. Whatever is coming, let it come. For I am already blessed and loved for all eternity, and therefore immortal.

Father McCartan was not at the rectory when Éilis called in the afternoon, but she was expecting this. After expressing both delight and concern at Éilis's return to Dublin, Mrs O'Grady explained that the Gardaí had rung earlier in the day and he had rushed off without explaining what had happened. She showed Éilis into the study and said she would make up a spare room. Mrs O'Grady then returned from the kitchen a quarter of an hour later with tea and scones, only to discover that Éilis had vanished. There was a note: "Staying at Dawn's tonight. Don't worry." Mrs O'Grady rang the priest straightaway but his mobile phone was switched off. Why was Éilis not in Gaoth Dobhair? Éilis, after greeting Our Lady in the square, went to Wakefields to leave her bag with Dawn, and then she went over to Deirdre's house for tea.

Heffernan Moves Quickly

FIVE HUNDRED NOTES wasn't much. A spit in the Liffey for Heffernan, but he always made sure it was paid immediately. So when a local taxi driver who worked for Spanzo as a courier of drugs and brass—that is, prostitutes—reported that he'd seen Éilis Devanney in the square, he was paid up front. Never mind that she was talking to the statue of Our Lady and that the girl was half-mad and needed help. Should be in hospital that girl. Danger to herself.

As Ned Behan gave orders as to the manoeuvring of a wind machine into its position outside Connolly's, Jimmy Heffernan was in his office unwrapping the dress he had ordered from Paris. By now Heffernan had established that she had gone to see her friends Deirdre and Sinéad, who were going to a rave party in Drumcondra. The media arrangement was supposed to happen on Saturday, but Heffernan ordered that the whole thing be moved to that Friday night. Selected journalists were notified that there was to be free champagne all night, and gossip editors were warned that the story about Connolly's going nationwide had been brought forward a day. Heffernan's own newspaper, the *Dublin Tribune*, immediately made space on its front page ready for Saturday morning. Most of the food the exclusive caterer was preparing was already done, but they had to move heaven and earth to get the canapés and salmon ready in time.

By the time Éilis got herself ready to go out, she was well aware that Finn was not actually in Dublin. So why not even a text message? Still though, she was on alert for his return that weekend from what her vibes were telling her, but at least she had got ahead of him. Could ward him off. Thus much more relaxed, she was delighted to be back with her friends again and admitted to herself that she probably could not move permanently to Gaoth Dobhair without regular trips back to Dublin to see them and take part in their mad chat. For the moment, and in the safe company of her best friends, Father McCartan's strictures about keeping away from Dublin and her own fears about her future had faded. The tom toms in her heart were not there and the Morrígan had vanished. As the first heavy spots of properly Irish rain for a month fell on Dublin, Deirdre and Sinéad raised their arms to the heavens in exultation and kept up a barrage of questions to Éilis about what Deirdre called "mango-crunching land" and whether there was any talent up there. So quickly had time passed, that it seemed to the three girls that they had hardly been walking for ten minutes before they reached a large Edwardian edifice overlooking the Tolka valley, De Courcey House, where the rave was being held.

Éilis immediately attracted attention the moment the girls turned into the driveway and proceeded to walk up to the big house. She had borrowed a backless black dress from Deirdre, who admitted that she could no longer fit into it. The dress was long and close-fitting around the legs with a flare at the bottom. To add to the effect, Éilis had let her dark-auburn hair tumble onto her shoulders and across her beige shawl. Some youths at the front gate wolf-whistled and Éilis became flustered, partly because she was very aware that all the attention was placed on her.

As darkness fell, light spilled from windows and doorways onto the large gardens surrounding the house. Éilis saw that the place was alive with youths in all kinds of weird garb, including Goths who could have stepped right out of scenes from the house's imperial past with their stiff collars and cuffs. Inside the hall, there were girls spraying a tattoo with a stencil over another girl's back. Another gang of young men stood near the entrance to the door as Éilis, Deirdre, and Sinéad pushed through the throng outside the house. Éilis could hear a Bob Marley song from somewhere upstairs, Amy Winehouse from somewhere else, and she made a mental note to explore exactly where the music was coming from. She had always liked to listen to Bob Marley. In with them to the large downstairs ballroom where techno-pop was being played. They bought drinks of lager in plastic glasses, found a table in a dimly lit corner, and soon got up to dance and laugh, laugh and dance, make fun of each other, admire and "rip" the other dancers.

The girls returned to their seats and gulped at their beer. Laughing again and Éilis saying she was already feeling woozy. No more drink for her.

—Ah, it's about bleedin' time E. Sometimes you just have to let go, you know.

A man with rings on his face and his exposed navel lurched into the girls' table at that point.

—Howya, D. Howya, Éilis . . . jeez, fancy seeing you here. Suppose a ride would be out of the question?

Sinéad, Éilis's lifelong defender, stepped in with a friendly but firm slap for the inebriated interloper.

—Howya, Gerry. I might take you round the back for a snog if you're lucky.

Deirdre then turned to Éilis as Gerry shambled away in pursuit of other distractions.

—No, Éilis, this'll do you good. No harm at all. Get rid of all that tension, Deirdre said as she slurped a drink. Aargh . . . life's bleedin' hard enough as it is without being hard on yourself. Few nights like this will break the waiting up for ya, Éilis. The time will fly by, don't you worry, and then you and Finn can get married and we'll have a huge party that day. I'll have me gorgeous Goth and Sinéad's bound to get someone.

A sombreness fell over Éilis at the mention of Finn's name and she asked the girls whether they had seen Frankie Byrne of late.

—Sure, isn't Frankie over in England with Finn? Sinéad asked.

—I'm not sure, Sinéad. In fact, I wouldn't be surprised if the both of them turn up here tonight, although Finn's not one for rave parties.

Another large group of youths pushed through the entrance to the house after negotiating a group of security men at the double doors at the front. The security men were all associates of Spanzo's, and whilst under strict orders not to consume any alcohol or drugs themselves, they had made a killing on the sales of amphetamines and E tablets to the scores of youths entering the premises. Sinéad pulled Éilis to one side as the crowd, cheering, punching the air, bowled around the ballroom, heads nodding, jiving and dancing, and then pushing out the ballroom doors again and farther on into the house.

—Is there something wrong, Éilis?

—Well, if there is, Sinéad, I'll find out about it soon enough.

—Will we go home? I don't like the way you look all of a sudden, Éilis Devanney, you're as white as me ma's tablets.

—No, thanks, Sinéad. I've a feeling that this is where I should be. Anyway Dawn's coming for me at midnight, before I turn into a pumpkin!

The Downfall of the Goths

MRS O'GRADY SAW that things were very bad when Father McCartan arrived back from the Garda station. His face was drawn and it was obvious that he'd been crying. She followed him around the house hoping that he would finally explain what had happened, but he seemed preoccupied, as if searching for something, and he lost his temper when she once again asked to have a word with him. Father McCartan and his housekeeper had not exchanged an angry word in the twenty years that they had known each other. As tears started to brim in her own eyes, the priest put a comforting arm around her shoulders and apologised for his behaviour. But nothing would he say about Darren Bulger. Rose O'Grady finally saw a moment to mention Éilis.

—It's just that Éilis Devanney, Liam.

—What about Éilis?

—She landed back at the house this afternoon.

—*Íosa Chríost!* Where is she now, Rose?

—May God forgive me. I went into the kitchen and then I put the kettle on because I know she loves real tea. But she left this saying she was staying at Dawn's.

Father McCartan gripped his housekeeper almost roughly by the shoulders.

—Yes, yes, Rose! but where is she now? She is in very great danger!

—That's just it, Liam, I haven't a clue where she went to.

With this, Rose O'Grady let out a wail and rushed off into the kitchen. Father McCartan ran in the opposite direction and out of the house but with no real knowledge of what he would do next. Dived into the car to Dawn's but she was not there. Then a thought occurred to him. The Goths by the flats may have seen Éilis going by and she may well have stopped to chat to them.

Many of the Goths who would normally have been assembled by the brazier and sofa near the flats had already gone to the rave party but a few remained, sheltering from the rain in a roughly constructed tent. Father McCartan recognised two of them from the day they'd sung in his church, an event which seemed like a past and happy life to him compared to what was happening now. In his cold wet bones he felt that he was entombed in a personal Valley of Death. What horrible, stupid, naive choices he had made.

The Goths seemed to sense the priest's distracted air and offered him a cracked mug of tea which had been brewed from a large and blackened kettle, but he declined on account of the urgency of his errand. Father McCartan became desperate when none of them could give him any word on Éilis and he was just about to leave their makeshift campsite when the young man with the blue stripe in his dark hair—Turlough, yes—entered the tent with what looked like a box of crisps and a plastic bag full of large bottles. For some reason, the youth's whole demeanour had a calming effect on him and he sat on a tea chest and remained silent whilst beer and crisps were distributed amongst these gaunt and serious youths. Father McCartan even accepted the next offer of tea and only then did he move the conversation back to Éilis and her whereabouts.

—I saw Éilis with her two mates. Er, sorry, what's your first name again?

—What? Oh, yes, Liam, Liam McCartan. It's Turlough, isn't it? I saw you once when we moved a certain thing, if you remember?

—Of course I do, Liam. People just call me Blue. I'm a poet but don't sing, so never joined your Goth choir. I'm going over to the rave later on and if I see her I'll let her know you're anxious. But I wouldn't worry. There's a full security team over there. I mean a proper security company, not local heads, and they look mean, so she'll be fine while she's in there at least.

—Blue's not telling you, Liam, that he's big into Éilis's mate Deirdre! came a cry from the back of the tent.

—Ah, I know Deirdre. She's a lovely girl. But Deirdre and not Éilis? enquired the priest with a wink.

—Éilis? Blue replied. Éilis is too good for any of us. You don't court the Godhead, you honour it and cherish it. Besides, she doesn't have long left.

The priest jumped up with a start, spilling his tea and nearly bringing the whole tent structure down around him.

—Good God. What do you mean?

—Sit down, Liam, and I'll tell ye, like I have tried to tell the boys here. There's no point rushing because it won't change anything.

The priest sat down again. The fire from the brazier outside flashed across the face of this young man called Blue and sent intermittent pulses of heat and light into the primeval gloom of the tent.

—We're finished, Liam. Our little sideshow here. And we are only the novices pining for a world that's already passed away. And all the poets, seers, visionaries, all the people we wanted to learn from. People like Éilis. They are all being swallowed up. The snakes have returned to Ireland and Patrick has been banished. Not Patrick the priest, if you'll forgive me, but Patrick the visionary, Patrick the poet, Patrick the liberator. Only yesterday, we had security men in big yellow coats with dogs coming to clear us off this strip of dirt. They reckon they can build five hundred dwellings here, as the new courts have been built and all the legal eagles want yuppie pads nearby. They see me as the ringleader so I'm heading to the hills tomorrow, and yes, hopefully the beauteous, bountiful Deirdre will follow me, because they'll be back with their snarling dogs and court orders. They won't be happy until every blade of grass in the country has concrete poured over it. We've learned nothing as a country. It's like the people have been injected with some kind of collective hysteria. You can see it in their faces, in traffic jams, bus queues, clothes stores, land sales, distressed auctions, motorways, shopping malls. Jackals and hyenas get vicious and frenzied when they sense a kill, and they have proliferated across all our cities and towns, snapping and snarling and turning on each other for that extra cut, the choicest parts, that inch of extra space.

As the youth moved into Father McCartan's space and placed his hand on his shoulder, the priest was not sure whether he heard a rumble of thunder or whether a lorry had just driven by.

—In the face of the dogs and their new masters, we have to melt into the hills and mountains, let the old world embrace us and protect us like it has done so many times before. It's too late for Éilis. She was ahead of her time. She could have . . .

The priest had disappeared into the teeming rain, even before Blue could finish his sentence.

Éilis was in a fit of laughter. She just could not stop laughing. Deirdre had been telling a typically dizzy story which was hilarious in itself, but the effect was increased by the presence of a huge video screen in the room in which the three friends were sat. The screen showed sequences of shots from hidden cameras with modified lenses which distorted the images that were being shown to everyone in the room. Just at the moment when Deirdre was telling her story, she would appear in close-up and then suddenly as a figure with three heads in a deep space.

—What's so funny about that, Deirdre cried. Sure, I only said I had to take the plunger to it because it was blocked!

Éilis laughed again, but then an image flashed before her on the screen that froze her very breath so that it became a blue frost in the half-light of the room. Éilis looked about her but nobody else seemed to have seen what she had seen. She put her head down and closed her eyes, purposefully willing the image to come back to her. It was a young man. He was strapped by sturdy wires to a ladder in a drain. Black mouth like he was roaring.

As Father McCartan drove away from the rectory in his car, his mobile phone rang but he flung the phone into the back seat and started up the engine. He had switched it back on in case Éilis would ring him, but he could see that Mrs O'Grady was ringing from the rectory. The phone rang again and he ignored it. It rang again and again just as he arrived outside De Courcey House. Father McCartan uttered a rare curse and finally answered the phone and saw that the call was from the local Garda station, which had been trying urgently to contact him. Darren Bulger had finally been brought out from the drain.

—He is of course dead, Sergeant?

—He's very dead, Father, and it's a blessing. And here's a strange thing. That box that was strapped under him?

—Yes, what about it?

—Well, it wasn't an IED. An improvised explosive device. I mean, not a pipe bomb or anything. It was a small television. One of those hi-tech things. Must've cost a bomb, er, if you know what I mean. And his tongue was in there as well. Amazing case. Father, the guys who brought him out are going to need counselling after this and you were saying you'd like to offer some prayers for the victim at the scene. He may have been a pusher, but the guys are still pretty shook. Holding their position there. I think as much for themselves as for that poor little bastard . . . sorry, Father.

Father McCartan put his phone gently onto the front passenger seat and placed his head on the steering wheel. He looked at the crowds of youths milling around the driveway to De Courcey House, blessed the security men at the door, invoked the protection of Bridget, and whispered a promise to Éilis with a kiss on his cross that he would return to collect her the moment his duties had been performed. With God's grace she would be fine. He then turned his car right into the rain to face into the horror of it all. He could remember giving young Darren Bulger his First Communion and now here he was losing yet another young soul from his community who had apparently suffered a lonely, excruciating, and terrifying death. The car disappearing into the rain. The very fact that Éilis so wanted to be a normal girl that she refused the sudden alarm bells in her head telling her to flee.

Peck Peck Peck

EARLY FRIDAY EVENING. A weekend off after lots of pats on the back for James Tierney. The polluted-rivers film due to be screened on Monday. Hard-hitting and legally tight as a witch's ass, as the lawyer had put it. Now some rumour that he was to be rewarded with a staff contract. He was the man.

Ronagh beaming at him across the canteen. Then her raging when her supposedly, allegedly, self-proclaimed best buddy, Úna, flaunts herself in front of her Jamesie. Linking his arm at the cappuccino table, that cow, and calling him the man with the child in his eyes. Absolutely blatant . . .

James sitting at his dining table smiling for a moment. But then Tommy Baker gone. And yes, he would be in touch, and Eileen would be back in a week. Cool the jets. Let me get better, then you'll see.

There was something seriously wrong with this. James Tierney stood up. One thing, one of the many good things from his extended family, his country family, was the wisdom. If things were going well, you'd better get ready for the landlord, the bailiff, the RIC, the rentman, the pitchcapper, the Redcoats, the Blueshirts, the informer, the long journey, the hunger, the anger. The time to act.

James Tierney pushing his chair back. Pushing his hair up. Filling the room. His kitchen-cum-dining room and get me out of here to the quiet of Loch Derg, and he pulling Éilis's diary from a false panel he had put in the radiator flue. Thinking about ringing Dawn but to say what?

He was sure he had missed something. The buzzer goes. The buzzer for the main entrance to the apartments. Go away. Still buzzing. Go away, Ronagh. Still buzzing. He walks to the intercom and tells the person down below (Ronagh) that he needs an hour maybe two. Still buzzing. James Tierney rips the box from the wall. The buzzing stops.

Kill all the lights. Kill the phone. Place the lamp on the table and think only of this from the pieces I cut out:

Fire for the brightness
After the shadows of Samhain.
Fire in the heart.
Fire in the dark.

Finn, her little hound, except that he was big, handsome and carefree. He laughing like a puppy. Wouldn't he wag it if he had a tail? Éilis's mouth broadened into a grin as she again turned her head on the pillow. Now she saw Finn's brother Séamus and her smile faded. He already too serious for one so young—prepared. What's wrong Séamus? she mouthed these words in her trance. Then, a young man was injecting drugs into his arm on a stairwell in the flats. Rooftops echoed with the sound of children playing in the streets below. Éilis smiled but was suddenly racked by a spasm of fear. All the sound was going in and out of phase. It was wide and tight, raucous, then soft. Just in that distance there was something wicked, waiting, biding its time. What was that horrible smell? Now a group of tough, well-dressed men were gesticulating. Peck peck peck. To blind the eyes of the dead. Riddle me that? Éilis laughed again but through tightly pressed lips as if holding grimly to the edge of a cliff. Eejits, she half cried, her mouth suddenly chalk dry and the words grating on her teeth. Rank smell of animal now.

She turned on the bed and saw the Raven. It was on her dresser next to her picture of Finn. The black bird was bigger than before. Its shard of beak snapped up her ornate blade, a letter opener which was a present from Finn. The bird shook it like a worm newly plucked from the heart of the world, and Éilis arched in the bed and flung out a sharp and anguished cry.

For the first time ever, the bird spoke. It hopped onto her bed in familiar, jaunty steps. Her breath was caught in pain and a putrid stench. She saw that the Raven was alive with fleas, which it was picking from its body with its beak, and with each bite it jerked a self-satisfied nod in her direction and repeated the word

Duibhegáin. —Duibhegáin, Duibhegáin.

Éilis rolled in her spasm across the balconies of the flats into a square near a skip where two children were playing and a woman stopped to inspect something that might be of use to her. A man staggered towards her. Hands flailing. He was in her room. She turned her face on the bed to avoid his hand and grabbed for her letter opener to use as a weapon, her hands feeling in the blindness of sudden sleep, but the bird cawed loudly and hopped into flight. Effortless, omnipotent, circling the bed above her head, sprinkling wriggling fleas from its plumage like the myriad lies of politicians and soothsaying journalists she could hear from the television below. Slit slit slit.

What I am saying is that given the chance
We will reform the banks
Turn away from corruption and sleaze
Look to ordinary people's needs

The man was still trying to put his hand on her face and he strung out and waving angrily.

Éilis willed herself to waken but could not suspend her utter belief in her vision or look away to other distractions. The bird was so real it was beyond nightmare. Why is it saying duibheagáin, "abyss"? The shocking blue of her quickly opened eyes. Not blind. Oh no. Seeing everything. Finn. Then Jimmy Heffernan. Heffernan is saying something . . . something important. He was beckoning her to him. The Raven's shadow blackening the room before coming to land on the dresser again. Now Éilis knew her tormentor.

—Morrígan, you are the Morrígan!'
The bird seemed to nod and caw in sarcastic agree-
ment. It's speech was machine-gun staccato.

The House of Devanney
Is the House of the Duibhegáin
Neville is Nimhtheanga *who any price will pay*
Bernice is Bécuma *who seeks to betray*
Her sex
Hex Hex Hex.
She is the Hex
Peck Peck Peck.

No that wasn't it. Or. It wasn't the whole it. The rain battering against the window. Wind. Like no wind for months. Pulling the double-glazed windows in and out. The rain and the lamp. James Tierney was close to remembering what he had forgotten. It was coming now. But Ronagh? Ronagh is still outside, I bet.

He went down the stairwell of the private apartments. He never used the lift, but hated the stairs, the communal smell of warming rubbish. Upmarket apartments and the Appian Way be damned. Give me a field and a run of water for Jesus' sake. James saw a shape beyond the frosted glass of the door at the main entrance.

—You deliberately stood in the rain, you total weird.

—Yes I did. Now will you let me in?

Standing embracing in his hall. James tasting her salt tears as they kissed. Hot mouth of pangs of emotion and a pool of water at their feet colouring the welcome mat.

James undressed her. Put his big housecoat around her. Made her a hot brandy and ran a bath. Ronagh understood him more, he understood her less, but wanted her the more.

Midnight Ravers

You can't tell the woman from the man, no, I say you can't.
'Cause they're dressed in the same pollution.
Their mind is confused with confusion.
With their problems since there's no solution.

THE THREE GIRLS entered a large room where there was a light show. Two men wearing masks were playing at computers, selecting words, shapes, and sounds with a large pen that they were moving in a tandem-dance fashion. These images were mirrored on a sheer transparent screen. CHILL. FLOAT. BREEZE. BEAT BEAT. SO TRANNY. FLY BABY FLY.

Deirdre wanted to go out the back to smoke a cigarette in the large tent which had been provided for that purpose, and Sinéad wanted to follow her, as a young man for whom she had a notion had also gone outside to smoke.

—Éilis, we're going out for five, said Deirdre. Do you want to come with us?

—No, D., I'll stay inside, but I'll probably head upstairs.

—We'll be back in five, so don't move till then!

Éilis's keen intelligence discovered that a part of her welcomed this whole dance towards the end of something. She had the feeling that she was becoming weightless and that all the fears and obsessions in her life were lacking in substance and leaving her body. She saw herself as a pulsating chrysalis shedding layers of skin in preparation for flight. Her eyes became glazed, unfocussed, shiny, happy. And yet, the leaving of her friends saddened her beyond all measure.

—Work away, I'm grand here anyway.

—Are you sure you don't mind, Éilis, said Sinéad.

—We'll be back for you ASAP, said Deirdre. Anyway, my dreamboat blue Goth will be here in an hour, so you can stick with us then if you want, darlin'.

—No worries! Sure, I know nearly everyone here anyway. See you in a while. Enjoy!

She began to wander around the house in search of the Bob Marley room. The bright lights of before seemed to her to have been replaced by shadows and recesses. As she passed people she realised that their images were becoming blurred and staying in her vision. Dragged. Drugged? A knife went across flesh and Éilis now recognised where it was happening.

Jesus. *Tá sé i mo sheomra.*

As she turned to go back down the stairs and look for Sinéad, a youth—who went by the name of Roly, or Rollerball, one who lurked on the fringes of the Untouchables—emerged from a dark corner all dressed in tight ski garb and made a grab for her. Éilis mumbled as Roly tried to feel her backside. She pushed past him, she hearing the sound of a heart racing like a thunder of horses.

—C'mere ya good thing, Roly called, catching Éilis's scent and turning his head to his friends in a frenzy of encouragement.

What to do when heroes and poets hide their faces?

What to do when innocence is no longer safe?

Éilis's words were nonsense and of no weight to him or those who surrounded her.

—Hero?! Is it a hero ya want? Here's your hero for tonight, ya good thing. I tell ya boys, I'm fucking havin' some of this.

Éilis pushing on. Trying to be urgent. Looking for a face she recognised who could lead her away.

—In your dreams, Roly . . . you've no chance, someone said.

—Do you wanna bet? I'll let the lot of ya ride me if I don't get this one within the hour. Eh! Do yez wanna come and watch me fly? This stuff is the business!

He rips off his ski mask. Produces a phial of pills from a small bag he carried on his back.

—Didn't I drop a big dose of Fuckbomb into her drink about an hour ago. And her mates. Come on!

Deirdre and Sinéad were half staggering around in the smoking tent waving away young men who were attempting to kiss them.

—I tell ya . . . Sinéad, said Deirdre, I have never been so pissed, and so happy. Yet we didn't drink that much, sure we didn't?

Deirdre stumbled, and Seánie Heffernan appeared and stopped her fall.

—Howya, Seánie, did ya see yer man in the chiffon?

—Who? the guy dancing on the stage?

—He was deadly. What a dancer. But you could see his whole body. And the screens in the room where you saw all that old film stuff. Seánie tried to kiss her but she pushed him away.

—Sorry, Seánie. Promised to a Goth.

Sinéad moved over to the young man who had taken her eye inside the house, and he pulled her into his space with relish.

The eyes and throat of a dragon tattoo stared out from a reflection of Éilis's back in a ceiling mirror above a large ancient bed where she lay moaning and sprawled face down and slightly sideways. Somebody had asked her did she want an instant paint tattoo, and she, in turn, had asked for a Celtic dragon, but when she would not sit still on the chair, a dark man with a massive bald dome and huge thick hairy arms had winked and thrown her onto the bed.

—Ah . . . fuck. Éilis stuck her hand into her mouth in an attempt to retch her stomach free of the demon writhing within her. In the doorway, the heads of the two youths in ski garb appeared. Éilis could see Roly in the mirror as he approached the bed. To her, it seemed that his head was detached from his body as he moved towards her across the space of the bedroom. Roly gave the bald artist two hundred to take himself and his paintbrushes somewhere else. The man pocketed the money in his leather waistcoat and winked, but then said he had to finish the head. —Professional pride, he said, dipping his fine brush into the red part of a wide palette.

—Finish the fucking head, said Roly. So do I, so make it fucking quick.

A large and heavy limousine, a beautiful and rare Daimler with smoked windows, pulled up outside De Courcey House. The doormen peered closely at it, looked at each other and shrugged their shoulders. However, when they saw the back part of the car dip slightly and Vincent "the Cube" Duffy extract his bulk from the car, they stood to attention, eyes widening as he walked towards them. His grin that no grin was. Something that in most other people would have been a rueful grin but with the Cube was just his laughing at the world. A world full of people who made life complicated and he loved grinning at them. His wide smile and slight surfeit of saliva along his naturally and perfectly white teeth. Life wasn't complicated and knuckleheads like him, he knew, enjoyed it best. The Cube should actually have been nicknamed the Killer White, except that he had early developed a penchant for pushing cubes of all shapes and sizes up the anuses of those he wished to terrorise.

In the artificial brightness of the entrance hall, the Cube called the doormen to him. Eventually, one of the men to whom he was talking grasped what he was referring to and nodded, pointing towards the central double staircase and the room where the tattooist had been working.

In the demi-light of the room. In this demi-world where the walls shook slightly with noise and boom, boom, Roly was trying to straddle Éilis from behind but was having trouble lifting her long dress. Éilis was vainly trying to prevent his actions by trapping her dress underneath her legs. She then began to cry loudly which made the youth accompanying Roly very nervous and increasingly scared.

—Hey, Roly. Hey, come on, Roly, for fuck's sake. That's Éilis from the flats. If they find out you spiked her the whole fucking lot of them'll be after you.

He pulled at the would-be rapist but was violently rebuffed. He tried again and received a stiff punch.

—It'll be me they come after, Roly, not you. You're not from round here. I'll be torched.

Roly was desperately trying to lift Éilis's dress and now had it lifted around her thighs. —I thought I knew her face from somewhere. Don't you be saying nothing now, Danny. Sure, who's to know? I'm fucked if I'm stopping now, she's a beaut.

—I'm getting out of here, Danny cried as he ran to the door only to turn and rush back to his crazed friend.

—No. We're getting out of here. Roly, listen to me. Snap out of it man and fucking listen!

With this, Danny pulled Roly from the bed and the force of his landing on the floor seemed to break his frenzy. Both boys looked down at Éilis's tattooed back. Still, Roly was reluctant to leave her. He bent down to look at her face and kissed her just as the door opened again and somebody else entered the room.

Ireland's New Face

ÉILIS COULD FEEL waves of pleasure running through her body but she also felt a heightened sense of hearing, taste, and smell which made her slightly nauseous. The smell and sound of paint, the booming bass line from powerful amplifiers in a room below. But she wasn't there.

The smell of a man. A smell she recognised. Her face was now upturned. Black now. And when she awoke again, Jimmy Heffernan's hands were gently tapping her cheek. Holding her at her shoulders and looking into her eyes and stroking her upper arms. She had to giggle. Laugh, in fact. This man. Her cousin Jimmy Heffernan told her that her beauty and renown had saved her. Word spreading like wildfire about Éilis so that she was found very easily and quickly. She didn't care. Started giggling again and held her arms out to him in the Devanney way. He stood her up and eased her black dress down and away from her body. Her perfect back with the curve of a Monet in half-light now washed of tattoo paint. Never would he. Never would he because she was of the Divine. But now a mythical Divine. Past. Here he was. Jimmy Heffernan. Holding an exquisite past and future in his hands. In his gentle hands in the upstairs rooms of his club. His will be done.

Holding Éilis at a stiff arm's length, he surveyed her in the way of a merchant squaring a prized horse, quizzing her perfect teeth, her flanks, lifting her ankles and drawing a line down the straightness of her spine. He then took a brush from her bag which was at the side of the bed and brushed her lustrous hair so that it swayed across her back. Then he cupped his hands around her face. She giggled and leaned her head upon his shoulder but he firmly placed her back into her standing position.

—Éilis, how are ye doin' . . . you all right?

—Ahh, Jimmy, *nil fhios agam cad a tharla. Tá mé as mo mheabhair.*

—Don't worry, Jimmy's here now. Here, put this on.

Seeking respite from a world where her realities were shifting from moment to moment, Éilis grabbed onto Heffernan. She stepped into a new green dress that had a lustre of diamanté-type filigree running as a sheen through it. A fine light-green under-lining, also.

Éilis swooned and Heffernan flipped her gently back onto the bed. Heffernan then left the room for a moment to instruct one of the men whom he had posted on the door to go and fetch a large jug of water and a glass from the kitchen down the corridor. When the water arrived, Heffernan raised Éilis to a sitting position and brought a glass to her mouth. She drank a full three glasses with great gusto, wanted more, but not the pill that now rested on her tongue. Éilis moved her face away, but Heffernan tugged her hair slightly so that her head fell backwards, mouth apart, and the pill went down, along with another mouthful of water. Sleep a bit more.

His henchmen, who had apprehended Roly and Danny in no time, discovered the substance used to spike Éilis's drink. They were then made to take two tablets themselves and stripped to their underwear. Just a message. Heffernan judged that Éilis could take an upper again after she had slept for two hours.

It was 00:30 and nearly time to move. The intercom went at 00:45 with Ned telling him that the press and catwalk was ready. But before going down to the club entrance, Heffernan dimmed the lights in the room and had Éilis stand either under or just below pools of light from the lamps on his walls.

He stood back looking at her. Pressing both hands to his lips as she flattened her dress down. Shaped in the body, swishy all below. She looking down so that her hair caught the light, she cooing admiringly. He took pictures. One hundred and twenty. The last of them with her fine, off-white Celtic shawl across her shoulders. He adjusting it so that her upper arms were more visible. Her arms made him shiver for something. If it could just be that. He could sire a nobility. The classic shape of her seraphic feet also. If simply caressing and adoring these could release.

—You are Ireland's Ingrid Bergman . . . Ingrid Bergman, Jean Shrimpton, and Audrey Hepburn all rolled into one.

—And you are weird, Jimmy Heffernan. He-he . . .

He observed that Éilis had taken to cocaine like a swan to a lake; this caused him to laugh aloud. Never did he.

—What, Jimmy? What's funny? Well, everything's funny and you are sooo funny. You're like a severe, desiccated woman dressed in a man. *Tá tú ait ar fad guy.* You don't do funny. You're queer.

Heffernan put his palm to her mouth. —The funny is, Éilis, that for a moment, a dangerous, dangerous moment, you had me around your little finger. But you didn't know it, or care. Others would have killed for that.

He proffered his arm. —Come on, Éilis, put your shoes on, as well. We are going to a party and you are the star attraction.

—Oh cool. But can the star attraction use the bathroom before we go?

—Éilis, tonight you get to do what you want. Party like there's no tomorrow, girl. Your carriage will be waiting when the clock strikes.

She half moved was half directed into the bathroom and got a huge surprise when she looked in the mirror, because the dress was sensational and thrilled her to her core. So 1950s. She leaned forward to the mirror and applied lipstick from her bag and pushed her hair up. Looked at herself again, swung her hips, swished her skirt, laughed, and put out the light.

The original idea from the world-renowned Fijian choreographer had been for Jimmy and his Queen to stroll down the catwalk (covered in Perspex glass almost to its fan-shape end amid the crowd) and then for the dancers to entertain, but the

choreographer took one look at Éilis and decided to send her
down accompanied by her dancers and by Amy Winehouse's
"Stronger Than Me." Éilis strutting down the board to the end
where the crowd went wild, she shimmering to the sax and the
flashes, whoops and cries—the wind-machine men asking for
a steer from the art director, he asking for instructions from
Heffernan. Send them down again. Hit it when I say. Amy
Winehouse pumping out again, the lithe black-clad guys walking, quick-stepping, gliding in and around Éilis back towards
the whole crowd digging the groove, girls jumping on guys'
shoulders, a forest of smartphones—Éilis mouthing the words.
Dipping her head forward. Then lifting her face to the light.
Pop, pop, pop, pop, pop, pop, pop.

I said, You don't know what love is, get a grip.
Sounds as if you're reading from some other tired script.
I'm not gonna meet your mother anytime.
I just wanna grip your body over mine.

Éilis grooving on over the blowhole and Heffernan raising just
one finger.

Ahh! Whoah! Gasped the crowd. Éilis's shawl sailing into
the drenching night sky. The rain and the million slices of light.

Camera lights popped and the world stopped when Éilis
stood over the vent where the wind machine thrummed the
skirt of her dress almost above her head. The soft rain in the arc
at the front of the Perspex gave an aura to the scene as if conjured
by Hera herself. As Éilis struggled to keep down her skirt against
the upward draught, she laughed uproariously and swayed
her knees, which showed the tops of her bare thighs to great
effect. Now she's led back, with Amy still belting out the beat,
to Heffernan's arm, and back they go like the biggest celebrity
wedding in town. Fireworks blazing up all around announcing
the nationwide Connolly's club venture—huge screens projecting the couple of your dreams and fantasies—the cool, austere,
sixties mod–suited guy and the Celtic babe from heaven. All
this can be yours.

Finally, Jimmy Heffernan led her away to cheers from the crowd and walked her up the red carpet, turned for a final pose for the photographers in front of his club, and then handed his filly over to Ned Behan.

—She's all yours now, Ned.

Ned Behan winked as he handed Éilis her jacket, an act of kindness for which Éilis expressed her extreme gratitude. Behan turned to Jimmy Heffernan, who was taking the lift down to the car park where a non-traceable car waited to take him to his ocean-going yacht on the south coast.

—Have a safe journey, boss! he called, but Heffernan was already gone.

Éilis, meanwhile, was placed at a table with Pierce Beaumont and other celebrities, who were all keen to make her acquaintance, and more champagne and gourmet sandwiches were consumed. She accompanied a female journalist from Dublin to the bathroom where more coke was inhaled, and Éilis felt that the party would go on for ever. Saturday night truly became Sunday morning and the crowd at the table thinned, Ned Behan turned up to swat away a young fashion designer who was making advances to Éilis. Éilis thanked Ned and called him to her as he moved to walk away. She motioned with her finger to indicate that she wished to whisper something in his ear.

—A hotel? Sure, Éilis. Your accommodation awaits you, Madame.

Éilis nodded in an arch and pleading manner. Ned Behan then led her outside and hailed a specific cab that had been waiting for just that purpose. He gave precise instructions to the driver and then got Damien Kelly to follow his instructions to the letter, to accompany Éilis back to Star of the Sea flats.

The cab pulled up at the arch and Damien did as he was instructed and led Éilis to the flop-pad next door to Nora Farrell's flat. Éilis was roughly pulled into the flat and shoved into a dark room which contained nothing other than a bed with a low table, upon which was a small box and a lamp, and a chair in the corner. Damien narrowed his eyes, made himself not stare at anything, hit the main light, a bare bulb, but it didn't make much difference. Now alone, she, Éilis. Silence, then a distant noisescape she half recognised. Some minutes later she heard the front door go and the first real alarm in her head—freezing goose-bumps, a head of ice bucket, she lay down on the bed as if asleep.

A man came into the room, alcohol fumes and dope. He seemed to stand and look at her for a long time before leaving again. Bang, bang went the doors and two locks. Sleep. Ah! Sleep. No way, wakeup, Éilis! Ah, just two minutes.

This is Spanzo running back down the stairs. Bit of a sweat on. There she is, half-conscious. There for the taking and I forgot the fucking camera. I mean I have the fucking fishnets, I have the jacket, but he wants to see them on her—he is a fucking total beast. Says I have to show them first, then I can do what I want, but have to dress her. When I'm done take more pics. But what the fuck? For ten grand. Jimmy wanting to see the moment before she loses it. Says she's a virgin. Jesus, no way is there a virgin left in Dublin. Not even the Virgin Mary, coz she's fucked as well, herr-herr. Now where's me keys to the caff?

Éilis wakes, sees the lines of coke on the table. Goes back to the door but finds it locked. The room begins to change colour and shape and she now really understands. Breathe, pray, think. Drags the table to the middle of the room, stands and removes the bulb. Heart banging somewhere near her mouth. Adrenaline sobering her body now. Put the table back. No, properly. That's the way it was. No needle in the box. Shit. But this will do. Crack pipe and a light bulb. Place them there. Here he comes. Breathe. Steady. Bulb from ceiling balancing in the belt of her dress at the back. Slim metal crack pipe inside the hidden palm of her left hand. Puts this hand by her side. Table to your right near the lamp. Stand and breathe big breaths. One chance, Éilis. You have once chance. The bang of the front door being kicked open and Spanzo shutting it again with his heel. Breathe. One chance. His bulk in the room.

—Ah fuck, bulb's gone again. Spanzo throwing the clothes on the bed.

She speaks softly.

—You're Spanzo, aren't you?

—That's me, darling. The famous Spanzo, your ride for the night.

He walks right to her and his grip on her right hand is so powerful she wants to scream, but he lets go. —Let's put the lamp on, eh? Help the atmosphere coz I believe you're a bit fucking touchy.

He lights the lamp and she steps back and holds her right hand out to him, and part of her left.

—Spanz. All I ask is . . .

—What? Do you wannit up the back first or in yer mouth? Don't worry, girl. We've all the time in the world

She holds her free hand towards him.

—Just don't hurt me, okay?

He roughly pulls at her right hand and brings her into his body. And Éilis pushing her breasts and leg into him and very slowly and deliberately, but with all the final force she can muster, pushes the pipe into his left eye as he grabs her neck and goes to kiss her.

Roars. The insane roars of Spanzo. The minotaur. The unbottled djinn that knows no fear suddenly stricken and in a place beyond primeval shock. He fucking and blinding and lashing out, but Éilis already well to his right side and smashing the bulb into his other eye but missing and striking his nose. More roars and her hand bleeding. Spanzo dives in her direction near the bed and half pulls her, but she kicks his face and manages to tip him back into the bed.

The door. He has left the door of the room open. Éilis ignores her bag lying on the floor, praying, praying, praying that he had not Chubb-locked the front door

Neither he had. She closes the room door behind her and then opens the front door onto the landing—sweet air of freedom, but now the flash of a torch.

—Mrs Farrell. What are you doing out? Get in quick.

—I've called an ambulance, no point calling Guards. What's a nice girl—

—Mrs Farrell, do you have a key to this flat? If you do, give it me quick.

Mrs Farrell fished a bunch of keys from her housecoat, which Éilis grabbed to the point of rudeness. Fumbling now at the lock as the roars in the flat grew louder, then Spanzo out in the corridor just as she turned the Chubb-key to lock the front door, leaving the key there.

Closing Mrs Farrell's door quietly but urgently now and guiding her down the stairs to Mrs Nolan's flat. Nora Farrell explaining that she'd already complained about the noise to Mr Gregory and the priest, but wasn't there going to be a film about the estate. Spanzo not roaring anymore, just letting out gasps and grunts as he tried to kick the front door down from the wrong side. Lights going on in some flats and the shadows of heads and then the blue light of an ambulance coming into the square.

Once Mrs Farrell had told the paramedic where the injured man was and she was safe inside Mrs Nolan's house, Éilis emerged from the opposite stairwell to tell the women that she would be back to explain everything.

Then the wind carried her feet to the rectory and Father McCartan, who, despite her initially vehement protests, insisted that she be taken to the Garda station for her own protection. And anyway, she would have to explain that she had apparently inflicted severe injuries upon someone and none of this would have happened if you had done as you promised and stayed in Gaoth Dobhair.

The tick of the big clock in the priest's study was all. Éilis big-eyed and hurt and also understanding the priest's anger. Rose O'Grady coming in, placing a hand on his shoulder. It was her hand that he clutched that made him break down.

—Poor Darren. What an awful ordeal. A terrible death.'

When the paramedic opened the front door to the flop pad, he stood back, but there was nothing. The Garda arrived, and he strode more confidently into the flat, pushed gingerly at the half-open door that led into the downstairs room as the Garda stepped in, flashing his torch shouting: Gardaí! There was a young man on the bed. Hair stiff with blood for about an hour, the paramedic estimated, still breathing but severe blood loss. From a cut artery or what. Then he rolled Spanzo onto his back.

—Jesus, he said.

Flame Grilled

THREE O'CLOCK ON Saturday morning in a nighttime café. Finn
Dempsey finally switched on his smartphone. All he wanted
was coffee and a large grill. No more drink. His family had left
him a massive number of messages, which he decided to read
as he ate his food. The coffee came first, and what he saw on
the front page of some of the newspapers from home for that
morning made his legs weak, and he dropped his mug onto the
table, just about managing to keep it from falling onto the floor,
but scalding himself in the process. His mouth clamped, hunger
gone. Some other punters looked round at him and shook their
heads. It was always terrible to see a young man with the shakes.
And typical Irish.

Finn looked out the window at the passing traffic. The
motion of the cars and the odd lorry was all wrong. People were
talking, laughing even, at a moment when the world was col-
lapsing all around him. His eyes moistened and he took a deep
breath and looked again at the picture on the front page.

The headline above the picture read: WHO NEEDS A
MARILYN WHEN YOU HAVE HEAVENLY ÉILIS. Below
the headline, Finn saw a woman who looked remarkably like
Éilis and yet was not Éilis at all. This Éilis looked like a film star.
She was in full makeup, even her long legs were tanned, and
she was giving a laugh to the camera like Éilis never laughed.
Deep throat. Something about Amy Winehouse. A heaving
crowd dancing madly. Strangely, one paper then asked readers
to go to the business section to get the full story. Finn turned

311

to the business section and saw a headline about Connolly's nightclubs cleaning up in the club trade and he saw a smiling Jimmy Heffernan leading Éilis along the Connolly's catwalk. He dropped the paper to the floor like a lost thought.

Finn walked straight out of the café without so much as a backward glance. A large man entering the café was bulldozed back into the street as Finn walked right through him on leaving the premises. The young waitress ran out from behind the counter and caught up with Finn as he made to cross the road. She'd seen him a number of times and liked the look of him.

—You all right, mate, is everyfin all right?

—Sorry? No, it's the end of the world.

—Wot, mate? Cam back an' eat yer grill. It's ready for ya, doll. Fings are always better after yev had a bite to eat.

—No, I've to go home and die.

—Oh Lor', I am sure fings are not that bad! Well, you have to pay for your mee-ul.

—What? Oh yeah, sorry, here.

Finn placed a twenty-pound note into the young woman's hand and made to move away.

—An' can I have the cup back?

Finn Dempsey looked at the mug in his hand and realised that until that moment he had been asleep whilst a thief had ransacked his very house, and a great and terrible anger rose within him. The flames of his anger fanned further by the knowledge that he had seen the prowler's face and decided to look away rather than confront the truth. Slowly, he squeezed the mug until it shattered in a thousand shards across the pavement.

—*Smidiríní*, he said, paying no attention to the young woman, who now stood cowering in the doorway of the café, where she had sought refuge from this madman.

He flagged a cab, but the normal black cabs wouldn't take him. Eventually he found a private taxi firm and asked to be taken to Heathrow, but then changed his mind and said Ealing Broadway. They wanted money up front and extra for his shredded hand pouring in blood. Finn simply threw a hundred pounds at the man and the owner came from behind a screened counter to wrap his hand in tissue paper. In every inch of his huge frame, Finn Dempsey bore the resemblance of the fighting Irishman of myth and legend. But in reality he was already a ghost. He stopped the cab at an area he knew well, and went to an Irish pub that had an early licence. The landlord and punters watched him warily but eventually realised he was in there to drink. The landlady brought him a pint but he said he wanted whisky as well.

At two p.m. the next day, Finn was poured into a taxi and taken to a local B & B to sleep off the drink. At four o'clock the next morning he opened his eyes. Strange bed, strange smells. Frankie Byrne. What was that about Frankie Byrne? He fighting the images of Éilis away from him.

—What would she want? No. What would she understand? What message? How could be the bravest and tell her she'd been right?.

He rose fully clear now and happy that he could act. Perform a clean simple thing that at the same time would take courage and endurance. He showered. Studied his hand and reminded himself to buy some large plasters. He had to wipe the blood away. For this was a pure act. He left the B & B with more than enough coverage for the room and the mess his hand had left on the bed. He went out to the shopping centre near Ealing Broadway and bought a suit that the salesman told him was perfect for him. Then he went to late Mass at St Patrick's near Soho and asked a priest to hear his confession. He took a leisurely, if solemn, evening meal and then walked from Soho down towards the river, the Barbican, and St Paul's. Finally painting a river in his mind and it was good. Then on to Smithfield Meat Market, where he watched for an hour or so. Reduced activity, but all he needed was one delivery going in or out of one of the ice rooms.

The lorry backed into the bay and the cooler doors were opened from inside, Finn walking out of range of the light. The driver took his bill of lading round to the shop area and Finn Dempsey darted quickly into the back of the room where he could not be seen. What happened next was exactly what he hoped would happen, there was no excruciating chill, just a numbing quiet, ice steam, and digging in to wait for the drowsiness that came before he actually began to freeze. The chill already settling in, he took his chain from beneath his new shirt with its junior All-Ireland medal and his Celtic Cross and stood fully upright against the wall, but with frozen products hanging right in front of him, he soon found it was easier to let his body tip forward and place his head against the hanging carcass. Twice his resolve almost failed him. Where was Frankie Byrne? My parents. My poor parents. But thoughts of Éilis abandoned and his deeply felt sin of despair riveted his mind back to his desperate task, his continually thumping, searing headache that nothing mattered or could be changed. Only she will understand. His last conscious thought. Ah sleep. Here it is.

Finn Dempsey very quickly began to sleep the sleep of the ancient warrior.

When next we meet
Frost will crush the heat.
The spring that creaks.
The hero's last croak.

Éilis back in her old room. No longer fearing the swirling raven. For all was done. Bone bleached. Distraught that she in her delirium had stabbed Finn to death. As her dreams had predicted. The quicker to get him to heaven. She watched Finn's last icy breath expire and the mask of death stiffen his once gentle features. She lay across him and held his blood-soaked curls in her right hand and with her left hand she repeatedly ran the blade of her letter opener across her wrist until she was sure her main artery was severed. As the blade fell, it gave a soft tinkle in the crush of ice and bare bone and Éilis stared and stared again at the mirror until it cracked and she was brave enough to face her horror and offer up her soul and her repentance to God.

She tried to speak but nothing came and then a whiteness and peace.

—Mise Éire. Mise i mo smidiríní, is what she was trying to say.

Four o'clock on Sunday morning. James Tierney threw back his duvet with such a violence that it half roused Ronagh Durkin from her sleep.

Through the fog of drowse, she could hear James throwing things about in the sitting room. She made three attempts to rise. Fell asleep again, and then finally with a huge effort and dark mutterings rose from the bed, then reached for his overcoat as she moved to the door.

There James was in that familiar pose. Reading a sheet of paper. But standing this time.

—It's here. This bit here is the key, Ronagh. I've read right over it a thousand times. Hit me like lightning. The key point is . . . that's it's not just about Éilis at all. In fact some of the crucial issues are about Finn and Séamus! How could I be so stupid.

—I have to agree.

—What a story. Two brothers. It's such a huge story.

—Right. And what?

—We have to tell this story, Ronagh, is what. Jesus, we have to tell Ireland about this. The whole thing. Get right to the bottom of it. Not just Heffernan but the media, the Guards. Then the personal stories. But how did we get where we are? In this mess?

Ronagh beginning to wake up slightly. Glad that the focus was moving from this Éilis one.

—Okay, great. Now come back to bed, Jamesie.

—I will when I've written this note. It's important I do it now. It won't be the same if I wait.

—Right. See you in the morning.

—Look, the fridge is full and there's loads of bread if I'm not here when you wake up.

—What?

—I have to find where Finn Dempsey is.

—I stood on the step for an hour and a half. I'm dying of a desperate dose. Flu or something. Maybe worse. And all you care about is Finn fucking Dempsey. Either you come back to bed or I'm going home. Ring me a taxi.

—You're right. Sorry. Just ten minutes to write this up. Have to do it now. Did you just say what?

—James.

Finn Dempsey putting his hand up apologetically, okay, silently, okay, shapes of mouth—looking lovingly at his papers on his table. Making a mental note of where each piece was, ready for the morning. Then looking with affection, nay a burst of huge love, at Ronagh Durkin as she moved, with that innate grace she had, back into the bedroom.

James Tierney turning off the table lamp. Standing in the half-light of the room. Éilis Devanney's diary somehow luminous. James Tierney pushing his hair up, smacking his forehead lightly with his palm.

James Tierney, laughing, happy.

At the root of it all. The answers were simple. Blindingly obvious. Éilis had got so much wrong. But so much right. Part poem. Part jigsaw. Part cry for help. Then all her mad ravings. Now what he had to do was put it all together. Hold the mirror of truth up to the populace. His duty. His call. The ancient oath of the scribes.

DEIREADH/END

MICHAL AJVAZ, *The Golden Age.*
The Other City.
PIERRE ALBERT-BIROT, *Grabinoulor.*
YUZ ALESHKOVSKY, *Kangaroo.*
FELIPE ALFAU, *Chromos.*
Locos.
JOE AMATO, *Samuel Taylor's Last Night.*
IVAN ÂNGELO, *The Celebration.*
The Tower of Glass.
ANTÓNIO LOBO ANTUNES, *Knowledge of Hell.*
The Splendor of Portugal.
ALAIN ARIAS-MISSON, *Theatre of Incest.*
JOHN ASHBERY & JAMES SCHUYLER, *A Nest of Ninnies.*
ROBERT ASHLEY, *Perfect Lives.*
GABRIELA AVIGUR-ROTEM, *Heatwave and Crazy Birds.*
DJUNA BARNES, *Ladies Almanack.*
Ryder.
JOHN BARTH, *Letters.*
Sabbatical.
DONALD BARTHELME, *The King.*
Paradise.
SVETISLAV BASARA, *Chinese Letter.*
MIQUEL BAUÇÀ, *The Siege in the Room.*
RENÉ BELLETTO, *Dying.*
MAREK BIENCZYK, *Transparency.*
ANDREI BITOV, *Pushkin House.*
ANDREJ BLATNIK, *You Do Understand.*
Law of Desire.
LOUIS PAUL BOON, *Chapel Road.*
My Little War.
Summer in Termuren.
ROGER BOYLAN, *Killoyle.*
IGNÁCIO DE LOYOLA BRANDÃO, *Anonymous Celebrity.*
Zero.
BONNIE BREMSER, *Troia: Mexican Memoirs.*
CHRISTINE BROOKE-ROSE, *Amalgamemnon.*
BRIGID BROPHY, *In Transit.*
The Prancing Novelist.

GERALD L. BRUNS, *Modern Poetry and the Idea of Language.*
GABRIELLE BURTON, *Heartbreak Hotel.*
MICHEL BUTOR, *Degrees.*
Mobile.
G. CABRERA INFANTE, *Infante's Inferno.*
Three Trapped Tigers.
JULIETA CAMPOS, *The Fear of Losing Eurydice.*
ANNE CARSON, *Eros the Bittersweet.*
ORLY CASTEL-BLOOM, *Dolly City.*
LOUIS-FERDINAND CÉLINE, *North.*
Conversations with Professor Y.
London Bridge.
MARIE CHAIX, *The Laurels of Lake Constance.*
HUGO CHARTERIS, *The Tide Is Right.*
ERIC CHEVILLARD, *Demolishing Nisard.*
The Author and Me.
MARC CHOLODENKO, *Mordechai Schamz.*
JOSHUA COHEN, *Witz.*
EMILY HOLMES COLEMAN, *The Shutter of Snow.*
ERIC CHEVILLARD, *The Author and Me.*
ROBERT COOVER, *A Night at the Movies.*
STANLEY CRAWFORD, *Log of the S.S. The Mrs Unguentine.*
Some Instructions to My Wife.
RENÉ CREVEL, *Putting My Foot in It.*
RALPH CUSACK, *Cadenza.*
NICHOLAS DELBANCO, *Sherbrookes.*
The Count of Concord.
NIGEL DENNIS, *Cards of Identity.*
PETER DIMOCK, *A Short Rhetoric for Leaving the Family.*
ARIEL DORFMAN, *Konfidenz.*
COLEMAN DOWELL, *Island People.*
Too Much Flesh and Jabez.
ARKADII DRAGOMOSHCHENKO, *Dust.*
RIKKI DUCORNET, *Phosphor in Dreamland.*
The Complete Butcher's Tales.

RIKKI DUCORNET (cont.), *The Jade Cabinet.*
The Fountains of Neptune.
WILLIAM EASTLAKE, *The Bamboo Bed.*
Castle Keep.
Lyric of the Circle Heart.
JEAN ECHENOZ, *Chopin's Move.*
STANLEY ELKIN, *A Bad Man.*
Criers and Kibitzers, Kibitzers and Criers.
The Dick Gibson Show.
The Franchiser.
The Living End.
Mrs. Ted Bliss.
FRANÇOIS EMMANUEL, *Invitation to a Voyage.*
PAUL EMOND, *The Dance of a Sham.*
SALVADOR ESPRIU, *Ariadne in the Grotesque Labyrinth.*
LESLIE A. FIEDLER, *Love and Death in the American Novel.*
JUAN FILLOY, *Op Oloop.*
ANDY FITCH, *Pop Poetics.*
GUSTAVE FLAUBERT, *Bouvard and Pécuchet.*
KASS FLEISHER, *Talking out of School.*
JON FOSSE, *Aliss at the Fire.*
Melancholy.
FORD MADOX FORD, *The March of Literature.*
MAX FRISCH, *I'm Not Stiller.*
Man in the Holocene.
CARLOS FUENTES, *Christopher Unborn.*
Distant Relations.
Terra Nostra.
Where the Air Is Clear.
TAKEHIKO FUKUNAGA, *Flowers of Grass.*
WILLIAM GADDIS, JR., *The Recognitions.*
JANICE GALLOWAY, *Foreign Parts.*
The Trick Is to Keep Breathing.
WILLIAM H. GASS, *Life Sentences.*
The Tunnel.
The World Within the Word.
Willie Masters' Lonesome Wife.
GÉRARD GAVARRY, *Hoppla! 1 2 3.*

ETIENNE GILSON, *The Arts of the Beautiful.*
Forms and Substances in the Arts.
C. S. GISCOMBE, *Giscome Road.*
Here.
DOUGLAS GLOVER, *Bad News of the Heart.*
WITOLD GOMBROWICZ, *A Kind of Testament.*
PAULO EMÍLIO SALES GOMES, *P's Three Women.*
GEORGI GOSPODINOV, *Natural Novel.*
JUAN GOYTISOLO, *Count Julian.*
Juan the Landless.
Makbara.
Marks of Identity.
HENRY GREEN, *Blindness.*
Concluding.
Doting.
Nothing.
JACK GREEN, *Fire the Bastards!*
JIŘÍ GRUŠA, *The Questionnaire.*
MELA HARTWIG, *Am I a Redundant Human Being?*
JOHN HAWKES, *The Passion Artist.*
Whistlejacket.
ELIZABETH HEIGHWAY, ED., *Contemporary Georgian Fiction.*
AIDAN HIGGINS, *Balcony of Europe.*
Blind Man's Bluff.
Bornholm Night-Ferry.
Langrishe, Go Down.
Scenes from a Receding Past.
KEIZO HINO, *Isle of Dreams.*
KAZUSHI HOSAKA, *Plainsong.*
ALDOUS HUXLEY, *Antic Hay.*
Point Counter Point.
Those Barren Leaves.
Time Must Have a Stop.
NAOYUKI II, *The Shadow of a Blue Cat.*
DRAGO JANČAR, *The Tree with No Name.*
MIKHEIL JAVAKHISHVILI, *Kvachi.*
GERT JONKE, *The Distant Sound.*
Homage to Czerny.
The System of Vienna.

JACQUES JOUET, *Mountain R.*
  Savage.
  Upstaged.
MIEKO KANAI, *The Word Book.*
YORAM KANIUK, *Life on Sandpaper.*
ZURAB KARUMIDZE, *Dagny.*
JOHN KELLY, *From Out of the City.*
HUGH KENNER, *Flaubert, Joyce
  and Beckett: The Stoic Comedians.*
  Joyce's Voices.
DANILO KIŠ, *The Attic.*
  The Lute and the Scars.
  Psalm 44.
  A Tomb for Boris Davidovich.
ANITA KONKKA, *A Fool's Paradise.*
GEORGE KONRÁD, *The City Builder.*
TADEUSZ KONWICKI, *A Minor
  Apocalypse.*
  The Polish Complex.
ANNA KORDZAIA-SAMADASHVILI,
  Me, Margarita.
MENIS KOUMANDAREAS, *Koula.*
ELAINE KRAF, *The Princess of 72nd Street.*
JIM KRUSOE, *Iceland.*
AYSE KULIN, *Farewell: A Mansion in
  Occupied Istanbul.*
EMILIO LASCANO TEGUI, *On Elegance
  While Sleeping.*
ERIC LAURRENT, *Do Not Touch.*
VIOLETTE LEDUC, *La Bâtarde.*
EDOUARD LEVÉ, *Autoportrait.*
  Newspaper.
  Suicide.
  Works.
MARIO LEVI, *Istanbul Was a Fairy Tale.*
DEBORAH LEVY, *Billy and Girl.*
JOSÉ LEZAMA LIMA, *Paradiso.*
ROSA LIKSOM, *Dark Paradise.*
OSMAN LINS, *Avalovara.*
  The Queen of the Prisons of Greece.
FLORIAN LIPUŠ, *The Errors of Young Tjaž.*
GORDON LISH, *Peru.*
ALF MACLOCHLAINN, *Out of Focus.*
  Past Habitual.

  The Corpus in the Library.
RON LOEWINSOHN, *Magnetic Field(s).*
YURI LOTMAN, *Non-Memoirs.*
D. KEITH MANO, *Take Five.*
MINA LOY, *Stories and Essays of Mina Loy.*
MICHELINE AHARONIAN MARCOM,
  A Brief History of Yes.
  The Mirror in the Well.
BEN MARCUS, *The Age of Wire and String.*
WALLACE MARKFIELD, *Teitlebaum's
  Window.*
DAVID MARKSON, *Reader's Block.*
  Wittgenstein's Mistress.
CAROLE MASO, *AVA.*
HISAKI MATSUURA, *Triangle.*
LADISLAV MATEJKA & KRYSTYNA
  POMORSKA, EDS., *Readings in Russian
  Poetics: Formalist & Structuralist Views.*
HARRY MATHEWS, *Cigarettes.*
  The Conversions.
  The Human Country.
  The Journalist.
  My Life in CIA.
  Singular Pleasures.
  The Sinking of the Odradek.
  Stadium.
  Tlooth.
HISAKI MATSUURA, *Triangle.*
DONAL MCLAUGHLIN, *beheading the
  virgin mary, and other stories.*
JOSEPH MCELROY, *Night Soul and
  Other Stories.*
ABDELWAHAB MEDDEB, *Talismano.*
GERHARD MEIER, *Isle of the Dead.*
HERMAN MELVILLE, *The Confidence-
  Man.*
AMANDA MICHALOPOULOU, *I'd Like.*
STEVEN MILLHAUSER, *The Barnum
  Museum.*
  In the Penny Arcade.
RALPH J. MILLS, JR., *Essays on Poetry.*
MOMUS, *The Book of Jokes.*
CHRISTINE MONTALBETTI, *The Origin
  of Man.*
  Western.

NICHOLAS MOSLEY, *Accident.*
Assassins.
Catastrophe Practice.
A Garden of Trees.
Hopeful Monsters.
Imago Bird.
Inventing God.
Look at the Dark.
Metamorphosis.
Natalie Natalia.
Serpent.
WARREN MOTTE, *Fables of the Novel:*
French Fiction since 1990.
Fiction Now: The French Novel in the
21st Century.
Mirror Gazing.
Oulipo: A Primer of Potential Literature.
GERALD MURNANE, *Barley Patch.*
Inland.
YVES NAVARRE, *Our Share of Time.*
Sweet Tooth.
DOROTHY NELSON, *In Night's City.*
Tar and Feathers.
ESHKOL NEVO, *Homesick.*
WILFRIDO D. NOLLEDO, *But for*
the Lovers.
BORIS A. NOVAK, *The Master of*
Insomnia.
FLANN O'BRIEN, *At Swim-Two-Birds.*
The Best of Myles.
The Dalkey Archive.
The Hard Life.
The Poor Mouth.
The Third Policeman.
CLAUDE OLLIER, *The Mise-en-Scène.*
Wert and the Life Without End.
PATRIK OUŘEDNÍK, *Europeana.*
The Opportune Moment, 1855.
BORIS PAHOR, *Necropolis.*
FERNANDO DEL PASO, *News from*
the Empire.
Palinuro of Mexico.
ROBERT PINGET, *The Inquisitory.*
Mahu or The Material.
Trio.
MANUEL PUIG, *Betrayed by Rita*
Hayworth.

The Buenos Aires Affair.
Heartbreak Tango.
RAYMOND QUENEAU, *The Last Days.*
Odile.
Pierrot Mon Ami.
Saint Glinglin.
ANN QUIN, *Berg.*
Passages.
Three.
Tripticks.
ISHMAEL REED, *The Free-Lance*
Pallbearers.
The Last Days of Louisiana Red.
Ishmael Reed: The Plays.
Juice!
The Terrible Threes.
The Terrible Twos.
Yellow Back Radio Broke-Down.
JASIA REICHARDT, *15 Journeys Warsaw*
to London.
JOÃO UBALDO RIBEIRO, *House of the*
Fortunate Buddhas.
JEAN RICARDOU, *Place Names.*
RAINER MARIA RILKE,
The Notebooks of Malte Laurids Brigge.
JULIÁN RÍOS, *The House of Ulysses.*
Larva: A Midsummer Night's Babel.
Poundemonium.
ALAIN ROBBE-GRILLET, *Project for a*
Revolution in New York.
A Sentimental Novel.
AUGUSTO ROA BASTOS, *I the Supreme.*
DANIËL ROBBERECHTS, *Arriving in*
Avignon.
JEAN ROLIN, *The Explosion of the*
Radiator Hose.
OLIVIER ROLIN, *Hotel Crystal.*
ALIX CLEO ROUBAUD, *Alix's Journal.*
JACQUES ROUBAUD, *The Form of*
a City Changes Faster, Alas, Than the
Human Heart.
The Great Fire of London.
Hortense in Exile.
Hortense Is Abducted.
Mathematics: The Plurality of Worlds of
Lewis.
Some Thing Black.

RAYMOND ROUSSEL, *Impressions of Africa.*

VEDRANA RUDAN, *Night.*

PABLO M. RUIZ, *Four Cold Chapters on the Possibility of Literature.*

GERMAN SADULAEV, *The Maya Pill.*

TOMAŽ ŠALAMUN, *Soy Realidad.*

LYDIE SALVAYRE, *The Company of Ghosts.*
The Lecture.
The Power of Flies.

LUIS RAFAEL SÁNCHEZ, *Macho Camacho's Beat.*

SEVERO SARDUY, *Cobra & Maitreya.*

NATHALIE SARRAUTE, *Do You Hear Them?*
Martereau.
The Planetarium.

STIG SÆTERBAKKEN, *Siamese.*
Self-Control.
Through the Night.

ARNO SCHMIDT, *Collected Novellas.*
Collected Stories.
Nobodaddy's Children.
Two Novels.

ASAF SCHURR, *Motti.*

GAIL SCOTT, *My Paris.*

DAMION SEARLS, *What We Were Doing and Where We Were Going.*

JUNE AKERS SEESE, *Is This What Other Women Feel Too?*

BERNARD SHARE, *Inish.*
Transit.

VIKTOR SHKLOVSKY, *Bowstring.*
Literature and Cinematography.
Theory of Prose.
Third Factory.
Zoo, or Letters Not about Love.

PIERRE SINIAC, *The Collaborators.*

KJERSTI A. SKOMSVOLD, *The Faster I Walk, the Smaller I Am.*

JOSEF ŠKVORECKÝ, *The Engineer of Human Souls.*

GILBERT SORRENTINO, *Aberration of Starlight.*
Blue Pastoral.
Crystal Vision.

Imaginative Qualities of Actual Things.
Mulligan Stew. Red the Fiend.
Steelwork.
Under the Shadow.

MARKO SOSIČ, *Ballerina, Ballerina.*

ANDRZEJ STASIUK, *Dukla.*
Fado.

GERTRUDE STEIN, *The Making of Americans.*
A Novel of Thank You.

LARS SVENDSEN, *A Philosophy of Evil.*

PIOTR SZEWC, *Annihilation.*

GONÇALO M. TAVARES, *A Man: Klaus Klump.*
Jerusalem.
Learning to Pray in the Age of Technique.

LUCIAN DAN TEODOROVICI, *Our Circus Presents...*

NIKANOR TERATOLOGEN, *Assisted Living.*

STEFAN THEMERSON, *Hobson's Island.*
The Mystery of the Sardine.
Tom Harris.

TAEKO TOMIOKA, *Building Waves.*

JOHN TOOMEY, *Sleepwalker.*

DUMITRU TSEPENEAG, *Hotel Europa.*
The Necessary Marriage.
Pigeon Post.
Vain Art of the Fugue.

ESTHER TUSQUETS, *Stranded.*

DUBRAVKA UGRESIC, *Lend Me Your Character.*
Thank You for Not Reading.

TOR ULVEN, *Replacement.*

MATI UNT, *Brecht at Night.*
Diary of a Blood Donor.
Things in the Night.

ÁLVARO URIBE & OLIVIA SEARS, EDS., *Best of Contemporary Mexican Fiction.*

ELOY URROZ, *Friction.*
The Obstacles.

LUISA VALENZUELA, *Dark Desires and the Others.*
He Who Searches.

PAUL VERHAEGHEN, *Omega Minor.*

BORIS VIAN, *Heartsnatcher.*

LLORENÇ VILLALONGA, *The Dolls' Room.*

TOOMAS VINT, *An Unending Landscape.*

ORNELA VORPSI, *The Country Where No One Ever Dies.*

AUSTRYN WAINHOUSE, *Hedyphagetica.*

CURTIS WHITE, *America's Magic Mountain.*
The Idea of Home.
Memories of My Father Watching TV.
Requiem.

DIANE WILLIAMS,
Excitability: Selected Stories.
Romancer Erector.

DOUGLAS WOOLF, *Wall to Wall.*
Ya! & John-Juan.

JAY WRIGHT, *Polynomials and Pollen.*
The Presentable Art of Reading Absence.

PHILIP WYLIE, *Generation of Vipers.*

MARGUERITE YOUNG, *Angel in the Forest.*
Miss MacIntosh, My Darling.

REYOUNG, *Unbabbling.*

VLADO ŽABOT, *The Succubus.*

ZORAN ŽIVKOVIĆ , *Hidden Camera.*

LOUIS ZUKOFSKY, *Collected Fiction.*

VITOMIL ZUPAN, *Minuet for Guitar.*

SCOTT ZWIREN, *God Head.*

AND MORE . . .